The HOUSE of the Wind

By Titania Hardie and available from Headline Review

The Rose Labyrinth
The House of the Wind

The HOUSE of the Wind

TITANIA HARDIE

headline
review

First published in Great Britain in 2011
by HEADLINE REVIEW
An imprint of HEADLINE PUBLISHING GROUP

1

Illustration on p. 433 by Chris Boehm.

The law case in *The House of the Wind* is inspired by several legal cases
that were settled out of court without an admission of liability, but the
story and account of Maddie's case is entirely fictional as are all the characters,
organisations and events described in the book in relation to it.

Cataloguing in Publication Data is available from the British Library

ISBN 978 0 7553 4627 1 (Hardback)
ISBN 978 0 7553 4628 8 (Trade paperback)

Typeset in Garamond by Avon DataSet Ltd,
Bidford-on-Avon, Warwickshire

Printed in the UK by CPI Mackays, Chatham, ME5 8TD

Headline's policy is to use papers that are natural, renewable and
recyclable products and made from wood grown in sustainable forests.
The logging and manufacturing processes are expected to conform
to the environmental regulations of the country of origin.

HEADLINE PUBLISHING GROUP
An Hachette UK Company
338 Euston Road
London NW1 3BH

www.headline.co.uk
www.hachette.co.uk

For Samantha and Zephyrine; and for Amanda and Jane.
With my real love, and my deep respect. TH

'Do you not see how necessary a world of pains and troubles is to school an intelligence and make it a soul?'

John Keats, 1819

PROLOGUE

The path down the hill from majestic Volterra towards the tiny village of La Chiostra snakes away into the Tuscan horizon – a shade of magenta at the end of the day – along a smooth, ancient outcrop of lava flow. The vista to each side of the narrow road will catch your breath at any hour, in any season: the beauty of the wild colours and fields in one direction, and in the other a timeless moonscape of strange geology, where the sensuous undulations of the hills are starkly replaced by the crags – the *balze* – created by a thousand years of landslides. If your interests are classical or historical you may be looking for the spot where the most ancient of the Etruscan necropolises was destroyed by the erosion; or you may be curious about the ruined eleventh-century *badia*, or abbey, or the earliest Christian churches, all swallowed by the landscape centuries ago. But if your soul is romantic, or you are interested in riddles, then perhaps your journey is to an obscure location a kilometre or two along the road – somewhere between the modern house with the barking dogs, and the ancient farm with the rows of vines and sunflowers. There is no sign, though, and the uninformed traveller may pass by unaware of the mystery.

Here, if you are looking for it, is the ruin of a house on the ridge positioned perfectly to look back up the hill at the imposing wind-blown town of the Etruscans. Legend says this is all that now remains of a small, late thirteenth- or early fourteenth-century manor, which was once the home of a comfortably genteel family and their bewitchingly lovely daughter. Her name we should – perhaps we must – dispense with, for a tapestry of tales has grown up around her, and the truth of

1

her name is part of the riddle. It's enough that, in a Christian age, she was a disciple of Nature. She preferred the company of animals and birds, and chose to pray to Diana, lady of the moon and the great patroness of one of the ancient temples that had dominated Velathri, as the city was then called.

Before it became a deserted ruin, this house held secrets. It was once her childhood home, and here she came to be confined by the council of the Bishop of Volterra with the absolute consent of her parents. It may have been less about her religious outlook than that she had disobeyed her parents' implacable wish for her to enter the convent and chastely serve God. She remained true to her more ancient goddess, and wanted to marry the man she loved. For such defiance and impiety she had been imprisoned and punished, and was now to be tried and tortured, despite her youth and charm, her intelligence and beauty.

Late, however, on the very eve of her terrible fate being acted out, something extraordinary happened. Permitted to walk only in her garden, closely watched, to offer a last prayer to her own deity, a freak storm suddenly rose up and whipped along the ridge, clenching the landscape in its fist and razing the house to the ground. Perhaps it was the same storm that gobbled one of those tiny churches, a kilometre or two away.

But sheltered in moonlight in the doorway of an outbuilding, the girl – and only the girl – walked free! Free to escape into the night, and the storm, and to her lover. This ancient house and land, its near neighbour new and buttressed against the medieval ruin, has been known ever since as the *Casa al Vento* – the House of the Wind.

PART ONE

1

20 January 2007, San Francisco

In the calendar of seasons and times, January is Janus-headed: the patron month of gateways and doors, of looking forwards and backwards. Back over what has been, what brings us to this point; ahead to what may be, anticipating the dreams of future days.

Perhaps today, laughing and circling the date on her calendar with a bright pen, Madeline Moretti had given some thought to this, at least unconsciously. She'd certainly been revising in her mind Christopher's favourite foods – his preference for salads and seafood, his enjoyment of full-bodied red wines more than champagne, his very British love of crumpets (accompanied with quince jelly!) instead of croissants, his funny thing for rose Turkish delight and dates dipped in dark melted chocolate – so that when she opened the cupboard tomorrow on his first morning in San Francisco she would be able to supply his most eccentric wish effortlessly, with dainties that had been shipped in anywhere from Maine to the Napa Valley, from London to Provence, 'from silken Samarcand to cedar'd Lebanon'.

She had dwelled a long time on the question of the bed linen, remembering how much comment some pale green sheets in a luxurious Venice hotel room last September had drawn from him; how he liked plain things rather than patterns. This had propelled her onto the streetcar at the end of her long working day yesterday, from her office near the Ferry Building through the Financial District towards Union Square – out into the cold and the crowds searching for bargains in the sales – to buy something new and lavish. Scheuer had amply supplied her needs with something smooth and blanched and with a heavy thread count, which had cost her a week's wages. What did the expense matter? She hadn't seen him in four months, and everything must be – would be – perfect.

Aside from these retrospective thoughts, Madeline hadn't had time to look backwards today. In high spirits, which were a feature of her personality, she had sprung from a light sleep at seven and kept going without a break all day. It was an ordinary Saturday with an above ordinary workload: collect her dry cleaning, fold away the exercise bike, tidy away the music on the piano into the stool, mend the broken tie-back on the bathroom curtains, get gas for her car, some white tulips from Jimena's shop for the table. The maid had been yesterday, had swept, vacuumed and polished within an inch of the little apartment's being, and there was nothing more to do. But Madeline did most of it again. When her cellphone rang she let its answer service dismiss her girlfriends while she lit scented candles in the living room, plumped cushions on the sofa and tidied the last of her work suits into her closet.

The moment for lunch came and went, but Maddie had no appetite for food. She had an hour's paperwork to do for her law firm and knew she couldn't relax into her looming time off until it was emailed back to her boss, the good-natured but very precise Samantha. Her mother and sister would drop by around three, and she wanted to wash her hair before that.

Madeline thought her face was really nothing special, and her tall, light frame actually rather unseductive, but her thick mane of dark curls was Christopher's delight, and though no one ever knew how much effort it took to untangle them, she needed an hour to make sure every spiralling lock was glossy and perfect. This would be the last opportunity for such lavish care, as the flight from London came in late tonight.

It was already five minutes to the hour, however, when she pushed the 'Send' button on her Vaio, got up from her hyper-neat desk in the corner of the sitting area and walked to the street-facing window. She checked for any sign of her mother's car in the tree-lined avenue below. Having overlooked breakfast as well as lunch, she was faintly light-headed, and anxious she hadn't yet showered. Nevertheless she felt that serene pleasure that comes when everything is very nearly in order, when pains taken for another person's pleasure are just about invisible, and when work can be packed away, to look forward to the thrill of a reunion with someone you quite literally adore, in a quantifiable number of hours.

Her disproportionately expensive apartment on Broadway, at the lower end of Pacific Heights, was tiny and, technically, facing in almost the wrong direction, away from the water; but she felt it was worth such a slice of her wages because, thanks to a shorter neighbouring building, it offered up one unexpectedly lovely side view of San Francisco Bay, courtesy of a small balcony. From here a week or two ago, on a fog-free night, it had given her a glimpse of the meteor shower just visible over the dark expanse of ocean to the north and west, in the clear California sky.

Now she noticed it was oddly dark for close to three o'clock. The skyline offered several colours: the stippled dove greys of the clouds, deep slate grey of the facing hills and a pale lemon yellow of shrinking light in between, all dissolving into the muted steel that was now the water. The city was trapped between two weather fronts. The morning had kept faith with the foregoing week of almost unbroken sun – a Californian winter that was mild, crisp, bright – but Madeline saw that a change was coming. The fog would roll in and a new weather cycle would begin. What a shame, with Chris's arrival only hours away. She grinned at the irony of his arriving in California to find English weather.

They were late. How uncharacteristic. It must be Barbara. Her older sister was sharply clever, usually well organised and a shrewd judge of character. Maddie was relishing the prospect of hearing her vivid sense of humour relate her first impressions of her future brother-in-law. But Barbara felt no reluctance in claiming the right to her own life and needs, when occasion demanded. She could be relied on to have lost track of time on a cherished Saturday, to cram in a clandestine cigarette, away from their mother, or to share some gossip about the latest scandals in the Castro with Drew, her gay neighbour and best friend. Dinner at the family home tomorrow night was one thing, but Madeline rather resented that they were coming today, breaking into that air of sanctity she wanted to create in the countdown to Christopher's arrival. She didn't want to speak to anyone; wished to focus only on *him*. But her fairer side acknowledged it was natural for her mother to be overeager to meet the Englishman who'd changed her daughter's life so completely in one short year of post-grad study abroad.

Or even on one short evening, she thought. She understood the cast of his mind, the sensitivity and playfulness of his character from a single evening. The rest was all affirmation.

She'd gone off dreamily to dinner at the Oxford Union that previous January (was it only a year ago?), in a chic black dress draped with a skimpy pashmina and her best black heels, despite the chilly air and hint of ice on the cobbles. Who on earth could wear Louboutins on the medieval pavements of Oxford? Pride before a fall, her grandmother would have cautioned. And sure enough, coming out a few hours later, beautiful unanticipated snow flurries were painting a fairytale landscape, making a white frozen ground. Her East Coast education had never quite inured her to the surprise pleasure of snow, and the Californian girl had laughed aloud, enchanted by the shapes and swirling movement. But there was no walking home now. Too late to hail a taxi easily; too far to walk to get one from the rank on Gloucester Green, in conditions like this. She'd shouted to a friend in a group behind her to phone for one, and almost lost her footing. This was the cue for a man in white tie and formal scarf, who suddenly appeared at her side. He was grinning, seemingly amused by her wide-eyed reaction to the weather. With exactly as many words as were necessary to introduce himself, final year medical student Christopher Taylor hoisted the lady elegantly on a shoulder and carried her back over the cobbles, past the bemused porters and right to her stairs at New College.

Though it was far from her longest journey, she later thought, it surely rated as among the most significant of her life.

She was still laughing, brushing snow off her shoes in her mind when an intrusive sense of the present brought to her notice the cry of the gulls, wheeling and taking refuge under the eaves of some buildings in her middle distance. The wind must have been rising steadily over the Bay. She glanced at the clock on the wall, and though the hands had hardly shifted she felt irritable. She was habitually good-natured, but her time was being broken into, and her hair still unwashed. Everything was suspended until her mother and sister had been and approved the decorative order of her apartment, had some coffee and biscotti, and left her to her own quiet rituals of preparation again.

Her thoughts were disturbed by the buzz of the intercom. They'd arrived and parked unseen. She pressed a button to bring them up, unclicked her lock and swung towards the kitchen to flick on the

La Gaggia. The greeting called over her shoulder to the visitors at her doorway merged seamlessly with one to the voice on the other end of her telephone, which had rung simultaneously in the kitchen. She spoke casually – the only half-phrase she would remember passing her lips that day – without turning at all to collect her mother's kiss.

And then a door closed.

A bitter chill from across the Bay accompanied Madeline Moretti to the bed she had freshly made up early that day, of finest linen. No words passed between them as Barbara unbuttoned her sister's collar, freed her from the simple cream wool dress, which fell to her feet, and unpinned her hair. Madeline was surely unaware of her darkly ironic shadowing of the rhythms of so many young women on this date, over so many previous centuries: but she couldn't turn round, couldn't speak or look to either side – her eyes staring straight ahead, unseeing – until her head was on the pillow and her bruised eyelids closed, a prelude to a drugged sleep of haunted dreams. To everything else in the world around her, she was dead.

The phone call just after three o'clock that afternoon – past eleven at night in England – had bolted the door to her future and left her a prisoner of the past; had changed her life unutterably. There would be no flight to meet that evening, no lazy Sunday brunch to enjoy, no cupboard of delights to open, no overnight at the wineries, no week of holiday to begin. There would be no Christopher to collect.

Her bed was a shroud, her mind numb in half-sleep. She could still hear his mother's soft English voice in a dull misfit tone, a cracked bell, words related without sense. They were words about his last overnight shift as the most junior of doctors at the John Radcliffe Hospital in Oxford, before the journey that would bring him to see her and meet her family here; about a car full of teenagers travelling back from an all-night party in the city, the driver drunk and overtaking another car on the bypass, leaping the barrier, catching Chris head-on, coming back home in the early morning to college to sleep for a few hours, before he was to pack and fly to Maddie. It was a collection of clauses, but for her they were words without sound or meaning in a rational world; words she had no expectation could ever be meant for her, yet could never erase.

St Agnes' moon had set.

2

Now, past the hour of three, the air had the taste of snow. Hurrying back from the abbey along the riverside path, Mia saw a frozen hare limp across the icy ground just in front of her, away into the scant cover of the bare willow trees and weeping pears. But if the wind kept up and the snow continued to fall, the creature would soon be well camouflaged.

It was not usual, even on a January day. Their home nestled in a valley of such beauty and shelter that it was known as the *Valle Serena* – the Valley of Tranquillity. While the proud hill town of Chiusdino a mile or two to the west could often be covered with snow pricked into quilted patterns by the Tuscan roof tiles, in their world below everything was mild. Winter was kinder, the bustle of life wilfully hushed. But not on this day, when the weather had turned and the villa was brimming with pilgrims and guests waiting out the conditions for a fairer road south.

The chill in the air thrilled the girl. She wondered if, on such a day, one might glimpse a unicorn, or some other wild and mystical creature, in the magical woods that bordered her home. Aunt Jacquetta may think that only wild boar and deer, and at times a few wolves, inhabited the woodland, but Aunt Jacquetta didn't know all the answers.

Mia tucked her dark braid under her hood and wrapped her mantle tightly around her, protecting the delicate cuttings of plantain, which had been the reason for her errand. A few days before, a pilgrim had arrived asking to rest with them, unable to walk the extra miles to the Cistercian brothers' famed abbey and from thence up the hillside of Montesiepi to the sacred shrine of Galgano Guidotti, a local knight turned holy man. The pilgrim's foot was badly bruised and misshapen. He had come far along the Via Francigena, like many before him; a man with pale eyes and skin, straw-coloured hair, and fine clothes tailored in a northern land. Though he was plainly in pain, he never lost his gentle manners, this man who must be in search of redemption and the purification of his soul. Aunt Jacquetta recognised the need for the unusual variety of plantain grown by the monks, to halt the inflammation and treat the bruise that had changed the colour of his skin beyond recognition. This had granted Mia the chance for a breath of air by herself in her mission to Fra Silvestro at the monastery, to ask for a little of the herb, with its strange, thread-like foliage, from his still room. Though the brothers would be busy with preparations for the holy feast day of Agnes tomorrow and would not welcome the disturbance, no one knew better how to grow the healthiest specimens in his garden of *simples* than Fra Silvestro.

He had confided to Mia that the secret lay in planting his garden according to the moon. 'The first quarter of the waxing moon, child, for the leafy herbs and plants that bear no seeds in fruits.' And indeed, it seemed to work, for he always had a plentiful surplus from the warm months, which he dried out carefully for winter use. The potency of just a few dried leaves was such that, in a day or so, all would be well and the pilgrims' road would carry him away again.

Mia's pattens were just starting to slip on the icy track when she came in sight of the villa of Santo Pietro, a home of simple beauty and purity looked after by her aunt. Sometimes the gossip among the servants made her believe the house must have belonged to her father, a man she never recalled meeting. Sometimes it seemed as if the Church must have owned the house, and that her aunt was only the custodian. But it had been Maria Maddalena's home since she was a little girl of six, and she remembered no other. For more than seven years she had been shaped by the rhythms and spirit of the house. It smelled, even in winter, of the beautiful iris that grew in masses over the hills of the Tuscan countryside: its delicate scent escaped from the linen press and the laundry room, the kitchen, the chests of clothes and the vats of soap being prepared in the outhouse from the crushed powder of the rhizomes and pure cow's milk, and even from their own small still room where it would be used in her aunt's recipe for aqua vitae. And Mia knew it well as her medicine, to help her breathe when she sometimes struggled to get air.

Mia came through the door of the scullery and found the sweet-tempered Alba – prettiest and youngest of the maids – with water still scalding for a guest to wash. She gestured whether she might have some, and showed her the plantain to explain. Alba and her aunt were the two dear souls who always understood Mia best, and never made her feel awkward or simple. For Mia never spoke, and had not done so since she first arrived at Santo Pietro. Her hearing was sound, and no one knew if her muteness were an affliction from God or a choice self-imposed by the girl, but she had contrived an excellent way of communicating to her two favourite people, and to Fra Silvestro in particular at the abbey.

'How do you want me to prepare it, Maria?' Alba asked patiently.

Mia indicated the use of three leaves only, in the smallest amount of water, then pointed to the linen and demonstrated rolling it up in her hands.

'It's to make a strong steeping for a linen wrap, around the *signor*'s foot?' she asked. 'And not too much water?'

Mia nodded with vigour and tapped her on the wrist, showing her the leaves once more. She mimed taking the leaves from the basin and back against the linen bandage, then gestured with a winding motion.

'I'm to keep the leaves and place them back inside the hot wet wrap, to remain against the swelling,' Alba said. 'And that's the advice of the tonsured one!' she smiled, perfectly interpreting Mia's hand patting the top of her own head to indicate Fra Silvestro.

Mia laughed soundlessly, and hugged her.

'Don't forget the vigil of Holy Agnes, Maria Maddalena,' Alba's voice followed her as she slipped through the scullery door into the kitchen. 'To bed with you tonight and no supper; nor turn round to look at a thing!'

Mia smiled at her, and pinched her lips between her fingers.

'That's right,' she agreed. 'No talking!' And they both laughed, the one warmly and the other soundlessly.

Alba had told Mia of the ritual of St Agnes for the first time this year, now that she was almost fourteen, and ready to think of husbands, perhaps. All the servant girls knew that a maiden – if she kept silent vigil

all the day long and went supperless to bed without looking behind her
– might be granted a dream by fair St Agnes of the man she would
marry. It was said he would appear to her in her sleep and offer her a
feast, with a pledge of his undying love. But if a single word escaped, or
she forgot the ritual and glanced backwards, all the charm was fled, and
Agnes would be deaf to all entreaty. No vision would come! Mia had
no idea that a man might exist for her – who would match with a girl
who was mute, and whose father was unknown to her? – but she would
act out the ritual, if only to please Alba.

The sound of bells from the abbey carried in the still air. Together
with the fading light, this told Mia it was near four. She must light the
tapers, and then find Aunt Jacquetta to sit with her and read her lesson.
Today she must do abacus, not her favourite; she would read or do Latin
translation more willingly. Though perhaps as the villa had guests
in overplus – one couple even willing to stay in garden rooms that were
used only in the summer months – she might help with the meal tonight
and do some chores in the house, rather than study.

She had started down the hallway to find her aunt when she heard
her name called from the door of the solar in the opposite direction.

'Maria Maddalena! I hope you have just come from Loredana's
kitchen, and helped her wash the capons? And Giulietta was looking
for you earlier, too, to help her in the laundry. And you were so long
about your errand to the monastery that you weren't here for the bread-
making. Have you been dwelling this whole afternoon inside your own
imagination, *ma donna mia*?'

Her aunt's voice was tempered with humour, despite the pretence of
being cross. Mia knew she was permitted to laugh as soon as her aunt
mentioned capons! This list of hers – the duties of housework longer
than a skein of wool – was her aunt's favourite tease to her niece. It came
on the back of an advice book by Signor Certaldo as to the management
of wives and daughters. From weaving purses and embroidering silk, to
sieving and cooking and darning socks, a young woman was to be as
gentle upstairs as she was to be ready to roll up her sleeves below. And
though boys must be fed well, it mattered not how girls were fed, as long
as they had sufficient but did not get fat. Mia's young aunt, though, was
fiercely independent, and raised her niece in similar vein. Free of artifice
and without the pressure of parents keen to betroth her well, neither was
concerned to follow the book of advice. They had strong affections and

lived simple, good lives, being kind to others. That was all the advice Aunt Jacquetta wanted to pass on to Mia. She came forward to embrace the girl.

'Have you brought *plantago* from the monks?'

Mia's hands told her aunt that the herb was with Alba, and in preparation for its way above stairs to the guest's chamber.

'I shall go to him now, then. But bring some clean linen and your own garments up from the laundry to your chamber, to lessen the burden on Giulietta, with the house so full.' She smiled at her, knowing of the ritual her niece was pledged in semi-secrecy to follow on Agnes' Eve. 'I'll have Chiara bring hot water to you to wash now, and then we must all help out in the kitchens for the supper tonight. Not everyone is fasting, as you are!'

It was late, in shadowy light cast by a bright full moon, when the poor girl – drooping from many hours of unexpected labour and the noise of too many people – at last lit her taper and started up the stairs to her own attic chamber, overlooking the pilgrims' way below. Light splashed through the gules of glass on the half-landing and Mia, her mind swimming in thoughts of sweet St Agnes and her lambs, and promises of gentle sorcery, forgot her hunger and the chill wind outside. Catching up the hem of her chemise, she gained the top stair, her lips moving silently in supplication to the saint. Her hand was on the latch of the door and her breathing quiet, in respect for Agnes, when horses were heard on the cobbles below. '. . . Or all the charm is fled,' she remembered Alba saying. But while she hesitated, a knock came at the doorway. What could she do, with the few servants spoken for in duties, and her aunt ministering to the pilgrim? Unwilling to turn, she slipped backwards down the stair, her hand on the rail and her footing surprisingly sure.

She was there before the second hesitant rap at the knocker. She slid back the bolt from the hasp and was quickly joined by the steward, Cesaré, who helped her pull open the heavy door. She protected her flame from the night wind with her spare hand, and squinted at the surprising amount of light. Silhouetted in front of her were a couple: a young man in fashionable clothing, dirty with travel; and a girl whose face was a mystery to Mia, backlit as she was by the huge moon and the torches retreating along the path to the villa gate.

Mia wondered for only a second who had unlocked it for them. All her senses were drawn to the young woman, framed against the light. In the cold darkness of the hour, she seemed to drink up that brightness: *Una raggia*, Mia thought, a lady wrought from a ray of light. And completely unafraid, without consultation with Cesaré, she moved her candle to usher them inside.

3

Immaculately dressed in a black coat and matching tailored suit out of respect for the loss of someone she'd never met, but who meant everything to someone she loved, Isabella Moretti came and went from Madeline's apartment. She took charge of those invisible duties of making coffee for a stream of shocked visitors and putting floral offerings in vases and food in the overstocked fridge. Amid the incongruous scent of a paradise of lilies and hyacinths and white daffodils, which stole the air in a confined space, she watched her eerily quiet granddaughter. Sometimes they exchanged a few words. Mostly they just sat.

For a week the weather had been as changeable as the seas: heavy storms and rain for a day or so, punctuated with crisp, bright weather and evenings offering up the ethereal beauty of a white plume of fog lit by a breath-taking sunset; then, storms again. The weather seemed able to express an intensity and emotion that her granddaughter could not, and Isabella couldn't stop her thoughts from drifting back almost twenty-five years.

When Madeline was born, Isabella had arranged to have a birth chart drawn up for her new granddaughter. It wasn't something she'd have thought of, but was prompted by a dispute over whether the child was born under the sign of Taurus or Gemini. Most newspapers said the first, but at least a journal or two weighed in with the latter. May the twenty-first seemed a day straddling a divide, and Isabella felt a professional should settle it. So she'd been directed to the elderly Signora Angela, a respectable milliner whose hats graced many well-to-do heads

16

on Church feast days, communions and at weddings. As a spirited sideline the *Signora* was talented at preparing astrological charts, something she'd inherited, she liked to say, from her Etruscan forebears! She was regarded by many as an eccentric, by some as a good angel, others a wise old crone, and at least a few as a *strega*, or witch. A few sceptics went so far as to call her weak in body and mind. But she was a tough old lady with an odd elegance and energy. She lived on one of the lanes in the North Beach area – a generations-old Italian immigrant, like Isabella herself – and so Isabella had gone to the *Signora* with Madeline's birthday details, including her weight and length, and the odd but interesting detail that she'd been born 'with a true knot in her cord'. The *Signora* assured her that date and hour were enough.

Seven days later, when she'd returned to collect the chart, the older woman looked at her client so seriously it had almost made Isabella laugh.

'The child is born on the Pleiades,' she told her, pulling her down onto a seat at a table strewn with felt and pins and stiffening fabric. 'They dwell at the very last degree of Taurus, though she is more under the care of gentle Maia, I believe, than ambitious Alcyone. Her moon is also in Taurus – an old moon, before it was born anew in Gemini a day or so later.'

Isabella's curiosity was satisfied. She rose to go, smiling kindly and feeling that settled the whole interest in the subject for her. But the *Signora*'s finger, dusty with tailor's chalk, hesitated in the air, her face alive with such an expression that it puzzled Isabella. She seemed like someone deciding whether to keep closed a wondrous riddle book; and after a moment, she added something.

'An old moon is an old soul with promises to keep; but mercifully her moon is not at Caput Algol, the Medusa's head. All of her planets after fiery Mars are travelling *retrograde* – moving backwards. Her whole chart harks back in time, you understand.'

Isabella didn't in the least understand, and the mention of the Medusa hardly worked any bright charms on her imagination, but the woman talked on without explanation of either point.

'The Pleiades are a very significant cluster of stars, Signora Moretti. "The sailing ones", they are called, or "the doves", as well as the "guardians of the harvest". But also they are known as the "weeping women". The little girl will be progressive, with a shining personality – certainly the cleverest in her class – strong-minded, yet also feminine. Watch her skip lightly through her life without concerns, hardly pausing to look deeply into things and never back over her shoulder, until the day comes early in her young life when she will suffer a terrible bereavement, and do nothing but look back. For some time she will be as a woman locked in stone. Only then will she begin her journey to understand the mystery of who she is. *That* is when she must travel backwards and become a pilgrim, and she has far to go.'

Then Signora Angela had given Isabella the girl's horoscope chart, sealed in old-fashioned brown paper, with advice to hold onto it for her and never to yield it up unless the time was right.

Isabella Moretti had found herself outside the woman's door in bafflement, even a little disturbed. She was not especially superstitious. She kept the observances demanded by her Catholic faith out of respect and still more as a matter of tradition, knew the important saints' days, but she was not devout. Yet in spite of her more rational self, she'd never quite managed to shake off the memory of this strange information, partly because of the starkly serious tone in which it had been delivered. She couldn't say if this event had ever unconsciously contributed to her special relationship with Maddie, to the way she thought of her as something of a favourite person of hers. This was deserved anyway by the girl's sheer vitality, her curiosity about and zest for life. Madeline was a child who had never walked, if she could run; never had to be taught that well-chosen language had the power to determine events. Enthusiasm radiated from her and uplifted others. Even at her most determined and reckless – when it was clear she was still young and needed some governance – Maddie was a shining soul, and very easy to love.

But, quite suddenly, remembrance of that day had come back to Isabella with stark clarity. So she stayed even closer to Madeline, which also kept the girl's endlessly chattering mother away. Isabella's daughter-in-law was a good person, but completely unable to read the signs or understand the requirements. Her over-cosseting and bustle wasn't helping her daughter's quiet grieving process. Perhaps for the first time in her life, Maddie needed some stillness to process the events. The poor child was struck dumb. A 'weeping one' indeed, although, Isabella thought ironically, the actual ability to release some tears would be a relief, if only she could do it.

That first week – Maddie's scheduled vacation time – was drawing to a close. In a benumbed state her only move from her apartment was a seventy-two-hour dash, against everyone but Nonna Isabella's advice, to London for a funeral she had no stomach to attend. She chose to go out of feeling for Chris's devastated parents, but declined their invitation to stay with them for a few more days. Madeline understood they needed her as extended access to their lost son, but she just couldn't help them. Now was not the same as before: those few lovely weekends down on the train from Oxford with Chris, last spring and in the early summer, when his parents had opened their elegant south-west London doors to her, made her welcome and at ease. They had lunched every day on the lawn, only so many months ago; but each hour of the present week was about what would never be again. Winter had a grip on the garden, and Chris was gone. What an extraordinary idea – that he was gone. It was an unbearable weight on her, and the feeling of grief was like cold fingers closing on her throat, choking both tears and words. She must get away from London.

And yet nowhere was there any respite. While others dozed on the overnight flight home to San Francisco, her mind haemorrhaged memories. She tried to recall each feature of Christopher's face. The dark unmanageable hair, which he'd promised her was genetically engineered never to be tidy, but also never to be thin; the dimple in his squared chin; the strangely long eyelashes she'd teased him about, saying any girl would covet them! And, of course, there was the scar where he'd bitten right through his lower lip as a child. She could see his very physical shoulders and his neck, which were well developed because he rowed for his college; and the mischievous brown eyes, which betrayed a warm humour. She could see the details, but it didn't add up to his whole face somehow. She had fallen in love with his intelligence, not his face at all; Chris's being was communicated in a visceral sense of his whole presence more than in any individual features. She could hear him, and possibly smell him too; she remembered his smell. But how he'd looked on their last couple of meetings she couldn't really recall. His expression evaded her. She couldn't haul him back, in any way. And by some perverse fate the photos she had were also a little unclear: off angle, or too middle distant. He'd a habit of putting his hand up to obscure the lens in pictures. So for most of the week she'd felt sightless – or at least, unable to see what she wanted to see. She had to live with her mind in sharp pain, though she was herself in a cloudy state.

19

By Saturday, a week to the day of her receiving the news, and the day after her return from London, Maddie reached a point of paralysing loneliness. It seemed so much more acute in the midst of too many visitors, who had once again taken up their watch in the time-honoured fashion of Italian condolences paid to the family and to friends. Apart from the gentle ministrations of Nonna Isabella, and the firm grip of Barbara, who came and went for just a single visit each day to hug her sister without words, Maddie knew she needed to recapture at least the appearance of normality if she were to survive this strange ordeal. It was a premature widowhood, the jarring sense of sterility she felt in a room set-dressed by sympathisers to resemble a bridal bower. She had to escape for air.

She concentrated on the idea that hard work would be a solace to get her through the days ahead, one at a time. Maddie believed that Samantha would be in the office, despite its being a weekend, and she rang demanding – with as much strength as she could summon up – to be allowed to come in on Monday morning for a normal week of work.

'Hmm. I think you could have another week.' Samantha had carefully chosen 'could' rather than 'should', but however little her employee was revealing to others of her feelings, Samantha realised she'd have suffered too many blows in the last seven days to be functioning soundly, and the work could be both shattering and stressful, even for a strong person.

But Maddie had needs of her own, and stalled her answer. She heard the tone of good sense in Samantha's voice, but didn't want to comply.

Samantha guessed some of this, and pushed a little. 'You're in a kind of war zone, Maddie. How are you *really*? Are you eating anything?'

Maddie smiled wanly into the phone, but realised she had to use words. 'No, not much. But I am breathing,' she answered softly. 'I just keep concentrating on breathing. I'd be grateful if my mind were busy.'

Samantha understood the pain. She respected Maddie's determination, hesitating only for a moment longer. 'There's an important briefing in the bull ring, first thing Monday. We've reached an interesting stage, and I'd be glad to have you in there.'

Madeline's voice steadied. 'See you then.'

4

29 January 2007, San Francisco

Madeline Moretti recalled the day of her interview at Harden Hammond Cohen only too well. Staying with her sister for a week of job hunting, she'd left the apartment on that late September day looking beautifully groomed, and giving herself ample time to find the address without rushing. Light rain had been falling, but it soon became heavier and, as she reached the Embarcadero, an autumn breeze had turned into a real wind gathering strength off the water. She remembered the wave of rising panic as her umbrella blew inside out and her hair escaped its combs – not the picture of business-like calm she'd wanted to present. Outside the building, a taxi pulling along kerbside into a puddle had splashed her down, and she felt that luck might be against her. But she'd liked Samantha at once, and soon eased into the meeting, picking her way through tough moral questions like an agile boxer, thrilling at every test of her mind, and cajoling her would-be boss into laughter. Maddie wasn't arrogant, but she knew she had the place after, at most, ten minutes of energetic discussion about her views on retributive justice. It seemed a perfect fit.

Three weeks later she'd arrived for her first day with a hangover from too many celebratory Margaritas with Barbara the night before, having spent half the night in her own bathroom and then half the morning throwing up in Harden Hammond Cohen's comfortable rest room. Yet she'd managed to charm the tough new partner, David Cohen, with a savvy appreciation of the artwork in his office, and make herself invaluable to old-school New Englander and the firm's trial lawyer, Charles

21

Hammond, by finishing an article he was writing for the *New York Times*, when he was suddenly called away to court. A quiet series of victories despite the headache – and every day since had been plain sailing.

Until today. Today she felt empty. She'd pushed everyone away, refusing to share her private emotions with friends or cry to a soul. Perhaps she hadn't even started to grieve. Today, she was exhausted. And she needed to be focused and prove she could still do her job as relentlessly as Samantha did hers.

This was a law firm where no one left before six at the earliest: no one wished to. Though the partners were not ungenerous, extremely high wages here would have been the wages of sin. Samantha's was a human rights firm, unquestionably one of the best on the West Coast, attracting grudging admiration from even their grittiest foes. Anyone with a tale of blatant sexism or abuse in the workplace, or serious corporate negligence, or deserving of workers' compensation, would knock on their door. The New Jersey daughter of community-minded parents, and educated at Harvard, Samantha herself seemed sewn from gentle threads, but she was a terrier who would fight to the death if her spirit was engaged and her sense of injustice aroused. She had a reputation that had reached some ears in Washington, and she relied on her team of stand-out youngsters to hold the fort regularly while she was away on advisory committees or lobbying for legal reforms in the workplace.

Anyone focused on their career opportunity would almost have worked here without a pay cheque, without expectation of financial gain, without incentive other than to watch and learn. This was a life-changing place of work, a firm acquiring an extraordinary name for its dedication to changing the lives of people with apparently ordinary names. Chris had remarked to Madeline that they 'sounded like dangerous lefties' from the city that had given the world the UN. But her faith in his values had been repaid when he declared himself ready to up sticks and come to live right there with her, in this city – *her* city – with her dangerous lefty colleagues. Chris sounded intrigued with her view of the ocean and her life and her law office, so she started out buoyant, and remained so every day from that first when she'd got the nod from Samantha.

Except for today. Clouds had no silver linings, but only promised rain.

Getting out of her exquisite sheets early on this Monday morning, Maddie felt sick about facing others. She had no real understanding of the kind of semi-madness overwhelming her in her unvoiced grief; she could only promise herself to try not to let the world outside break her any more than it had done. She would concentrate on surviving, follow her feet and see where they took her. She had no other designs, no future plans.

An early morning phone call had broken into her half-sleep with Samantha's voice full of an urgency and excitement Maddie envied.

'The documents we've been waiting for from Stormtree are on their way to our offices in San Jose. We'll have them tomorrow morning. There's a meeting today at nine to bring everyone up to speed and brainstorm some aspects of the case, so I'm taking you at your word that you're ready to get straight in.'

There was no pause for breath. Maddie realised Samantha had rung with this news to try to enthuse her – and more than a week or two ago, it would have – but today she had to work much harder to care about anything at all.

Aware that she'd said 'for sure' without vigour – but which would, she hoped, be read by Samantha as tiredness – she put the phone down and embarked on the meaningless rituals of coffee, shower, bed-making, dress for the office, in something of a haze. Her window revealed a foggy drizzle and she fished for suitable shoes, trying not to react emotionally at seeing the black Louboutins positioned at the front of her closet. She scooped them to the side, grabbed her running shoes and shoved smarter chocolate pumps into her tote, picked up an oversized document case, her umbrella and purse, and closed her door on the hothouse full of flowers.

It was still early enough for the grey of the city fog to be lying in the street, and it seemed to move with her as she walked around the corner and headed downhill towards Union Street, unable to view the sea behind the wall of fog. She ran for the bus from Cow Hollow that would take her down to Union Square, and wondered where her head had been when the journey was suddenly over and it was time to switch for the streetcar to her office. On a nice day she'd have walked: not today, when she could barely muster the strength to stand in the crowded public transport.

She tried to use the short walk along the Embarcadero to get hold of the implications of Samantha's news. The California Superior Court must have finally forced Stormtree Components Inc. to release almost ten years of documents – including the crucial in-house memos – which had been subpoenaed months ago. Aware of the threat of such disclosures, Stormtree had been stalling ever since Maddie had joined the firm. Samantha was surely jubilant that after so many months of legal gymnastics on the part of Stormtree's lawyers, the Court had finally lost patience and ordered them to deliver the material – or face charges of contempt.

But once they'd picked over the minutiae of this tonnage of paper, would they find within it that one small piece of information they sought? Was there anything that could indisputably prove Stormtree had been aware of the toxicity of their materials, but refused to do anything about it to protect the workers? Assuming such a paper trail might have even existed, could something so sensitive have escaped a paper shredder? The idea that the company was bound to be at least partially aware of its negligence was what had catapulted Samantha into the fray to take them on, years before Maddie had become part of the team. Samantha and David were in no doubt that the varied critical illnesses and numerous fatalities of about two hundred workers, employed by Stormtree all around the US to assemble electronics and mother-boards for computers, were more than just an embarrassment for the corporation. They deserved far more, they believed, than just a hands-up apology and plea of ignorance about the chemical poisons used in production. Stormtree surely *knew*, Samantha believed. It was literally inconceivable that they could have been blind to – and uninterested in – the growing catalogue of sick workers in their cohort. But now the test results and recommendations from Stormtree's in-house scientists would be on their table, and they would go a long way to proving, or disproving, Samantha's hunch. What would it all yield?

Maddie walked under the shadow of the beautiful glass buildings that had been home to her bosses since they relocated from their traditional turn-of-the-century Bay Area office after the 1989 earthquake. Samantha joked that going more modern and quake proof might be a blessing, given the explosive nature of the cases they so often fought, but despite the appearance of luxury in the new premises, the heart of the old firm stood tall against the wind – almost literally on their high-up floor – as they continued to take on their unusual and *pro bono* cases. It was this that had so strongly appealed to the idealist in Maddie.

Maddie felt the fog had clung to her clothes, and it seemed to follow her into the lobby and even the elevator as she exchanged running shoes for pumps, and then rose up the ivory tower. She braced herself for the lipstick-immaculate smile of Jacinta Collins – a pout so perfectly applied that Maddie had witnessed it slurp through innumerable luncheons of truffle linguini or spaghetti marinara without a trace of disturbance afterwards. One of the few blondes in an office of varyingly attractive dark-haired women, Jacinta was employed to be PA to both senior partners, though each had a personal aide as well; but Maddie always felt Jacinta's reach exceeded her grasp, and that she liked to exercise a firm control on all that happened at Harden Hammond Cohen. She was someone to respect more than you might wish to.

Right now the perfect lips had puckered into a drawling look of sympathy at Maddie.

'Oh, I'm so sorry for your loss, Madeline. I didn't think we'd see you back here for some time yet.' Her expression of distaste at Maddie's choice of demure brown suit was not quite stifled. 'Just look at you! I can see how much you've suffered. You're so brave to come back at all.'

Maddie swayed a little as the extended arms moved towards her in hug formation.

'Thanks,' she answered in a woolly voice. Her tone invited no further conversation.

Maddie was rescued from physical contact by the appearance of her equal number, Yamuna Choudhury, who had joined the firm as a junior to Charles Hammond only a few weeks before Maddie. She had been top of her class at Stanford, and oozed the sophistication of a girl who was quietly aware of her unusual beauty. Brought up between California and Jaipur – which her father seemed to own parts of – she sparked Maddie's admiration for her ability to think deeply, but only to speak if she had something relevant to say. Her smile spoke of her sympathy better than words, as she handed Maddie a slim file of papers that exactly mirrored her own.

'The latest depositions, and some other documents that will bring you up to date, Maddie. Glad to see you. I'm afraid the gang are in the bull ring already, wanting to start at nine on the dot!' Yamuna's efficiency was not devoid of humour and fellow-feeling for the enormous task she knew her colleague faced: to wake herself from shock and be alert for the dramas of the next hour.

'On the dot,' Maddie nodded, a little unconvincingly.

The doe-eyed receptionist, Teresa Suarez, who was in her mid-twenties but only seemed about seventeen, waved at Maddie quietly before picking up a tray of coffee. She mouthed 'Hello' to communicate respect for her loss without encroaching on her private thoughts. Maddie smiled back, suddenly picking up her pace to hold the huge glass doors leading to the inner sanctum open for her. The grand meeting room beyond was affectionately known as the bull ring, more for the matador-like manoeuvres planned against adversaries within, than because of its shape or size.

As she passed her, Teresa apologised: 'I put a small mountain of post in your office, Maddie. And I'm sorry to say that your pretty pot plant looks very unwell. I tried to water it while you were away, but I might have done more harm than good.'

'Don't worry, Teresa,' Maddie answered. 'It's sweet of you. I'll take a look.'

She rounded the corner into her own tiny office. Maddie glanced at the small framed print of Oxford on her wall, the neatly arranged files in her own choice of soft colours, the photo frame on the bookshelf behind her desk. What sort of person had inhabited this space, she wondered. Someone she could hardly remember now: a distant relative, a cousin. She wanted to pick up the photo of Christopher so she could look at him before the meeting, but equally, she didn't want to think of him just now. She glanced instead at the desk and, despite the warning, saw the post stacked high alongside the unmistakable vision of her once beautiful white orchid shrivelling, the waxy leaves turning necrotic from water that had pooled at their base. She didn't blame Teresa. Few people realised orchids required very little water, and it looked as though hers had been drowned in a mistaken goodwill gesture. But it was the saddest sight, this proud phalaenopsis that Chris had sent for her first day of work four months ago, which had flourished ever since with a succession of flowers on two spikes, now drooping pitifully. She put her briefcase down and considered whether to give in to a tear, but she swallowed hard, tossed her coat onto a chair and threw the orchid into the waste basket. Then she turned deliberately on her heel with the newly acquired paperwork, grabbing freshly sharpened pencils and a yellow pad on her way back out towards the meeting room.

Entering the circular space, with its wonderful view across the landscaped plazas and elevated walkways below, Maddie was aware that the animated chatter of her colleagues abruptly broke at her appearance. She found her place in a spare chair near Samantha's position under the window and pretended everyone was not trying to avoid her eye.

'Good morning,' she said as unemotively as possible. But, she thought, how should you respond to the quiet sympathy of strangers? What was expected? No one had written a conduct book for those who were victims of a failed fairy tale, whom the world seemed to pity but not know how to approach.

The quiet was interrupted by Samantha springing through the glass doors. She seemed in possession of a fine joke, and threw a copy of *San Francisco* magazine into the centre of the table. She rested a hand very lightly on Maddie's shoulder as she spoke, before sliding into her seat.

'Just in case any of you here are in doubt as to the kind of character we're dealing with at Stormtree, here he is! Fighting his personal war of attrition from the cover of our city's cherished self-image. Behold the fine, upstanding figure of Mr Pierce Gray, benefactor of the newly refurbished wing of the art gallery – and, of course, none other than the President of his family firm, Stormtree Components!'

'Inc.!' laughed the handsome Tyler Washington, the firm's top paralegal. Tall as a Harlem Globetrotter, his physical presence dominated the table. 'That man Gray is the consummate press and public relations expert! No jury is ever going to believe he's not the all-American success story with a heart of gold and a wallet open to every charity.'

'Yes, except the charity of those who work for him,' Samantha frowned.

Charles Hammond smiled quietly to himself from the other side of the circle. Immaculate in his Brooks Brothers style and old-fashioned manners, he rotated the photo of the bespoke-tailored man – perhaps just prematurely greying at thirty-nine or forty – towards himself, and asked his partner, 'Ah, but have you been invited to his lovely country "cottage", as he calls it, in the heart and soul of California's wine country, to taste his much-heralded new vintage Sauvignon? Because, I have to confess, I have had that honour!'

Samantha was mock open-mouthed. 'Charles, supping with the devil? At "Château Pierce"?'

'I believe he calls the new release "The Gray Lady", in honour of the ghost of some scintillating French Château Cabernet Sauvignon from before the war,' Charles answered. 'A reminder to his contacts in Bordeaux that they owe some of their own grapes to his grandfather's viticulture, all those years ago when the French vines were almost wiped out with fungus. They've actually gone so far as to give him a bit of their hallowed French earth, for his vines.'

Tyler laughed. 'The whole of the French wine industry must be aware of the merits of Mr Pierce Gray of Napa Valley. There's no dirt under his fingernails!'

'Let's check for some dirt then, shall we?' Samantha addressed them all seriously. 'Tyler, you and Charlotte have some updates to give us on the medical reports?'

The slender blonde sitting beside Tyler Washington was a violet-eyed beauty from Indiana, and also his romantic partner. Charlotte Baxter and her handsome co-worker had come together within a week of her joining Harden Hammond Cohen a few years before, and they mostly managed to keep their personal lives sacred. It was Charlotte – cool in a lace blouse, her hair neatly caught in a chignon – who took over the summary of their research.

'Absolutely, Samantha. We have almost four hundred requests now from Stormtree workers, or retirees, who have serious illnesses they believe they can lay at their employer's door. Everyone thinks they have a claim, but some we've looked at in detail have nothing to do with this case. One, for instance, had a road traffic accident on the way home . . .'

Maddie took her eyes off the cover of the magazine to watch Charlotte's lovely classical face, her earnestness, as she relayed the facts of the people who had suffered from Stormtree's negligence. Or was it their ignorance? She seemed so impassioned. How could anyone let themselves care so much, and yet function so clinically? Maddie listened as Charlotte was describing someone who blamed the conditions in the 'clean room' for making him drowsy and unfocused, giving him a migraine headache, which caused him to drive into the back of a lorry. An excuse? Maddie wondered.

'So, he wants the injury to be Stormtree's problem. But, to be brutal, we're not going there.' Samantha shook her head. 'It might even be true, in some way, but we need cast-iron cases. Who are our strongest starters, Charlotte?'

Maddie tried to concentrate and took in more than she would have thought possible as Charlotte presented a summary replete with numbers of cases and statistics. About one hundred and fifty people were involved, some from states other than California. A few were on the East Coast, near Boston and up in Maine, with strong similarities to the cases here. Did Samantha want to focus only on those closest to home? Charlotte asked her.

'I'd keep them in the basket, Charlotte,' Charles said. 'You never know how – or where – things may pan out over time. They could be useful down the line, if we get some intransigence from the California judges . . .'

Maddie's eyes flitted around the room, unseeing, then came to rest again on the face of Stormtree in the middle of the table. She heard Samantha agree with Charles, and then there was Tyler's voice. Charlotte again. Samantha. Now Tyler sounded agitated, and Maddie gave him her attention.

'We also have twenty-five "probables", right here in the Golden State. I'd stake my life that they've been poisoned by Stormtree Inc. I mean, yeah, we can prove the toxicity in the materials because our own commissioned report states clearly that they demand handling with extreme care. But, there is the crucial onus of proof that Stormtree knew *exactly* what they were doing. We have to demonstrate that they were just cost-cutting *not* to do it.'

Can you demonstrate that they knowingly took risks with other people's lives? thought Maddie. Prove that they didn't stop to think about how their actions could terminate some people's dreams? Tear away hopes and happiness, break up families, cause suffering for people on a daily basis? She wanted to say something, but then Yamuna had put down a pencil she'd been toying with so it rapped loudly on the surface, startling Maddie. It was she who spoke.

'Tyler, I want to be clear. I'm sure I ought to know the answer. But if the toxicity of the heavy metals used in the construction of the motherboards and chips is not in doubt, and these people are definitely sick because of working there, even though they worked in clean rooms, then why is it so important to prove Stormtree knew beforehand? Surely they're culpable even if they didn't know the stuff was killing the workers? Isn't the only important thing that we have to prove the indisputable fact that the illnesses arose from the workplace?'

Samantha held her hand up with quiet authority. 'Let's clarify that point. It's not the metals themselves that are the demons.'

She glanced in sequence at each face, and Maddie felt caught in the current. She looked straight back at her, thinking she was being quizzed, and answered her boss. 'The poison emanates from ethylene glycol ethers, benzenes, epoxy resins and so on, which are the kinds of solvents that can cause carcinogens.'

Maddie was wondering where that had come from, when she realised Samantha was nodding at her.

'Correct. All these have been a mainstay of high-tech manufacturing for decades. But,' she turned to Yamuna, 'you are right, too. One part of the puzzle for us – a huge part – is in proving beyond reasonable doubt that the cancers and other critical conditions are down to their work environment, which is not straightforward. You can bet Stormtree's team will claim that the illnesses their workers are suffering from are perfectly natural – within demographic lines.'

'They all argue that Mexican workers and Hispanics, or whatever other group we're going out there for, are more likely than richer whites to have a higher instance of liver cancer, or breathing complications, or spontaneous abortions, or children with leukaemia et cetera!' Charlotte said in frustration.

'But the point about them having prior knowledge is crucial, Yamuna,' Samantha went on. 'The settlement for a mere misdemeanour of, "Oops, gosh, sorry, everyone, we had no idea these developmental toxics could do our workers any serious harm" would be substantially less – almost a goodwill gesture on the part of Stormtree towards its employees. They'll remind the court that they pay their employees' health insurance as part of the contract, so they already look like good guys to some. But if they've cost-cut, or been negligent, or even just lazy in their checks – to the degree it's played God with their workers' lives and health, and that of their families – then, we're talking serious damages.'

'Not to mention the moral point,' Maddie said quietly, with her eyes fixed on the image of the man gracing *San Francisco* magazine. She glanced up to see everyone was looking at her.

'That too, yes,' Samantha nodded at Maddie, 'which is exactly why we have to take pains to get accurate depositions from our clients. We need to be sure that what they tell us about joining the corporation, the conditions they endured, the nature of their illnesses, and anything else they can remember about working there, is clear and precise and not one bit embroidered. It's got to hold water in court and win a lot of sympathy in front of a jury, too.'

'No one needs to embroider. Less is very often more with juries,' Charles suggested.

Tyler picked up a cover sheet from his pile and passed it to Samantha. 'We've had our own people go over all the medical records again with a fine-tooth comb, and there seem to be about one hundred and fifty more cases of cancer of various types per thousand people among Stormtree's workers, than in the population at large. The toxicology reports are—'

Samantha's eyes rested on Tyler. 'Can we prove that last thing?'

'We still need some more detailed investigation. I'm just getting hold of a first-class epidemiologist from Princeton. Lots of Stormtree people dying of cancers has been pronounced "bad luck", caused by their low-income backgrounds, according to Stormtree. So we've asked them to run tests on their clean rooms, just to eliminate them. But they say there is no scientific evidence that the clean rooms weren't clean; so, the response from them to our request is: no need to run tests!'

Charles was more than *au fait* with Samantha's suit, but he would not become closely involved with the finer details until they proceeded to trial, when he would be the advocate. So he asked something for clarification. 'The term "clean room" means they are working in a sterile environment, yes?'

Charlotte shook her head. 'All that is "clean" about them is that the workers have to use gloves and headgear and sterile suits to protect the integrated circuits they're producing. If you get a speck of dust on a computer chip, for instance, it doesn't work. But it's to protect the *manufacturing* – not the workers at all.'

'It's what they're breathing in, Charles,' Samantha added.

'But if their clean rooms were squeaky clean,' Yamuna persisted, 'wouldn't it be better to prove it? Fighting us in court is much more expensive.'

'And they could make their own findings and settle out of court, too.' Charles was almost thinking out loud.

'Pierce Gray is just the kind of man who won't face up to his shortcomings, or admit any wrongdoing at all.' This came from a quiet young woman of about thirty, sitting to Maddie's right. Daisy Chang, whose great-great-grandfather had come to California with nothing in his pockets during the gold rush, was a brilliant young advocate, a trial lawyer in waiting, who worked now for David Cohen. He was abroad this week, and she was sitting in and listening for two.

'He's sure to have a cuddly side,' Marni Van Roon said tonelessly, so that no one was sure if she was being ironic. A final-year international law student from Rotterdam, she was spending it at Berkeley on exchange, and had a few weeks interned here at Harden Hammond Cohen, but she didn't belong to anyone. She had shared some lunch breaks with Jacinta, who seemed to be quite impressed with the debonair Mr Gray, and it was Jacinta's opinion she voiced when she said: 'In the interests of being fair, you may not be able to prove that they knew the chemicals were carcinogenic.'

Maddie stared at her, but refrained from commenting.

Samantha smiled ruefully. 'True,' she said. 'But let's hope we can get at the truth, for the sake of a lot of people who are in terminal wards in hospitals, without much hope and the clock ticking against them. To which end, Maddie,' she looked at her neighbour, 'I'd like you to visit a couple of our best possible cases for me, and get depositions from them all over again. Tyler?'

He filled in as prompted. 'Yeah, the nice lady of about sixty, Maddie. You've met her already – Marilu Moreno. She's in San Jose, and she liked you very much when she met you on your own a month or so ago. Hers is a breast cancer case. Do you remember?'

Maddie nodded with an opaque expression. Yes, she remembered this extraordinary, gutsy woman. But to have to go see her *now* . . . Why me? she thought.

Samantha answered unwittingly. 'You're super with people, Maddie, and Marilu needs sensitive handling. She's bright, and tough – and pissed at all the delays and tricks coming from Stormtree's lawyers. And there's a new girl too, isn't that so, Tyler?'

'A Native American girl of maybe thirty-five. Her father is in Nevada, and she helps to support him as well, because he looks after her child. She's been well educated and has a boy who's ten. She seems to be pretty seriously sick – an inoperable brain tumour, among other things. But she's got the sweetest disposition, and refuses to give up hope. She's also in Jose. You can probably see them both together, Maddie, and I'd be happy to come with you.'

He placed another sheet in front of her, and offered her an encouraging smile. Personally, he didn't envy anyone who had to go and talk to this poor girl. She was almost certainly not long for this world.

Maddie, her gaze still struggling to wrench itself from the face on the table, was only dimly aware of the bustle of activity of those around her. Samantha was closing the meeting, allocating tasks and setting the 'reconvene' for a week from today. Maddie was lost in her own thoughts, wondering about Pierce Gray, wondering how she could be of any help to anyone. She felt quite hollow inside, as if she had somehow, someway, lost her hopes for life. But, maybe that was the point. She could walk among the dispossessed, she thought, and still feel the same immunity, the same numbness, that she felt now.

She almost absently picked up the magazine with the image smiling up into space, trailed back along the hallway to her office after everyone else had emptied the room, and was surprised to find Samantha there, waiting for a quiet afterword. She was looking at the orchid in the bin, but turned to face Maddie as soon as she heard her step.

'I feel for you, dear girl, more than I can articulate. But you'll recall why I took you on?'

Maddie looked slightly away from her, not quite sure which bit she wanted.

Samantha looked at the shadow of the girl who'd seemed like a breath of fresh air when she'd met her at interview. She'd eclipsed every other candidate. 'I told you, "I'll take you, Madeline. Not for your experience – that will come – but because of something I see in you. Your energy, your ability to think laterally, to understand people's complexity. I think you're someone people will feel they can talk to." Do you remember?'

Maddie nodded, clutching her file, yellow legal pad and the magazine to her chest.

'I know you're raw and hurting right now,' Samantha continued. 'I know that life has little joy in it for you. But I *need* those special qualities from you, Maddie. You do have the chance to make a difference to these two women's lives, and they are playing a tight game against time. So, you need to find some way to believe in a cause again, and get ready to look the Pierce Grays in our story right in the eye. Please, don't give up on us all,' she smiled at her softly.

She then bent into the bin and picked up the orchid, passing it to her struggling fledgeling lawyer, and left.

Maddie took the orchid, set it again on her desk, making up her mind about something. But her thoughts remained with the man in the picture – the human face of Stormtree Components Inc.

She'd looked at him, all right, up close and very personal, on an occasion or two before this. They shared a history which Maddie had tried very hard to forget.

5

LATE JANUARY 1347, SANTO PIETRO IN CELLOLE, CHIUSDINO, TUSCANY

The quiet hours had denied her sleep; Maria Maddalena's eyes were open early, but still heavy. At the last, going to bed the night before, she'd had to move items from her own room to make way for the late arrivals. Asked to share a bed with her aunt, and still wild with curiosity, she'd been unable to still her mind for hours. With the wind in the right direction she'd heard the bells of compline from the abbey, but they were long finished when she'd finally drifted into some kind of rest.

Now she was fully awake and aware of the sweet smell of bay enriching the smoke of the morning fires, like incense. Only then did she recall the feast day of Agnes. Ah! The patron saint of betrothed couples!

She washed, dressed quickly, and hurried along the hallway of the ground floor to look for Aunt Jacquetta. Though she expected to discover her in the library, working early, Mia found her in the larger kitchen, writing up the day's regulations and receipts for the meals and the smooth running of the household. Although it was a feast day, sweet Agnes was deemed neither sufficiently demanding nor locally significant to interrupt the flow of work or daily duties of the people in their part of Tuscany. The law courts would not close for her, nor would the artisans be expected to halt work in her honour. Anyhow, no one at Santo Pietro had to fear the penalty of the one-hundred-soldi fine for presuming to work on a holy day; the butchers, spicers, bakers and innkeepers were each free to maintain their activities and supply the

35

services required for living even on the most important saints' days, saving only the Christmas fête day of San Stefano, whose feast must be kept free of any work whatever to ensure clean water and the absence of hail.

Mia laid an urgent hand on her aunt's arm and held out two fingers to her, pointing towards the front door with a look of enquiry.

'They're still sleeping, Mia, the couple from last night,' Jacquetta answered. 'But we must go shortly into the village for church, so collect your cloak and purse, and make ready.'

Mia looked defeated, and her aunt smiled.

'They'll be here when we return – and perhaps risen, too. Their journey yesterday was long, and they'll need more rest before we ply them with questions. And,' she added in response to Mia's expression of frustration, 'if they prefer to remain quiet, and say nothing to us about why they came so late, and from whence, that is their right.'

Aunt Jacquetta was stubbornly resistant to any further questions now, even under pressure from Cook, whose raised eyebrows showed that she, too, was engaged and curious about the wanderers who had pointedly given no name, but woken most of the guests and stirred up the whole house in the late hours.

'Ay, we'll hear no tales from them,' Cook stated flatly, 'nor have a florin for our trouble.'

Her lips and facial expressions communicated to Mia that she fully expected them to rise and leave as mysteriously as they had come, probably without remunerative thanks for their bed and board. Pilgrims came and went like this, their tales of travel and news from distant places often standing in for payment. It was the next best thing to making a pilgrimage yourself, to offer charitable hospitality to those who did. But the better sort always left something for the house and servants, and many were generous in their appreciation. Jacquetta's villa was so much more comfortable for the lay traveller than the sparse rooms put aside for pilgrims at the monastery. Her house was warm, the rooms clean and well-furnished – some almost palatial, as though expecting an unannounced visit from the *signori* – and the table more substantial (even providing eggs at breakfast!) than the simple nourishment they would receive from the monks. The travellers' payments supplemented the income from the land, in a house of this size. And, situated close to the shrine of Galgano and the abbey that grew up in his honour, giving lodging to pilgrims or travellers on business to the abbey itself was surely half their purpose. But if some came and went without payment or talk, that was immaterial to Aunt Jacquetta: she was clear about their obligations, whoever the passer-by, wherever they came from, whatever their business with God.

Yet to Mia's joy and almost everlasting faith in people, she and her aunt returned from Mass to find the mysterious couple in the vestibule off the panterer's room, with only the fair-haired pilgrim and the laundry maid's small child for company. The young woman had on a simple dress of cream with a fashionable tabard of green silk over it, proving she was high-born enough, though not over-ornamented. Mia thought it was the same dress she'd worn last night with only a travelling cloak covering it. She couldn't have packed much for a change of clothing. But what attracted Mia was that the delicate sleeves were carefully rolled back, an apron over her dress, and there were instruments about her on the small oak table. The visitor's whole attention was with the pilgrim's foot, so it was her young husband who spoke to them.

Mia heard his fine words make an apology for disturbing the house so late last evening. In a voice barely accented by Tuscan rhythms he explained their progress had been slow on the higher roads because of the snow. They'd been forced to take the horses carefully through Casole d'Elsa, and were quite unable to make it into Chiusdino to look for lodgings, as the roads had become impassable and the light gone early. With no hope of reaching Siena, they had had to follow the road where the weather was gentler – here into the valley.

Newlyweds, Mia thought, and she wondered if the man's speech rhythms suggested their starting point might have been Lucca, which the pilgrims' road passed through along the Via Francigena, all the way to and from France, or beyond on the route to Rome and the Holy Land. But if so, they hadn't taken the best or most direct route to make Siena. From San Gimignano the pilgrims' road went through Colle di Val d'Elsa, not Casole, and nowhere near Chiusdino. At Siena travellers made their choice whether to include the sacred shrine to Galgano, with his sword thrust into the chapel floor, on their route towards Rome. It was not the main path, though many came on, out of their way, to see both the shrine to the saint and the exquisite abbey, where miracles were said to happen. Did these two completely lose their way, or simply confuse the destination?

But for all this conversation between her aunt, who listened politely without putting many questions, and the young man – who had still given no name – Mia's eyes were fixed on the young woman. Her face, her work, enthralled Mia. Unusually she had a high forehead and, unlike Mia, was fair – the kind of lighter colouring that the painters chose in their depiction of the saints and the Holy Virgin at the Duomo in Siena. And her hair curled a little, though nothing as much as Mia's. Her face was not docile with the forced expression of humility that many young wives wore in public. Barely more than a girl herself, Mia decided, this young wife had *life* in her eyes.

What she was doing, which so fascinated Mia, took some stomach. While her man had been speaking, she had been dipping one of Chiara's longest darning needles in a little of the aqua vitae from their stores, then held it for some time in a candle flame until her own fingers must have felt they were glowing. This she took to the pilgrim's foot, which Mia noticed had gone from a large inflammation to a festering wound, probably from having rubbed many days against his shabby boot. It looked raw and ugly, and Mia would have looked away except for the fascination of watching how the visitor was treating it.

'Courage!' she said to the pilgrim in a clear, light voice, and she smiled at him.

The hot needle now sank into abscessed skin, and white mucilage spurted from it. The pilgrim grimaced but said nothing, and half a moment later the young woman was bathing it, applying a salve of her own, then wrapping it again in linens dusted with iris root and enclosing some of the plantain leaves Mia had brought yesterday. No one spoke, but all watched. Her movements showed no hesitation.

'The salve is of local white iris root and flowers of wild thyme, to kill the poisons that would infect your blood,' she explained to her patient, as she finished. 'And I have continued with the *signora*'s wise use of plantain leaves, besides,' she said, nodding respectfully at Jacquetta. 'Their treatment in such wounds is not widely understood. You have had the best care here to get them. Now you must rest, and drink the tisane I have made up of wild thyme to counter fever. I must do this again tonight, if,' she glanced at her hostess, 'the *signora* will permit us to stay a day or two?'

'Of course you must stay,' Jacquetta answered. 'And I believe from watching you that you must be the child of a surgeon, or one of the doctors from a good hospital? More than a mere bonesetter, certainly!'

'I have been taught by the daughter of one such . . .' she replied.

This was all the history they would learn for several days.

Mia pondered the strange road they had taken; the sound of her voice, like running water, and the fact that her speech was certainly Tuscan. Perhaps she had started in San Gimignano? And she considered the modest changes to the beautiful young woman's wardrobe, over the passing days. She noticed the husband rarely went into the village to hear Mass; and the young wife, never. Other visitors left, new guests came with better weather, and the couple stayed on to the end of that week. The young wife was ever present, though, to keep watch over the wound of the pilgrim – a man who, it was revealed, started his journey in the south of England. He had to remain with them to mend. The young wife – still without a name – helped in any way she could around the villa, gathering and arranging the scarce winter flowers and greenery in the rooms, mending garments and chamber linen, and she never lost her sweetness towards her young husband. Can married life be like this for long? Mia wondered.

While she considered these questions, Mia was in ignorance that she had equally attracted the interest of the young female guest, whom, without a name to bestow on her, Mia called 'la bella pellegrina' to herself, and wrote the name out for her aunt: 'the beautiful pilgrim'.

Mia first came up in conversation late in that week, when the two women sat in the solar. The girl's husband had gone with the steward into the forest to check the traps and snare some rabbits. The young woman was drying on a linen cloth the seeds of a pomegranate she had eaten, ready for replanting in the spring. Jacquetta, making up pomanders, felt comfortable enough to question her a little.

'You are no ordinary pilgrims, I think.'

'We are all such: travelling through life in quest of beauty and truth,' she said. She didn't raise her head while she toyed with her seeds, but smiled almost imperceptibly.

'I don't think you are going to rejoin the Via Francigena, or have missed the road to Siena.' There was nothing alarming in Jacquetta's voice, and she laid her head slightly to one side, looking at her guest, who nodded at her.

'We are not foreigners, certainly,' the girl answered Jacquetta honestly.

This was the unstated implication of being a pilgrim, as the word meant 'foreigner' in its strictest sense.

'Perhaps you and your husband are heading for the Bagni di Petriolo, a few miles away to the south?'

Jacquetta had seen many couples come to her as they picked their path to this alternate place of pilgrimage. However, most couples travelling that way had been significantly older than this young pair. If a marriage had not yet been blessed with children, a stay at a spa was recommended by Church and physicians alike, and the wonderful hot springs of Bagni di Petriolo were justly famed for their general curative powers and their capacity to help barren couples get children. But, Jacquetta knew, this seemed odd so early in a marriage.

Yet mention of the place made the girl look up.

'Bagni di Petriolo? That is near to you here?' she asked. 'My mother visited these *bagni*, before my own birth.' She seemed lost in a long train of thought before she added: 'They were a long time waiting for me, and there are no other heirs to my father's house.'

Jacquetta considered very carefully, then asked her a serious question. 'Do your mother and father not approve your choice of husband, *Signora*?'

She knew all too well the pain that could be inflicted on young people in love, when the civil law of so many Italian cities protected the jealousies and rights of a parent – and even older siblings or relatives – to decide who would marry whom. Clandestine marriages were expressly forbidden, even though canon law required only the consent of the couple concerned. Of course, they had to make their vows in a public place, but they were not to be impeded, according to the words of canon law. Jacquetta found it an outrage against God and his laws that a civically imposed requirement for parental consent should be allowed to thwart two people's happiness. Any person who was a legal witness to such a marriage – without the parental approval – every witness and the notary, besides the couple themselves, were liable for a hefty fine. Sometimes it was as much as one hundred livres. So, she wondered sympathetically, was this the reason for their quietness and their journey? She would be the daughter of Ghibelline parents, she didn't doubt, older landed gentry who still bore allegiance to the idea of the Emperor, and who had no trust in – nor political accord with – the son of some new-town family in commerce, who had made their living out of trade and supported the Pope's party.

Jacquetta knew only too well that such factions had caused terrible suffering and bloodshed in every city in Tuscany and to the north. Had these two married, then, and fled without the girl's parents knowing or agreeing?

'Not approve . . .' the girl said in a tone that was difficult to read.

Jacquetta was wondering whether she had reiterated the question, or given half an answer, when she continued speaking.

'We are none of us permitted to be individuals, *Signora*. Everything, every choice, is for Church or city or family. We have a low expectancy of our ability, or right, to change the destinies of human beings.'

This was sudden and honest, and it struck Jacquetta. She had deep and complicated thoughts on this question herself, from the history of her own family.

'But if we could . . . ?' the girl was almost thinking aloud. She looked at Jacquetta sympathetically. 'Why does your daughter not speak, *Signora*, when she hears so perfectly?'

Jacquetta looked at her young guest seriously. She was surprised, but not offended, by her question. It took her a moment to answer.

'Maria Maddalena – though every bit a daughter to me – is my niece,' she said, 'and the question of her speaking is impossible for me to answer. It is tied to her childhood and the dark time when she was forced to leave her mother.'

The two women looked at one another. Each seemed to be thinking and choosing whether, and what, to say next.

'In exchange for her speaking, God has seen fit to give her other gifts in richer measure, I think,' Jacquetta said.

'Yes. I have seen this. But did she cry as a baby?' the young woman asked gently.

Jacquetta nodded. 'Oh, yes. She spoke when she was a very young child.'

'I would like to try – rather, I believe I could –' the visitor said to Jacquetta, 'bring her voice out of the darkness.'

6

29 January 2007, San Francisco

As the working day ended Maddie had slipped out of her office shoes, and away.

She did not want to do the usual post mortem on the day with her colleagues at one of the watering holes along Embarcadero. Instead she walked, carrying the drooping orchid in her canvas tote bag, in her mind heading for the cable car turntable at Montgomery, but her steps took her on to Third Street. She was hardly aware that she had arrived at the door of Jimena's flower shop. Today the violet-sweet scent of iris, which greeted her as she opened the door, took her to a foreign place, somewhere that happiness still was.

A voice from behind the row of huge vases brimming with flowers greeted her.

'*Hola, chica, qué tal?* I'll be with you *en un momentito!*'

Jimena's voice had the singsong lilt that was full of its usual joy. Maddie marvelled at her zest for life, and hope.

Jimena came from behind the display of blooms, carrying a number of luxuriously wrapped bouquets.

'*Madre de Dios, Señorita Maddie,*' Jimena smiled sadly. 'I don't know which of you looks worse, the orchid or you. A broken heart I can't fix, but the orchid I believe I can bring back to life. I think some good neighbours will help her, poor thing.'

She took the orchid from Maddie's tote and put it on the wrapping bench as though it belonged to the angels, then moved quickly towards

42

the door, turned the lock, put up the 'Closed' sign and pulled the blind down.

'*Carita*, I was just closing. I hope we have a moment together before I am picked up. You sit for a second, while I finish packing the deliveries – and then we will talk?'

She vanished again, but her voice trailed back over the flowers. 'Oh, that rich admirer of yours – the one who's on the front of the magazine, who sent the biggest bunch of flowers for your loss – Mr Gray?' She was content that she had found his name. 'He was in, today.'

'Oh, really,' Maddie said without wanting to betray any curiosity. Here was the man she'd been thinking about for much of the day. She dropped onto the stool at the wrapping bench and looked about. 'He stopped being an admirer of mine long ago, Jimena,' she said politely but firmly.

'*Sí?*' Jimena said lightly enough. She dismissed the statement, because she knew very well that nobody sent bigger flowers for Maddie's birthdays or seemed to have a closer watch on the events of Maddie's life. Still, it was Maddie's business, and she obviously preferred to stay quiet about it now. 'Oh, well, anyway, he was asking if you got the flowers he ordered the other day? I told him: *Sí, seguro*, because I delivered them myself.'

Though the subject of Pierce Gray might have made her uncomfortable, Maddie was caught by the charm of the young woman rather than fixated on what she was saying. Even now, when she was weary of so much in her life, Jimena's little space had the magic to lift her spirits. She had adored this shop since she had found it, one sunny day on a slow walk home from work. It always contained things that were fresh and usually different. Apart from the obvious bouquets, herbs and rare and strange flowers that were often on display, Jimena had an art that made the beautiful more beauteous: little carts with cream enamel pots of lavender that made you feel as though you were in the country outside of Paris; casual ceramics blooming with pink roses and sweet peas in every season, that would look at home in a cottage in England; and Delftware jugs crammed with jonquils, blue daisies and stems of veronica, like a Dutch still-life painting from another century. Where they came from, or how they got there, was a mystery to Maddie.

When she first told Nonna Isabella about the shop, her grandmother said that Jimena's family had grown and sold flowers in San Francisco for *forever*. She could remember Jimena's grandfather, Gonzalo, selling flowers and herbs in North Beach. That was from a horse-cart, before the war. Also, she'd told her, if Maddie's own father was to be believed, the family might have been descended from the herb gardeners of the first Mission in San Jose in the 1790s. And at Mission Dolores after that. 'Before the gold rush,' Isabella had clarified to Maddie, 'before the coming of the "gringo", when the town was called Yerba Buena.'

Good herbs, Maddie thought. That was then. Now the herbs were grown in a greenhouse and sold here in a gleaming modern kiosk that stood on the pavement outside a shining modern building.

Suddenly, Jimena stood before her. She took both of Maddie's hands in hers, and her rich brown eyes looked deep into Maddie's soul, almost moving them both to tears.

'I'll save the orchid from your Chris, Maddie, and in time you will be someone new. But now is not the moment to think about that.'

A quick series of toots on a horn broke the hush.

'*Dios, Enrique!* Is it that late? *Mi hermano.* He is here to pick up the deliveries, but if he stops for too long the police get *muy feo* – you know, Señorita Maddie – very ugly!'

Her haste was so calm and sweet that Maddie felt under a spell.

'Take these out for me, please, and I'll get the rest,' Jimena said, as she pulled the door open and pushed Maddie towards the street with an armload of flowers. 'Go! *Vete!* There'll be police here in a minute.'

Struggling with the floral offerings, Maddie went. She dodged through the ebbing tide of homeward-bound commuters to reach Enrique's pick-up truck. She felt she might be sucked away by the sea of humanity, but Enrique saw her and leaped out to open the passenger door, taking the flowers and placing them on the seat.

'Thanks,' Maddie breathed out. 'Jimena is coming behind me. Give her my love and tell her I had to scoot off. Tell her I'll drop by later in the week.'

Then Maddie let the anonymous sea of humanity carry her away in its flow, hoping that Jimena could save the last living vestige of Chris.

7

1 February 2007, San Francisco

In the first days back at the office – and in her life in general, post the trauma of losing Chris – Maddie's life seemed surreal. She was suspended between cycles of heavy clouds and sunshine in her physical landscape, and the melancholy of Chopin's Nocturnes and Mozart's Requiem playing over in her psychological one. She avoided everyone, refusing dinner invitations, which would open the way for friends to be sad and gushy on her behalf, or, God forbid, to exhort her to be strong and then look forward. Because, the emails and sympathy cards read, she was by nature such a positive person with her 'whole life ahead of her'.

Seriously?

What did they know? The friend who'd just been dumped by her boyfriend of a few weeks because he said it was 'getting too serious'; or another who'd broken up with someone who 'didn't seem like good parent material' . . . Their concerns were what *might* be. But Maddie knew with Christopher what *was* – what should have been. She had no time for platitudes. She blistered her heels walking miles, everywhere, nowhere, with her iPod, to exhaust herself and strangle emotional thoughts. She had no interest in the arrival of her 'whole life'.

For two days she'd kept her head down with work any trainee secretary could have done: requests for information from specialists, compiling files from cases with similarities, catching up her own paperwork. She dreaded the trip to San Jose on Thursday. How would she face the strain? Talking to people with terminal illnesses was no one's idea of an away-day. When she'd started, weeks ago, half a carat set in white gold on her finger seemed a metaphor for her unsinkable faith in something bright and beautiful in this world, her talisman against the dark. Many people she'd talked to were without hope or anger, some tearful, others resigned; but Maddie had energy for all of them and promised to be the voice they lacked, to speak up against their expendability. She understood how to choose details that would clinch the hearts of a sober jury. Somewhere between objectivity and empathy, you had to establish trust with the victims, yet stay focused and not allow sentiment to cloud good judgement. But this took stamina and an unwavering belief that you could make a difference. She had neither that fortitude nor confidence now. In ten days, the world had come to look very different to her.

On Tuesday afternoon, she'd thought of speaking to Samantha to be excused, but decided not to. And by Wednesday lunchtime, she'd recognised such a request would make her seem weak. Then, without warning, it was early Thursday morning – the first day of a new month – and she was being picked up from her apartment by a coffee-toting Tyler, threading a route out of the city with its low-lying tule fog still clinging to the ground and slowing the traffic, until it eventually began to lift and the miles to pass a little more quickly.

Once they cleared the centre, her companion began to chatter in a tone that belied the seriousness of what he was telling her. Maddie wondered if he was nervous about what to say to her, which everybody seemed to be these days, studiously avoiding the subject of Chris's death and just making meaningless conversation that made her feel even more isolated. Tyler was doing the same, covering territory they both knew fairly well: that Stormtree had its own in-house health insurance scheme for the employees; that it was much lauded as a very good deal for the workers because it covered the hospital bills in a country where health care was always a guaranteed hot topic and political football. Tyler was saying that most of the workers couldn't have otherwise afforded medical insurance.

'Of interest to us, perhaps,' he said, 'is that Stormtree is a major supporter of the St Catherine's group of hospitals, including the two sister hospitals here in Jose. The company makes charitable donations and receives significant tax rebates for it.'

'Somehow I'm thinking their altruism is not your point, Tyler?'

Maddie twisted her hair into a high knot that held itself in place with a strand of curl, inviting him to make his argument clear. Tyler, however, had his own style, and took his time.

'There's also a magnificent "retreat" – that's the word they use for it – which hospital directors can enjoy around the lake at Gray Pines, near Tahoe. New England-style guest houses – you know, Maddie, all shingles and shutters and steep roofs – which were once a rehab facility for the hospital. Gray bought them up and improved the amenities for the hospital's benefit,' Tyler grinned.

Maddie couldn't help liking Tyler. He was a man with such a conscience, it was as though every breath of air meant something more to him than to other people. He'd signalled his distaste for Pierce Gray's attempts to import some New England polish and invent for himself some revised family credentials. It made her smile.

'This is circuitous, Tyler,' Maddie said drily, 'but I believe you're suggesting that Stormtree and the hospitals are so closely intertwined – or the hospital so tied to this fiduciary help – that criticisms from any of the staff concerning Stormtree would be an unlikely prize?'

Tyler shrugged. 'You'll say I'm a cynic . . . yeah, maybe.' He looked over at her. 'But, babe, this is the world of the big corporations, wheels within wheels – and Pierce is a genius at laying down stores for future payback. How can so many bright people be fooled by this guy?'

And Maddie pondered this question until the jigsaw of streets that made up the urban sprawl of Santa Clara County, in Silicon Valley, started to engulf them.

Marilu was Maria Luisa Moreno, and she'd been very pretty once. Her heart-shaped face and trim waist were still those of a younger woman.

She'd left the white iron gates open for them, and now watched Tyler pull his Chevrolet into her concrete driveway under the arms of an Elephant Foot palm, from the porch of her 1950s wood and stucco home on South White Road. The rain had stopped an hour or so ago, and she'd been keeping watch for them.

Marilu nodded respectfully at Tyler and offered Maddie a hug, but was surprised with the young woman's reserve. This was something odd. When they'd first met she'd been struck with Madeline's easy charm and, most significantly, the fact that she didn't seem to have that inherent condescension towards her. Marilu had lived her whole life with the awareness that most of the white population treated her and her family as second-class citizens: most of them weren't even aware of it. But Maddie had been so very different. She'd had energy, and warmth, which were not regularly offered to someone like Marilu; and she'd rewarded this openness with a rare sense of trust. Today, however, the rules seemed to have changed, and Maddie had a distance that was a contrast to her previous self.

Marilu looked at her, and checked her own behaviour, but Tyler saw all this and spoke to the older woman quietly.

'She has just suffered bereavement, Mrs Moreno. Someone young and very close to her.'

Marilu led them through her front door. 'I am sad for you, Miss Maddie,' she said softly. 'You are not yourself, I think. It was very deep, yes?'

'My fiancé was killed recently in England. His car was hit by a drunk driver.'

Maddie's voice sounded strained, Marilu thought, rather than devastated. Now she recognised the loss of weight, the papery thinness of her skin, the tangible stress in her – something borne of days of denial and an inability to confront the pain. She'd done that herself, once.

She sat her visitors in the vibrant living room – set-dressed with a riot of colourful ceramics and fabric and a picture of the Virgin – while she went to get coffee.

Maddie had noticed on her first visit here how house-proud Marilu was: how she'd explained the huge step up from the mobile home she and her husband had lived in twenty years before, to this substantial house with three bedrooms and a good-sized bathroom that working for Stormtree had afforded her. One hour here in her home, she'd thought, and the paradoxes were clear.

Tyler was taking out the recording equipment and setting it on the table when the cherry-pink coffee cups and cookies arrived.

'I know you must feel we've discussed everything before, Mrs Moreno, but we'd like to go over it all again just in case there is some detail you forgot, or that springs to mind now.'

Maddie tried to smile. 'Can you start by giving us your name and date of birth? Your place of work? Then we will ask you some questions.'

Maddie heard Marilu reiterate these details, then posed some questions that she knew would start her talking. She remembered Marilu Moreno's story well enough.

She was the child of Mexican agricultural workers who had almost nothing. They had given up what little there was so Marilu could get an education. She was bright, and driven, had faith in the virtues of hard work and was destined for university, with a wish to go into journalism. But her life had changed for ever in her last year of high school. Her father had contracted a lung condition, caused by the inhalation over a long period of time of the organophosphates used for years as pesticides on the fruit crops. Her parents had wanted her to continue at school, but she knew the family could never survive without the income from her father. So, aged seventeen, she took his place in the fields.

Peaches were harder than grapes, and almonds kinder than both. But she worked hard, and with her mostly optimistic outlook on life, the years had seemed to smile on them all. The agro-industry had declined in San Jose, but was replaced by the big-name computer companies. And Marilu – ever willing and agreeable by nature – was lucky. She had just enough education – and a surfeit of desire for a better life – to secure an assembly job in the fledgeling manufacturing industry with Stormtree Components, in the brand-new plant that rose out of the ground where the lemon trees had once grown.

God had blessed them, she believed; and it seemed he had. A quick learner, and with hands well-trained for delicate work, she rose to become a section leader, married, and she and her husband were able to buy a little house – not much, but it belonged to them, along with the mortgage company. In time they extended to create an extra room for Marilu's widowed mother.

They had three children, the eldest at last able to live out his mother's dream and go to San Jose State University, where he'd studied engineering. The last one, sadly, had not been so lucky. Born with a congenital heart defect, little Jorge had died before he reached his second year. In telling the bare facts, Marilu's voice still betrayed the emptiness that she'd felt at the time. But her sad tale was not done. Two years after the death of her boy she herself contracted breast cancer. Then, she thought, the company had been wonderful: kept her job open, insurance met the bills, family survived. Not what her poor father had endured.

Returning to her job as a supervisor, she gradually became aware that there were a disproportionate number of colleagues in the clean rooms getting serious illnesses – many more than in the other departments. This was made even clearer from discussions with her workmates over lunch in the company canteen. During a routine check-up she asked a company doctor about this. He assured her it was because of her background, and the history of exposure of people like her to what were now known to be carcinogens in agriculture. It was very sad, but to be expected; wasn't she lucky to have the company's support now?

But on another day, in a different mood, she'd passed him in the corridor. He said that he had looked at the questions she raised about her illness. There might be something to it, he agreed nervously. A week or so later, though, before she could question him further, she discovered he'd been transferred to another facility on the East Coast. She had pushed the doubt to the background, accepting his original explanation. Now, she couldn't even guess at his name.

At the distance of ten years, though, her cancer had returned. She wasn't angry. She was disgusted at the injustice. When her second in command also got breast cancer, and the number of sick staff in her area had increased again, she was determined to find out why and make some noise.

'After all,' she said flatly to Maddie and Tyler, 'somebody should.'

Maddie reached across and switched off the tape recorder. Tyler Washington smiled at her. He obviously saw something in what had been said that might take them a little further, but it was not yet clear to Maddie. All she could see was a sick woman who was fuelled with anger enough now to raise the devil. Maddie almost felt her loss of Chris was nothing compared to the ongoing suffering of this woman. She marvelled at Marilu's ability to divorce herself from the life of the person she was describing on the tape. How could an individual step back from their own reality and examine it in such a detached fashion? It seemed such a hopeless situation.

As Marilu held the security door for them, she asked how the case was progressing. Maddie knew it all seemed interminably slow, but Tyler was more positive.

'You've given us something today that may help a great deal. It was very useful.' He shook her hand in a gesture designed to encourage her.

'Thank you for your time, Mrs Moreno. We're going to help you make some of that noise!'

She nodded at him, but her words were only for Maddie: 'Be patient with yourself. Grief is a terrible companion. If it takes you over it will eat you from the inside – eat away at all your hopes and happiness, Miss Madeline.' She squeezed both of her hands. 'That's a thing worse than cancer,' she said firmly. Then she waved them away.

'God, you're hard work, Maddie. Where's the real you?' Tyler complained as they climbed back into the car. He waved to Marilu as they drove off.

'Sorry?' Maddie asked.

'Did it slip right past you?' Tyler almost snapped, but he checked himself a little, remembering the 'real' Maddie was lost in a widow's clothes. 'Look, we have copies of the medical records in our paperwork. Somewhere in among them we can find that doctor's name. If we can find him, we can ask him what he meant about Marilu. It's a starting place. Don't you see?'

If, Maddie thought. 'If' was a word that ran unchecked into wasted years. But she said, 'Maybe you've just convinced me that he'll never speak out against the company – *if* we can find him.'

Tyler instinctively wanted a sharp response – some pithy remark from the impressive young woman Samantha had hired – but the change in her made her sound flat and resigned. It was light years from the shining girl he'd first met. He understood; but it couldn't continue. He turned the car away from Marilu's enclave, and tried something different.

'Henry Ford . . . you know, Maddie? My mom drummed his philosophy into me as a kid. "Whether you think you can or think you can't, you're right." It's always been true.' And he gave his attention to the road again.

They drove in silence, lost in their own thoughts as they passed the verdant parkland around Stormtree's ultramodern San Jose plant, subjugating the countryside. For blocks and blocks, it seemed to announce its presence in a kind of feudal dominance over the human dots in the landscape. Then, a quarter of an hour further down the road, St Catherine's sibling hospital, the Mater Misericordiae, loomed large. Overly clean and sterile in some ways, it was nevertheless shaded by a cluster of unexpectedly lovely Mediterranean umbrella pines, which caught Maddie by surprise.

Tyler pulled the car into the visitors' parking lot, and they entered quietly by the main desk. Pointed fingers sent them on their path to find a young woman neither had met. At the end of a corridor, in a room facing onto an inner courtyard with a giant cypress pine, serene and poised even from a prone position, they found Neva Walker.

Dark silky hair tied loosely around her face, Neva smiled at them as they came in. She voicelessly commanded that they leave their tensions and their noise, their worldliness and woes, at the door: this was her domain. Maddie saw immediately that she was not angry at all – or not in the way that Marilu seemed to be. Marilu's sense of a fight was what kept her going; but Neva appeared to be a completely different human being.

'Thank you both so much for coming down here to see me,' she said simply.

Maddie heard a song-like quality in Neva's voice, and wondered at its richness in the frame of such an apparently fragile body. But Neva was not fragile at all, as Maddie soon saw.

'Can you sit?' she asked. 'And I will tell you my story.'

But even Tyler was so unprepared for this beautiful, gentle woman, who looked younger than her thirty years, that he forgot to put on his tape recorder. Instead, the two visitors sat and listened to a tale.

'The snow fell in San Francisco on February the fifth, the year I was born. My father took it as an omen. He named me, his first daughter, after the surprise weather, but also after the place he originally had come from – his home state of Nevada – the land of snow.

'My mother, who was Muwekma Ohlone, told him the story that her own grandmother had been born on just such a day, this very same date. She could recall the family history, that on February the fifth in the year eighteen eighty-seven, her father's mother was born on a day with snow deep enough to bury your feet! She was a wise woman, renowned for her cool head and her warm heart. She had been given the name "Nevie", which is Spanish, you see, but so much of the Costanoan languages and names have been lost, that we share. But you must understand, Miss Moretti, Mr Washington, such a thing was a tiny miracle to my father. Two women, two snowfalls in a land of heat, and one date. He felt blessed.'

Maddie sat, her hands resting together in her lap, and let Neva's voice pour over her like a balm. The details made her shiver with a strange kind of pleasure. Neva told how this way of naming people was the choice of her father's people for millennia, to mark the events of births by tying them to something beyond the person, linking them to a moment in time.

His people were the first Americans. Though precise time-lines were still under debate, a conservative estimate meant they had arrived in North America at least twenty thousand years before the Bible had been conceived. Fewer than one in ten of her people had survived the colonisation, first by the Spanish in the eighteenth century, then later by the arrival of other European whites in the nineteenth. But whether you believed the world had been created six thousand years ago by God, or a little longer ago than that – when Neva's maternal ancestors were farming along the waterfront and fishing from the great ocean – the truth was that she had already been treated for a lesion on her brain and was still struggling with a colon tumour and metastatic disease to her liver. She was young, and sweet-natured, and very beautiful; and in Maddie's mind, perhaps alongside Chris's death, this was the most unfair thing imaginable.

How could the lovely creature in the bed, surrounded by medical apparatus and tubes, seem to accept these circumstances with such equanimity? And Tyler, Maddie observed, was caught in the same mood of silent amazement. Neva's smile was so warm and welcoming that the nurse had to come and prise away her guests after half an hour, to remind them they had promised not to stay long. They got to their feet, embarrassed, but Neva reached for Maddie's slim hand with her own, to stop them leaving just yet. Maddie felt an unexpected strength in Neva's grasp.

'Thank you. I am glad you have come for me.' She smiled. 'Sometimes, Miss Moretti, there is nothing you can do about the inevitable. But do not think of me as a victim. I have whatever time is left to me on this earth. I will find a way to enjoy the sun on the hills, and the moon coming and going, and my son getting older, learning new things. There will be days of pain, but also of pleasure. What is the point of anger? It would steal from me everything that I value. I do worry, yes, of course.'

Neva's eyes were so enormous in her petite face that Maddie couldn't look away, nor add a word. Neva continued talking as though she were confiding to an old friend.

'What will happen about my father and my son, when the time arrives for me to go to the place of my ancestors? My mother is already there, so this journey holds no fear for me. As for my father, he says that he has been here in the world a very long time; he can still drive the lumber across the state lines; he knows the old ways, and can look after them both. He is strong in his mind that they will be fine, so I should make the most of the time I have. But . . .'

Neva changed her hold on Maddie's hand to a gentler one, and her eyes intensified as though she urgently needed to communicate something to Maddie that language couldn't quite convey.

'. . . . Yes, I do worry about them. I believe there is something you can do – *you*, Miss Moretti. You have been tossed in a storm out at sea, haven't you? But you survived. You will be the one who ensures that when there is a settlement, my people are not overlooked because one is old, and the other only a child.'

Maddie found herself a little unnerved, but deeply moved; and she realised her head was nodding without her apparent volition.

Neva laughed, understanding, perhaps, the crosscurrents of Maddie's emotions.

'So,' she added, 'with this promise from you, I too will promise. I'll stay away from the ancestors for as long as I can. I want to know that day has come before I go.'

Maddie couldn't speak; and the normal banter and chat of Tyler had been snuffed for three-quarters of an hour. The nurse now rounded on the pair and took Maddie gently by the arm, indicating 'out' with her head.

'She has the patience of Santa Fina, that one,' she said to the departing pair with a mild Irish accent. Then she ushered them into the corridor, and closed the door firmly. Neva and the cypress were left alone again.

Tyler looked at Maddie as they'd reached the front door of the hospital, unaware of the track their feet found to take them there. Each looked as shattered as the other, and he took her hand to lead her back to the hospital's small coffee shop. He placed a hot drink in front of her in an automatic fashion, then sat unusually close to her. She exhaled; and he nodded. No one spoke. But it was another half-hour before they walked to the car for their journey home.

8

FEBRUARY 1347, SANTO PIETRO IN CELLOLE, CHIUSDINO, TUSCANY

How altered this morning was her cherished landscape of mystery and strange power! Exhaling warm breath on the leaded pain of her window, and then using her sleeve to clear it, Mia scrutinised the frozen stretches of ground below: a carpet of white as far as the eye could see. Only an animal's tracks broke the silk perfection of the snow; she thought, at this uncertain height, probably a deer. For days they'd been snowed in – so unexpected here by the river in the valley. The hill towns often had this, but only rarely did it get cold enough to stay on the ground at Villa Santo Pietro for so long. A short distance away in Chiusdino – or still further, in noble Siena – the business of life would be bustling along almost as usual: the baker would be shouted at for selling out of hot bread faster than he could make it; the bankers and justices would struggle into offices up icy, sloping roads from their town houses; the officials would come and go across the Campo Santo to the Palazzo Pubblico where they would govern, or misgovern, the people in town and the outlying districts, for good or ill – despite the famous entreaty in Maestro Lorenzetti's painting to strive for good government.

Here, in Siena's rural *contado*, snow drifts prevented much movement. No one had arrived or departed from the villa for some days together. The light-haired young nobleman with the lame foot had been the last to leave almost a week ago, walking upright and assured after days of ministration at the hands of the '*bella pellegrina*'.

Now they were completely snowed in, as if someone had pulled down a mantle of impenetrable weather to stop them all being disturbed. This also meant the suspension of attending Mass half a mile away in Palazzetto. Once they'd had a fine chapel themselves, right there at the villa, serving the grand house and small dwellings of the workers. But almost one hundred years ago it had been torn down: subsumed to the need of the monks to expand the abbey of Galgano, waived away by Bishop Ranieri in Volterra at the urging of Rinaldo, an overreaching rector of the now defunct church at Sorciano. Rinaldo had been a powerful and ambitious local cleric, always looking for ways to wheedle into the graces of the clerical and social hierarchy. And what were the needs of the villagers – how much heeded would their voices be – compared with the opportunity to enlarge the abbey and attract visitors and cash gifts from those on the road to and from Rome? This was a chance at salvation for the nervously rich, and at raising revenue for the Church. Gifts to an abbey guaranteed you a place in heaven, and the Cistercian brothers were guardians of a very popular saint. Every knight returning from the Crusades had learned of Galgano: the man who had thrown aside his gentle birth and life of privileges to follow the cross. In order for Galgano to pledge his agreement to give up warring and follow the Lord, the Archangel Michael had commanded him to plunge his sword deep into the stone ground on Monte Siepi, leaving just the cruciform-shaped hilt exposed above the ground to worship, instead of the earthly material life.

And there it remained to this day, guarded by the monks, a miracle for all to see: a sword floating benignly in the mighty unhewn rock, exerting wonder on the imagination of those hoping for miracles.

Aunt Jacquetta had taken Mia to the place a short distance away on the road to Ciciano, where Galgano's horse had kneeled at the appearance of the Archangel. The horse's prints remained, leaving a soft impression in the stone as though it were merely sand – as though it happened yesterday! The avenging angel had been just a mile or so from the villa, here among them, in the blessed countryside of the Merse Valley. *This* was why Mia knew that unicorns might exist in the forest near her home. This was a landscape that had witnessed the presence of the holy, touched deeply by *spirit*. Mia understood that just being here opened up a world of possibilities – which was why pilgrims came.

They were well prepared for the weather, the villa supplied with enough winter provisions to last a month, if need be, despite the reduced grain harvest last autumn, which had left some shortages in Siena. Mia could concentrate on her unicorns, and the lady with light in her eyes and her hair. For almost three weeks she had watched her, trying to understand her story.

Many things seemed strange. When it was customary for all young brides to have their bridegrooms matched for them, it was wonderful that there was obvious feeling and empathy between the young woman and her husband, whose name Mia at last knew! And that was another unusual thing. She had earlier this week heard him called 'Porphyrius' – a Latin name after the Greek – rather than the Tuscan 'Porfirio', in honour of the saint. Perhaps he came from an old family, as sometimes these conceits were kept among the upper classes. Mia recognised his name meant 'purple', a reference to noble robes and the blood of his family. Yet his clothes, though fine enough, were worn and stained with travel. Or perhaps his parents had bestowed his name for the learned philosopher, whose text on logic even Mia had been made to study by her aunt, though this wasn't usually encouraged for a girl's education. Or, was it just *her* chosen name for him? Aunt Jacquetta's choice of calling her 'Mia' was more than a contraction of her given name: it was her aunt's way of telling Mia that she claimed her as 'mine' – her own child. But whatever the reason for the appellation, his name stood out for consideration.

Other things piqued Mia's curiosity. The lovely pilgrim still had said nothing about herself.

In winter daylight she seemed rimmed by sunshine in her fair hair, and at night her whole presence exuded an uncanny aura of light so that she might almost be the daughter of the sun and the moon, rather than mortal parents. It was so ethereal, Mia wondered if she might be a 'holy' or a 'blessed'. Tuscany, with its landscape of sulphurous hills and dramatic chasms, seemed a nurturing ground for saints. But against this, the most notable feature of her character was that she didn't seem the least bit pious. She hadn't once attended the local church, or visited the shrine of Galgano or the abbey. She would walk from the house, even in the direst cold, and spend half an hour completely alone in the garden. When she returned to the warmth inside, she seemed touched by something special – touched by the Divine. She had the aura of a saint; or, Mia thought, at least what a saint ought to be. Possibly, like Chiara in Assisi, she had her own very simple way of wanting to worship.

Then there was the question of a ring. She wore nothing to show her marriage, though this was not *so* unusual. A ring was becoming customary in betrothals and at weddings, but it was not absolutely required. The husband bringing his young wife publicly into his parents' house to live with them was still the clearest token of marriage. Nor did she have a proper change of clothes, or a light pack for travel. He carried the little they had between them, and Mia thought she and her husband had left in a hurry, without much preparation. They surely had contracted a marriage for love, Mia thought, rather than to honour the wishes of the *pater familias*. Such a thing would be worse than heresy.

Coming downstairs to the kitchen, Mia found Loredana ready for her with a roll, hot from the oven, and an egg already boiled.

'Eat this quickly, Maria,' she told her. 'Your aunt's been waiting for you in the solar for some time.'

Mia tossed the warm bread between the fingers of each hand to cool it, then ate as quickly as she could. Leaving the egg, she wiped her hands and mouth and hurried from the kitchen towards her aunt, whom she found sitting in fact not in the solar but in the large room they used for music and reading. She was absolutely without sign of impatience. The fire was lit, fresh cypress shavings and mint had just been strewn to deter pests, which might venture in during the freezing weather; and Mia smiled seeing at once that their visitor was there. Her fair hair was twisted around her face with cord like a young girl's, and today she was dressed in a fresh kirtle of pale silk. Mia thought its appearance might explain Signor Porphyrius's mission in terrible weather to Siena a few days ago, perhaps for a bolt of cloth. And fine damask it was, which must have required a few florins.

'You've slept long, Mia,' Aunt Jacquetta said with wry amusement. 'Were you up late, reading?'

Mia didn't know whether to look apologetic; but she was saved from embarrassment by the young *signora*.

'It's the hush of the snowfall, and the feeling of peace in this house.' She rose from her low seat near the fire, and stretched a hand to Mia. 'I haven't slept so well myself in a long time. This house has some power over the soul.'

Mia accepted the hand and seated herself beside her, opposite Aunt Jacquetta. She noticed a slightly conspiratorial smile between them.

'The family of the *signora*'s husband, Mia, trade wax and rare spices into France, in exchange for Flanders cloth. We are lucky enough to have been given a gift of some we have never tried.' Jacquetta's voice was full of its usual warmth and enthusiasm.

The young woman picked up a small dish from the floor beside her and addressed Mia in the lightest voice: 'I have blended some of these spices for Signora Jacquetta, Maria, for use on the poultry dish tonight. But she says you have decided preferences, and is afraid you won't like them. Cloves you will know, and the cinnamon flowers and ginger. And you will have tasted saffron for special occasions. But I have here something we call "grains of paradise", and some mace, and cubeb – which is a spice some people feel has magical properties. Would you taste the mix for me?'

Mia looked at her aunt, and then again at her neighbour. She believed it was a test of her maturity – whether she was outgrowing the appetites of a child. She put her finger warily into the dish of coloured grains, and pressed so that some stuck to the pad. It seemed harmless enough, and she put the tip of her finger onto her tongue.

Such a sensation! Warmth, and richness – much greater than just salty or sweet. The small grains took her tongue on a journey it had never been to, and she couldn't find words for herself to describe the new pathways. She repeated the movement, allowing her tongue some time to play with the sensations, then she swallowed. But something caught in her throat: peppery, but much stronger. It took Mia entirely by surprise, and she coughed sharply, swallowed her own saliva, and then coughed again.

The young woman patted her on the back, then stood to get her a cup of water from a table near Jacquetta. But Mia noticed from the corner of her eye that she and her aunt were smiling at one another.

'Signora Toscano was asking me about your voice, Mia.' Aunt Jacquetta spoke gently. They'd never discussed this before, and she knew her niece might be sensitive to the subject.

Mia was wrong-footed, most immediately by the use of a name for their guest: 'Signora Toscano'. Whether or not the new young wife of a spice merchant, this was certainly a general name, not a true family name. She had already indicated to them that she was '*di Toscana*', a local; the name just underlined this. It was the name of someone revealing nothing about herself, remaining in hiding. But the lady in question put a hand comfortingly on Mia's shoulder again and spoke to her directly, as though she had nothing at all to hide.

'You coughed aloud,' she said. 'I believe this means that your voice cords still work, and that you could most certainly speak – if you wished to. If you had something you wanted to say. Perhaps,' she said softly, 'you have simply lost the habit. And I know there are often things we don't want to talk about, that make us go silent for a time.'

Mia looked very surprised. She thought for a moment. Using her voice wasn't something she'd considered – not in years. Why was it necessary? The people who mattered understood her, and it was less complicated, not being expected to voice her thoughts to any other people. Why would she want to start speaking now?

With a series of shrugs and a look of bemusement, Mia communicated this to her aunt. But the young *signora* persevered.

'There will come a time,' she said gently, but emphatically, 'when you will want to find words – careful words – to say what's in your heart. This is something I know.'

Mia's brown eyes looked at the *signora* searchingly. Yes, she was a little uncomfortable with the subject; yet she gave this young woman respect. There was something utterly unfathomable about her, Mia felt. It was unsettling not to know more, more about who she was and what she was thinking. But for all that, Mia trusted her too.

'Should you let me work with you, Maria Maddalena, to strengthen your throat and exercise your vocal cords against the day that you want to use them, I would mark that as an honour to me.'

'Would you be willing to try, Mia?' Jacquetta's voice was almost a hush, not wanting to put any more strain on the girl, who had already been tricked a little, to frighten her off if she were thinking of agreeing.

Mia's head felt light, and her breathing slowed. She wanted to escape the feeling of being closely watched for a response. She took her eyes towards the window and fixed them on the beautiful *monacordo* – an enchanting new instrument that plucked the strings with little brass hammers to release sweet sounds – which she'd received weeks before for holy season, an exquisite gift from her benefactor. This man she'd never known, never remembered meeting; but some of the servants gossiped that he was her father. A note came with it, entreating that it was a delicate instrument for making music 'to accompany the voice'. She'd known then that the gentleman mustn't have understood she had this malady – that she didn't speak, let alone sing. She'd felt sadness about that. She had spent hours at the pretty keys, learning its ways, mastering its touch to the best of her ability in so short a time. It was so very different from the *organetto* she had been learning with a lay brother at the abbey. She had already learned to produce pleasing passages on it, with her fingers skipping dextrously over the keys, but would she disappoint him if they met, because she couldn't sing?

She had thought sometimes, in moments of deep contemplation, it matters little what you would wish to do if you *knew* you couldn't fail. What is important is to look into the face of your fears, whatever they may be. Without courage to do that, good ideas and kind intentions were only half of your character.

She looked at her aunt, then seized Signora Toscano's two small hands. 'Yes.' Her nod was unhesitating.

So it was that many days passed with Mia in the close company of the young woman. On the coldest of those days Aunt Jacquetta offered them privacy in the warmth of the music room. Late in the week – when the snowfall had started to ease and the sun to reappear – they took up residence in the brightly lit solar, while Jacquetta worked from the small room overlooking the garden she called her office. The young husband left them again, this time for three days, and his wife, whom Mia still called *un' raggio di sola* – a beam of sunlight – gave all of her attention to Mia.

On the first day of their undertaking they had gone into the still room together, next to the dairy, and chosen some herbs. The young *signora* knew her way through this room better than Alba, better than Mia, better than Aunt Jacquetta herself. Mia was astonished by her knowledge of herbs and salves, and thought she could possibly teach even Fra Silvestro something new. She took the stems and flowers of agrimony and some costmary from the jars, and grated some ginger root her husband had given them. But she wanted something more, which she couldn't find – a herb Mia and her aunt had never heard of, which she described as having a long purple spiky flower and a distinctive scent. When everyone looked blankly at her, Signora Toscano directed her husband to an errand with the monks, before he made his journey away from them. And he duly returned, with something that made his wife kiss him warmly in front of everyone.

'*Salicaria!*' she enthused.

Now this little herb was blended by her with the others into a pan simmering on the fire. She had some winter berries, which she threw in at the last, leaving all to sit cooling for about an hour before she strained the odd-coloured mixture through fine cotton into a small vat 'for Mia's use alone', she said to everyone.

On that first day she asked Mia to let the liquid sit for a few moments in her throat, before swallowing it down. This she did without complaint: it was surprisingly pleasant tasting. The following day she heated a little of it just for warmth, asking Mia to keep it in her throat with a gurgle this time, for as long as was comfortable. On subsequent days they did this for longer periods, and the *signora* asked that Mia gurgle warm salty water in her throat too, in between the washes with the *salicaria* tincture. After five days Mia came into the solar to find Signora Toscano had a little polished silver glass in her hand, and was waiting for her.

'Come and sit facing the light,' she asked Mia. 'I wish to look down your throat and see its colour.'

Mia obeyed very dutifully. The polished glass was tipped by the *signora* to catch light from the sun, then reflected into Mia's wide open mouth. She sat very still for a while, and the *signora* made a few quizzical sounds. Mia's head was immovable, but she heard the bustle of Aunt Jacquetta's dress and the distinct tread of her foot, coming into the room to join them.

'Is it inflamed and red?' her aunt asked.

'A little,' was the answer. 'But not nearly as much as I had feared it would be.'

The *signora* withdrew the glass and allowed Mia to relax, then looked again at each of them in turn. 'Yes, pinkish rather than red; and much healthier than I expected. Today we can amuse ourselves with some new exercises.'

She demonstrated a series of very exaggerated shapes with her lips, mouthing vowels so comically that it brought both silent and loud laughter respectively from her audience of two. She laughed with them.

'And after that, Signora Jacquetta, I wonder whether Maria Maddalena and I might have some paper and paint, and your blessing, to design a quiet healing garden for her to use, where she might continue to look for her voice throughout the springtime?'

Mia looked at her aunt with a sense of wonder, assuming it was something they had talked about and already privately agreed, but Jacquetta's face was as surprised as Mia's.

'I have seen her small drawings,' she continued, 'and they are beautiful. We might sketch something together, to make a place of enchantment and miracles?'

'Do you have in mind a holy garden, Signora Toscano?' Jacquetta asked. 'We have made a start on this already, where our chapel of St Peter's used to stand.'

But the younger woman looked at Mia with a different light in her eye, and shook her head humorously.

'I thought,' she ventured, 'given the special qualities of your niece, perhaps a unicorn's garden?'

9

27 February 2007, San Francisco

Tuesday morning. The alarm went off at seven as usual, and Maddie opened one eye wearily on an apparently greyish day. Then she sat up slowly in bed, unable to comprehend why the room seemed so gloomy. It was as if it were still night outside, and the alarm clock misinformed about the hour. She shivered a little, sought the floor with her foot, and moved across the short distance from her bed to the partly closed curtains, which she left that way on working nights to help her out of bed next morning. Her view was obscured, and she was having trouble making sense of the apparent scene glimpsed through the space between them. She pulled back her curtains in confusion; then moved swiftly from her bedroom to the living room, right up to the French door of her tiny balcony.

Extraordinary!

The world before her looked like a grey and misty shimmering sheet, which stretched from her balcony towards what should have been her glimpse of the Bay. Instead, it offered a deceptive shroud of optical mist. She unlocked the door and stuck a toe outside, noticing it was definitely very cold, but the shock was not the chill. It looked as if a giant ice-crushing machine had been switched on and left running, spewing its contents over the San Francisco landscape. She pulled the door properly open now and gently extended her hand into the surreal world beyond – to be rewarded with the baby's-breath softness of some shining ice crystals – hail, in fact, but very close to snow.

'Neva!' Maddie whispered to herself.

She looked at her hand. The idea taking hold in her mind that this didn't happen in San Francisco fought with her certainty that she was really awake, so she flicked on the television for the breakfast news. There it was: images of children throwing Slush Puppie-like snowballs; a cut to the scene of a minor car prang; someone scooping a substance like mushy hail off their car window; stranded buses skidding on icy surfaces – all in quick succession. The weather was the news, and the anchor woman told her viewers in childlike glee that it seemed 'quite localised'. Maddie was in shock, but couldn't help herself smiling a little – until the full realisation of what this would mean for her day caved in on her.

One click switched on the coffee machine and her mind began to rehearse the day. She was due to have dinner that night with her family on the other side of the Bay, had planned to take the car into work so she could drive straight over the Bay Bridge as soon as her day finished. She'd promised her mother that she'd pick her father up on the way, at the university's Berkeley campus, where he taught at the Plant and Microbial Biology Department. 'Ohh', she sighed out loud. She certainly couldn't take the car to work in conditions like this. If I try to drive, she thought, I'll simply slide down the hill right into the Bay. The idea almost made her smile again.

'Very funny, Neva,' she heard herself say.

But not really amusing this morning! She made the decision to move to a Plan B. Yet, peeking back at the news over her coffee cup, it seemed that the surface transport was at something of a standstill, too.

After showering and dressing, she still hadn't resolved the problem, but looking outside, she saw that the strange crushed ice was still on the ground, even though there was hard icy rain falling. That would cause problems too, she thought, so Plan C was hastily constructed. Walking seemed the best answer. Then she could come back for the car at the end of the day. She would have to leave the office early to do that, but had got home late last night from San Jose, so she doubted Samantha would mind.

She reached for the television remote and just caught the comment that weather like this was 'something of a mystery', with two fronts colliding and creating the freak conditions.

'No one could have forecast this,' chirped an impossibly pretty weather girl in fitted cashmere; and Maddie clicked the 'Off' button.

To put Plan C into action, she grabbed the only thing she owned that she felt might save her from freezing to death on the walk to the office: an over-sized shaggy black faux-fur coat that her mother had given her for the Oxford winter. She'd managed to leave it at home for that trip, and meant to give it to charity months ago. She hated it but, drowning her lean frame in it today, she had to admit that, in these bizarre circumstances, it effectively covered her from head to toe. It blotted her out, actually – except for her feet, which stuck out at the bottom like penguin's feet. Feeling certain she'd win no style awards this morning, she addressed the footwear problem. Minutes later she was sporting a large pair of rubber galoshes, which her mother had also given her for England. Her mother, like so many of her generation, imagined that Britain was permanently gripped in a post-war time warp. She had no idea that people of Maddie's age couldn't spell 'galoshes', never mind wear them. Maddie hadn't ever taken them from their wrapping, and couldn't think why she'd brought them back from England. Her dislike of them was on a par with her feelings about the coat. But today it seemed her mother would have the last laugh; though not the only laugh, Maddie said to herself as she glimpsed her full-length silhouette in the hall mirror.

Maddie arrived at the office late, but not too wet or cold. Jacinta did her best arching-of-eyebrows mannerism and laughed unkindly.

'You look a bit like a yeti,' she said with a sarcastic smirk; 'but that would be a slur on yetis, who probably have more grace.'

Maddie upset Jacinta's rhythm by taking the jibe well, privately acknowledging the truth of the quip. Anyway, she had arrived, at least, and others had not. She knew she looked ridiculous and didn't need to have it pointed out to her by Jacinta, who, she thought, must have floated into the office in her Jimmy Choos like a revamped statue of the Winged Venus, never touching the icy hail that had collected thickly in so many places along the streets. There was something unnatural about Jacinta, Maddie thought, as she shook the ice off her hat and dived for the cloakroom to divest herself of the coat.

The first thing Maddie saw as she went into her office was a Post-it note on her desk-top screen. She reached across for it and read the fine black felt tip:

Sorry, can't trace
Dr (E for Elroy?) Macfadden.
T for Tyler

Maddie felt like popping her head through his door to say she'd guessed as much on day one, but that would be ungenerous. From the last interviews, the whole office had been confident that they might identify the doctor Marilu had mentioned. Maddie was the least optimistic, but she'd waded through a stack of medical notes and noticed a hieroglyph of someone's name on one of the clinic reports in the material they'd obtained most recently from Stormtree.

She'd shown the document to Marilu in Jose yesterday, and there was enough in the hen scratches to trigger her memory. 'Dr E. *Macfadden?*' Maddie had suggested to her. Marilu's face had brightened and agreed – and, the 'E' was for Elroy, she thought. This prompted Maddie to call Tyler at once so he could get on the phone and start the hunt for the doctor. But, in less than twenty-four hours, it seemed to be just another dead end.

Knew it was too good to be true, Maddie thought, scrunching up the yellow paper and tossing it into the trash. Suddenly she felt achingly flat and depressed. Why do people have to suffer for the negligence of others? Was nothing fair in this world? What had Marilu done but be a good mother, work hard for her family, and show just the right amount of ambition to be invaluable to her employers? Why couldn't they play fair, in return, and give her a safe place to work hard in?

This thought took her to another that had been bothering her unremittingly for weeks.

What kind of God is there out there? How can people sing his praises? She recalled it was her father who, in spite of his Catholic background – or maybe because of it – had put to her, when she was first old enough to think, the philosophical question posed by Epicurus two thousand years ago. That question echoed now, loudly in her head: a question about God that no one seemed able to answer.

'*Is he willing to prevent evil, but not able?*' She spoke the words out clearly, from memory. '*Then he is impotent. Is he able, but not willing? Then he is malevolent. Is he both able and willing? Then, whence is evil?*'

She sighed. 'Oh, but evil *is*,' she said softly.

She looked at the pile of papers on her desk, and started sorting through the day's chores. Predominantly there was a red-letter note from Samantha with a copy of a Stormtree Medical Department memo, asking her what she thought it meant at the bottom of the page? The typed words were asterisked in pencil: 'referenced – see also STC/CIR/425.272'.

Samantha had put her own Post-it just above the asterisk: 'Can you trace this cross-reference?'

Maddie knew she had to tackle this first. Samantha would want some kind of answer before she left, and Maddie realised it might help her ease her own mind – which was ruffled right now – to spend an hour looking for needles in haystacks. There'd be good reason, even if she herself couldn't see much in the footnote. Samantha was renowned in the legal world for her prodigious memory for detail. She could see something on a page and days later remember where it was, what it said. These were the details that supplied their trial lawyers with the kind of material that really shook their opponents. For this reason, their opponents insisted that every pre-trial submission was locked in stone before they got near a court. They were afraid of the killer detail Harden Hammond Cohen might produce in the eleventh hour, to destroy a case. The physically petite Samantha stood taller than her peers in this arena.

It was around three p.m. when Maddie pushed open Samantha's door. Her warmly dressed, rather than be-suited, boss looked up questioningly.

'I couldn't find anything more about that reference you wanted, Samantha,' Maddie said apologetically. 'I've called the department on the memo at the Stormtree Medical Centre, just on the off chance.'

'And?'

'I got a doctor who said he probably should not be telling me this – and I was not to quote him – but it referred to a complete record of all the known deaths of Stormtree's employees almost since the company started. "CIR" is Critical Illness Records, but he wouldn't say more.'

'Really?' Samantha's tone was pensive, and quietly enthusiastic. 'That's a kind of mortality record?'

'I imagine so. I've put it on the list of follow-ups,' Maddie said, 'for the additional material from Stormtree we're requesting through the courts.'

'Good girl.' Samantha began making a note to herself.

'Samantha, I'm supposed to go to Orinda to have dinner with my family tonight,' Maddie said tiredly. 'With the weird weather we had overnight, could I possibly leave early?'

Samantha indicated that would be fine. They both knew the journey could be an hour and more in traffic over the bridge and through Berkeley, even on a good day.

'Sure, good luck,' she said. 'I hope you make it, though it seems the ice has mostly melted now.' She looked up again at Maddie, grinning like a girl. 'It *was* weird, wasn't it? It was so loud it woke me in the early hours. I heard it was some kind of freak weather system that just blew up out of nothing from the Sierras.'

She returned to scanning her way through some Stormtree documents but Maddie hung on at her door, hesitating for a second.

'I had a very . . . well, *extraordinary* conversation with Neva yesterday,' Maddie said slightly tentatively.

'The Native American girl,' Samantha nodded, but hardly raised her eyes. 'Extraordinary?'

'When I told her that we really needed her testimony in court, she told me for the second time she would survive for as long as was necessary. She felt totally confident she could do that.'

'This is the girl who is terminal?' Samantha queried.

Maddie nodded, and Samantha took her glasses off to give her junior her complete attention. 'That struck you. I understand. But,' she said with animation, 'have you ever heard anyone say they have far too much to *do*, to get sick?'

'Sounds like you!' Maddie said, and they both smiled. 'But she told me that . . . Samantha, I had no idea that less than ten per cent of her people have survived to this day. The coming of the white Europeans with their diseases wiped out almost eighty per cent of some of the tribes. Many of the rest were enslaved, shot, or driven off their land.'

'Wow!' Samantha waved her into a chair. 'There were better odds of surviving the Black Death in thirteen forty-eight! That only *halved* the population of Europe.'

Maddie sat down. 'But,' her voice strengthened, 'she feels aware that she and her son, and her father, represent a line that extends back to the beginning of her people, against every odd. Her line has not ended, and she's determined that it must not. As Neva's people have suffered all the unimaginable pain and injustice the world can dump on them, what more can frighten her? And now she tells me positively she will stay in this world to help fight the case to the end. She's adamant that her boy will grow to become a father; and she believes that even I have to be prepared, when I come to face *my* adversary. I don't understand that at all.'

Samantha looked at her steadily. 'This is quite a privilege – this conversation you've shared, Maddie. Neva's story is unique to her, but similar stories are told across the world, by many races, down the length of days. None of us is ever really exempt. History shows us endless cycles of man's recurring heartlessness, and I'm sure our ancestors wielded sticks or worse, in their turn. The supposed superiority of religion or culture was all the excuse they needed. Maybe that's why we should make things better now, every time we can. David Cohen lost most of his family. His grandfather somehow got out of Dachau alive. He feels it rests with him to make good the survival – to do something on account. He always says we can't change the past, but we can change the future. We don't have to be bitter or retire from the human race, do we?' Samantha asked.

Maddie took a moment, looking away to avoid what seemed a suspiciously direct question.

'The oddest thing about our afternoon,' she resumed, looking at Samantha again, not knowing how her super-rational boss would react to what she was about to say, 'was when I asked her how she managed to be so focused and positive, after life had been so unfair? And, how could I find that belief? She looked at me quite unnervingly – not unkindly, though – took my hand and said, "I'll help you".'

Maddie felt self-conscious; but she wanted to talk about this, which Samantha must have sensed. It only took an encouraging nod for Maddie to go on.

'Neva explained, "My body is here in this hospital, and they tell me I'm dying. I can do nothing to change that. Instead, I take my mind and my soul to some other place I'd like to be, somewhere I've been completely happy – to draw strength. Your mind is always free, Maddie; never imprisoned unless you allow it to be. So, my mind and I go to the beautiful places I can think of, and I feel it as though I were truly there. This fills me with a *wildness* to live! Then, I could perform miracles! I can hear my son learning his math, and hear the sounds of my father's house. This makes everything possible. I can easily stay alive a whole lot longer for my son".'

Maddie paused and Samantha waited for her to continue.

'Neva told me to close my own eyes and think of such a place myself. "Don't think of *going* there," she told me firmly. "Think of *being* in that place, fully a part of its geography, smelling the air there, feeling the breath of that place on your face. Maddie, look down at your feet, in touch with that ground." And she held my hand tightly while we sat for some time. I went with it, Samantha – did this thing she asked. I went to the place in my mind that was the most vivid in my heart, where I'd been deeply happy, and where I wished I could be for just five minutes again.

'Strangely, when I opened my eyes, Neva was asleep in complete peace, in spite of the pain I know she's in. Now, I'm not sure how exactly to be prepared for what she says she sees,' Maddie concluded. 'But I followed her directive, and went to my special place; and I could really feel my cold feet and eyelashes. Then it snowed overnight – well, sort of, anyhow. Who could dream that would happen?'

Samantha smiled, and looked at her in a studied way. 'Some say the world will end in fire, some say in ice. Maybe miracles happen, for some.'

These words weren't what Maddie expected. She stood and turned towards the door, then left hearing Samantha's voice: 'Enjoy your evening.'

Even on the lower level eastbound out of the city, the sound of the wind on the open expanse of the Bay Bridge cables above her resonated with an ethereal harmonic. It was like the sound of wind playing in the mast and stays of a sailboat.

Far out, on the waters of San Francisco Bay, Maddie could see a lone white sail on the choppy sea. The boat looked to be in trouble – suddenly heeled over sharply in the gale, and then started to race across the blue and grey surface of the Bay, only to be jibed violently as the wind unrepentantly changed direction. Finally it seemed to escape the clutches of the gust and fled in front of the weather, leaving a trail of spray and foam behind. Maddie could imagine its crew fighting in panic to keep the boat from capsizing. The scene made her shudder, reminding her of an incident long ago that she'd pushed to the back of her mind. It was something that troubled her.

She changed lanes aggressively and pressed forward. She knew she needed to beat the rush of traffic that would spew from the city at any moment. On the Oakland side of the bridge she pointed her Mercury Cougar up the Eastshore Freeway towards Berkeley. Her mind was on autopilot. How many dozens of times could she remember taking this route? Her father had rarely driven himself to work. He saw no need for a car to stand idle all day long. In the summer he used to ride a bike, and it was only a short drive for someone in the family to pick him up when it was needed. When she first got her licence she used to offer to come, to give her an hour behind the wheel. Yet today the trip had little of the edge of pleasure it had had in the past.

The Plant and Microbial Biology Department, University of California at Berkeley, centred round Koshland Hall, which backed onto Hearst Avenue. Maddie swung into the familiar road, just out-side the green pastures of the university campus, which was bathed in an incongruous afternoon sun. She pulled into a loading bay on the side.

A tall, dapper man standing in the bright sun wore a warm chocolate sports jacket with a scarf. He had a profuse crop of curly salt-and-pepper hair, and was holding a well-worn briefcase of red leather, which Maddie had brought him back from Florence on a summer vacation, years ago. He smiled at her now, as she pushed open the passenger door towards him.

'Hi, Papa. I'm glad to see you're here already.'

'It was such a nice afternoon I thought I would just stand in the sun and think for a moment, while I waited for you. Looking at the internet news, I should think this is quite a contrast to what you've been having on the other side of the Bay? There's even some talk about landslides, so I hear.'

This was all spoken in that easy tone that characterised Enzo Moretti, or 'Laurie', or 'Lorenzo' still to his mother. But not 'Larry', Maddie thought. Only one person she had ever known had called her father that. And the person was Pierce Gray.

'Very different our side,' she agreed.

Enzo folded his long frame into the Cougar next to her, and she leaned over to give him a quick peck on the cheek.

'How you doing, Madeline?' he questioned. Her full name signified affection rather than formality, when spoken by him.

'Ho, Papa, I'm not sure. I go to work, do my job OK, I think. But, well . . . it's just "do". I don't know what I feel, or think.'

'And she forgot the stars, the moon, and sun,
And she forgot the blue above the trees,
And she forgot the dells where waters run . . .'

Enzo spoke these lines and smiled sadly for her.

'Kind of,' she said, and put her arms around him and kissed him a second time. She put her car into drive, and shot out into the traffic. 'It's real, and it hurts every second,' she added, glancing in the mirror and changing lanes.

Enzo nodded and looked at his daughter. 'I'm sure, so I won't give you the line about time heals. But, I think it will help.'

She nodded uncertainly back at him, and they drove in self-contained silence for the remaining fifteen minutes to the house in Wild Cat Canyon Drive, the house that had been Maddie's childhood home.

When they pulled into the yard it was just after six and the light was starting to fade, but the mellow wood of the cedar-shingled building was welcoming. The single-storey house, with its screened summer porch on one end overlooking the garden and vegetable patch and various sheds, stood on the rise of rough lawn. The indigenous forest – almost bluish in the late afternoon light – had been cut back hard to a wide perimeter from the buildings as a fire precaution. Maddie parked next to Barbara's new Nissan in the vast dirt parking area, rimmed with fragrant bushes, just to the left of the house.

It all looked as it had always done. Though it wasn't dark the porch light was on for them, and the windows of the house shone like welcoming beacons along its length. Maddie's bedroom was at the far end, with Barbara's room beside it; and here they used to chatter through the screened-wire windows to each other far too late into the night. Next space was the living room, with the old family grand piano; then the dining room; her parents' bedroom; and a guest room. Each had two windows looking out to wild, hilly woodland of Ponderosa pine and scrub oak. A long hall was in the middle, and a large kitchen – which was the centre of their home – contained a door that led the other way out into an 'L' shape. Here was a panelled den with an open fireplace, and this was mostly appropriated by her father. Two bathrooms at the back had small windows looking over the lawns on the other side.

Right now the associations of security and cosiness inherent in her childhood home fought to cheer Maddie, the garden as lovingly tended as ever by her father and mother. She thought of soon-to-be barbecues in the yard, swimming in Lake Anza in Tilden Regional Park, just a few minutes' drive away, and days at the beach. The fair-weather days – always inviting laughter from the past and the promise of more days like them in the future – made Maddie feel deeply sad and alone in this moment. She didn't belong to the happy people now.

She stood in the shrinking light and watched her father unwind himself from her car, aware she had not visited her family home since Chris's death.

'Go along, and say hello to your mom. She'll be pleased to see you. Of course she wants to talk,' he said, with an expression of some sympathy to Maddie. 'But Barbara has arrived, so she won't be able to go on at you for too long.'

Maddie grinned.

'Tell them I'm in the den. I've got a bit of work to do, but I'll come in a while.' Enzo looked at Maddie, sensing she'd rather he came at once and saved her from the over-solicitous care of her mother; but then he'd have his wife's wrath to deal with. 'I've got some really nice wine,' he told her encouragingly, 'a white, from Italy. It's as good as your grandfather's home-grown. We'll have a glass before dinner, OK?' He vanished around the side of the house.

Maddie acknowledged his departure with a nod. She knew this was, and had always been, her father's pattern of life, except when on vacation or the odd weekend days. He had always been entirely caught up in his work. His diligence had led him to become a world figure in the study of plant disease, but had perhaps also taken him out of the clutches of her sweet but over-bearing mother. And now her children had left home, she was possibly a rather lonely figure.

Maddie breathed in deeply as she trod along the path. Much as she loved her mother, she understood why she had been so long in coming home. A shadow crossed the light from the living room window, fell on her and caught her attention. It was her mother, Carol, and luckily also Barbara, whose permanently animated face smiled at her from the window, fervently waving at her to come in.

Everyone knew that Nonna Isabella had made sure, almost as part of the wedding contract with her new daughter-in-law, that Carol would cook well. Her beloved Lorenzo had to have good Italian home-cooked meals every night. Carol had risen to the task and learned well, but Isabella's fail safe – unbeknownst to Carol – was that her son himself was also an excellent cook, having spent much of his childhood watching and helping in the family kitchen. So, dinner – no matter what else was occurring – was always good and bountiful, frequently swelled with home-grown produce and even, at the right moment, with home-made wine, which was surprisingly excellent.

Barbara had just about saved her sister from the prurient questions of her mother, and she called out to her father to join them after what seemed, fortunately, a short enough interlude. The family gathered around the old oval maple table, glasses in hand.

'I had a crazy phone call from Nonna Isabella,' Carol said as they completed their toast to each other. 'She said she couldn't make it tonight as she had to find some old lady who used to make hats, or something.'

'Where in the world is she going, that she needs a hat?' Enzo asked, amused. He started to serve from a large bowl in front of his place of *crema di fagioli*, a bean dish, which used to be his and Maddie's shared favourite course for informal get-togethers.

But his wife ignored this question and began to ask instead those on her own mind, which Barbara had parried for Maddie in the hour before dinner.

'Maddie, do you have any news from England? Have they gaoled the man who killed Christopher yet?' Her mother rushed on from this without pausing for breath. 'I mean, there has to have been a trial by now, and a conviction, surely?'

Both her father and Barbara looked supportively across the table to Maddie, who had lowered her head. She managed an answer, in a small voice, 'No, Mom, I've heard nothing yet. The process of the law takes a long time, you know.'

'Oh, Mom,' Barbara said firmly, 'I'm sure Maddie will tell us when there is any news, or if she wants us to know anything.' Barbara tried to communicate a warning to her mother, which seemed to go right over her head, so she changed her tactics and turned to Enzo.

'Dad?'

Barbara always addressed their father as 'Dad'. Maddie had preferred 'Papa' from the time of the family trip to Italy, when she was twelve; or, 'Pa'.

'Dad,' Barbara said again, 'I see from the papers that the university is part of the new state-wide task force on Pierce's disease.'

This was a desperate attempt, really, just to steer the conversation in a new direction. She had no idea what she wanted to say after this. Her father, however, helped out, reading the signs.

'Oh, that's right, Barbara. The publicity machine is in place, it seems. Yes, the department is quite strongly involved,' Enzo replied.

Maddie was startled, and looked at her father. 'Is that seriously what it's called? What is Pierce's disease?' she asked, wondering if Barbara and he were sharing a joke.

'If you're asking out of real interest,' Enzo smiled, 'I shall explain, as simply as I can.'

'With you it's never "simply", Dad.' Barbara knew that her father seldom got to talk about his work at dinner. But, once started, he would vanish into his science, leaving all else behind.

'Simply,' he looked at her with a smile, and then at Maddie, 'Pierce's disease is a lethal bacterial disease of grapevines. It was first identified in California in the late eighteen hundreds, and has caused millions of dollars in damage to the state's vineyards. Berkeley scientists confirmed twenty years ago that the disease is caused by the *Xylella fastidiosa* bacterium. It's spread by certain types of leafhoppers known as "sharpshooters". It's a national, as well as a state, problem.' He shot Barbara an amused glance. 'Is that simple enough, miss?'

'Yes, Dad. Stop right there!' Barbara laughed.

'I'm advising, but I'm not part of that team. I'm doing something else.'

'Who is this Pierce?' Carol found something that interested her, and joined the conversation out of context. 'Does it have anything to do with your friend and colleague Pierce Gray?'

'No, dear, absolutely not,' Enzo almost laughed. 'In this case it's a last name, not a first, after a researcher in the late eighteen-nineties. He was Mr N. B. Pierce, and is credited with discovering the disease. But,' he continued, 'Mr Pierce Gray has in fact helped to fund part of the taskforce on Pierce's, as well as the research I'm working on. It's important to the wine growers in Napa. Gray is a major contributor to the costs – along with the other growers. It's in his personal interests, of course.'

'He always looks such an interesting man, so handsome and powerful,' Carol enthused, almost to herself. 'Haven't you girls been out on his yacht once or twice? I seem to think so. Everyone says he gives such nice parties. Your father has been a few times in the past, though I've never been included myself.'

'They're always work-related occasions, Carol,' Enzo answered her, refusing to rise to the bait. They'd been invited more than once for purely social reasons too, but Enzo had never been very interested in going and always made his apologies without consultation with his wife.

'Never mind, Mom,' Barbara added, knowing some of this. 'You haven't missed anything. From what I've seen at the "Gray Parties", they tend to be either very large and rowdy, or very private and over-intimate.'

'He gives a lot back to the community, you know,' Carol challenged. 'Look what he has done for the City's Art Gallery just recently. And that affects your job, Barbara. While you're busy hunting out all these works of fine art, someone has to be the patron and pay for them.'

Maddie put down the fork which had been toying with her beans. And think what he has given to his workforce for the past twenty years, she thought. Of course, she could never discuss this outside of her office. Suddenly, though, she wanted to speak in spite of the politics of keeping silent. She wanted to say what she knew about Stormtree, to confront her parents' perception and see how her always-wise father would respond. What did he really think of Pierce Gray, she wondered. Just at that moment, his voice distracted her.

'I've found him interesting on each occasion I've dealt with him. I quite like the man.' It was as though he'd heard her. 'In his arrangements with me and the university, he's always been more than generous. I remember you interviewed him for the university newspaper years ago when you were an undergraduate, Maddie, and you were very impressed with him at the time.'

'I was a child, Papa,' she said almost as a protest. 'I hardly had the maturity to evaluate the man himself.'

Enzo grinned. 'Well, he produces one of the consistently fine wines in the Napa, and has a huge reputation to keep up. His close involvement is surprising for someone who says grapes are just a hobby. Whenever we talk he is well researched on viticulture and wines. He has such passion you'd think he was speaking about women.'

Barbara had heard enough of this eulogy. 'On that subject he is more than well researched,' she commented with an ironic smile. 'He's had a lot of women to show for it, and keeps changing concubines like some Italian medieval potentate.'

'A succession of trophy wives, you mean,' Maddie sparked.

'Catas-trophy wives, in fact,' Barbara laughed, enjoying herself.

'You could have done worse than to be one of them, silly girl,' her mother said. 'You had a bit of a chance once; and I'm sure he looks after them very well,' she added. 'There's nothing wrong with a generous divorce settlement.'

'There is, if there's been a pre-nup,' Maddie joked grimly.

Enzo seemed to be wondering aloud whether being an Italian duke would have suited Pierce Gray. 'He'd have style and passion,' he said. 'Remember, when the bankers took over the Medici's art collection in Florence, Lorenzo told them the world would always remember them for the art, and not for the money they'd lost.'

'I was thinking more of Browning's poem, "My Last Duchess" – the one her husband kills off!' Barbara laughed. 'It was the Duke of Ferrara he had in mind, I think – the serial marrier who ended up with Lucrezia Borgia as the ultimate duchess. A giant among patrons, no doubt, but a monster with his control of the law, and his power, and no concerns about who got hurt. Pierce would go the same way, if he could.'

'"O, it is excellent to have a giant's strength! But it is tyrannous to use it like a giant,"' Enzo suggested.

That's a point Pierce Gray should bear in mind, Maddie thought, her anger rising. She could see Neva's patient face, and Marilu's photos of her kids; but she clenched a fist on her napkin out of sight, and said nothing.

A door suddenly banged at the back of the house, and made her jump.

Enzo rose. 'I must have left the window open again and a breeze has come up. I'll catch it.'

Barbara stood. 'Don't worry, Dad, I'll go close it. I'll take these through to the kitchen on the way,' she said, as she started clearing the first course. Maddie rose to help, but Barbara stayed her. 'I'll get the chicken dish, and the *contorni*. Sit down.'

Maddie turned to Enzo. 'Papa, what are you doing for Pierce Gray?'

'I'm looking at plant DNA and allelopathy,' he said, knowing she wouldn't understand the word. In reply to her puzzled expression, he tried to explain without becoming technical. 'It's a study of the relationships plants have with each other, to see if there is any long-term correlation between the allelopathic effect and the earlier species plant, which could be introduced into the plant biology of grapevines. Allelopathy is—'

'Help! Maddie, I need a hand,' Barbara's voice came from behind the swing door to the kitchen.

'Coming.' Maddie rose. 'But do tell me when I come back?' she asked, moving towards the kitchen with some plates. Reaching Barbara, she said under her breath, 'That was hardly subtle, Bee. Are you worried it sounds like a long one?'

Barbara handed her a serving dish to carry out. 'It is. I wouldn't get into it unless you want to stay the night and go back in the morning. I'm leaving early-ish, as I have to open the gallery for a delivery first thing.'

'OK then, I'm with you,' Maddie agreed. Then she paused. There was a child's painting on the kitchen wall that had been there years, but it caught her eye tonight. It was ambitious, and well executed for a little girl. She looked closely at the framed watercolour of a woman with streaming hair in a wild landscape, struggling to hang out washing in very gusty wind. The back of a child's head and shoulders was in the foreground, sheltering in a doorway out of the weather, watching her mother. The child's curly hair whipped across one side of the painting and, as an optical illusion, extended outside the frame. This made the viewer the child.

Barbara came up beside her. 'It's good. It's very true-to-life of Mom, and she thought it captured the moment with such feeling she had it properly framed. Do you remember? You did it when you were about eight, and had been sick at home with terrible fever – chicken pox, I think. I tell you, girl, you had talent. Now I'm the one working in Fine Art, and you're the lawyer.'

'Funny, I don't remember painting it, but I can still remember hearing the wind,' Maddie said, her voice almost lost. 'And by the way,

Bee,' she whispered, needing to tell her sister, 'my firm is in fact involved in a huge case against Gray's company. Best not to tell Pa.'

'Ooh.' Barbara's eyebrows lifted. 'For sure I won't. It's none of my business. My own dealings with him are not like Dad's. Every time we sell him a painting he tries to renegotiate the price, just before closing. It leaves us in a very bad position with the sellers, who feel they're being manipulated. They are. We've lost a couple of prestigious sales because of this. And I know what I'm saying about his attitude towards women.'

Maddie gestured at the steaming dish in her hand. 'I'd better get this on the table,' and she pushed against the swing door. 'Looks good, Mom,' she announced as she re-entered the dining room.

For half an hour her father explained his ideas, ending with the fact that plants are able to emit very complex chemical signals, which repel, or attract, others according to their individual interests. 'Algae can actually affect cloud formation, and therefore the weather,' he said finally, downing the last drops in his glass. 'But that's a story for a night when you can stay,' he said, noting she had never shown quite so much interest in his work over dinner before.

'I'm afraid I can't, Dad,' Barbara apologised. 'I'll clear for you, Mom, but then I'll have to head back.'

'Me too,' Maddie smiled softly. 'Work is pretty full on at the moment, and I don't want to be too late home.'

Maddie helped Barbara clear, but as the door swung shut she asked Barbara a question that had been growing for her over the course of dinner: 'What is Pa actually doing with Pierce Gray? I know they've always had a passing association, but he seems cosier than ever with him just now.'

Barbara had her own opinions. She spoke quietly while stacking the dishwasher. 'I may be wrong, but I think Pierce sees dollar signs and kudos in what Dad's doing. So he has set up what he thinks is going to be a profitable side bar, using Dad's reputation and expertise. He is funding a private research project, and has convinced Dad it's for the good of America, California, and the grape industry.'

'Papa at least seems aware it's in all the Napa growers' interests, which certainly includes Pierce Gray.'

Barbara nodded. 'Also, this research will give Dad a permanent place in the pantheon of plant scientists. Not that he hasn't got one already.'

'I think Pierce is sharp about business and entirely self-interested,' Maddie said. 'But I think Pa can look after himself, don't you?'

'It helps that he isn't a woman!' Barbara said wryly. 'With any female who crosses his path, he seems to feel he can buy whatever catches his eye. Another one for the collection – all the better if she's an unusual piece. He has an autocrat's sense of entitlement.'

'Bee, are you telling me anything personal here?' Maddie asked. 'I remember he tried to wine and dine you before wife number two, but I thought that was long ago and of no interest to you, even at the time?' She rinsed the last plate and handed it to her sister.

'Oh, I can take care of myself, hon. I've never seen his appeal. But he's been a total bastard to a friend of mine.'

Maddie didn't want to know more about this. She'd had Pierce Gray up to her neck today. So she hugged her sister and picked up her bag and coat, to say goodbye to her parents in the next room.

'You aren't eating,' Barbara announced flatly before Maddie could open the door. 'I saw you play with your food tonight, Maddie. I know every damn day is a bitch for you just to get through right now but you have to eat. Starving won't bring him back.'

Maddie nodded. 'Just not hungry. I'm never hungry any more.'

Barbara put her arms around her baby sister and said very simply, 'I know.'

Enzo walked out into the night to see his daughters away. He kissed them, closed their car doors, waved and watched as they drove out of the yard towards the Bay Bridge, not in the least unaware of the suffering of his younger child. Maddie had always been different. She'd been born with a knot in her umbilical cord, and was lucky to be alive. He'd always believed it showed her instinct for survival, but . . . her fate was not the fate of other people's children. He wasn't sure what to do for her, but felt a rush of hope as he watched her taillights vanish.

The sky was clear, and filled with a million stars. Just above the hill behind the house, to the north-east, there was an especially bright cluster. Enzo addressed it with a smile.

'Many a night I saw the Pleiads, rising thro' the mellow shade,
Glitter like a swarm of fireflies tangled in a silver braid.'

Oh, yes, it's a tangle, he thought. Then he turned off the outside lights and plunged his hands into his pockets.

10

Nonna Isabella had never thought of herself as the least bit superstitious. She might not 'tempt fate', as people put it: she wouldn't willingly walk under a ladder, for instance, or put shoes on a table, or open an umbrella inside her house. This just seemed sensible, rather than preventative of bad luck. Ladders were uncertain things, umbrellas opened inside houses could poke somebody in an eye, and shoes . . . well, shoes might have been about not tempting fate. Friday the thirteenth, though, was an ordinary day for her, and she could leave a pin on the sidewalk if she noticed one, despite the caution never to 'let it stay' if you wanted to be lucky. Like Neva, she came from a long line of women of whose heritage she was fairly aware, stretching back in time – in her case, to the people who inhabited Tuscany at least from Roman times or before, when the world was still the centre of the universe. Nonna Isabella, however, was happy to be a very modern woman – for all her lineage.

On the night of the ice storm, Isabella had sought and somehow found the lady who made hats. She'd been old twenty-five years ago: and Isabella thought she must be a nonagenarian or gone to God by now. But she'd sounded very much alive, engaged, and willing to see her old client, when Isabella told Signora Angela what had happened to Maddie over the phone. The lady suggested that she do a few things, and then come and see her the following night.

Isabella had to pore through the drawers of the old family desk, which had been her grandfather's proud purchase for the first home they had managed to buy in San Francisco. There it was that Isabella found a selection of family papers dating back to the 1890s, and a few old family photographs. Eventually she put her hands on Maddie's astrological chart, in its original brown paper wrapping and still with the seals unbroken.

These she brought with her to the venerated milliner, and the two ladies met at the *signora*'s same little home in North Beach over coffee, a slice of *torta caprese*, and a glass of iced Strega.

'Strange weather we had yesterday morning,' the beldame said to Isabella with her eyes glowing. 'Apocalyptic, some would say.' Her voice was quiet and clear, especially for one of her age.

Isabella only half listened to this, though she agreed it was highly unusual in their fair-weather city. But she politely came to the reason she had rung, and placed the items she'd been directed to look for onto the table in the *signora*'s workroom, which, amazingly, still bore signs of hat-making for what must surely be just the occasional client.

Signora Angela first placed her hand on the brown-wrapped packet she had tied up in string with her own hands all those years ago, then she spoke. And what Signora Angela had to say this time was more carefully attended to by her guest than it had been twenty-five years earlier.

'I don't have to open this,' she said, her eyes fixed on Isabella. 'I know its contents well.'

Isabella looked at her with disbelief.

'Understand, Signora Moretti,' Angela said in answer to that look, 'I have drawn charts for many hundreds, maybe a thousand or more people, over the ninety-one years of my life. I still use my own mathematical equations; still have a book of tables with the planetary movements. I don't let computers short-cut my work, and I am as busy now as I have ever been. The young generation are reverential, interested again in the wisdom of our Etruscan ancestors. Etruscans, of course, used to divine for their Roman conquerors, and were deeply respected for their knowledge of the mysteries.'

Angela's voice resonated in the small room, and the effect would have been theatrical to Isabella had she not been entirely magnetised by what she was saying.

'In all that time I have seen only three that I could never forget. Usually natal maps contain what one would expect: love, contracts, births, travel, and heartache. They are written on a palimpsest, you see:

one writes them, and erases, then writes another over the old wax impressions. They are inscribed upon sand.

'But of the three I well recall?' she said softly. 'One was for a man who became a bishop – and a good one, God rest his soul.' She took a sip from her drink, and added more from the bottle to each glass, then continued. 'Another was for a lady with unusual gifts and human sensitivities, who sadly took her own life when the divine seemed to have asked more of her than she had strength left to give. If only she had been able to hold on a little longer, her world should have changed for her. I think she lost all her hope. Her very grasping son benefited from what should have been hers. All too often, life is not fair.'

At this moment the old lady paused. Isabella wondered whether she was required to make some philosophical comment. She noticed, though, that Signora Angela seemed to be somewhere in her own mind, in a territory all her own, not of this world. Then her eyes returned to fix on Isabella.

'And then, there is your granddaughter. Madeline Moretti, May the twenty-first, child of the Pleiades. She is the owner of the third nativity, printed for ever on my memory. I recall the main details of the chart and I have wondered what has happened in her life. You know, charts are only celestial guides, Signora Moretti. They are a weather map, offering some way to navigate our lives. They indicate the road, but they are not the journey itself. That is in the hands of the traveller. Everyone has challenges in their lives. It is how they meet those challenges: that is the thing that marks them apart. That is what counts. And so,' she sat back in her low armchair, 'how is Madeline dealing with this loss?'

Isabella was very struck by Signora Angela's revelation about the special nature of Maddie's horoscope. She had assumed the older woman was being polite, or pretending an interest she didn't really have, when she spoke with her on the phone and was told she 'remembered' her granddaughter. Now, listening to her speak, she felt she was sincere.

'Madeline,' she replied, 'is, I would say, *meno male*. I don't know, not too badly; yet, she has lost all her zest. She eats, but is thin; she speaks, but has nothing to say from her heart. She was such a child of passion and brightness. In a line of pretty girls her age, she would stand out for her sheer personal fire. Now, it seems, that enormous spirit has abandoned her.'

Signora Angela nodded. 'I wasn't sure how it would happen. Like an eclipse of the sun: everything growing very suddenly chill and drear in her life. We must be careful, or she will become the *ombra della sera*, the evening shadow.'

Drawing her thoughts together, the *signora* asked Isabella for the photos of her own grandmother, who had come with her young husband to San Francisco so many years ago, and the family's embarkation papers. When they were handed to her, Signora Angela looked at them for some time, though Isabella couldn't decide what she was searching for. The face of the woman, in her simple Victorian clothes, a high pin at her lace blouse, captured the old woman's attention for a very long time.

'This was "Mimi", the enchantress,' Signora Angela said nodding, and it wasn't a question. 'I had always believed your famous grandmother was from Lucca, like my own family, Signora Moretti, but I see now that I am wrong about this,' she said rather elusively. 'But, how to get beyond this bereavement of your granddaughter's? I am quite certain now. You know of the saying that a good parent must give their child two things. That is "roots to grow", and "wings to fly". Madeline Moretti must at last dig for her roots, so that she can find her wings again. I may have told you before,' she added after a moment, 'that she has promises to keep.'

'Do you mean that we should send her on a trip – for some kind of holiday?' Isabella asked.

'The ruse you use? It really doesn't matter. Wherever you think to send her, she will still end up in the place she is meant to be, whether she designs it that way or not.' Signora Angela handed Isabella the photo again, and said firmly: 'She must be borne across that narrow bridge, back into the time of the ancestors. And she will find the Pleiades are already waiting for her.'

11

28 February 1347, Santo Pietro in Cellole, Tuscany

In the five weeks since the arrival of Signor Toscano and his wife, Jacquetta had learned more about them. Unlike her niece – who discredited the family name at once as an improbable fiction – she knew better herself and had guessed, rather than been told, that the young husband was likely to be related to the family of Giovanni Toscano, who had built one of the most beautiful *casa-torre* in town: a justly famous town house with a fabulous tower, a building of elegance and strength that had been the talk of the city in her great-grandmother's day, just short of a century ago. And so she knew, too, that his quasi-noble line had come not from Siena or from Florence, as she had originally supposed, but from Volterra, a city she knew well.

She had congratulated him on his ancestor, a man renowned for his taste and intelligence, and also for his rather unusual career. Giovanni had been employed many years as treasurer to the illegitimate son of Federico the Second, the Holy Roman Emperor. King Enzo of Sardinia was said to be Federico's favourite child, despite his illegitimacy: a poet and a falconer, like his father. But the poor young king had spent more than the last twenty years of his life imprisoned in Guelph Bologna, Jacquetta recollected. The treasurer, unable to change the outcome of his master's fate, had returned to his native city where he settled his family and built himself a very fine home with an emphasis on security, as the quarrelling times demanded.

Whether it was from modesty or a tacit request for privacy, the young

86

man had only inclined his head to acknowledge Jacquetta's identification, and said nothing more. But she was not so surprised at this. Though Giovanni Toscano had been a celebrated man in Volterra, and left a legacy of church donations and buildings that touched many people, one of his sons had fallen into disgrace some thirty or so years ago. Like his astute father, Fortino Toscano, too, had been a leading citizen of the city, an elder, and also served as *podesta*. He had received public honours and been praised for his charity, wisdom and dedication to the good of the people. Some years on, though, in ways she could not now recall, he must have upset his peers and lost his post, and thereafter been entirely excluded from public office, along with his heirs. Jacquetta knew that the climate in Volterra a generation ago had turned from a pro-Ghibelline politics – those who supported the Emperor – to the papal party of Guelphs. This change had come with the arrival of the hungry and ambitious Belforte family into political prominence. Of *this* family Jacquetta had significant experience. She was sure the enmity of the Guelph Belforti had been a principal reason for the slide in fortunes of the Ghibelline Toscano family. These feuds were biting and vicious, with lasting consequences, and at this moment – after many changes of fortune of their own, which had seen the Belforti out in the cold for years – their star had risen again and they had seized every key office in the city. Jacquetta was relieved to be raising Mia at some distance from the vacillating fortunes of life in Volterra, while the family of Ottaviano Belforte remained in power.

She couldn't remember the reasons, but she knew that another of Giovanni's sons had fared better. There was a daughter, also, who had been a close friend of Jacquetta's grandmother; Finapietra, she was called. She'd married very well into the family of the counts of Pannocchieschi, who were landlords across Tuscany, with properties dotted from Siena to Pisa and across the *contado* again to Volterra. Which of the brothers might have been her guest's ancestor, she would not ask. If Signor Porphyrius's family had chosen to move into trade – as many nobles and members of the upper middle class did – that, too, was their affair. It meant nothing to Jacquetta if they were on the social scale sliding upwards, or down; if they were now Guelph, or Ghibelline; or if they had counts for cousins from here to Jerusalem. She knew she liked him – liked his patience and kind eyes, his careful way of speaking, and his obvious education – and she liked his lovely wife. No one she could ever recall had reached out to Mia so effectively. They were welcome for as long as they needed lodging, which the young man paid for honourably on a weekly tally.

Jacquetta had to select a pig for killing today, and she wanted Mia out of the way, sequestered in the shining presence of her new companion in the solar. It wasn't that Mia was squeamish about the realities of butchering animals when it was required. Even though she was tender-hearted she understood that the beautiful fallow deer in the woods were killed for their table. She was up to the task of plucking a fowl by herself, if she had to. But last night Mia had come suddenly into Jacquetta's room, her heart pounding, in genuine distress. She had heard – her hands explained with some difficulty in near darkness – the terrible howling of an owl. 'Howling', like a dog, was what she mimicked to her aunt, and this had terrified the girl. Everyone the length and breadth of Tuscany accepted that the howling of an owl in the night was a terrible omen. So, this morning Jacquetta preferred to see to the pig without Mia witnessing the event.

The nearby bells in the abbey had signalled ten o'clock some time ago, and Jacquetta passed quietly by the solar, but found neither the one nor the other. She slipped up the stairs, looking to see if they were in the small library on the landing, but again found no one. One more flight, however, brought her a glimpse of both the young women through the open door to Mia's chamber. They were working together mixing pigments into paint to create their design for a physic garden. She heard the chatter from the *signora* and saw Mia practising her vowel shapes, smiling as usual; so she waved, and left them to it. Porphyrius and Cesaré had taken the cart into Chiusdino for salt and some few provisions, so this was the moment for Jacquetta to go quickly down the stairs and out to the barn, along with the feisty Alba, to see to the pig.

But, turning on the landing, she was suddenly aware of the sound of hoofs on the cobbles, the iron ringing out on the cold stones. It seemed many days since pilgrims or visitors had come, the weather having kept most at bay for weeks. Yet, there was something about the sounds – some urgency and sharper noise than was normal, coupled with the shouting of men – that struck Jacquetta's notice. She glanced back upstairs as if by instinct, hesitated, then returned quickly down again to see to the arrival.

With Cesaré gone she opened the heavy front door herself, and a swirl of movement and clatter of hoofs and boots startled her. Four men – or rather, five, as she now saw – in heavy leather coats, their breath frosting in the still sharp air, were marshalled in the courtyard. Two had already swung into a dismount. There was haste and gruffness about them, and the strong smell of leather suggested they'd had a hard or long ride. Loredana's boy came scampering from the stables to see to the horses, but he saw he would need help with the numbers.

'Is the master of the house in, monna?'

This came from the heavy-framed rider at the front, and it grated on Jacquetta. The question was perfectly reasonable, and 'monna' a perfectly polite contraction of the usual greeting to a housewife, 'madonna'. But for some reason just now it sparked a little lack of courtesy in her reply.

'I am the master of this house, *signor*,' she replied coolly. 'It may not be the custom in every corner of the country, but so it is here, with me.'

The man wore a heavy sword, and thick leather gauntlets. Jacquetta thought him a jumped-up member of the citizenry, rather than a nobleman, but his tone towards her altered to one of slightly improved civility.

'Very good, madonna,' he said. He passed the reins of his horse to the boy without looking at him. 'We are here on business from the Bishop of Volterra. May we come inside?'

Jacquetta knew this was a question that wouldn't be satisfied with a 'no' from her: yet, again, she was bristling; and it was cold, which made her unexpectedly nervous.

'You confuse me a little,' she answered him. 'Of which bishop do you speak, sir? The one who is legally still in office, but was forced from his post some while hence? Or the nominee, waiting to take power, who has nevertheless already stepped in to perform that role in the bishop's stead, these few years past?'

The man looked at her, his lip curling involuntarily. Her politics seemed transparent from these remarks. But he wanted something from her, so he struggled to find his best manners. 'I come on an errand from Bishop Filippo in the City, monna; not from the exiled Ranuccio in his outpost. And more importantly, perhaps, I come from the Gonfalonier of Justice; and from the Governor of the people of Volterra.'

'The latter offices belong to one and the same man, *signor*.' Jacquetta kept her voice level. 'But, of course, if there is anything I can do for you . . .' She moved from her place in the centre of the threshold to one side of the stoop, permitting them access. She understood that pragmatism might be wise. 'You and your men must come in, and have something warming. I'll bring you to the fire in my kitchen, if you won't take it amiss. It will save you having to take off your boots.'

She kept her cordial smile despite the smell of horses and sweat, leather and urine, which passed by her as they entered her home.

From her leaded panes two floors above, Mia watched in absolute still-ness. She followed the movements of the men, and strained to hear the words they spoke. In an agony of curiosity she was finally driven to pull on the catch ever so gently, almost without breathing, and open one of the windows just a crack. This allowed her to hear the muffled voice of one man and that of her aunt – but nothing distinct could be understood. So her eyes darted furtively, from one to another, as she tried to understand who was calling, and the purpose of their journey. And then it was that she saw one man, distinctively short. He was standing a little away from the group – bearded, sullen – and her face drained quickly of colour.

Communicating something of anxiety, she gestured to Signora Toscana to come and join her. But as troubled as Mia was herself, she was absolutely unprepared for her friend's reaction once she was standing beside her. The young woman seemed to glimpse something that panicked her, and her whole body swayed backwards, out of any possible line of sight. Her hand had shot up to her chest, and she looked paler than Mia.

'They've come for me,' she whispered. 'I'm so sorry. I've brought this on you.'

Mia looked at her, unsure how to react. She'd wanted to say something on her own behalf, and had desperate concerns, too, but these she put aside for a second to try to comfort her companion. She grabbed both of the *signora*'s hands, and held them tightly to offer solidarity. At the same time, though, her expression craved explanation.

'We fled,' she told Mia directly in a hushed voice, pulling her close. 'It was exactly as your aunt has said. I upset the wishes of my parents – went against their authority.' She walked Mia backwards from the window, and added, 'It's too much to explain it all now, Mia, but there will be terrible consequences if they find me here. They'll take me back to Volterra.'

Mia took her firmly by the hand and waved away her words with the shaking of her head, to tell her not to consider that. She found some strange strength in the situation, in Signora Toscano's need, and she led her quickly down the steep stairs and across the lower landing, away into a hiding place in a recessed space behind the book shelf where the servants came up from the scullery below to access the rooms. Mia hoped this was a caution more than was necessary.

Jacquetta, having seated the men in the kitchen, took an iron poker from the fire and plunged it in turn into mugs of ale, which sat lined up and ready on the refectory table. It immediately released an exotic scent of spices – and diluted the smell of the unlooked-for arrivals. She had no wish to entertain them for even five minutes, so strong was her dislike of the man who had dispatched them. However, she knew well enough to be cautious until she'd learned their business.

'What can it be,' she asked brightly, 'that brings you out on such a day when the weather will surely turn again at any moment?'

She spoke only to the man who'd addressed her – she thought perhaps the captain of the guard. No one else warranted a second glance from her.

'The weather has held us back indeed, monna, for weeks. We have a mystery to solve – a disappearance.'

'Indeed?' Jacquetta replied. Her eyes were steady, betraying not a flicker of emotion even while she was assembling ideas in her own mind quick as lightning.

'It is a strange tale,' he said, drinking the warm liquid between his sentences. 'A young woman who staunchly resisted the wishes of her dear parents . . .'

'We take pilgrims in here, *signor*,' Jacquetta soothed. 'Those headed for Rome or Jerusalem, stopping to see Galgano's shrine *en route*. We are not in the business of harbouring children or runaways.'

'You mistake me, monna.' He looked at her. 'For I do not suppose you would knowingly aid such a felon. We are simply checking, from guesthouse to guesthouse along the road from Volterra, to see if someone may have been duped by the fair appearance of the maiden we are looking for.'

'If maiden she still be!' One of the group laughed heartily as he spat this out for the amusement of the others.

'Felon?' Jacquetta's eyes arched. 'Can you mean the young woman you seek has committed a theft? Stolen bread for her existence? Or coins from her family?'

'Sit, monna, if you would,' the leader insisted. 'It is a tale you would do well to attend to.' His physical bulk dominated the space as he raised one foot on a bench, but remained standing.

'Please, you sit. You are tired; and I am comfortable.' Jacquetta refused to be told what to do, and stayed upright herself. 'But I am fascinated by your story. Has one girl – a "maiden", you have called her – been the means of drawing five strong men from their home, attired in swords? What can she have done?' Then she thought for a split second and added: 'Who is it you come to warn us about? Who would you wish me to keep a watchful eye on the road for?'

The short, bearded man darted up. 'It is more than the strength of one girl we are dealing with, *signora*.'

'Forgive my men, monna,' the captain said, shooting a withering look at the single individual who had interrupted his contrived process. 'Ildebrando forgets himself. We have been many hours in the saddle, and combed many routes from the city.'

'Do you come with news to alarm me, then, sir?' Jacquetta asked.

'The young girl we are looking for may be alone. She may be with someone – a young man of very good family.'

'They have married against parental instruction?' Jacquetta moderated her tone to make her sympathies harder to read.

'She has defied all that is true, and godly, and just, in this world. She refused to enter the convent, as her parents had arranged. And her reason, monna?'

'Perhaps she was in love, *signor*?' Jacquetta's voice was still gentle, as she realised any hint of defiance would work against her. 'It is surely for each to worship according to their capacity? It cannot be for all people to take an oath of chastity – or the human race would die out.'

'The young woman refused to enter the holy sisters' house, monna, because she is a heretic!'

'A Waldensian? Or perhaps a Cathar?' Jacquetta questioned.

This was an interesting departure, she thought. There were a handful of Cathars, still, in the Italian cities – those who had been careful to keep their religious beliefs quiet enough to avoid confrontation. Some last of their faith had joined them here from France, as Jacquetta knew. Was this Signora Toscano's secret: that she adhered to a belief system condemned by His Holiness?

'She is a witch, monna.' The captain's face showed rage, but also some fear. 'She is in league with the devil, mark me. On a clear night some weeks ago, a malefic force – some blizzard that blighted one place only on the ridge travelling west along the *balze*, but witnessed by men from the City gates – utterly destroyed her parents' home, and everyone inside it.'

'My brother was one among the number,' Ildebrando said sharply. 'He had been placed there to guard the girl, the night before her trial and certain execution.'

At these words Jacquetta sat, struck by a rush of unexpected feelings.

The captain raced on in his speech. 'We thought the girl had been killed, crushed by the fallen masonry, along with her parents and the guards. But,' he said, breathing in deeply, 'after the weather let up we began to clear away much of the rubble, and while all other bodies have been recovered, she appears to have vanished. There is no trace of her. It is witchcraft!'

'And the young man she plighted her troth with this last year or so – expressly against her parents' permission – he has gone too,' another of the men said gruffly. 'Though his own parents insist he is merely away from home on business.'

'It is our belief, monna, that this girl has the devil in her and has used such spirits against her own mother and father, to steal her freedom regardless of the human cost. She must be shunned, as the incarnation of evil and sin . . .'

'. . . in the body of a saint,' dwarfish Ildebrando finished his captain's sentence.

Jacquetta's wide eyes and startled look translated very well to the men: her shock was sincere. She stood to top up the mugs with the dregs of the warm, spicy ale. After a moment she spoke slowly and very deliberately.

'You frighten me,' she said, 'and I understand the importance of your journey. Leave this intelligence with me. If there is anything I can report to help you – or that I hear of – I will get word to you.'

Jacquetta sent a message to the stables for the horses, and no one said more on the subject until she walked the men out into the courtyard once more. An icy wind had stirred, and there was a look of snow in the clouds again for the first time in many days. Jacquetta smiled.

'You regain your road in good time, I think, gentlemen,' she said. 'You have an hour or two, I would guess, to get to Siena before the weather seriously threatens. But I'll save you a trip along the road to San Galgano and see the abbot myself. Though, from what you say, I imagine this would be the last place she would go.'

Men and horses trotted down the pathway towards the Maremma road. Jacquetta looked away up to the window of her niece's bedchamber. No one was visible, and she considered going up to talk to their guest. Then she reached inside the doorway for her cloak, stepped from the portal into the freezing wind, and walked towards the stable herself.

Minutes later she was on her own mare, cantering purposefully along the track beside the river, through her own woods, towards the neighbouring abbey.

12

The slant of the early morning sun reflected off the yellow sides of the cable car onto the Cellophane-wrapped bunch of flowers Maddie was carrying. This bathed her whole body in a yellow glow and, with her dark hair floating above, she looked like an angry bee. She stepped down from the cable car at the Powell Street turnaround and headed towards Jimena's shop. Last night she had been close to tears, but this morning she was mad as hell. This was the fourth time in as many months that she had received a large bouquet from Las Floritas. Always, the flowers appeared without a card, and when Maddie rang Jimena to ask who they were from, she was polite but evasive.

Maddie certainly did not want this level of intrusion into her personal life. She'd had enough. It was strenuous and depleting dealing with the pressures of work and the almost stifling internalisation of her continuing grief. There was no room left over to deal with an unknown admirer – no matter who he was. Prince or pauper, staunch supporter or stalker, these tokens were most unwelcome to a woman whose heart was still utterly broken. This morning she had decided to put a stop to it.

The sun was just hitting the front of the shop as Maddie stormed down the hill towards the door. Jimena, in a bright waterproof apron with impressionist poppies on it, and long rubber gloves, was pulling the plant stands out onto the pavements to set up for the day.

'Jimena, what are you trying to do to me?' Maddie began, her ire defeating her habitual grace towards someone she really liked. 'Who are these from?' she asked impatiently, waving the bouquet at Jimena. 'You

95

really have to tell me. It is insensitive and cruel, sending such unsolicited romantic gifts to a woman who is still drowning in sorrow, feeling thoroughly isolated from the world; and I am completely bemused that you would be a party to it.'

Another human being might have been affronted by this. Jimena, however, unschooled in any language of bitterness or resentment, looked at the angry whirlwind that had blown in to confront her, and just laughed.

'*No mates al mensajero*,' she said. 'It is, as you would say, "Don't kill the messenger". It's not me with an admirer who does not want to leave his name, Señorita Maddie. I just sell the flowers. What is making you so mad? Are the *flores* not beautiful?'

Maddie's feelings had been choked for so long that it was strange to discover she felt so emotionally charged right now. And Jimena's inherent sweetness – which seemed to know no way to teeter into bad humour – made her feel guilty. Yet she remained distressed by this situation.

'Oh, Jimena, of course your flowers are beautiful. But every time they come it makes me think about who they are not from, and can never be from again. You know.'

Jimena recognised that Maddie was deeply upset, and put an arm around her waist. '*Sí*, I do know. But what should I do? It is your Mr Gray, who has sent you lovely roses many times before – and he has given to me six hundred dollars in cash. He said I must keep it a secret, because he is just trying to cheer your spirits and he doesn't know what to say to you. But I am to send you my best flowers each month, for six months. I hoped it would make you happy because you are someone whose soul is very touched with flowers; so I said yes. I am sorry if it makes you so sad.'

Maddie looked at the tear just forming in one of Jimena's lovely brown eyes, and she recanted. 'I'll tell you what: can you take these back from me and send them to another person?'

Maddie dug in her bag and produced a little pen and her agenda. She started to write Neva's name and hospital address.

'Am I right, that there are two months left after these have gone?' Maddie asked.

Jimena nodded.

'I'll pay any delivery charges,' Maddie continued, 'and that might be a lot more, because they have to go to Jose. Is that OK?' Maddie wrote another name without looking up at Jimena, and added, 'Please can you send next month's bunch to Marilu Moreno, at this address, and the July bunch to Samantha, my boss, at my office address? She has been very patient with me since I lost Chris.'

Jimena looked wary. 'Señorita Maddie, this can land me in very big trouble with such an important client as Mr Gray.'

'Jimena, please understand how much pain this is giving me. I'm asking you to do this to spare me that pain. We don't have to tell anyone. You can put my name on them, if you like, so everyone concerned will know exactly who the flowers came from. If you only knew how much more than this they all deserve – and Pierce Gray's role in their individual stresses and strains.' Maddie decided she'd better say no more on that head.

Jimena's face brightened, conscious that she would be doing something to please one of her favourite clients. '*Sí, claro*. And don't worry about the delivery. Enrique can drop them off on the way out to our farm, where he must go twice a week.'

While Maddie finished writing a note to accompany the delivery, Jimena busied herself setting out some faïence-blue delphiniums in the outside stands, and turning their neighbours front and centre so the blooms were at their best for the passers by. Stems of fuchsia and white dappled camellias were crammed in with an apparent carelessness next to deep red roses, creating artful perfection. Then she straightened up to look at Maddie. She lifted a single exotic cream bloom from a deep vase by the door. It had an overwhelming scent that called to customers on the sidewalk. This, she passed to her early visitor.

'This one is so special, Maddie. I hope you will accept it from me?'

Maddie sniffed the flower head and closed her eyes. 'This is like something from paradise, Jimena. What is it, and where do you get these extraordinary flowers from?'

'*Es bonita, verdad?*' Jimena said. 'This one is a tuberose. They come originally from the Far East, but we grow them on our own farm now that it is late spring. Will you come to see it one day, maybe? And I can give you some wonderful food and a glass of wine. We can grow almost everything there if we plan it well. St Agricola of Avignon protects us. He brings the rain for me, exactly when I ask for it to come. But sometimes not in the hot times, of course; so we catch his blessings and keep the extra rain he sends in the big cisterns we built, which my grandfather says are like the old Roman wells in the city squares in Spain and Italy. This is how we irrigate in the dry times. We are very lucky because we are small, and a family business. When times are hard we work more and charge less, and go on. The big growers, they must just fire the workers.'

Maddie smiled at Jimena's rain saint: why didn't that surprise her? But she preferred not to get into a long discussion about flower farming right now so she said, 'I'd love to come out and see it one day, yes, please. But for now I must get on to work or I'll be late.'

Her briefcase and the tuberose in hand, she was nearly out the door when Jimena called her name.

'*Ah, una cosa más,*' she said. 'I forgot to say to you, Señorita Maddie. Your lovely orchid – Paloma, I have been calling her, because her colour is the dove – she is very happy now! I have put her with some other plants that are friendly to her, and I will look after her a little longer, yes? She starts to come to life again, but still she needs to be with friends *un poco más de tiempo* – a little more time. But she will come home to you one day soon.'

Maddie was unable to speak. She just bit her lip, and hugged Jimena. 'Thank you,' made a quiet effort to come out, and Maddie left quickly.

'*Adiós, Señorita Maddie,*' Jimena smiled, and gave her a little wave. Then she lightly turned on her toes and followed a customer into her shop.

The thought of the orchid stayed with Maddie all the way to her office, opening a little place in her heart that had been empty for months. By nine o'clock she was seated looking at the single exotic stem – which had found a home in a small Perrier bottle – and a styrofoam cup of cold caffè latte side by side on her desk. She had picked up the latter on the way along Market Street with her mind and her hands too busy to drink. It should perhaps be filed in the waste-paper basket, she thought, and she should get on with the day. But she didn't much feel like it.

She reached out to remove the coffee, and her cellphone rang. Maddie looked at the screen: 'Caller Unknown'. She opened it warily.

'Hello?'

She eventually recognised the voice on the end of the line, but it took a moment. It was not a voice she was expecting. Only about a dozen people outside of the office used her cell number, and they were all family and close friends. How had this caller got the number?

The voice on the line was authoritative: a clear tenor, male, and Californian. 'I have two tickets to the opera next Sunday. I thought we could have dinner afterwards.'

'The opera season doesn't start until June,' Maddie responded carefully. 'It's very kind of you, but, anyway, I'm not free.' She hesitated for half a second and added, 'I have a lot of work to do.'

The voice persisted: 'I know the Opera House is closed. But there are other places to enjoy the show. I know you've been having a torrid time, and I was told you really love the opera. So it seems the only proper choice for a slightly early birthday present.'

Maddie was irritated, but also mildly curious to know quite how the great man would manipulate the calendar. 'A giant's strength . . .', she thought. But her irritation won out, and she interjected another, firmer excuse.

'Well, it's intriguing, but I've made other arrangements, which can't be broken.'

'Yes. The work. You mentioned it earlier. But you couldn't be expected to do office days every Sunday, surely?'

Maddie grimaced. She'd been caught out in the disparity between her first excuse and her second.

'A colleague and I have made definite arrangements, and it would be rude—' she tried to cover.

'Nonsense,' the man came in quickly.

His tone spoke of a habitual attitude of never being put off. Despite herself, Maddie was quietly fascinated with his manoeuvring of the situation.

'We both know that a constructive half-hour with me would – could – be beneficial to your working cause. And I have something I've decided to share with you. It's in everyone's interests for you to come meet me. And the social nature of the occasion won't be unwelcome to you, I can promise.'

This was a thunderbolt. What was he considering? Was it possible that he was genuinely thinking of sounding her out, to make some kind of proposal *ex judice*?

The voice went on in a cool tenor, 'Madeline, it's your birthday in a week. This will be an adventure. Life's been tough for you lately – for us both, actually. And I think we should enjoy it. I want to talk something over with you because I believe you are sharp enough to see the sense in what I've been thinking. And, as a final temptation, your favourite opera is *La Bohème*, is it not? And that is exactly what I have tickets for. Now, aren't you just a tiny bit inclined to join me?'

Maddie couldn't speak. She was caught in crosscurrents of anger, fascination, surprise, and even a partial sense of being flattered. But it was the curiosity to know what he was thinking about her 'work' that won the day.

'Yes, all right,' she said without wanting to betray any emotion.

'Excellent. I'll have my car pick you up from your apartment at nine on Sunday morning. That's the thirteenth.'

Maddie was thrown. 'That sounds very early.'

'It's not an evening performance. Didn't I say? Nine. Enjoy your week.'

The caller rang off. She had amazed herself. What had she agreed to? Was this a conflict of interest?

What kind of idiot am I to refuse this man's flowers and then accept his opera tickets? she wondered. How have I just said yes to a social invitation from Pierce Gray? And do I need to tell Samantha?

But these thoughts resonated every remaining day of the week without her taking action to cancel the plan, or talk to her boss, or even further debate her folly, and when the doorbell sounded on Sunday morning, she was ready in spite of herself. In a simple cream lace dress that drew attention to her too thin waist, she'd teamed her choice with plain shoes and bag, and a toning pashmina for a day that might yet prove hot or cold. Her hair was loosely pinned up to be both chaste and suitable for an opera, and she almost laughed at her reflection, feeling she would look perfect for a Victorian afternoon tea. She had no idea if what she had on was right, but consoled herself with the idea that it really didn't matter.

'I'm just coming,' she told the intercom.

Maddie opened the glass front doors to the street and was greeted by a perfect breath of late spring air: sunshine that was yet to warm the ground. She heard birdsong, and a sideward look showed her that sunrise yachtsmen were already out on the Bay. It was a shame, she thought, that she couldn't feel more enthusiastic about the day. She glanced up the road, expecting to see Pierce Gray in something like an open-topped car, but parked just a couple of spaces from the front of her apartment building was a neat black four-door Mercedes in the possession of a driver wearing a jacket but without a tie. He was waiting for her by the rear door.

'Miss Moretti,' he said politely; and Maddie noticed it wasn't a question.

She nodded, and stepped up to the open door he was holding for her. 'It's going to be another beautiful day,' he said cheerfully.

'It seems so,' she agreed. She sank into the seat and dived into her bag for sunglasses. 'It's been a little too hot for about a week. But I feel a change might be coming,' she suggested, not knowing what she was saying.

'I hope so.' The driver checked that her dress was clear of the door before he closed it gently. Climbing into the front he added, 'A little breeze would be nice.'

Maddie settled in the air-conditioned car. 'Where are we going?' she asked.

'Oh, I'm sorry, ma'am. Mr Gray told me quite specifically not to say anything. He's hoping to kind of surprise you. So, please, you just sit back and enjoy the view. We'll be about a half-hour, then all will be clear.'

The car headed south of the Bay onto the short freeway 101 towards San Jose, which meant her first guess – that he'd arranged a small private performance on his own lawns in Napa – was wrong. Oh, well, she thought, he's not as stylish as that. Something was obviously happening in Jose. But to Maddie's confusion they swung off onto route 380 and then onto the airport perimeter, following the north access road along the edge of the airport. The car pulled up outside the private charter terminal.

As the driver opened the door, he said, 'If you'll just go straight to reception, Miss Moretti, and tell them you're joining Mr Gray, they'll show you where to go. I'll see you myself later this evening. You have a great day, now.'

Maddie breathed deeply as she got out of the car and headed into the glass building. She wondered again – not for the last time – what she was doing. Did she need one of Charles's long spoons, to sup with the devil? Or was she behaving with independent business maturity – to learn what the other side was thinking?

She pushed her sunglasses up onto her head and turned the door handle. At the reception desk, Pierce Gray was in conversation with another man in a pale cream spring-weight suit. Pierce was dressed in a light navy blazer and flannels, and Maddie had to admit he looked a picture of casual elegance. Around his neck he'd chosen an unusual light green almost blue silk tie, and his shoes were two-tone. A flower for his buttonhole was an interesting finishing touch, and the whole outfit suited his medium-broad build.

Pierce held out his hand.

'You look lovely, Madeline. Thank you so much for coming. The opera would have been no fun on my own.'

He gave her his complete attention when he said this, and though determined to find a little fault with him somehow, she thought he sounded sincere.

'This is our attorney, Gordon Hugo. Perhaps you two may have met?'

She shook her head.

'He's very kindly dropped some paperwork off for me, but Gordon's not coming with us,' Pierce added.

Maddie lightly took the lawyer's proffered hand.

'Actually, I believe we've met before, Miss Moretti,' he said.

'I don't recall,' she replied.

Maddie wondered if he was lying. Gordon Hugo had the kind of face she would surely not forget, with heavy jowls and slightly pockmarked. He was a big man, with a mop of curly greying hair. His eyes were circled with dark under-tissue, like a former pugilist. Maddie knew exactly who he was by reputation: he had called the office a number of times trying to negotiate with various members of the firm. He was respectfully considered to be smart, but a bully.

'Another time, I'll remind you of the occasion. But I shan't detain you now.'

He spoke this only to her, which seemed rather unpleasant to Maddie. Then: 'I'm good to go, Pierce. A pleasure to see you again, Madeline.' And back to his boss: 'I'll be with you in Napa on Tuesday, around noon, if that still suits?'

'It still does,' Pierce replied.

They watched him go, and Maddie started to speak. Pierce, however, held up his hand rather mysteriously.

'Follow me. All shall be revealed.'

The receptionist led them through the building to a security checkpoint, and then onto the edge of the taxiway. At the pavement a Mercedes M-class vehicle stood with its doors open, the driver waiting with the uniformed pilot and stewardess, who were chatting to each other. Maddie and Pierce Gray were ushered in the rear door while the pilot, stewardess and driver clambered into the front. They pulled away down a long line of gleaming private jets.

'Good morning, Mr Gray. You've chosen a great day for it. Looks like clear air all the way up,' the pilot said. 'My co-pilot – Richie Mayes – is already on the flight deck preparing for our trip. And, Miss Moretti, we're delighted to have you with us today too. Your flight time should be around an hour and forty if we make our slot.'

'Thanks, Jeff.' Pierce spoke across the seats. 'Madeline, I'd like you to say hi to Captain Jefferson Sands. He has a degree in astrophysics, I believe. But he does this for me now.'

Point taken, Maddie thought. 'How do you do?' she said, and the pilot's broad smile beamed over the seat at her. 'You're giving up your Sunday for us,' she added.

'That's no problem at all,' he said pleasantly. 'This is your cabin crew, and also my wife – Cat,' he said.

'Good morning, sir, Miss Moretti.' She also looked as though there were nothing she'd rather do with her Sunday than this. 'I think we've got everything you asked for. I'll make some breakfast once we're airborne. Anything special happening where we're headed today?'

'Miss Moretti and I are going on a pilgrimage, Cat.' Pierce looked at Maddie and said, '*Hic locus est.*'

Maddie was surprised by the Latin reference: 'Here is the place.' 'The place' she remembered was a special location where something iconic, which one wanted to be part of, was kept. This she recalled from her studies about the development of law in the medieval world. In context, she thought, it referred to a shrine where a particular relic was housed. But what a very unusual usage now.

Pierce chatted to Cat as they passed along beside a second fleet of small private craft.

'Today our pilgrimage will grant us the therapy of distance,' he smiled.

Maddie was amused, and thought the day might yet prove more interesting than she had first considered.

The people carrier turned left and stopped alongside a sleek, twin-engined jet in Stormtree Components' company livery.

'This is one of our Gulf Stream Fives,' Pierce told her as they got out.

The ground crew had the plane steps down and the door open, and Jeff boarded first. Cat assisted Maddie and Pierce, and then pulled the cabin door closed behind as the engines began to rotate into life.

Maddie's eyes took in the smart interior, wonderfully appointed, with a galley towards the rear and then three distinct areas for seating. One section looked like it could be converted into beds, and the other two were conference and relaxation areas. Each had a table and four plush, leather armchairs in shades of bone.

Pierce indicated that Maddie should sit anywhere. 'We are the only passengers, so take your pick.'

She selected a window seat and, to her surprise, her companion took a place by the window on the opposite side. If he was being considerate and deliberately not pushy, it was welcome and unexpected.

'No matter how often I fly, I still watch the take-off. It's irrational, but it makes me feel nothing can go wrong.' He smiled across at her, and then turned back to his window as the plane manoeuvred onto the runway.

Maddie smiled to herself. He's a little like an eager schoolboy, she thought, with his fear and his larger-than-life toys. Then she remembered Marni Van Roon proposing that Pierce might have a cuddly side, and she wondered if she were getting a little glimpse of this.

Maddie began to relax as the plane swung onto the runway, closed her eyes and felt the aircraft lift off gracefully through the low mist that often surrounded San Francisco below the golden cloud above. As the plane rose skyward she could see the distinct line of the San Andreas Fault, a dividing line between worlds, she thought. One day, as her father always said, smiling incongruously, next year or a thousand years from now, the whole coast would just slip into the sea. 'We live like our ancestors, cradled on Vesuvius,' he would say philosophically.

She wished this wonderful day were unfolding with a different man from the one sitting across from her, but, perhaps as San Franciscans knew, there was a keener edge to life when you sat on the brink of peril, sensing danger. Or, maybe today she would learn something unexpected. She felt she had nothing to lose. On the edge of an earthquake or a volcano, or walking with eyes open into the Phlegraean Fields, there could be no one more willing to sacrifice her own comfort. What were the risks to someone whose life path had been so suddenly aborted? Let's allow the wind to ruffle my hair a little, she decided, and see if it can make a difference for anyone at all.

The plane returned to Napa County Airport, rather than San Francisco, and on landing Pierce helped Maddie into the same car that had brought her in the morning.

'I'll call you in a week or so, to give you time. Thank you for your company. It was a very memorable day.'

Maddie thanked him without hesitation, saying the pleasure was shared by her. He offered only his hand, not even a cheek to kiss. God, she thought, he is either very good at this, or really a more complex man than we give him credit for.

What, she wondered, as the car door closed, had changed Pierce Gray? She recalled their first encounter a few years earlier – before she'd gone to graduate school – when he had awarded a prize at Berkeley, where she did her first degree, and met her on duty for the university paper. He'd connected her at once with her father and pretty sister, and flirted so charmingly. It was bold of him to invite her to an afternoon sailing party, when he was famously and publicly between marriages. He'd been very different at that time – arrogant and over-confident of his charms – but the memory – the extraordinary avalanche of events that had really thrown them together – still made her nervous.

As the car pulled away she watched him vault over a rail like a man in his twenties and head for a sports car that stood waiting in the parking area. Her own car paused at a traffic control light so she saw Pierce's car lights come up, then his vehicle departed in the opposite direction from hers. She was outside her apartment before ten, as promised.

She'd sat in her own silence the entire way and the driver had respected her privacy, but opening the door for her now he asked: 'Did you have a good day, Miss Moretti?'

'Yes. Thank you. It was lovely.' She replied in expectation it would be reported back to his boss, but it was also the truth.

She turned the key in the lock, tossed down her wrap and bag on the piano stool to the left of the door and moved fluidly to the kitchen cupboard. Here she'd stored the unconsumed feast that had lain in wait for Chris's arrival. She took out an unopened bottle of single malt

Scotch, bought for him months earlier, and in a second she'd cracked the seal. She took down a glass and poured herself a large slug.

Maddie had little taste for whisky. It had been Christopher's tipple – she was a wine drinker by preference – but tonight her thoughts were in turmoil. She took a sip of the liquid and let it release its fire into her throat. She moved to her glass coffee table and took the bottle with her, collapsing into a large lounge chair. She longed for someone to talk to. This was when Christopher's absence caused a physical ache in her, because she wished she had his cool head with which to analyse the implications of the day. She'd lost her lover, but she had also lost her best friend and wisest counsel. The Scotch couldn't take his place, but it was his and offered the nearest thing she could get to reflected comfort.

Barbara's attitude to Pierce was clear, probably just, and yet one-dimensional. Maddie swallowed another mouthful and articulated her sister's position for herself, as an exercise. She would say Pierce had one goal: to use Maddie in any way possible to find out what her company had on his, then to persuade her bosses that they could never win, and should settle. In this scenario Maddie would be the perfect go-between, with Pierce the adept, who could confuse the issues in Maddie's mind to his own advantage. And, Barbara would possibly add, if he could seduce Maddie herself along the way, why wouldn't he do that, too?

Isabella was Maddie's anchor, and she understood every unvoiced syllable of her granddaughter's suffering, but though she would always have Maddie's security at heart, she simply wouldn't understand the implications surrounding her discussion with Pierce, wouldn't be able to advise her. And her father – undeniably extremely clever and a sound philosopher – was too deeply involved with Gray to be objective. Although he would view any discussion fairly, she'd told him nothing of the case Harden Hammond Cohen had against Stormtree, and it would be unfair and unprofessional to do so. So, any conversation with her father would have to be in half-revelations, and this would make it impossible for him to counsel her.

There was Samantha, naturally. Maddie respected few people more than her boss, but she was a little nervous not to have come clean already about her acquaintance and family connections with Pierce, and she knew she had to think deeply over each ramification.

Cupping her Scotch, she got to her feet and crossed to her balcony door, then walked out into the soft night. She did now sense a change in the weather – maybe because distant dogs were barking in an odd way, or there was just the hint of a breeze – but it was still warm enough to be an early summer evening, almost a month ahead of the calendar. She pulled the comb from her hair and shook it out, and there was just enough movement in the air to tousle one or two strands. She leaned over a rail and watched the sky absently while she revised the day.

Did she still think her first thought had merit – that the whole event had been an elaborate attempt by Pierce to seduce her? He'd always been very pursuant with women who were hard to get: and yes, however unintentionally, she'd been one of those. But there were so many super-attractive fish in the vast California sea. Would he take such pains for her?

She had to admit that his power to arrange things was impressive, even though she was not of a mind to be impressed by sweeping gestures. But it was hard not to be a little flattered. Cars, and people waiting for her with her name on their lips, had flowed seamlessly from her pick-up in the morning through to their arrival in Seattle. A wonderful – if slightly flawed – production of Puccini's *La Bohème* had been followed by an early supper at Volterra, an authentic Tuscan-style restaurant, which Pierce said was the best Italian on the West Coast; and then back to the airport, and home: just for the opera!

In the hop to the theatre Pierce apologised that he had no idea what the production would be like, but laughed, 'On the bright side, Seattle Opera has a beautiful new home in the city, so let's take a look at the stylish venue and a company on the way up, who everybody is talking about.'

Maddie had assured him she didn't care because she truly loved Puccini, knew the music and libretto of most of his operas; but she was delighted and amazed by how much Pierce knew about them too. She hadn't reckoned on that – had no idea it was a genuine interest for him.

The breeze came again as she thought of the opera itself. God, yes, she loved the music, and she'd been enthralled by the production. As always the solo of '*Sì, mi chiamano Mimì*' had sent shivers through her, and brought her close to tears. If she'd been more herself, she'd have let them flow with pleasure. She noticed Pierce was pleased for her, but more overtly critical of the overall production than she. In the interval, over champagne, he explained there was double casting for major operas in Seattle to allow them to run for fourteen consecutive days, and he'd apologised that the alternate cast's singing was not as good as he'd hoped.

Over dinner, he was very funny. He thought the soprano didn't look at all bad as Mimi, but insisted her voice seemed harsh and a touch out of tune for much of the first act. 'She wandered around some of those arpeggios, hunting for the melody without much success,' he chuckled. And it was true, really, and most noticeable when she sang with Rodolfo, whose performance they both thought was inspired. Enjoying a glass of Vernaccia, and feeling surprisingly in her element, Maddie had taken up a vigorous defence of the afternoon, pointing out that Mimi had sung liltingly in the third act, and that everyone had a few off moments. Pierce countered this with a suggestion that the lady had sung too loudly until then: 'Well, she shouldn't have gone into open competition with the orchestra!'

They both laughed. It was the first time in a long, long time that Maddie realised she could still make that sound. It came as a shock to her.

'The next time we see Puccini,' Pierce added, 'I'll take you to Lucca, the real home of his music.'

Maddie looked across at him, taken aback. 'Well, that sounds surreal. My great-great-grandmother was nicknamed Mimi, you know; and she came here to San Francisco from Lucca.'

Maddie was astonished with his answer: 'Yes, I know. I understand from your father that she and her husband came in the eighteen nineties, and she was a very famous and much-loved soprano. He accompanied her, I think?'

Maddie nodded slowly, unsure what to make of this. 'They were both involved with the opera from the very beginning, and they stayed. He taught, more than performed. But, I've never been to Lucca – where they came from.'

'Then we really must go one day,' he said; and with that, he moved away from such a personal conversation before she could feel uncomfortable.

Maddie was so relaxed and enjoying herself that she'd almost forgotten the original source of her curiosity to join Pierce for the day. Then suddenly, over dessert, he picked up with the subject he'd mentioned on the phone. She had to cut through the relaxed haze of the wine to listen very carefully. She made no comment, merely listened to his ideas. And, as they finished their dinner, she said she would have to think over what he'd suggested. It was the wrong moment for a serious business discussion, or to say what she might otherwise say to Pierce. It would have been rude, and inappropriate to the more social nature of the day.

Now the wind came up more, and refreshed her. The current lifted her hair, cooled her neck, and cleared her head. She looked out from her balcony into the north-eastern sky and could see the collection of seven bright stars her father loved, the Seven Sisters. Perhaps fuelled by a little too much Scotch, Maddie found she'd made up her mind what to do; and she walked swiftly inside.

13

21 May 2007, San Francisco

A few minutes before nine Maddie met her own reflection in the glass double doors bearing the company name. She then looked beyond her ghostly self into the foyer of the main reception area, where she could see a rather discomfited Teresa Suarez at her desk. The receptionist with the habitual easiness was unusually furtive, open-mouthed and trying not to look to her left, where something must have been bothering her. Maddie's eyes investigated and sure enough, in the corner of the foyer, beside a seating area, Jacinta was helping a forty-something man into a coat. Her body language, Maddie saw, was that of someone simpering over the visitor.

Teresa sighted Maddie coming through the entrance and signed wildly for her to come in and do something. Maddie's ears burned as the doors closed behind her and she caught Jacinta's drooling voice.

'I'm sorry Miss Harden wasn't available. I'll talk to her later, and when she's free I'll give you a call myself. Would you tell Mr Gray—' she changed the subject but not the fawning tone – 'that I love what he's done at the Art Gallery. I went to a reception there last week. Awesome – his concept for the new wing, the use of space,' she gushed.

'You tell him – if you'd like to meet him? He'd be pleased to hear that. Join us there for lunch one day, and he'll give you a private tour. I'll arrange it.'

He spoke to Jacinta, but his attention shifted past her to the new arrival through the glass doors.

'Hello, Madeline! How nice to see you again so soon.' Gordon Hugo picked up his document case and moved towards her. 'I came on the off chance of a meeting with Samantha, but the lovely Jacinta tells me she hasn't come in yet. Let's catch up when I come back – but I must rush now. Have a nice day, everyone,' he called to her and to the others before pushing through the main doors.

Jacinta and Teresa responded to his back, the one over-enthusiastically and the other politely, 'Bye, have a good day!'

But as the door closed again, Maddie said quietly, 'No, thanks, I've made other arrangements.' She wondered what on earth brought him here, and her look said as much.

'I can tell you why he came.' Charles was unusually flustered, opening a side door into the foyer, and coming over to them. His expression conveyed some amusement and more irritation. 'Thank you, ladies, for seeing him off. Mr Hugo just tried to crash in on Samantha unannounced. Luckily she went east over the weekend on business and isn't coming in today. Otherwise that encounter would have come to blows. What an arrogant man.'

His expression struck a chord with Maddie. He looked as though something slightly unpleasant-smelling had just been waved under his nose. She decided to seize an opportunity.

'Charles,' she asked, 'I needed to speak to Samantha, but could I trouble you for half an hour of your time?'

'If I'll do?' He gestured towards the door leading to his own office and put on his most avuncular manner, lowering his voice. 'Let's step in out of the circus.'

Charles's large square space had its own distinctive style. It reminded Maddie of a more prosperous version of a don's room at Oxford – full of first editions and elegant prints, bespeaking an intellectual shabby chic that was not a lie. She could have lost herself in here for hours, with the oak-panelled walls, comfortable armchairs and roll-top desk with captain's chair. A few pictures on a side-table were of family and friends; a smattering of traditional hand-clasps with the rich and famous. Maddie had the impression these latter were for their effect on his clients. She felt that personally he might think them ostentatious, although he was proud of the people he called friends on both coasts. She noted – not for the first time – that Pierce Gray was not represented, though they belonged to the same yacht club, and there had been a picture of the two of them together in the press a few weeks ago.

Charles held a chair for his guest, and then sat opposite her.

'What a furore this morning,' he confided. 'Samantha's father was taken to hospital in New Jersey over the weekend, and she's flown east. I ran into Hugo in the foyer, and I don't much like him. He wanted to chat about a new deal, but it's all a bit cloak-and-dagger, and he shouldn't open it up with me. No proper meeting or tabled discussion, all very underhand. I gave him short shrift and told him to put his ideas on paper.'

Maddie was surprised, and a little annoyed. Over the intervening week she'd considered several scenarios regarding Pierce's discussion with her last Sunday, but now she wondered if the events of the morning threw a new light. Did he know his head-of-legal was coming here today? Surely yes; so, had he grown tired of waiting for Maddie to call him?

'That's exactly what I wanted to talk to Samantha about his morning. I met Gordon Hugo quite incidentally with Pierce Gray, the weekend before last. My appraisal of him matches yours. He's a man who looks at you and thinks he immediately knows everything about you.'

'Is that a strange social outing for you, Madeline?' Charles asked humorously. 'Gordon Hugo and Pierce Gray?' He went quickly to his door and called to Yamuna to arrange some tea, thinking this might take longer than he'd realised.

'Pierce took me to the opera in Seattle. But I'm beginning to think I was lured there on an elaborate ruse. Perhaps to recruit me to the same idea Gordon Hugo wants to put directly to Samantha. I believed Pierce was genuinely consulting me about the chances of a negotiation – testing the water with me, if you will – but I flatter myself thinking he had the slightest intention of listening to anything I might say. And his lawyer has either less patience or less tact than his boss.'

Still wondering whether her 'date' might have contravened good policy or good sense, Maddie cautiously reiterated Pierce's words on that Sunday evening. The arrival of the tea was the only interruption, and Charles's eyebrows arched only mildly as he listened attentively to her analysis of the man they were dealing with. He smiled sympathetically when she expressed her concern as to whether she were being played for a fool; yet she spoke simply about her decision to listen open-mindedly to what he'd had to say. She'd been eager to hear anything that might prove helpful for their plaintiffs. Then she came to the pith of their after-dinner conversation.

'Pierce was in a reasoning mood, I thought,' she told Charles. 'I'd drunk a little wine, but I was focused and clear in my mind when he admitted that the cost of defending the law suit would be a lot of money. Stormtree have set aside a huge reserve for their defence; but, Charles, I almost believed him when he said he'd rather use that directly for the workers. Of course, he said that his legal team didn't rate our chances of winning in court, and I dismissed that as the inevitable poker hand. But I also wondered whether he's the one having doubts that they can beat us.'

'He's a strategist,' Charles nodded. 'And the idea that it's costing him money to fight us, which would be better given to his victims, was designed partly to make you feel guilty, in fact. There again, Pierce is perfectly capable of sounding gracious – which you're describing – when his back is really against the wall. Who knows how confident they are? What was the nub of his suggestion?'

Maddie smiled. 'I told him it wasn't the moment to go into details or talk sums, but in essence he proposes his company might use the money they've set aside for the case to swell the benefits to the workers and their dependents. He made it clear that there's a long queue of employees ready to fill their jobs, and that Stormtree Components is under no obligation to make such an offer. But he argues, with some merit, that it would help their suffering immediately and end the hiatus everyone is trapped in.'

'Ah, yes.' Charles interlaced his fingers on the desk. 'Pierce wouldn't want to see the workers suffer because of court delays. And we know he's sure there's nothing abnormal in the conditions at Stormtree compared with similar companies.'

'I understand the note of irony, Charles,' Maddie said. 'You're gently suggesting he's made me change sides and advocate his position to my own bosses. Maybe I should feel a bit naïve. And yet, I thought he might really want to press for a way through without his lawyers dictating to him, and I read this as a real possibility. It must cut the company's costs if they settle directly. But I know it's Samantha he should be talking to.'

'Maybe,' Charles said pensively. 'But it's a very different conversation he'd have with her.'

Maddie smiled to herself. 'Charles, I could only tell him I'd think about what he was saying, talk to Samantha – and address my family's personal connection with Pierce at the same time. I've been looking for the right time to do that, but last week she was impossibly busy. What do you think? If Hugo has the same script, what was the point of taking me to one side?'

'Well, it's a cogent argument Gray makes, Maddie, and you're not at all naïve.' Charles poured out more tea from the silver pot. 'In my book there's a lot to be said for negotiation – not least for the time it saves. It depends on the size of the settlement he has in mind. If it's limited to the sum he has in reserve for legal, that's not really a discussion. It needs to be much more. But in principle, I'd hear him out. Samantha, though, has different needs.'

'Do you think she really wants to test this in a court – even if we could lose?'

'She's brilliant, and fired up, and wants to win. It's about setting a precedent for her. She's not only fighting for the people in this case; she wants it to pave the way for change for all high-tech workers, across the board and in government legislation. Only a high-profile court case will do that.'

'And I see that such a precedent is exactly what Pierce wants to avoid.' Maddie looked at Charles and grinned. 'Flying me to Seattle for an opera was worth his trouble, wasn't it, if he could undermine my confidence in the cause of the fight?'

'Maddie, some might call me pragmatic, and others have accused me outright of being unprincipled. But, like you, I've enjoyed Gray's hospitality on more than one occasion. There are facets of his personality that fascinate me. Have you noticed how like a modern example of Machiavelli's Prince, he seems to be? I might even say he has a medieval mind. He's superstitious, powerful, feudal – and yet charitable, erudite, and urbane. But he's blind to – and unwilling to see – any worldview that doesn't mesh with his own.'

Maddie almost laughed. 'My sister would agree with you and say that Sunday's show was about making me alter my attitude towards Pierce himself and Stormtree Components Inc.'

'Much more than that,' Charles rejoined. 'I'm sure he enjoyed himself immensely – the company of a bright, highly attractive young woman. He loves opera, and it appears you do. So, don't think of it as a wasted day. Most people would give their eyeteeth for the opportunity you've had – even if he didn't succeed in turning you. Give him credit. It was a stylish attempt, and it won't be his last move. Plus, it reveals something about the way he's thinking. He may not have complete faith in his lawyers. Or, he may be unable to delegate.'

Maddie shook her head. 'That would be the medieval prince. Gosh, Charles, they didn't teach this at law school.'

'No,' he laughed. 'But now, think like a lawyer. Would capitulating at this moment be in the interest of our clients? We shouldn't think to lead them, but to advise them. Flexibility is essential for survival. Give me your opinion as a lawyer, and not emotionally.'

'I can't tell,' Maddie answered. 'I see such suffering. These are people with no voice, no power, and very little time. Might they be better off to have something now? If the sum were fair it could settle their bills, reduce their worry about their families.' Maddie lifted her head and decided to add something. 'My grandmother says there is an old Italian saying: that it is better to bend like the grass than break like an oak against the wind.'

'A wise woman, and very true. Let me say right away that your personal life is your own. A close involvement with Gray might throw up a conflict of interest, but if you keep us apprised of the situation and pledge complete discretion about our details of the case, I see no problem. It may help, actually, that you have a level of access very different from the rest of us.'

Maddie wondered if Charles were thinking aloud here, until he asked her again: 'So, now you've thought on it, what do you think is the right thing to do?'

'Well, I must tell Samantha about our outing, as a matter of real priority. I don't want to be duplicitous. But then, I think if there is a reasonable chance of our winning – and for the reasons you mention about Samantha wanting a precedent – we should persist, and fight on. As long as we're not just shouting against that wind,' she added.

'How do you assess our chances?' Charles leaned forward in his chair.

'Honestly? I can't judge at this point. A lot depends on what comes out of the next batch of disclosures we've had from Stormtree. Then we'll have a better idea. But I take comfort that Pierce is contemplating ideas to settle. His confidence might not be as sky-high as he professes.'

'I think you have your answer,' Charles smiled at her.

'It could be months – another year.' Maddie was anxious.

'Yes, and more people may die. The firm's been at this for almost five years, and we're here to win, but we're not fools.'

Maddie thanked him and left, closing the door. She had one kind of answer, yes; but she knew that Pierce Gray was up to something.

It had been a benign but joyless day that ended with Maddie crying off drinks with her peers once again, without giving a reason. Not even Teresa – always reliable for a celebratory message – had noticed anything about today's date, so Maddie didn't feel the least bit guilty not staying behind. Now, as the late spring warmth had come to an end, she was glad of her trench coat as she walked, casting a long strange shadow in the early evening. She balanced her briefcase with a beautiful bouquet from Jimena's shop, heading towards Beach Street in the Marina, where Nonna Isabella lived.

The last earthquake twenty years ago had affected the Marina area badly, but for some reason hadn't touched her grandmother's house. The front garden was filled with convolvulus and lavender, asters and magnolias, roses in bud, herbs of differing heights, and various late spring flowers now cascading from pots at the height of the season. The black railing fence, with gold-tipped fleur-de-lis, made the house look like a Victorian, and this was because it had been built as a copy of the first family home in North Beach, when her grandfather had made money from property in the area so long ago and built this house near to the sea for his beloved Isabella.

A bird bath was almost grown in amongst the plants, and mourning doves used it for a cool-down most days at first and last light. Always in pairs, they would add their eerie call to the sounds of the day, and today Maddie recalled how they used to wake her when she stayed over at her grandmother's house when she was little. She would lie awake listening to the doves, overlaid with gulls calling into the wind from the water, until the rest of the house started to move about. Only then would she get up.

When Maddie was young she had thought of Nonna Isabella as old; always beautifully dressed, but of an age that seemed unfathomable to a child. But today, on her twenty-fifth birthday, she only thought of Isabella as an older friend. While her maternal grandparents had seemed to grow old, Isabella had gone the other way. Maddie thought Isabella's house never smelled like 'old people', as she had said as a child about the contrasting smell of her mother's family home. There, the furniture, the kitchen, the linen all smelled old. But the house in Beach Street smelled of salty air and sunshine and cleanliness and flowers. This was partly from the distinctive iris soap that Nonna Isabella had always used, imported at considerable cost from the apothecary of Santa Maria Novella in Florence. It was an odd vanity, perhaps, but her grandmother insisted this was what kept her skin perfect; and now, in her late seventies, Nonna Isabella still had the complexion of a woman thirty years younger. It pleased Maddie, just as her grandmother's energy and elegance pleased her.

Maddie pushed the gate open into the front yard. It squeaked and she knew that was the signal for Isabella to open the front door. And as always, she'd barely reached for the bell as the door swung open to reveal her hostess stepping back with welcoming arms to let her into the hall, take her coat, and receive the floral offering, all without a hint of fuss.

'How beautiful they are! Now come in, *bella faccia*! It's a surprise. Guess who has come. Isn't it wonderful?'

'Happy birthday, little one,' Barbara said, hugging her sister.

'This is so nice. I thought you had a busy day or I'd have met you for lunch,' Maddie told her sister.

'Yes, it was a bit of a bitch,' Barbara said quietly. 'I spent many and fruitless hours searching for a needle in a haystack. But I shut the door on it eventually and decided to come to you.'

She handed Maddie a glass of wine while their grandmother found a vase. Then they moved together into Nonna Isabella's living room.

The focal point of the house, this airy room was a mixture of modern and antique. Beautiful big sofas and comfortable chairs positioned to maximise the water view emphasised the generous space; striking Murano glass vases adorned two of the tables; and there was a finely carved white marble statue of the Roman goddess Diana, which had always stood in the corner near an antique lamp. It had come from the old country with Maddie's great-great-grandparents. Everyone believed it brought a benediction with it; and those who would doubt it laughed at their peril. It had survived the quake and fires that had racked North Beach at the turn of the century; and while other houses had been felled or fractured more recently, here it stood – like Isabella – showing not a crack or a wrinkle, in what must have been the eye of the storm during the last disaster. Lorenzo might mock, but Isabella would have nothing said against her protective goddess – even if she weren't superstitious.

Maddie came forward into the centre of the living room now and saw the large round walnut table festooned with lights. Her grandmother had set out twenty-five candles in exquisite crystal holders in a large semi-circle, which lit the room diffusely at this early evening hour.

'Ah, Nonna, how beautiful. Thank you,' Maddie said, and she swung round to hug her grandmother. But her brow wrinkled when she turned back. In the centre of the circle, surrounded by the candles, was a collection of oddities. There was a large package wrapped in brown paper, secured with string tied up with what Maddie thought were sailor's knots. The parcel was sealed with red wax. What was in that? Beside this was a selection of what looked like old photographs and hand-written letters on fading paper. The entire pile was wrapped with a wonderful pink ribbon; and finally, there was an envelope with Maddie's name inscribed on it tucked into the bow.

Maddie's hands went up to her flushed cheeks. 'What's all this?' she asked.

Isabella never ceased to amaze Maddie by the inventiveness of her gifts, but this was like a small installation in a gallery.

Isabella looked pleased with her granddaughter's response. '*Mia Maddalena*,' she said, 'you have been through so much in these last months. I wish I could suffer your pain for you, and leave you free to be young again. But now, I have been talking to my friend, Signora Angela—'

'The woman who makes hats . . .' Barbara interrupted, with an expression impossible for her sister to caption.

'And she says,' Isabella resumed, 'that you have a long way to go if you are to find yourself and your purpose again. She insists you have promises to keep.'

Both girls looked at each other, Maddie quite uncomprehending but moved by her grandmother's emotions. Barbara felt like laughing, but understood that to do so would be very ungracious and cut through one of Nonna Isabella's special, if rather opaque, gestures.

'So,' said the older lady, 'this is for you, now. And I wish you "*buon compleanno*".'

Isabella reached onto the table and picked out the envelope. But then, instead of giving it to Maddie, she put it into her jacket pocket.

'You can open this in a minute. But first, please let me say something. Grieving makes us become someone we're not. It makes us dark and lonely, without the brightness and humour that was there before. We suffer depression, which becomes a habit. We lose our way. People talk about closure, but, closure isn't what we're looking for. We want to keep the door open – keep the loved one alive with us. I know this, Maddie. I have buried several people dear to me, including your grandfather a few short years ago. Now I am the last of my generation, but my memories are not all behind me. Some have yet to come, and I want you to find a way forwards to your share of them.'

In this moment, Maddie felt saddest of all to hear such expression of her grandmother's worry. Yet, even with this clarity of understanding, she felt powerless to throw off the terrible malaise. It was her twenty-fifth birthday; and while she wasn't looking back, she wasn't looking forwards either.

She watched with affection as Isabella lifted the rest of the things wrapped in ribbon from the table, and sat down on the couch, patting the space beside her, inviting the girls to come over, sorting through the pictures. Maddie was very moved by these efforts, and she joined the other two, and sat down.

'You know me, both of you,' Isabella laughed. 'Your mother thinks I have some strange ideas. I've not discussed your gift with anyone else. They wouldn't understand. I'm not sure I do; but I think it's right for you. First of all …' She paused, with dramatic effect, and held an ageing sepia photograph in its original mount in front of the two sisters.

'This is your great-great-grandmother, girls: Mimi – you've heard me speak of her a little before. Maria Maddalena, my grandmother. She was a singer with a voice that would have torn Ulysses from his mast, it was said. A true siren.'

'I've never seen this photo before,' Barbara declared. 'This is dated at the bottom, and must have been taken in Lucca before they left.'

'Yes, look on the back,' Maddie said. '"Signor Giuseppi Chiarella, Lucca, eighteen seventy-seven."'

'Just before she got married, before she and my grandfather came to America,' Isabella agreed. 'She must have been about seventeen or eighteen here. She knew Puccini, of course. She sang in the Oakland Opera before there was an opera house here in San Francisco; and at the Tivoli; and at the Palace Hotel, for President Woodrow Wilson. They didn't build a proper opera house until nineteen twenty-four, not long before I was born.'

'God! A time before you were born, Nonna,' Barbara teased.

Isabella growled playfully at Barbara; and Maddie took the picture from her hand. She examined the image, looked searchingly at the young woman who smiled knowingly at her from the frame. How strange, Maddie thought, to be confronting the very woman who'd engaged her thoughts off and on ever since her visit to the opera with Pierce Gray a week ago. Now she took in the details of her straight pleated silk skirt, traditional high-buttoned blouse, and long curls carefully pinned and elaborately styled to show off her graceful neck. Maddie noticed a wide black ribbon around that neck. Pinned to the ribbon was a finely carved cameo brooch depicting a pair of doves lifting two garlands of flowers between them. She felt she could remember it.

'What a fine-looking lady she was.' Maddie sounded surprised. 'Why haven't you shown us this before?'

Isabella nodded, and slipped on her reading glasses to look closely at the photo. 'I remember her from when I was young. We lost her around my tenth birthday, when she was in her seventies, but she's always stayed in my mind. She was an amazing woman, with her pretty gamine face, like you, Barbara; and her wild curls like yours, Maddie. Her hair was still thick and not altogether grey when she was old. Now –' Isabella took her glasses off again – 'I have that cameo some place, but I can't find it. That will worry me until I can remember where I've put it.'

'How odd, Nonna,' Barbara said suddenly, a postcard from the remaining items catching her eye. 'What's this?'

'Yes, that's the last card she had from her own mother, Maria Pia, in Italy – before the old lady died. It's rather a strange picture, isn't it?'

Barbara took it from her grandmother and studied the image, ignoring the message written in Italian.

'What is it, Bee?'

Barbara scrutinised the sepia photo, taken on a very old-fashioned camera. It was of a bronze statuette. Though unfamiliar to her, it nevertheless excited her.

'It looks modern, doesn't it?' she said. 'But I'm as sure as I can be that it's Etruscan, and probably more than two thousand years old.' She passed it over to Isabella to read the Italian, which Barbara had little command of.

'Yes. Yes, you're quite right.' Isabella had put her glasses on again. 'Her mother explains here to Nonna Mimi that it was being used as a fire poker by a farmer, who ploughed it up in his field near Volterra just before the date of this card. And yes, it seems it is Etruscan. It was nicknamed the "*Ombra della Sera*" – you'd say, "Shadow of Evening".' Isabella took her glasses away and said almost to herself, 'That is odd, because I feel as though I've heard that somewhere recently.'

'It's actually weird when I tell you I spent the whole day scouring upcoming auctions and international dealers looking for an Etruscan artefact, for a client who was quite specific. It had to be Etruscan, and not Roman, and it had to be soonest – tomorrow, if possible.' Barbara looked at Maddie and arched her eyes, as though her sister shared the secret. 'And I've never been asked for such a thing before; nor do they exactly grow on trees!'

'No, but they can be dug up in the right field,' Maddie joked.

'Well, then, before we eat let me give you this, *nipotina*,' Isabella said to Maddie. She took a deep breath, as though she were parting with crown jewels, then drew the card from her pocket. 'You need to do a bit of digging yourself.'

'Nonna?'

Maddie carefully broke open the envelope. It took a moment for her to make sense of the older woman's words on the card.

A parent should give their child two things. Roots to grow; and wings to fly. Your roots here are strong, Madeline, but you've forgotten how to fly. If this can help you find other, older roots, perhaps you will remember you also have wings.

Maddie gently drew out an airline ticket from the envelope and a few banknotes in a foreign currency. These were relatively unfamiliar, but she quickly recognised they were euros. Reading the details on the ticket she saw she had been gifted an open return to Pisa, via Rome. And cradled in the seam of the envelope, her fingers freed a shining silver disc on a chain, which she knew without need of inspection would be a St Christopher's medal.

Now her throat caught, and it took a moment before she could free the sound.

'Nonna-bella!' she said, feeling very emotional. 'This is so generous, and such a lovely idea, truly. But what about my job?'

'You'll go when you're ready to, Madeline,' she said firmly. 'And they're already waiting for you in Tuscany.'

Isabella raised her hand quietly to signal that enough had been said for now. 'Shall we go into the dining room for birthday dinner?' she smiled.

14

During the last stretch of the ride to the abbey of her Cistercian neighbours, Jacquetta realised snow was indeed beginning to swirl again and leave white patches on the ground. But her horse was sure-footed, and beast and rider passed quickly around the bend in the river into the eventual clearing of the meadows. In summer these would be lush with grasses supporting the abbey's justly famous sheep and horses; and the bordering fields that ran as far as the eye could see would be rippling under a warm wind with the nutty-flavoured grains that fed the brothers.

Today that seemed a long way off. All was grey, the ground frozen and unyielding. Smoke rose from the forge where the monks worked their secret alchemy, turning rock into iron; and water wheels turned to crush the grains, make beer, and warm the domestic buildings with hot water. But in this harsh season most of the activity within the walls was at a minimum. Within weeks, Jacquetta was thinking, the monks and their equally hard-working lay brothers would bring all the fields under the plough again, working from sun-up to sun-down to renew the cycle of planting that so generously supplied the abbey's many residents and provided surplus for sale in the markets. As the days lengthened, all would be a hive of industry again.

Jacquetta slowed her horse's step as she rode towards the arched gate that marked the main entrance to the fraternity. It was still before midday, when the monks would take their meal, but she was aware that the privilege of being both friend and neighbour would assure her welcome even at such an hour. And as she hoped, the porter came quickly to give her admittance, beckoning her out of the worsening weather and into the care of a brown-robed lay brother, who opened the door for her into the guesthouse, then took her horse.

The beauty of the Cistercians' abbey complex struck Jacquetta anew, whenever she came. It was a beauty of elegant restraint. The strength and simplicity of line, the cleanliness of the white stone buildings arranged together seemed to embody physically the original doctrine of the brothers at Cîteaux, in France, who preferred the simple purity of work and meditation to one of comfort and excess enjoyed by some of their more worldly ecclesiastical peers.

A fire was lit in the guesthouse, but Jacquetta lingered at a window and gazed across the cluster of other buildings to the graceful form of the abbey church. It was whispered that the Cistercian masons had built the whole monastery, and especially the church, following plans of sacred and magical geometry. Only those who knew could hear the music of its stones, read its message and learn its spiritual secrets. But Jacquetta felt she was under its spell of harmony and serenity – though she knew nothing of the story in its walls.

'Ma donna Jacquetta! You are welcome.'

The visitor turned her head from the window towards the front door. She had been hoping for an audience with the prior, who often saw her at short notice even though the presence of women allegedly rather frightened some of the monks. Today, however, it was Abbot Angelo himself who came graciously to her.

'Do I intrude?' she asked. Silence was more or less a rule at the abbey, or at least unnecessary talk was discouraged. Visitors were always politely welcomed, but she knew enough not to waste words or time with the abbot and his order.

A kind shake of his head reassured her, though.

'What would bring you here, in such weather?' he asked, gesturing hospitably for her to sit at the good fire. He placed himself in a chair opposite her.

'An unsettling visit from Volterra,' she answered quietly.

The abbot nodded, and waited. He knew all the sad history of the house of his neighbours, knew of their tangles with the bishops – old and new, ordained and not ordained; was privy to the violence and injustices that had been done to Jacquetta and her sister. He was no stranger himself to the knotty politics of Volterra, as his abbey and the church properties of his neighbours were in its diocese.

'Is there news of Bishop Ranuccio?'

'I've not seen him.' Jacquetta shook her head. 'But visits from Volterra bode ill to me and mine while he remains in exile.'

'The rest of his family are returned there,' Abbot Angelo told her, aware that she probably knew this. 'His Grace, though, will come to us here at the Abbazia. He has refused to go back to Volterra himself, though the Belforti have at last stopped harassing him. His intentions are for us to become his beadsmen – when the time comes.'

Bishop Ranuccio Allegretti was like a father to Jacquetta, and she hated to talk of his end, whenever it must come. But she knew the ageing man had struggled in recent years, sent into exile by the malice of the Belforti. They had a score to settle with Ranuccio, who'd been chosen as bishop when the Belforti's own incumbent, Ranieri, had fallen foul of the Pope and the people, and been driven from his office. It was twenty years before his brother, Ottaviano Belforte, managed to raise a coup against Ranuccio. The vendetta of the Belforti went deep, and Ranuccio was forced to flee with his family in mortal fear. In the first weeks of his absence, the Belforti clan confiscated all the personal and family properties of the Allegretti in Volterra, then further sequestered lands given to the Episcopal office as well. Bishop Ranuccio lived in exile, still anointed; but it had aged him, and he was not the man he had once been.

'This is a conversation I must have with Maria Maddalena, one day soon,' she said to the abbot. 'But I do not come about that today.'

'All is well with the child, I hope?' the abbot asked. 'We have a great affection for her, but I've not seen her come for music or drawing with the novitiates these several weeks past, I think.'

'Because of the weather,' Jacquetta smiled. 'And this is why I have come.'

She looked into the fire, gathering her thoughts. She recognised the privilege of having, as neighbours and acquaintances, some of the finest minds in the country. The monks of San Galgano had a reputation for their intellects, their fairness and wisdom. Their abbey was not unlike a university and – besides theologians – lawyers, architects, engineers, men of medicine and music could all be found here. They had settled arguments between the great Tuscan cities – very recently between Siena and Volterra; they had supplied a treasurer in Siena for close to a hundred years; they had helped to draw up property documents for their neighbours; their engineers had improved the water supplies in the city of Siena and the local towns; and their architects had drafted the plans for the building of Siena's magnificent Duomo. Now, Jacquetta had come to her friends for advice.

'Do you believe God can, and does, control the weather?' She looked up and smiled doubtfully at the abbot.

'A strange question, donna Jacquetta!' he answered with a fusion of humour and seriousness. 'With a deeper question still that lurks behind it, I should think. But shall I put on the mantle of Thomas Aquinas to answer you? Or are the views of William of Ockham of more help to us, I wonder?'

'Answer only as Abbot Angelo of San Galgano,' she smiled gently, 'and I am satisfied.'

'Things are never so simple,' he said, and he drew his hands out from the sleeves of his white robe, and placed them together. 'The head of our order, some decades ago, exhorted those who would listen to follow his call to arms in the Holy Land. Bernard was a magnificent orator, challenging ordinary men to take up the cross against those in other lands, with other beliefs. Whole villages emptied, leaving young wives as widows to yet-living husbands, and when the campaign failed Bernard threw the blame back at the sinful nature of the men who had fought it.

'Yet,' he continued slowly, 'was the sin only theirs? Perhaps he had not considered Friar Bacon's view. The Franciscan had learned something of Mahometan culture and science, and believed that it might yet displease God that we take such measures against them unto ourselves. He suggested – and surely with some wisdom – that those who survived the terrible slaughter would only become more deeply entrenched against Christians.'

'What says Abbot Angelo?' Jacquetta asked.

'I am in accord with my Cistercian brother abbot, Isaac of Poitiers. I cannot agree that Christians become martyrs for dying while despoiling non-Christians; nor that converting members of Islam by force is in any respect the right action for a true Christian.'

'But,' Jacquetta asked, 'do we have free will to resist such direction placed upon us? When the Pope calls for the fight, do we have the right – as ordinary people – to debate this?'

'If the leaders calling upon us are committed to a rigid set of beliefs even before a debate can be had, then our enquiry is not impartial, and becomes meaningless.' Abbot Angelo smiled, knowing this complex argument was one that many churchmen would discourage; but he knew Jacquetta would relish the philosophical discussion. 'I believe,' he continued, 'that it is required of us – is vital to our conscience and our individual relationship with God – to subject those beliefs to the utmost scrutiny; and I must be prepared to live and die by my own convictions.'

'Volterra's acting bishop,' said Jacquetta, 'young Filippo Belforte, may disagree with you. I think he is a politician first, and a man of God after that.'

'He would certainly disagree,' Abbot Angelo laughed. 'And what has this to do with the weather, you may ask?'

'I think you may be saying that God is responsible for the weather if it suits us that He should be?' Jacquetta's question was more a statement.

'The Bible tells us of many occasions when the will of God has been expressed through the weather,' the abbot replied. 'Floods and famines; the clouds darkening at Our Lord's death; the frankly terrible punishments enacted on Job's family; God smiting the Egyptians with the East Wind. But I think it could be a dangerous practice to ascribe every squall and every snowstorm to his Divine action.'

The abbot's expression was now one of question, as he looked at Jacquetta with a slight frown. She realised he was curious about why she had asked this.

'A young girl,' she said softly, 'came to my home to stay with us. And I have since learned from Belforte's men that she refused to enter the convent at her parents' wishes, has married instead, and that when her family and the authorities imprisoned her – prepared and ready to execute her – something of a miracle seems to have happened. The wind shook her family's house to the ground, and killed every inhabitant, including her guards, but spared the girl so that she walked away freely.'

Abbot Angelo placed his elbows on the arms of his chair, and brought his hands to his chin almost in prayer. He pondered this for some moments.

'I am reminded of the storm that saved the virgin St Agnes from ravishment in the brothel in Rome,' he said at last. 'Perhaps her piety need not be expressed in a life at the convent; and the Lord has truly spoken through such an act.'

'If she were a devout Christian,' Jacquetta asked, 'would we have no difficulty in saying that she had been spared for something, by God?'

The abbot's brows knotted and he half-smiled. 'You have said, "if", donna Jacquetta. Is she not devout?'

'I cannot answer,' she said honestly. 'I've not asked her about this; and everything is dangerously told from hearsay. It's reported she is a "heretic" – but who am I to be her judge?'

'No more can I be,' he said. 'But I believe that civil law should not impede her marriage; and that canon law should have the spine to insist that a union honestly contracted is a matter for the couple. There is something touching the divine in this event. It is the kind of tale that makes us think of the miracles of the Lord and his saints.'

As he finished speaking, a single bell note rang out from the campanile in the abbey grounds. It simply marked the rhythm of the monastic day, announcing midday's approaching meal, but now, within the confines of their current conversation, it struck Jacquetta as other worldly.

'And if she were truly pagan?' Jacquetta asked.

'Eusebius is clear,' Abbot Angelo answered. 'Miracles not born of reverence for God the Father or Jesus the Son are the work of demons. Eusebius isn't always comfortable with Christian miracles either, feeling them dangerously close to works of "magic".

'Then again,' he added, 'there is an intriguing rain miracle that occurred on the Danube, in the second century after Our Lord's birth. The Roman army, fighting the Barbarians on a sweltering summer day, were prevented from getting their wounded to the river for fresh water. They fully expected to die, unless a miracle might save them. Within moments of their various prayers – to a collection of deities, including some from Christian soldiers – clouds gathered and broke into a heavy rainfall, which allowed them to quench their thirst. Precisely at that moment the Quadi troops decided to attack them, when fierce thunder, lightning and hailstones fell on their side of the river, killing some of the Barbarians. It is written that fire fell in one half of the sky, and nurturing rain in the other. No account at the time could decide whether the miracle belonged to the Christian God, or to Jupiter, or to a Persian magus named Julian.'

'I knew nothing of pagan miracles,' Jacquetta said, looking surprised.

'It is nearly impossible for us to understand the will of God, donna Jacquetta,' Abbot Angelo told her. 'I venture only that some power intervened on this young woman's behalf; and I would be cautious myself about quarrelling with that power, without being privy to God's mind. Which,' he added, 'is something disclosed to men only, it seems, after a fevered state of fasting.'

'This is not something I ask of you, Abbot Angelo,' she said, quickly coming to her feet. 'Your refectory will be filling. Please go to your meal, with my deep thanks for your time and wisdom.'

In the rhythm of her horse's canter, Jacquetta's head swam with the ideas the abbot had shared with her. He was a man she respected, with taste and generosity and a strong sense of his own responsibilities and limitations. In the many years she'd known him, he could be relied upon to have an opinion of his own that was not shackled to any centralised dictates. She was still mulling over his willingness to see some divine intervention in the events related to her house guest, revealed to her only that morning by the men from Volterra. Now, she strongly felt, she wanted to talk to Signora Toscano, and hear her side of what had happened.

She stabled her horse herself quickly to prevent calling Loredana's boy up from the house in the bad weather, then hung her coat in the hallway; but when she turned into the entrance chamber that served as a small audience room, she was completely unprepared for what she saw.

Gathered before the fire in a group of three, Signor Porphyrius had a hand on his wife's back, and she – perched on the low arm of the settle – had a protective arm around Mia; and the child was sobbing gently, but aloud!

She looked up at her aunt. Very slowly, very deliberately, very precisely, words came from her. 'The *nano* – the short man – he watched, and I watched. His brother killed my mother.'

Jacquetta moved toward her niece swiftly, kneeled at her feet and took her free hands in hers; but she said nothing, and let the child continue at her own pace. Her voice was soft, just audible, but it was clear:

'They came into our house, that May morning. The sunlight was thick, incongruous. I stood behind a partly open door. He called his brother "Maurizio"; and he laughed while the man forced himself on my mother.

'She screamed,' Mia went on quietly. 'And when it was finished, he stopped her screams. He sliced through her pretty throat, Aunt Jacquetta. Then he pulled her tongue right through the gaping hole. I heard a gurgling noise, like water; and a sputtering sound. And then it stopped. Everything stopped.'

PART TWO

15

MONDAY 11 JUNE 2007, NEAR SIENA, TUSCANY

After a strenuous twenty minutes along a mountain road winding through thick woodland, Maddie emerged at last, and with some relief, into a watercolour landscape. Her road skirted a yellow-gold hilltop town shimmering in heat on a perfect June day. She shook off the trance of a long journey to look up at it, guarding the route below. Red roof tiles and quaint chimneys rather like small dovecotes created a soft silhouette, though the town itself was ancient and imposing.

'*Non è lontano adesso!*'

This was her ever-cheerful driver, Gori, who had collected her smilingly from Pisa airport; Maddie marvelled that the smile had barely left his face, even in brutal June traffic along a famously named and even more famously busy motorway, the Via Aurelia. But Maddie was growing weary from the hour and a half in the car, and regretting the last airline breakfast before these miles of meandering motion; she was very glad to hear it wasn't much further.

She'd come away barely prepared for the trip, leaving Samantha and Neva and Stormtree to themselves for three weeks. A rational mind made her wonder now just how her boss had agreed so willingly to her coming away at all. The Stormtree paper trail was still long, and much nit-picking work was yet to be done; but Samantha had told her unequivocally that the break would do her good, sharpen her mind and give her a fresh appetite for the fight. So here she was, a large and a small bag behind her, eyes and thoughts private behind large sunglasses, and

133

without a clue as to what she would find. A friend of her grandmother's here in the south of Tuscany was ready to welcome her and, though Maddie had never met her hostess, she felt a desire to come away; to have a change of air and faces – even if Nonna Isabella's riddles about 'finding herself' were too muddling to engage with.

Gori pulled off the road on to an unprepossessing dirt track fringed on one side with oleander bushes, and on the other a few tall poplars that seemed to lead nowhere. Then the car swung unexpectedly to the right towards what was once a magnificent gateway, now graced with slightly rusting wrought iron. Maddie glimpsed mellow ochre stone-work and the typical line of a large Tuscan roof of red double Roman pantiles; then suddenly, without having an idea of what she would find, she was able to see the house. She sucked in her breath. It's a Renaissance palazzo! she thought; and she felt a shiver of pleasure, as though she were a little girl again. She was thoroughly awed by its appearance.

Gori had parked and was already pulling her bags from the boot when Maddie sprang from the car. A beguiling dog with a very human, wrinkled face greeted her, trying in vain to catch her full attention. Maddie couldn't, however, take her eyes from the building in front of her. Two storeys of large, elegant windows underscored with a row of neat iron balconies spoke of its quiet nobility, and she wondered how it could be that this was her hostelry.

'Eleanore,' Gori told her, pointing at the dog.

Maddie nodded and bent down to pat her, then followed both of them past a low border of box and a higher hedge of laurel. She entered a courtyard in the centre of which was an olive tree that looked as though it had flourished in the same spot for a thousand years. Her feet crunched on the white pebbles under her, and she moved behind Gori and the dog, past ancient urns of flowers, towards a pair of perhaps eighteenth-century folding wooden doors. Before Gori's fingers reached the handle the doors opened, and an elegant blonde woman of thirty-nine or forty smiled openly, extending arms towards her.

'Madeline! You don't know how welcome you are,' she said warmly. 'I'm Jeanette, and we're so happy to have you.'

She spoke perfect English in a gently accented voice, which Maddie thought might have been northern European, not in the least what she expected.

'Thank you so much for extending the invitation,' Maddie answered. 'I'm in a bit of a daze from the beauty of your house.'

'Well,' Jeanette laughed, 'it didn't look quite like this when we found it a few years ago. But I'm happy you like it; and it's yours to share for a while. I expect you to make yourself completely at home here.'

'You're very kind,' Maddie answered. But she felt the words were meant, and not just said from politeness.

'If you're tired,' Jeanette offered, 'I can show you your room right now? Or if you'd like to stretch your legs, maybe you'd enjoy walking a little with me in the gardens, and we can get Gori to take your bags up so they're waiting for you later.'

'Definitely stretch the legs,' Maddie nodded. 'I've been sitting a while.'

'Perfect. *Gori, porta il bagaglio in "Pellegrino", per favore*,' she said, 'and, Madeline, let's get something to drink and then stroll together.'

Maddie's hostess walked her through a large entrance hall with a Chesterfield and two leather armchairs grouped around a low table in front of an old stone fireplace. A faint odour of wood-smoke suggested recent weather might have been mixed; and an impressive staircase opposite the doors ascended along with Maddie's curiosity. It was up these stairs that Gori now disappeared with her luggage while the two women walked through a short hallway and into an enormous kitchen.

Maddie felt an extraordinary sense of personal calm, yet there was a quiet bustle of activity all around her. An electrician was working on a fitting and getting ready to hang a chandelier; a joiner was finishing a cabinet; and through glass doors Maddie glimpsed a slim, dark-haired man with a cigar hanging out of his mouth intently painting with fine brushes onto the wall. She could hear Jimi Hendrix playing, as company for him.

'It's a work in progress,' Jeanette told her, walking over to an industrial-sized coffee machine. 'I've been at it so long now, I don't know how I'll feel whenever it's completely finished!'

'When did you buy it?' Maddie asked, nodding her head for some milk in the coffee.

'It's six years ago already,' her hostess answered. 'And I was sure it would be perfect in seven, when I want to open it as a small hotel. But I wonder if I'll get there!'

'It looks amazing already to me,' Maddie said. Her eyes drank in the tall ceiling, the cosy French or even Gustavian feel of the kitchen, with its nineteenth-century glass-fronted cabinet, which covered a wall, a modest refectory table with antique chairs. 'Is there a lot more you want to do?'

Jeanette smiled, and her eyes suggested there was too much to say on that subject.

'Let's bring our coffee into the garden,' she said.

She led her guest through another pair of double glass doors onto a broad stone terrace that ran the length of the building. Maddie couldn't speak. Her first impression of the low white armchairs placed near an outside fireplace, and the pots of lemon trees heavy with fruit on the lawns in front, was enough to delight the eye, but they faded almost into obscurity next to the view that beckoned just beyond the edge of the garden.

Jeanette registered Maddie's response, and was pleased.

'It has two names,' she said. 'In the oldest documents I can find it's called the "Val di Cellole", and from about the end of the medieval period it's recorded as the "Valle Serena".'

Maddie walked across the grass with Jeanette. 'The Valley of Serenity.' She nodded, seeing without explanation why it deserved the name. Hills, almost like mountains and blue in colour, stretched the eye across an undulation of green fields without a road, an electric pylon or a telegraph pole in sight. It looked, surely, as it must always have done.

'Maybe it's because our neighbours were the monks at the abbey a mile or so along the river – and I'm told they had a vow of near-silence. But it's just as peaceful today!'

'It is,' Maddie agreed. 'And I imagine it was the view that made you want to buy it in the first place.'

'Funny thing is,' Jeanette shook her head with a smile, 'we never even knew the Valle Serena was there. No one did.'

Maddie looked at her, tilting her head in question.

'When we came, that whole edge of the garden had pigsties in it, and you couldn't see past them. It wasn't till we took them down that we found the valley. Not even the locals knew it was here.' She laughed. 'Those pigs had the best view.'

Maddie was transported. The two of them walked together through the grounds, from the lemon lawns into an English-style rose garden, stepping across fountains and rills, while Jeanette told her of the lengthy project that had started so many years ago when she and her husband, Claus, had found the house on their honeymoon. Maddie couldn't imagine how much money had been invested into it, but she could see that a lot of love and vision had been. It was just like a secret garden, a place where time and no person had been for years until Jeanette had hacked back the thorn trees and kissed the house alive again.

'We even found some bodies buried right here, near where we've put the wall for the rose garden,' Jeanette said. 'And we weren't sure if it was a job for the police or an archaeologist. But that's a story for a glass of good wine and some supper later on.'

Maddie's face registered amazement.

Jeanette laughed again – a wonderful earthy sound. 'I think right now maybe I should show you your room, and you might want to rest for a while before we have some late lunch?'

Maddie nodded. 'Please.'

She followed Jeanette back into the house, where she collected a key from a small office near the kitchen. As they retraced their steps, Jimi Hendrix was supplanted by the soft strains of opera in the entrance hallway. Maddie said hello to a girl who was now pinning up a curtain hem in the enormous window that lit the stairs opposite the main door, and a man working near her on the lower steps with an artist's fine brush. She saw that he was painting a *trompe-l'oeil* of a rope banister, and grinned.

'This is Peter,' Jeanette said, 'and he's been here for months painting the frescos you'll see in some of the rooms. There's a particularly special one in yours.'

Maddie smiled a hello. 'I like your taste in music,' she said, and he nodded back at her emphatically.

They'd soon reached the top of the stairs, and Jeanette produced a tasselled key from her pocket. Maddie waited while she unlocked the door, and her eyes read the words painted over the lintel: 'Via del Pellegrino'.

'There are some wonderful stories about this room, Madeline,' Jeanette said, as she turned the handle, 'but it is called the "Way of the Pilgrim" because it overlooks the ancient pathway below that twisted along to the hermitage of San Galgano.'

The door opened, and Maddie stood rooted to the spot. Her mouth formed an 'oh', without her knowing it had. Her eyes went first across the space to an ensuite bathroom, where a glorious free-standing Victorian claw-foot tub, gold-leafed under its lip, stood proud behind glass doors that sparkled like crystal. Then she saw the beautiful antique bed, a soft feminine blue, and the fresco positioned opposite it that Jeanette had mentioned. It was of a man leading a laden packhorse along a track lined with pencil pines towards a rotunda on a hilltop. All the hues were creamy soft, with a rose-tinted sunrise or sunset; and as they stepped together into the room, the whole of it had a palpable effect on Maddie.

'It's just exquisite,' she said, and bit her lower lip.

'The villa served the pilgrims' route for hundreds of years,' Jeanette explained, 'and this room overlooking the old road was immediately special to me. I saw it at once as the place to be scrubbed clean – to get free of clutter and worry. It's a place to renew the spirit. That's why you see the bath as soon as you open the door, and the painting leading you to your own place of pilgrimage.'

'I don't know what to say. Just, thank you for having me.' She gave Jeanette a hug.

'I'll leave you to relax and unpack your things, maybe have a shower if you want to,' she smiled back at Maddie. 'Come down when you're ready and we'll find something to eat.'

Maddie took a further stride into the room, then noticed a large envelope with her name on it set on the little writing desk.

'Oh, yes, I forgot about that,' Jeanette said. 'It came a day or so ago, special delivery. I had to sign for it! I wonder what's inside.' Her eyes sparkled at Maddie. 'Anyhow, see you shortly. Isabella says you have good Italian, so, *ci vediamo presto.*'

'*Grazie mille, Jeanette,*' Maddie said meaningfully; then, when the door was shut, she took up the envelope and sat on her bed.

The package had been overnight couriered, and came from the USA. She opened it carefully and found bubble wrap and tissue protecting its contents; then, at the heart of it, a note and another tissue wrapping enclosed a small box. She got through the last of the tissue and opened the box to reveal an old irregular-shaped silver coin, with two faces looking in opposite directions. A small typed provenance inside said: 'Janus coin, second century BC, probably Etruscan or possibly Etrusco-Roman, and from Volterra.'

Now Maddie unravelled the note, and was astounded.

'This little guy is the guardian of doors and gates. I hope your sojourn opens something interesting for you. Belated birthday wishes, and kind regards, P.G.'

16

Last night, under a canopy of stars, Mia had watched while Signora Toscano had stood in their special place at the extreme edge of the orchard, making measurements with her thumb and forefinger outstretched against the skies, and then noting it down with strange symbols on their garden plan. Clearly she was making alignments to plant by the moon and stars. As Mia herself had been taught by Fra Silvestro at the abbey to respect the lunar rhythms for planting, she found nothing peculiar in this; but she was fascinated watching her friend doing something she had never seen. She had opened her arms wide and lifted her forefinger to each corner of the heavens, searching – Mia thought perhaps – for the wind. She had again made note on their drawing, then taken Mia's hand as they retraced their steps to the house.

Through seven years of acting with her aunt as a comfortably born hostess to pilgrims from every corner of Christendom, Mia had been privileged to open up their doors, and her mind, to the worlds of the rich and the poor alike. Counts and courtiers, even a king and two queens had passed through the villa in their turn; but so had nuns and monks and mendicants, knights and their ladies, merchants, clerks and common folk. She knew something of their simple lives and struggles, of their quest through pilgrimage for a life of spiritual rescue and enlightenment, their hope of cleansing their souls and easing their pains through honest work and pure faith. Often, at odds with this avowed intention, some were full of jealous passions and prejudice and

140

hatred; and they seemed to Mia to have irrational beliefs and fears of anyone different from themselves, with an unyielding conviction of their own superiority. Others, of high and low birth alike, were mindful that the purpose of their journey was to seek the almost unattainable, to unburden their souls through compassion and gentle treatment of their fellows. It had been an education, affording her a powerful sense that life was very often not fair, and full of unsettling instabilities.

In these years of helping her aunt offer refuge to pilgrims she had never met anyone like Signora Toscano. She still named her '*la raggia*' – the lady of light; and Mia knew that the servants called her '*la bella pellegrina*' – the beautiful pilgrim – as she herself had first done. Cesaré, who was equally charmed by her radiance and sweetness, called her 'La Toscana' which not only followed a convention of feminising her married name, but also imparted a sense that she was the physical embodiment of everything beautiful and natural in Tuscany. He named her as though she were the spirit of the Tuscan hills, the sun and the moon and the countryside – not from Firenze or Pisa or Siena or Volterra, but part of the land itself. Yet, to Mia, *la raggia* was less earthly than this, and had stars in her soul. But whatever names they accorded her, Aunt Jacquetta never asked for her given name. After the loss of the young signora's family in such complex circumstances, her aunt had thought it sensitive not to enquire about her family name either. It wasn't relevant to her existence here, at Villa Santo Pietro.

And Mia knew that, just as she herself did, Aunt Jacquetta had come to care very much for their house guest, this young woman who – though none of them spoke more than a word or two about it – had through the strangest events become orphaned, like Mia. Far from being alarmed by what she'd been told, Aunt Jacquetta seemed to have become more protective of the couple. Mia realised this when she admitted to her niece one evening that she 'could hardly imagine what the girl must have been through'; and she'd immediately invited the couple to stay for as long as they wished. She then moved them into her best room on the first floor of the villa, overlooking the road below so they could see everything and everyone who came and went. It also looked onto the pretty patch of garden that had fronted the old church, where flowers and two precious bushes of Damascan lilacs, brought back by pilgrims, would soon appear; and it was Mia's favourite room, even though it was not the largest.

The reason for Aunt Jacquetta's hospitality was clear. Thanks to the *signora*'s patience and care of Mia, the girl had unlocked a part of herself that had been bolted shut for close to seven years. Stopping her voice had been an attempt to lock up the pain. She had been loving and affectionate with her aunt, but she recognised that a new strength was beginning to emerge in her. She had confronted her past, revealing the horror of a death of which not even Aunt Jacquetta had known the details. The image of her mother haunted her afresh, weeks after she had told her nightmare. Yet Mia felt free of a demon, the tacit caveat on her telling a soul what she had witnessed. Now she knew what had happened, and had started to understand it as an adult. Details were missing, as to why her mother was a victim of such violence, but Mia was ready to hear her own history whenever Aunt Jacquetta was willing to talk to her about it.

Today, however, early in the morning on the twentieth day of April – and three months exactly since the arrival of her friend – the spring had come, and everyone was up and already joyous and busy. The last heavy snow had been on that day when the men of Volterra appeared – when that leering face from her past had caught Mia like a bird of prey at her throat. The new and the older members of the household at Villa Santo Pietro had suddenly forged a powerful bond; and while they shared their griefs and nursed their starkly revealed wounds, the skies had spewed forth an unceasing torrent of ice. The snowfall that afternoon and evening had been deeper than the length of a human leg, which no one could remember for at least a generation. The old woman in the farm close to the villa told them she had never seen such snow here in a day and night – and she was more than seventy years old. But it had prevented the return of the Volterran guard, to everyone's relief; and Mia awarded responsibility for the weather to *la raggia*.

In the seven ensuing weeks the snows had gently melted. Fields were again lush, birds noisy, and peach and almond trees quickened with blossom. It was a celebration of life, and pilgrims and minstrels again came and went from the villa with news and stories from other lands. Most importantly to Mia it was the moment for the realisation of their design for a paradise garden, the place where – as Signora Toscano said – the unexpected could happen.

For weeks they had planned and drawn, painting in minute detail a garden space of simple design and soft colours, where the grim world of pain and distress would be excluded. In the words of Signora Toscano, here they could concentrate their minds and still their restless energies to a better purpose.

'We cannot create a better world,' she had said to Mia as they painted in rose trees and irises among herbs of every kind, 'until we can first imagine one. It must be a place of beauty and purity, but also of the subtlest enchantment. A tranquil spot, which might equally play host to a virgin, a saint or a goddess; somewhere your unicorn might venture.'

So, it was to be a garden where a better world could take root, both 'holy and enchanted'. It was planetary and also earthly; astrological and yet religious; beautiful and useful. And at its heart would be a secret.

Only last night, an hour before their walk to the bottom of the long and uncultivated outer gardens, the two women had finally completed their intricate three-part design. It was an accomplished work of art, decorated in gold leaf, with a dazzling blue dome stretching across the canopy of the picture. Within the azure heavens the lord sun and the lady moon lit the world below, and each was personified by Porphyrius and his lady, their beautifully painted faces watching from within the golden and silver orbs. Mia had given her own face to the watching wind, her hair gently blowing fertile seeds and cooling breezes into the landscape. This paradise – a walled herber edged with a water rill and containing exactly forty-two varieties of carefully chosen herbs and flowers, which filled out the planting – used a predominant colour plan of reds, yellows and creams. Very dark green and blue-flowering plants edged the extreme border, and at its centre was a special place marked by Signora Toscano for an old stone she wished to set there. Over this would be a central mulberry tree – the choice was important – and around it they would group all the plants and paths, which must also be white. There would be precisely sixteen planted spaces, corresponding to the divisions of the heavens their ancestors had consulted for words from the gods. It was sacred and powerful in Signora Toscano's eyes.

While Mia had sat beaming, proud and dazzled by the work they had achieved, they'd shared an unusual discussion as they waited for their last application of colours to dry.

'My teacher, Monna Calogera, was my governess,' Signora Toscano had told Mia. 'She was a lady instructed in the wisdom of her ancestors. Her mother came from a noble family who had lived in Volterra, she told me, even before the time of the Romans; and my mother and father wanted her to shape me with traditional manners, to turn me into a pious and obedient creature. But they knew nothing of where her heart belonged. She had learned other philosophies.'

Mia's voice, still soft but growing in assurance, gently enquired of her friend: 'She is the lady who taught you the use of herbs?'

'Her father was a surgeon, and a Jew,' she'd answered, smiling. 'He was a remarkable man who worked in the *ospedale* of the Franciscans in Volterra; and as your aunt guessed, he knew about much more than the setting of bones. He had travelled and learned from teachers in both Alexandria and Granada, was schooled in the most secret traditions of his people. He taught his daughter to think, and to heal; and her mother taught her other ancient wisdoms. Some of this Monna Calogera shared with me.'

In this sparsely furnished picture, Mia understood that her governess had been more of a mother to her friend than her real mother had been. Mia could not imagine the pain that must have been tangled with parents who would so willingly want their only child to suffer and perhaps die, in order to fulfil their plan. To cut her off without money, or to disinherit her – though awful – was not unheard of, and would have been punishment enough. To pursue her and threaten her life was unbearably awful to Mia, and she was pleased that her friend had a closer and kinder confidante to look up to.

'Then,' she said quietly, 'it is Donna Calogera's thoughts that will grow with us, in our garden. Do you think she knew anything of unicorns?'

Her companion put a gentle arm around Mia, and nodded. 'I think she did.'

And now, on this day of immaculate sunrise – the first, Signora Toscano pointed out, under the sign of the Bull – the two women took their painted plan out into the gardens of the villa to their designated place. They left behind the *forno*, where the bread was baked, then walked past the small farmhouse that stood in the shadow of the grander building; then they passed beyond the poultry house and the stables and the barns, along beside the orchard, and into the opening of a large meadow at the border of the property. Here, at this hour before the sun was high, dew still damped the grass.

Bells were calling the monks to prayer at the abbey as they began to pace out the first part of their plan on the ground. In perhaps an hour they had covered the space with string and stones, marking out rounded paths and circular spaces of precise dimensions. This first area was to be a preparation for the meditation and reflection that would feed the soul in the third part of the garden, further down. Most importantly, this section was dedicated to Mia's unicorn. The pathway looped and curled like the whorls in a unicorn's sacred horn. Surrounding this pathway would be holy trees – including olives and pomegranates, which were said to have grown both in Eden and in Elysium, and which *la raggia* said were both magical and sacred to every idea of heaven, no matter what your religion. The whole was to be set within a flowery mead, brimming with planting, which a unicorn sought and where the colours were carefully selected. This, Signora Toscano explained, was a labyrinth, like the one seen on the face of the Duomo in Lucca, and yet, much simplified. With its richly scented narcissi and aquilegias, its sweet violets and rocket and sweet cicely, and most importantly its Tuscan irises, it was an enchanted woodland with a well of truth at its core. The orchard of pomegranates was dedicated to the Virgin and the Goddess, and Mia associated these trees most strongly with her friend. Whatever else they would plant, she loved this grove best.

By the time the shapes were marked out in the rough field the sun was almost above them, and the girls sat. Porphyrius appeared with cool water for them, and Mia watched shyly while the couple embraced and kissed. She tried to look away, watching a lizard flashing green along some stones, enjoying the warmth. But Signora Toscano had noticed, and when her young husband left, she smiled at Mia.

'Let us go from here, Mia – from this first garden of preparedness. It is ready for us to plant tomorrow, when Porphyius will help us. He has brought cuttings from plants in many gardens, including one in France and another in Lazio. But let us leave for a moment this, and also the tiny second garden – the middle world, the resting place. Because I wish to take you at once into the third garden, while the sun is overhead. Here we will pace out the most important space, our garden of purest enchantment and deep religion. It will be woven with secrets that many men have forgotten, and few can tell – though perhaps a woman might. The Sun shall be the father, and the Moon the mother; the Wind shall carry the child, and the Earth be its nurse. Anyone who should merely doze there will find themselves asleep in the lap of legends old! And there, believe me, we will softly sing the song of the deepest past, that calls upon your future.

'We shall weave the garden of the lost mysteries. It is a paradise garden and an oracular garden; and the alchemy shall exude a giddying power. What we do here now will slumber while every new generation plays in the shade of the trees. But no one may undo the enchantment, or unsing the song. As we move from the Ram to the watch of the Bull, with the Sun at its peak of power in spring, the Moon in its most exalted house, witnessed by the seven maids of heaven, it is the right time.'

17

The French windows were open, and a grey-green silk curtain stirred. Maddie's slender fingers reached for the watch on the bedside table to discover it was just before nine in the morning. She had been unable to submit to proper sleep for five months; but last night was just as her first here at Borgo Santo Pietro. From a mixture of sheer exhaustion and the willingness to surrender a degree of the control she had imposed on herself for so long, her head and light frame had sunk into a cloud of goose feathers and rose-scented quiet. She knew no more until the same roses stole her breath again, intruding from the garden below. She was aware of the calm in the room, and opening her eyes to the fresco of the pilgrim moving slowly towards the shrine on the hill she knew exactly where she was, despite the chance that the rush of events and the long miles of travel might have left her disoriented. In two days, she had allowed herself to feel very much at home.

An aroma of good coffee teased her out of bed and into soft bamboo-fibre slippers, which Jeanette had placed for her. She pulled on a robe and made her way towards the source of the smell. A rosy light filled the kitchen, and she casually slipped into a chair opposite two clouds of blond hair. The lighter shade belonged to Jeanette and the deeper, golden colour adorned the head of her two-year-old son, Vincent, with whom the mistress of the house was busy enjoying breakfast.

'Good morning,' Maddie said to them both, gently taking the little boy's hand and shaking it.

'Your skin looks lovely this morning,' Jeanette told her, 'so I think you've slept well.'

'It's true. I've been tired for months,' she answered, 'and my plans to come to Italy were made in one breath! There was so much to finish up before I left. I've only just permitted myself to slow down.'

'Pain eats into a lot of things, doesn't it?' Jeanette looked matter-of-factly at Maddie. 'Sleep's not the first one we notice. But this house will put its arms around you, and you'll feel like giving in to that. You'll see.'

Jeanette's words were spoken with a lightness of tone in keeping with the gentleness she shared with her child; and while Maddie noticed it was the first glancing reference to her loss of Chris – her tacit reason for coming – she felt no secret admissions were asked of her; that there were no emotions she had to explain. It was a huge relief.

'Can I give you the spoon?' Jeanette asked her, inviting her to stretch across the table to Vincent. 'And I'll make you a breakfast cappuccino.'

Maddie walked around the other side of the long table to sit beside the child. She'd never been asked to do this, as she was the younger sibling and hadn't yet a niece or nephew. She wondered what language to use.

'*Ciao, Vincent!*' She thought this was a good beginning. 'Should I talk to him in Italian, Jeanette?' She grinned at the smiling face of the toddler and struck an instant rapport.

'I speak to him in Danish a lot of the time,' Jeanette answered, as the jet of steam shot into the milk. 'But English should be his first language. He'll get to Italian, too, one of these days. He understands quite a lot of it already, but it's good to have a clear mother tongue, do you think?'

Maddie shook her head in admiration. 'I wish my grandmother had started on me earlier.' Vincent took the first spoonful without complaint at the change of hand. 'When I travelled to Florence as a teenager, I realised how badly I wanted to learn Italian. Parents think they're being wise, not to confuse the child. But it's an advantage to speak more than one language. I think you're doing exactly the right thing.'

'He has to be at least bilingual,' the softly accented voice laughed to Maddie. 'His father and I speak to him in English, like his nanny. But he has to have some Danish as well, or else he's losing a part of who he is.'

Jeanette put the coffee mug in front of Maddie, with its perfect foam afloat.

'I don't know why,' Maddie said, continuing with the spoonfuls, 'but I hadn't understood you were Danish. How on earth do you know my nonna Isabella?'

'Your grandmother is one of those souls,' Jeanette smiled energetically, 'who simply makes it her business to be your friend, if she likes you. I've been fortunate to have that luck, and we more or less adopted each other. She became a great friend to me, just after my own mother died. Claus and I met her first in London, through an Italian friend; and then we found each other again in Como; then in Florence, where she's a friend of the Ferragamos. We were always being thrown together.'

Maddie recognised the portrait. Her grandmother felt two random meetings more than enough to suggest people were meant to be friends. Three would have been divine intervention!

'I'm very glad,' Maddie nodded, and passed Jeanette the spoon.

The conversation was interrupted by the arrival of Justina, Vincent's nanny, freshly showered and with a long day to begin. While the adorable child was extracted from his chair, Jeanette laughed. 'He looks angelic, doesn't he? But you have to be as fit as a marine to keep up with him!'

Maddie watched as the blond head and gurgle of laughter disappeared out of the room, and she gave her attention to the coffee and some fruit and cheese Jeanette was putting out on the serving table. They lifted the plates together and took them out to a table with two soft linen sofas facing each other on the terrace, where they'd breakfasted the day before. Maddie stopped to breathe in the beauty of the June morning over the Valle Serena. It was already getting warm, and she had to pinch herself to understand she wasn't going to work today, wouldn't be battling the crowds on the San Francisco transport.

Jeanette settled into the sofa opposite Maddie.

'Now you've had a day to catch your breath and unpack properly, I was going to take you into Chiusdino this morning, which you can see up on the hill. I thought you'd like a peep at an authentic medieval town that isn't quite as well-dressed as Siena – it doesn't set out its stall for the tourists,' she smiled. 'As far as they're concerned you can take it or leave it, which I love. But I've got a lot to do before Claus arrives from London tomorrow evening. He's coming early this week.'

Maddie understood from their talks yesterday that Jeanette's husband still worked in London during the week and flew in most weekends, but that left a lot of real physical work and organisation for Jeanette to do on her own.

She looked at Jeanette over the rim of her coffee cup. 'You must miss him.'

'I love showing him what we've finished in a week,' she enthused. 'But this time he's bringing something for me. An architect is coming with him, who might do our medieval garden – if I approve the choice.' Jeanette wrinkled her nose like a young girl.

'You're planning another garden?' Maddie asked, surprised. 'They already look perfect to me.'

'Oh, yes! We have the most important one still to do!'

Maddie tilted her head with curiosity, and Jeanette leaned across the cane coffee table to explain.

'We laid out the grounds first, before the house was even habitable, and it's taken six years to get them to this point. It's funny, isn't it? The infinity pool was in, so we could swim; and the fountains and orchards were developed; but we had nowhere proper to sleep until a year ago. Vincent and I were camped out in the old bakehouse, sleeping above the enormous oven where pilgrims got their bread. But, when I came down one night on my own with him from Milan and found a scorpion in our bedding, I thought it might be time to get the house fixed up!'

'Uggh!' Maddie's face distorted at the mention of a scorpion. 'In bed with you?'

Jeanette laughed out loud. 'It's not the worst thing I've seen. Believe me, you don't want to be out pushing your baby in his pram and come across a mummy boar with her kids! That's more worrying than a scorpion. And I don't mean in the forest. You can find one in the village without trying too hard – at the right time of year! Anyhow,' she nodded and nibbled some sliced pear, 'I made a hasty decision to do up the house, and put the gardens on hold for a while. Which leaves something interesting still to do, according to stories I've been told by the oldest locals.'

Maddie had been grazing through a light breakfast, and suddenly looked at Jeanette. 'What an enormous undertaking this must have been. How brave. Were there moments when you thought it was beyond you?'

'I felt unbeatable when we got out the pomegranate tree that had taken root in the house. Its arms had reached all the way into your room!' Her face shone with humour. 'And it was such a victory once we'd replaced the floorboards that were hovering over an empty space on the upper floor. Can you imagine, almost forty people had been sleeping on that floor during the war years, living off the pigs and a few chickens and what they could grow in all these acres?'

Maddie shook her head. She couldn't imagine it, really. The house was beautiful now, very large and accommodating, obviously once grand; but so many people eking out a rural existence at such a time of poverty and distress, in a noble ruin, was a situation beyond Maddie's experience.

'You're a strong lady, Jeanette,' she answered. 'It's astonishing you never lost sight of what you wanted to do here.'

'Oh ho!' Her response was delivered in a tone that said, 'On the contrary'. 'Maddie, I had a sign outside for a week, about a year ago,' she laughed. '"For Sale: One euro!"'

Maddie laughed out loud. 'Come on!' she said. 'How long was the queue to buy it?'

'Not a single taker,' Jeanette grinned. 'Everyone knows how long it takes to seek permissions, to wait for approval even to remove a toilet from the yard. We still hadn't found a good water supply – which required getting a diviner and hoping he was good at it. Verdi said, "You may have the universe, if I may have Italy." And he was absolutely right. But it's never straightforward, and it can wear you down.'

'Ah! And the bones you uncovered,' Maddie suddenly remembered. 'You were going to tell me about them but I've collapsed tired these last two nights, fuelled with a little too much of that delicious Chianti you gave me.'

'Mmm, stopping work for the bones,' Jeanette nodded, and smiled mischievously. 'Let's save it for dinner tomorrow night, when the men arrive. I've just learned a little more news about them, and Claus will be surprised.'

'OK, I can wait,' Maddie assented. 'For that story, and this mysteriously appealing thing the locals have told you. But,' she thought aloud, 'is there something I can do for you today, to help with the chores before they come?'

Jeanette looked like a pleased child. 'Absolutely! In half an hour Peter and Milo will arrive to try and finish painting the lemon-tree frescos in the dining room, before Claus gets here,' Jeanette replied. 'But, I want to dye some fabrics out here on the terrace, while the weather is so fine. Are you up for that?'

Maddie nodded. 'That's an appropriately medieval-sounding workshop. I'll rush and shower right now – before your lovely Bohemians come!'

'And while they're drying this afternoon, I'll take you up into town, just for a coffee.' Jeanette rose and added, 'Siena will have to wait until the weekend, if that's all right?'

'I still have almost three weeks of Tuscan summer, thanks to your generous hospitality and my boss's kindness. And every day there's something new to absorb me right here, Jeanette.'

Maddie said this with warmth and energy in her voice: but she was aware that this had become a sadly uncharacteristic note recently. She was just starting to recognise a little of her old self. As she got up from the terrace and started towards the French doors inside, she heard Jeanette's voice, full of good humour.

'Borgo's casting its spell upon you. I told you it would.'

18

21 MAY 1347, SANTO PIETRO IN CELLOLE, TUSCANY

The path down the slope from the majestic villa of Santo Pietro in Cellole passes small farm cottages and stables as it crosses the old pilgrims' road, used since the time of the Romans, and snakes gently towards the wild green fields that make the border of the property with the adjacent village of Palazzetto. The vista to each side will catch your breath at any hour, in any season, passing by orchards that stretch back along the river and marry with those of the abbey, blossoming profusely in spring and fruiting abundantly in autumn.

At six in the evening, with the light still soft and rosy and under the watch of the first star, two young women set out to consecrate their paradise garden. The elder spoke to the younger in a voice that piped sweetly, like the sound of running waters.

'Our people were the seafarers, masters of boats and the tides. The Romans gave to them the name of "Tusci", as we still do,' Signora Toscano said, 'for they built many-towered cities on the Tuscan hills like those of Troy, from whence it was said they had come long ago. But I know that they chose their homes in the highest locations because here were the places of sacred connection between the high realms and the low; a place for communication between the above, and the below. And our ancestors from Volterra and the other cities of their people gave to themselves the name of the "Rasenna".

'Legend says that even in the time of Caesar, there were some among them who could still hear and remember the lost chord.

'For they told that at the beginning of the world there was a tiny egg

153

cradled in the chaos of the heavens. Small as it was, one half of it was a perfect golden hue, shining like a gem in the blackness; the other half was of the deepest blue. In one profound moment, amid this chaos of black vapours and icy water, there arose a great thunderstorm. The sounds of the thunder were immense, unfathomable – yet neither deafening nor fearful. The sound was only deep, like the voice of the oldest and wisest man rumbling his call. This thunderous voice broke open the egg – and it was a violent birth – but the voice called its contents into being. You, Mia,' she said, 'would call this the voice of God. But our ancestors gave to him the name of Ani – Ianus, to the Romans. He was the first god, lord of the skies and the constellations.

'As the egg broke apart, another voice was heard from within. This voice belonged to a woman, singing a gentle lullaby in notes so beauteous and high that the human voice could only marvel at the sounds, and hardly hope to repeat them. The first voices blended in harmony, the highest and the deepest; from their song came the sun and the moon, the winds and the clouds. The storm raged on, and another great crash of thunder awoke the sentient plants and animals, and all forms of life here and in the heavens around us.

'When the egg cracked wide, one half moved into the highest heavens, the other into the depths of the world, and the sea and the sky became separated. I have been told that the egg still breaks in this way, with new stars born hourly in the realms beyond our sight. But, the brightest gold and the azure blue – the opposing halves of the egg – have lent their colours to make up our night and our day.

'In the beginning the music of the creation was known by all; there was no one unable to understand the melody, no one left out by it, for it was not a language but a song that stirred the soul as well as the mind. And the memory of both egg and song went to the east, and to the south; to the north, and the west; but few now can remember its tune. Some, it is told, were blessed enough to be still bound to that lost chord, to remember at least some fragment of its harmony. These were chosen as the augurs who read the messages of the one universe through the movement of birds – messengers from the heavens – through the sixteen segments of the divine sky.

'Yet though the first sounds were long forgotten by all but a few, the truth of the symbol of the egg remained and is with us everywhere, Mia. It hangs still in the great church of Santa Sophia, in Constantinople; and it hung in the temples of the Egyptians and the Greeks, and in the tombs of the heroes and martyrs alike in Rome; and Virgil remembered its power, and set it in the Castel dell'Ovo in the Bay of Napoli. And at the time you celebrate as Easter, beautiful eggs fashioned from marble or silver or alabaster are offered in churches.

'These also tie us to our earlier people, those who lived in Volterra before us. Recalling the enchantment of the first song they understood that Ani was also Ana, both male and female, with two faces; and they preserved this balanced status for the man and the woman in their culture. So it was that the women never lost their voices, or went unheard. And in their tombs and their temples, their houses and their gardens, they placed and revered the egg as the symbol of the start of all life, and the return to one.'

Signora Toscano and Maria Maddalena had now reached the gardens they had laid out as a reflection of paradise. One was the labyrinth garden, the realm of the walking meditation; and this gradually led into the second, an open chamber in which to come quietly to knowledge. Here was the resting place, the space in which to pause and bring the mind to a purpose, to concentrate the will. The third garden was sacred, enclosed with hedges, yet in their infancy. This was the place of action, the navel of their world. Such was the garden renowned in paradise where the divine tree was centre and the four rivers marked out the compass points.

Here, now, in the light of the first smattering of stars in a sky still made up of manifold colours of early evening, they placed together – and with great effort – an ancient stone brought by Porphyrius from the ruins of his wife's parental home in Volterra. It was a large oval – an egg, Signora Toscano said – and it was still possible to see carvings criss-crossing it in decorative patterns, like knots woven at intervals in a great net.

At the foot of the carefully chosen mulberry – the pivotal tree in their garden – they set the egg. Here they sang a lullaby with sounds each recalled from her earliest memories, when each had a mother and a time of safety. The song had few words, but a soft wind moved among the leaves to join them.

19

THURSDAY 14 JUNE 2007, BORGO SANTO PIETRO, TUSCANY

Maddie had been awakened by the sun's early coming to her window. It had smiled on her, but there was an unexpected chill in the morning air. She rolled onto her side and pulled the duvet over her head to try to doze a minute longer. She could hear a distinctive coo of pigeons on the roof above, which reminded her of home and Nonna Isabella.

The dreamy unreality of Borgo, and the strange effects of the whole environment, seemed to be raising her spirits. It was lifting away some of those empty feelings she had carried with her since Chris's death, rejoining her a little to her present world. Certainly her awareness seemed to be heightened, and she felt stimulated and alive which, she realised, was what her grandmother had hoped for.

There was no reason that anything important should have occurred in California while she slept on the other side of the planet. She knew everything in the world was moving on at its grindingly slow pace. Yet, Maddie had the sensation that news was trying to reach her. It was this curiosity that finally goaded her from the warmth of her feather bed.

She rose quickly, grabbed her laptop from the window ledge where it was charging, shivered as she pressed the power button, and dived back into bed, reaching for the duvet. She watched the screen from her position of comfort. In seconds the Vaio popped into life, and Maddie clicked Safari to watch her email browser appear.

Two emails caught her eye. One was from Harriet Taylor,

Christopher's mother, whom she hadn't heard from in some weeks. An inkling told her what this might contain, and as she felt her stomach lurch she decided it could keep for a while. She would need to be wide awake and braced for an emotional punch to deal with that one. But the other made her both reluctant to open it, and full of impatience: *YamChoud@hhc.com.*

She noticed immediately an icon for a video attachment next to the address. This was somewhat unusual, as Yamuna wasn't really one of her penpals. Important news would come from Tyler, and a communiqué from Samantha would either be from the lady herself, or relayed through Jacinta.

Is this bad news? Maddie considered; then she clicked to open Yamuna's offering.

An enlarged smiley face greeted Maddie, and she smiled herself and relaxed. Her eye scanned the number of exclamation marks and she grinned, then began to read the contents very quickly. An intrigued expression gradually morphed into one of confusion and incredulity. Before she had quite reached the bottom, she decided to go back and savour the whole thing again, reading more slowly this time.

Dear Maddie,

The attached is for your eyes only!!! A most exciting day!

The clip will reveal all, so this is just to put you in the frame with the essentials.

This morning I arrived in the office early. Shortly after, Samantha came charging in dressed in her sage linen suit and snakeskin slingbacks – 'something is definitely up', I thought. She asked if I would drive and said I had to 'be you' for the day. Stormtree had pressured some court official to spring a special hearing at 9:30, in Santa Clara – practically sans notice. She had less than an hour to get there – and you know that drive in traffic!

I turned into Cagney (or was it Lacey who always drove?) and listened while she talked at speed. For a woman who usually keeps things close to her chest, I have never heard her sound so pissed at Stormtree, with their evasions and legal shenanigans. Her brain was razor sharp and racing – she almost had steam coming out of her ears: sort of Portia meets Popeye!

We made the courthouse by a thread – I literally skidded to a stop, and Samantha ran in while I parked – God knows how she scaled the steps so fast in those high-heeled babies. No highway patrol cars on our side of the freeway or I'd have gotten a fist full of traffic citations.

OK, so, when I finally got to the courtroom Samantha was apologising to the Court for being late and explained the reason. Then a half-hour of claptrap by Stormtree's team – led by your friend Gordon Hugo, but more of him later, LOL.

Ha, well! Guess what! The judge just FLIPPED OUT!!! He looked up and said, 'I have had you in this courtroom now for the hundredth time, saying what has been requested is irrelevant and unimportant. I have listened with some patience to your arguments. I can find no merit in them. I have warned you people about your behaviour. So today is the end of your evasive stone-walling. You are now wasting this Court's time.'

Maddie, I mean, seriously! Then he almost made spittle with this bit—

'If you do not deliver every item asked for to these people in this Court in the next two hours, I shall instruct the Santa Clara Sheriff's office to put you in jail until I have had a chance to personally read and check every document. I am a very busy man, so it may take me several months to do this. Am I clear? Court is adjourned!'

Wow, Maddie, I thought Samantha was going to kiss him! Well, that's not the end of it. When we got back to the city, we went for a late bite at the Ferry Building, 'cause Samantha was in such a fine mood and said we'd earned it. And, can you just GUESS who was already there at the Slanted Door? OMG – watch and learn! This is what you would have seen if you had been there, and I was you, remember? This is your catch-up, then – my phone is your eye! Best to enjoy it, and perhaps not to analyse it too much?

PS. Should I post it on Facebook?

Mata Hari, a.k.a. Yamuna.   XXX Bet Tuscany is to die for!

By now Maddie was so intrigued that her fingers fumbled over the 'download' key and miscued twice. When it finally started to upload her bladder interrupted the process and forced her to hop into the bathroom while the clip prepared. She grabbed a glass of water at speed, then jumped back into bed and under the covers like a child with a guilty secret.

What can she have sent? Maddie thought.

She squinted to focus on the first image, somewhat blurred, of a female ear sporting a very fine diamond stud. Then almost surreptitiously, the camera swung round. It was as if Yamuna had been on the phone and then secretly started filming.

The camera moved to reveal the interior of a large modern restaurant, simple steel and wood tables and chairs, polished wood floor, clean and new. Maddie recognised it as the chosen lunching place where many of the denizens of the nearby legal fraternity paused somewhere between midday and one. It was good food and not too over-priced for its location on the harbour near the Ferry Building. As you entered you faced the large modern glass frontage, which also opened onto an outside eating area.

No one was outside today. The camera showed a typical 'Frisco' day, with the fine view of the Oakland Bridge shrouded in grey cloud. The passer-by along the boardwalk outside seemed rather warmly dressed for mid-June. It must have been chilly there too, Maddie thought as she snuggled deeper into her covers, watching with curiosity.

In the background the lunchtime crowd was thinning with a few empty tables here and there. Waiters moved dextrously between the remaining customers, hovering now and then, like black and white vultures in their uniforms, electronic card machines at the ready, quick with a smile, ever hopeful of the good tip. A pastiche of the good life, Maddie reflected.

As the camera steadied Maddie could see that the foreground was partly filled with the back of what looked like Samantha's head. Then, to Maddie's incredulity, she picked out the back of another familiar head. Those, she realised, were the unmistakable blond locks of Jacinta

Collins. Maddie wondered at this in light of Yamuna's suspenseful build-up – until the full implication was suddenly revealed when the camera found its true subject. Suddenly, centre frame, Gordon Hugo's standout build and facial shape appeared – and Maddie gasped.

'Oh, my,' she said aloud. 'This should be interesting.'

She saw that he was seated opposite Jacinta. Hugo was holding a napkin in one hand and about to pour from a carafe of red wine with the other. His eyes seemed to Maddie to be fixed rather lecherously on Jacinta's plunging neckline. Maddie could see he hadn't yet noticed the presence of Samantha or Yamuna, and she heard herself laugh aloud, then bit her bottom lip. She could hardly imagine what could be going on in his head as he looked up at the new arrivals, but the camera caught the look on Hugo's face, which told the whole story.

Here is a man caught with his trousers down, she thought, with someone else's wife or lover.

The pictures now showed the Stormtree lawyer turning his head to stare up into the hard, unsmiling face of Maddie's boss. A very brief flash of on-screen reaction from Hugo exposed the blinding realisation that he had been caught red-handed coming on to the office manager of the opposition's firm. Maddie only wished Jacinta's reaction to being flushed out was also on camera.

Maddie could almost see Hugo's mind whirring, his body language going into overdrive as he picked up, and immediately put down, his wine glass. This situation might be a little embarrassing, she thought, but she was even more certain that both he and Samantha knew the subtext of the look on Samantha's face. She was on the brink of expressing her feelings about what had taken place earlier at Santa Clara Court.

Maddie's attention was suddenly distracted as she heard Vincent and his nanny pass her door on their way down to the kitchen. She realised it was probably well past seven now, and there was a lot to help Jeanette with before her husband and the architect gardener arrived tonight. But she was riveted by her post from Yamuna, and couldn't draw her eyes from the screen, or her mind from the unfolding drama.

She looked at the man in the clip fidgeting with his napkin and his drink, and realised that what had been done – as Hugo himself would have known only too well – to get such a snap hearing without due warning to the other side was completely out of order. But Maddie was focused again on his lightning changes of expression, revealing anger, perhaps, and frustration, and guilt, and a little arrogance as usual. There was no way he was going to admit the truth of their attempts to wrong-foot Samantha with a hasty hearing she wasn't prepared for. And anyhow, Maddie thought grinning, Samantha was always ready.

'Someone in your firm, who must of course remain nameless, has obviously called in a favour. It back-fired badly today, but I see it hasn't put you off your lunch.'

This was Samantha's voice, off screen. Maddie now watched spellbound as the Rottweiler in Hugo recoiled into attack mode. But before he could say a thing, Samantha spoke again in a voice cool and unflustered. She didn't bother even to recognise the presence of Jacinta.

'But what happy chance to find you here, because there is something I wanted to say to you.'

Hugo placed the glass carefully on the table again, then threw down his napkin. He stood rather too quickly and opened his mouth, but once again Samantha was quicker.

'Three little words,' she said. 'Critical Illness Records. Do they have a nice ring to them? I don't know what game you thought your people were playing this morning, but I'm grateful, as it turns out, that it's given the judge a chance to speed things up. Not what you were hoping for – but we'll have a full report within the month and I'll send you a copy.'

Hugo's face turned a dark red, Maddie saw. 'There'll be nothing in there that you can use.'

'Are you sure there is nothing?' came the voice off-camera. 'Is that why your bosses were so eager that we shouldn't look at it?' Samantha's voice was quiet, but firm. 'Mr Hugo, one of Norman Mailer's most pointed observations on corporate awareness was that the Corporation, by its very nature, is as blind as it is powerful. Spiritually blind, morally blind. As a collective entity, it is worse than any of the individuals who make it up.'

'What's that supposed to mean?' the man in the frame retorted.

Samantha considered her answer for a moment and then said, 'I don't think anyone at senior level has ever wanted to look too carefully at this problem. But Stormtree is aware there is a steadily growing body-count rising among their employees in certain sectors of the company, and now it's registering among those employees' children. That is not good press for anyone's corporation.'

161

Yamuna's phone camera had just made use of the close-up, and Maddie saw at once the look on Gordon Hugo's face. My God, she thought, impressed. She's got to him with that.

Hugo scowled, then recovered to go back on the attack.

'That can't be proved. And anyway, what's it to a bleeding-hearts bunch of ambulance-chasers like Hardens?' He leaned forward towards Samantha, filling the camera which he, for some reason, had failed to notice was filming the chance encounter. 'You make your name by representing a bunch of society's marginals, pure money-grabbing losers who are the dregs of our country's business ethos.'

Samantha must have been a little shocked by this outburst, as she stayed silent long enough for Hugo to speak again, almost shouting: 'Everyone in corporate law knows you're only in this to screw as much money out of Stormtree Components as you can get. And where would we be without big firms who employ half the country, bring in millions from global trade, and finance the schools and roads in this country with their corporate taxes?'

Samantha's response was dignified, and without raising her voice she said, 'Your firm's fees for this morning's little screw-up would be more than enough to buy lunch for everyone in this restaurant for a week.' She waved her hands at the space around her. 'Don't try to shame me.'

Maddie could see from the screen that the argument was beginning to attract the interest of other patrons. The waiters had stopped and were standing neatly in a row, smiling to each other. Heads around the dining room were turned in the direction of the voices of the pair. 'Quel drama! Quel Hollywood,' said a voice somewhere behind the phone camera.

From Jacinta's body language, Maddie could see she wished the floor would open and swallow her. And Gordon Hugo seemed to be getting redder by the minute. Maddie wondered if he might go apoplectic or, she thought with pleasure, be seen by someone who knew his wife.

'We are worth every penny of our pay cheque,' was Hugo's response under his breath.

'Or do you mean, the longer you can run this the more you make, no matter who loses?' Maddie thought Samantha asked this question uncharacteristically loudly, as if she would be happy for anyone in earshot to hear. 'We'd love a resolution; so it must be your firm who are lining their pockets,' she added pointedly.

'We've offered you a parley,' Hugo grunted, 'and you don't seem a bit interested in a resolution. Not even the courtesy of an answer from your team. I could report you.'

'To the California Bar Association,' Samantha finished his sentence for him. 'I know that line,' she mocked. 'You do that! My moral conscience and my individual relationship to the world I subject to the greatest scrutiny, so Mr Hugo, do your damnedest.'

'You people are unbelievable,' came the answer. 'You have no case at all, and you try to use emotional blackmail to make us responsible for something we're not.'

This time, Yamuna had pointed the lens at Samantha, and her just-controlled anger was clearly visible.

'Well,' she said without colour in her voice, 'the consequence of your being wrong will be the continuing damage to the lives of not only this generation, but the children of the generations who follow. There is no price that can be paid to compensate a child blighted by unnecessary brain defects or physical handicaps. You're playing God with these people – and a malevolent God at that.'

'Nothing is proven, as you know very well,' Hugo said emphatically. 'And unless it is, it's not Stormtree's problem.'

Samantha held her gaze on Hugo, who looked around nervously. 'If we prove your clients are knowingly killing people, then it will be their problem, big time.'

The camera bounced back to Hugo, who was smiling somewhat inappropriately. 'You and I know that no company executive has ever been successfully prosecuted for corporate manslaughter in this state; so I wonder where a betting man would put his money?'

'Will Mr Gray's company be duly flattered, then, if they're the ground-breaking, history-making case? Somehow I don't think so. But be very sure what it is you're defending,' Samantha stated. 'No company will win friends playing games with children's health.'

Maddie had been watching the exchange for several minutes now, and could hardly believe it at all; but she certainly didn't expect what happened next.

'You'll never prove that accusation,' Hugo said calmly.

Here, Maddie saw a supercilious grin flit across his face, as if he knew that, no matter what, something would tip the balance in Stormtree's favour. What does he know? Maddie wondered. Why is he so confident?

Jacinta now rose into the frame, saying, 'Excuse me. I have to get back. It's late.'

She pushed past Yamuna's camera, making it wobble. Her voice followed her out of the picture: 'I won't be staying for dessert. He'll pick up the check.'

The frame showed the bewildered reaction of the now almost silent restaurant, with the diminishing staccato of Jacinta's stilettos on the hard wood floor.

Samantha turned to find a camera confronting her face, and she smiled into frame. 'Were you recording all that?'

The camera did a little nod of assent; then it zoomed behind Samantha to where Gordon Hugo could be seen, looking past the waiters. He picked up his napkin and reseated himself, as though nothing unusual had happened at all. The waiters moved in to clear the empty place setting from the table.

'Good,' Samantha's voice was heard again. 'That's given me an appetite. Let's get some lunch.'

The camera swung through ninety degrees to face the entrance, where Reception was finding the coat for a vanishing Jacinta Collins.

Off camera again, Samantha could be heard laughing. 'I'll deal with that later,' were her words; then the picture timed out and went to black.

'Whoa!' Maddie slumped against her pillows, barely breathing. One part of her felt pride in her boss, whose calm demeanour and steady addressing of the points had looked much better than her adversary's huff and puff. She knew a jury would think so, too. But the other side of her felt a cold void, a rekindled awareness of her own very recent loss of belief in humanity. Empathy for others seemed to be too much to ask; and this awareness took her back to the overwhelming sadness she had felt when Christopher had been killed so unnecessarily and without any expression of remorse on the part of the drunk teen driver who had killed him. This, she knew, she would have to address all over again when she opened Harriet's email.

Right now, Maddie stayed focused on Gordon Hugo. She wondered if he was a reflection of what Pierce Gray was, behind his charm and moneyed polish.

Her eyes went to her painted pilgrim for a while, struggling towards his holy place. How did one survive the sadnesses, the frequent injustices of life? How naïve medieval faith seemed to her – how impossible to believe in anything good.

She left the bed, pulled on a robe and walked to the window in the pretty bathroom. She passed the free-standing Victorian tub, and ran her hand over its back. Then she opened the window, which looked out on the sun-dappled pathway below. Leaning out of the frame, her eye searched right – towards the roof of the medieval bakehouse, and across the retreating path of the old pilgrims' way – just as in the fresco. Its ancient line could be seen very clearly, wandering over the furthest fields and then vanishing into the forest beyond, towards the ruined abbey of San Galgano in the distance.

What did the people here have faith in, she questioned, to keep hope alive? Did miracles ever really touch those who dwelled here?

20

For more than a month, the still high heat of September had kept the villa and farm and two tiny cottages almost empty by day. Every available worker, along with the residents of the large house, had laboured side by side from sunrise to suppertime. The men had been out with the huge white cattle of the Chiana valley, ploughing the fields; and the women had trodden the harvested grapes in great oak troughs with their bare feet, ready to transfer them to casks. Then in swift succession, with the first days of October and a modest cooling of the weather, attention had turned to the olives. Great nets had been spread out under the graceful line of trees for several days. Many slim hands – including those of Aunt Jacquetta and Signora Toscano – had wrested the fruit from the lower branches into baskets tied at the waist. Those on the ladders higher up – like Porphyrius and Mia – had dropped the olives into the waiting nets.

Now it was past mid-month, and leaving no time for respite from the hard physical work of the previous weeks, the orderly lines of chestnuts that shaded the roads and lanes offered up their own ripe harvest. Mia was happy to add her slight weight to the number of women picking them, and looked forward to the smell of the roasting nuts in the days ahead. She and Loredana had sore fingers, but Alba's were completely cracked and blistered from the cumulative weeks of picking. The work had to go on throughout the daylight hours, however, as chestnut flour was a valuable commodity and a speciality of Tuscany. Her aunt's trees were of two varieties, the fragrant *marroni* and weightier *rossalina*, and

166

Mia loved them equally. Her favourite food from now into the dark winter days was sweet chestnut cake made from the peeled fruits soaked in creamy milk and puréed with honey, eggs and almonds. She would be happy to prepare the first one herself, and take it in great ceremony to the bakery oven in just a few days.

The stage before cooking them was to dry them in huts at the edge of the estate; and as the sun had already passed its position overhead, this is where Mia and the others now headed to find her aunt and her friend, and have a rest in the shade and something to eat. At the end of the long path between the field and the road, she shaded her eyes from the strong sun and saw Aunt Jacquetta coming towards them, just ahead of Cesaré and Chiara. All three were carrying bread and olives, figs and cheese, jugs of water and wine, and aromatic dishes of cooked mushrooms, spinach and beans prepared with olive oil and lemon juice. Mia joined in alongside her aunt to walk the last yards to the huts.

'You're flushed pink, Mia,' Aunt Jacquetta fussed. 'You should have your sunhat on.'

'I'm fine under the canopy of chestnut boughs,' Mia said in her now familiarly soft, but confident, speaking voice. 'It's only when we walk the paths . . .'

'Mmm,' Jacquetta admonished her with a sceptical expression. 'But I got a touch of sun myself this morning collecting the honey, even though I had my hat on with the muslin, and my arms were properly covered against the bees. It's very hot, and you'll look like a heathen if your nose and cheeks burn.'

Mia returned her aunt's smile and mirrored her expression. It was territory they'd skirted before, and the real issue was one of Mia's stubbornness – her disinclination to start behaving as a young woman should, and to give up being a child. Since her birthday a few months ago in May there'd been a tacit awareness that it might be time to consider matching Mia for a marriage – if they were ever going to. But Mia wasn't altogether willing to change her life, and at one level she certainly preferred the idea of being her aunt's niece here at Villa Santo Pietro, and going on as before. She knew Aunt Jacquetta's single status was elective; and though the deepest reasons for her choice were still a riddle about which they never spoke, Mia was sure it had something to do with keeping command of her own property and personal freedoms.

Mia doubted her aunt would force the issue of betrothal on her or make her do something against her wishes.

As they came closer to the chestnut huts they found Signora Toscano sitting in shade, taking gentle breaths. Her shape had altered quickly over these last weeks, and the fact that she was carrying a child was much more obvious than it had been when she'd told them all a month ago. Mia hurried to her.

'You should be doing gentle labours in the house. It's too hot out here.'

'I've only just had to sit,' she answered Mia. 'I'm well enough to share the outdoor work.'

Jacquetta put the food on the largest drying table, and came over to Signora Toscano with deliberate calm. She placed a hand on her forehead.

'You are a little warm,' she agreed. 'Something to eat and drink will help. Though,' she added with a bigger smile, 'this will be the best medicine?'

Jacquetta drew something from her pocket and passed it to Signora Toscano, whose face immediately brightened. Porphyrius had been away for almost two weeks, having gone south to the port of Messina after the olive harvest to meet a shipment of spices from the East. His mission also demanded that he collect silks that had travelled from Samarkand for his wife and the coming child; and some rose and fruit trees from the Lebanon and beyond, for the new garden. They had heard no news from him in days, and his lady had been worried enough for it to enter the awareness of Mia and Jacquetta.

'It arrived this morning from Chiusdino, while I was busy with the apiary,' Jacquetta told her, passing her a mug of water Mia had poured out. 'And the messenger told Cesaré that his master – the man of law – had it from Volterra late last evening.'

'Ah,' she said, her fingers fumbling with the wax seal. 'It went by way of his mother, then.'

Mia was helping to lay out the food, but couldn't help noticing the beautifully formed writing on the letter and the way it was addressed. Her soft brown eyes became larger as she read the words, 'Signora Agnesca Toscano, Villa Santo Pietro in Cellole, Chiusdino.'

Agnesca, Mia thought; but the name lived on her lips so that she found she had spoken it softly.

'Yes,' Signora Toscano explained. 'It is *his* name for me. I like it better than "Agnese", which was my birth name.' She spoke very quietly, and then returned to give her attention to the first lines of the letter.

Mia looked at her aunt with some astonishment, but her aunt's face told her to mind her own business.

The team of chestnut pickers now began their meal, and Mia brought a plate over for her friend and her aunt, then sat and tried to find some appetite for her own, despite the quickening emotions she felt at the relatively casual revelation of Signora Toscano's given name. After all these long months without knowing it! She hardly knew if her palate were on vegetable or cheese, olives or beans. It hit her at once that there was a strange coincidence in the fact that the lady had arrived on the night she performed her vigil of sweet St Agnes – a far better prize, Mia had so often thought, than any appearance of a sweetheart. And now here was her name: a pet form of Agnes itself. She realised that the name spoke of a long betrothal to the Church, as far as Signora Toscano's parents were concerned. Agnes was the saint of virgins – of chastity and purity, of a vocation to refuse marriage and pledge one's life to the Lord. She understood that her friend's destiny had been chosen for her at birth, no matter what course events may have thrown at her.

Mia considered this very seriously now. It was a strange irony that her friend had qualities that were properly religious and imbued with a powerful spirituality, though it may not have been conventional spirituality. She was different from others; and she had a light within her that affected every person who came within her orb. She always spoke wisely and without malice, showing kindness to everyone; and Mia felt that, though Signora Toscano may not have chosen 'God', God had chosen her.

'He writes of a terrible sickness that has hit at the port of Messina,' Signora Toscano suddenly said aloud, her face paler.

'But he himself is well?' Jacquetta asked.

'I believe so.' She nodded slowly. 'It has delayed his return, because there is much trouble in the city, and no one from the mainland or the other towns in Sicily wishes to travel into Messina. He writes that there are rumours of people suddenly sickening with terrible fevers and falling slumped in the street, coughing blood; and that their friends and neighbours ignore them. Many residents of the city have panicked and fled into the countryside.'

'Has he reached Messina himself, then? Or has he been unable to get across from the mainland to the port?' Jacquetta wondered.

Signora Toscano read quickly, turning a page before answering the dozen curious looks that were now fastened on her.

'He has been to Messina, and had begun his return before this news overtook him,' she explained. 'He had trouble and excessive expense getting a ship back, and wrote me to explain the delay. He says that every man's sense has left him for the moment. But –' she turned to the back of the second page – 'he was hopeful of getting passage within a day or so, when he wrote this, and he gave the letter to a nobleman connected with the court party, to take to Naples and send on from there. Perhaps—'

Signora Toscano broke off, not knowing what she could surmise. He might be anywhere, unable to return for days. But Jacquetta finished her sentence for her:

'Perhaps people's tongues wag in ignorance, and the rumours have been greatly exaggerated. He is surely already halfway home by now, and we must expect him at any time, any day.'

'Yes.' Mia spoke quietly, and rose to place both hands on Signora Toscano's shoulders. 'He had been in the port, before the trouble began. He will return to us shortly.'

21

THURSDAY–FRIDAY 14–15 JUNE 2007,
BORGO SANTO PIETRO, TUSCANY

I t was near four in the afternoon when the wind came up to fulfil the promise of the chill that had disturbed the morning sunshine. It started flapping the pages of notes Maddie had been working from. Stiff currents of air now brought the sweet odour of the pilgrim's garden across the space to the loggia, where she was sitting with her open laptop. She sighed, and gulped strong coffee. It had so far been one extraordinary day.

Hours ago she had helped her hostess prepare for tonight's dinner, with Claus and his colleague due from London, by making an olive and pine-nut tart – one of her trademark dishes. Then she'd thrown together a quick pasta course for lunch – gaining particular compliments from Milo, the painter. Leaving Jeanette to fuss with too many duties to list she'd washed up and left the kitchen perfect, to allow all the artisans to carry on with their work uninterrupted before Claus appeared to see the progress and hopefully give it the thumbs up. Jeanette had pronounced her 'invaluable' and thanked her profusely. Maddie knew, however, that she had been deliberately seeking tasks that allowed her to procrastinate in opening Harriet Taylor's waiting email. It had been in her thoughts since early morning and, like a genie in a bottle, once released it would open up Maddie's studiously placated mind to a din of stressful emotion. But with the last wine glass washed and replaced in the antique armoire, there was no further delaying tactic she could legitimately employ. She'd retreated to her pilgrim's room to face it.

She'd too quickly found Borgo's moody broadband signal and signed in again as Jeanette had invited her to do with the given password. It seemed to take some time and test her determination to confront it before she was connected. Then another excuse offered itself up as she found her mailbox crammed to the nines. She deleted several circulars that had come in overnight West Coast time, including invitations from the Crocker Galleria and two from Bloomingdale's about events; and she put her credit card statement to one side. Then she'd glimpsed a tantalising title on a note from Barbara about 'Two-faced cheats bearing gifts', which was time-coded at near midnight in San Francisco. She had a sense it was about Pierce Gray, but she decided to save it for later, and stoically opened Christopher's mother's note instead.

It was, as she knew it would be, a request to prepare a victim statement for the pre-sentence report and initial hearing about Chris's death, which would be next week. This was a call to put down on paper – if at all possible – something of what it had meant to be an innocent victim of that January car crash. The more poignantly she could convey her loss, his mother believed, the more weight it would lend in determining the sentence of the drunk-driver.

'He won't get nearly what he should, Maddie,' she'd written, 'but try to give voice to some of your heartbreak, if you can. I shall do the same.'

Give voice? How? Maddie wondered. She'd not been able to confide this impossibly deep grief to a single soul. But she'd locked her hand around Nonna's St Christopher medal and closed her eyes; and for the first time in long months she could actually hear Chris's voice. The lovely preamble to his marriage proposal came straight into her head: that remarkable end-of-day on the terrace of the Danieli in Venice. No going down on his knee, no diamond in a cocktail glass. He'd simply chosen the most perfect location, a sunlit day, and asked her a question she had no idea was coming. He'd actually apologised for the absence of violins.

'Plain words speak best,' he'd said to her, and grinned; and then, very simply, he'd asked her to become his wife.

Maddie breathed deeply. 'Plain words,' she said softly to herself. So here she sat, committing them to paper.

The first draft she'd done by hand, and now she typed up her short letter authored from the heart. She trimmed away everything that seemed unnecessary as she went. It told of the end of the most important friendship of her life; of the loss of a human being whose only wish was to use his waking hours helping others; of the loneliness she felt now, knowing no card, no text, no phone call could ever again be from him; no voice in her ear would again be his. It stated, in pared down language, the horror of helping his mother select flowers for his funeral service and a suit to bury him in – instead of being able to approve Christopher's own choice of the clothes he would marry her in. In words of weighted syllables she expressed the pain of sending her love into the unknown without her; her irrational guilt at having not been physically present to hold him, as his life bled away. She was changed irrevocably, she wrote; she couldn't yet imagine a future.

When she'd done it was about twenty lines of heartache. The wind now threatened to scatter her notes, and she gathered her things together and made her way back to the sanctuary of her room. She thought she might be able to cry, but instead, blackness came over her and she shivered a little. Having articulated her pain for someone she didn't know, she found it hard to breathe. She lay down for a while.

It was almost two hours later when she woke, unaware she'd even slept. It must have been after six, and the skies had darkened. She thought she could possibly hear thunder rumbling in the distance and, slightly embarrassed, she got up and smoothed down her clothes, opened the door to go looking for Jeanette.

When she found her she learned the flight from London was already delayed. The incoming plane was about two hours late, and they wouldn't be getting away until nearer to eight. With the hour's time change from London to Italy it would be about ten thirty when they arrived in Pisa, close to midnight for Borgo. But Maddie felt weak and apologetic about her afternoon slump, and she told Jeanette she'd like to wait up with her for the late arrivals.

The house was now as quiet as a ghost town. Peter and his girlfriend had finished an hour or two ago, and set off for a three-day break to give Claus and Jeanette some peace for the weekend. Milo had returned to Florence, Justina was out with friends, and only Flora and Antoneta remained somewhere at hand to clean and help around the house. Once Vincent was in bed, there was a hush at Borgo – except for the distant roll of thunder, which had kept up its intermittent call across the Valle Serena.

Jeanette understood Maddie's mind was elsewhere tonight; she knew her companion wasn't in the mood to talk. Without asking much about it, she understood why. But they sat together as the hours passed, eating a little, drinking a glass of wine, and then piecing and stitching a curtain of magnificent antique fabric, which Jeanette had acquired for the large window on the staircase landing. In such relative silence, they provided perfect company for one another.

'The weather's worsening,' was all Jeanette said for an hour or so. She was thinking of the flight into Pisa with her husband on it; and the mountain road between there and here, in what would soon be heavy rain.

Maddie lifted her head from the tiny stitches she was hemming, and nodded. But the weather suited her mood, and she felt oddly reassured by it.

A text to Jeanette's phone broke the quiet and explained that the plane had only just touched down – that the rain was heavy in Pisa. The garden designer was collecting a hire car for the drive, Claus said, and they would be home as soon as rental desks and winding roads allowed. This solution to their journey had seemed good originally, saving Gori a late drive to the airport to collect them. Jeanette worried now, though, about them both being tired and the gardener not knowing the road. Maybe Claus would drive? So Maddie hung on with her, saying little but offering support by her presence, until it was long after midnight, the curtain completely finished, and Jeanette feeling in want of a cigarette. Maddie knew this was something she tried not to allow herself too often.

'You're exhausted, Maddie,' she said. 'Take yourself off to bed, and I can sit here without feeling guilty and smoke!'

Maddie laughed this off and said she'd have one with her, if that would make her more comfortable. She insisted she would sit up and wait. But Jeanette pointed out this would force them all to be sociable and communicative when the men arrived – maybe not before one o'clock – and they would really be tired and want sleep. This carried the argument. Maddie cleaned up the untidy threads and scissors and wine glasses, and hugged Jeanette without chatter. A quarter of an hour later she had started up the stairs – lit by the odd flash of lightning – towards her room. She was at the top when she caught the sound of footsteps in the courtyard, paused at her landing and looked over the banister when she heard the front door open. She saw the back of Jeanette's golden head embracing her husband, and another figure behind him; and she considered just stepping back down for a moment and saying 'hello'. She decided instead to slip quietly into her room. In moments her head had hit the pillows, with her mind still wandering over a day that had taken her from a restaurant in San Francisco to a hotel terrace in Venice, and with the thunder almost under her window and the rain coming down hard, she fell into deep sleep.

After a stormy night when Maddie felt she had heard the wind raging all through her sleeping hours, it was a golden start. The heat was already apparent at something a little after eight when she woke, and she felt the rain had washed away the indecision in the Tuscan June weather.

After showering and dressing in light clothes, she emerged from her room to a house of silence. Everyone was sleeping in – hardly surprisingly – and Maddie felt she wanted some time inside her own head before Borgo eased into its usual welcoming mode with Claus and his guest. With this in mind, Maddie helped herself to some walking boots in Jeanette's store cupboard and set off for the shrine on her pilgrim's hill. It was Friday morning and she'd arrived on Monday, but still hadn't visited this famous little chapel that drew visitors from the length and breadth of Italy, just a kilometre or two from Borgo's door. Half an hour later her boots were mired to the rim in mud from the track, but she'd arrived at the familiar round form of the age-old shrine.

She took off her boots and ventured in, slightly tenuously, for no one seemed to be there this early. Her eyes immediately noticed the protrusion in the floor, and she was vaguely aware that this was the object that still drew pilgrims and visitors from the cardinal points – this famously described 'sword in the stone' – which she had read in Jeanette's guidebook was regarded by most as the inspiration for the legend of King Arthur's sword. But this, fascinating as it was, seized her attention much less than the overwhelming interior of the cupola itself. It was a strange Romanesque dome, devoid of ribs, and Maddie's eyes drank in the alternating bands – twenty-four of each, as she counted – of brick and stone circles that took the rotunda from the floor to its ceiling meeting point. Multiples of twelve, she thought; twelve apostles, twelve tribes of Israel. She was sure it had sacred connotations, and found the whole structure and atmosphere within surprisingly moving. Had it really been just a cave once? And had a man truly lived here with only the wolves for company, as was claimed?

Maddie was unexpectedly affected by the space within the little hermitage, feeling oddly close to those past pilgrims who had ascribed power and potency to the very stones. '*Hic locus est*' indeed, she thought, smiling to herself. As the main attraction was deemed to be the '*rocca de la spada*', she dutifully walked over to the sword now safely encased in Plexiglas to preserve it, she guessed, from souvenir hunters or saboteurs. And yes, it was remarkable: a primitive shape of twelfth-century iron tantalisingly embedded in the rocky floor of what was Galgano's cave. But she wouldn't put it past the Church to have had a hand in anchoring it there against time – with any substance required – to entice pilgrims across the centuries and the long miles. It was an apparently preserved miracle communicating the supremacy of prayer over war, of the spiritual over the physical, which seemed to Maddie to offer up some unusual and conflicting messages. What on earth had returning Crusaders made of this?

Perhaps a half-hour had passed when she eventually walked outside into sunlight, surprised to find as she passed him that someone had come in behind her quite without her knowing, while she had been absorbed by sword and sepulchre. She looked down from the height of the hill over the romantic shape of the ruined abbey underneath her, floating in a field of wildflowers. It was beautiful, no doubt; and she noticed a few cars had begun to arrive in the parking area below. After a day of unusual weather yesterday, it was Tuscany in a hot June again, and business was soon to be as usual.

She sat on the step and inspected her boots, ready to put them on, when a clear English voice spoke to her.

'It looks as though you've walked the whole pilgrims' route to get here,' it said with quiet good humour.

Maddie turned round and squinted in the sunshine. She smiled at a man in jeans and a crisp white shirt, but she couldn't see his face properly at this angle, and against the rising sun.

'And my boots haven't quite been up to the task. My feet are going to be sharing the walk back with a layer of mud inside.'

He smiled, and came down the steps towards her. Maddie could now see a young man, perhaps in his late twenties, with dark brown hair, hazel-brown eyes, and a rather sensitive face, she thought.

'You're English?' she said, getting to her feet.

'I'm Søren,' he said, and offered his hand to shake hers.

Maddie heard not the hint of an accent, though she'd been told their architect-gardener was a London-based Dane, like Jeanette and Claus.

'Have you just come from Jeanette's?' she asked, shaking his hand with a small amount of confusion.

He nodded. 'At just the right time to save you a walk back, I think.'

He steadied her while she climbed back into her boots, and her expression of discomfort made him laugh. He walked her down to a concealed parking area just beside the shrine, where a lone white Mini was parked in the morning shade with its convertible roof down.

Maddie laughed. 'That shows optimism, considering the weather you arrived in,' she said. 'I'm Madeline,' she added, and waited while he opened the door for her.

Søren nodded appreciatively. 'Well, Madeline, shall we go and join the others for breakfast?' And he pointed the Mini back down the hill, away from the little hermitage.

22

The weather was still warm, perfect for drying the chestnuts and getting another late cut of grass for winter fodder; but the woodlands surrounding the villa had taken on new shades of reds and ambers, thanks to the cooler mornings, and there was a vivid beauty about the countryside that stirred Mia now just as it always had done. She understood it was tied to her feeling of security with Aunt Jacquetta. The colours of the rural *contado* had come to embody the peaceful existence she had found here as a little girl, in marked contrast to her life in the town, which she had started to recollect recently. She remembered a lavish tower-house, with so many stairs; the window of her room covered with pale parchment rather than glazing, to admit filtered light; and chambers decorated with colourful woven hangings. But she remembered she had always been uncomfortable with the stuffy heat, the noise and the smells of the crowds gathered in the nearby piazza, when she'd lived in Volterra. Something had made her wary then; and she was trying to piece together what that sense of danger had come from.

But now, here in the *borgo*, there was a gentle hum of labour in every field stretching away from the villa. And in such beautiful weather, visitors wearing the clothes of pilgrims came and went in their familiar rhythm. Mia had herself been busier and more independent in her duties this season, overseeing the making of the soap without her aunt's help. The irises had been collected from the hillsides and lanes with Signora

Toscano in the summer, and the dried rhizomes were now crushed and prepared for the full-fat autumn milk, which was at its best for the process of soap-making. Mia had collected the ash from the first season's fires to make the lye, and for the last several days she had managed the distilling, the blending of the milk with new pressed olive oil, endless stirring, and finally the pouring into smooth wooden moulds made especially for them by Signor Porphyrius.

The moulds were a daily reminder that he had not yet returned.

It left a terrible emptiness and anxiety, which couldn't be dismissed. Her friend had kept busy, occupying herself for hours selecting herbs from their fledgeling garden, drying and pulverising them, making simples and unguents and tinctures for the cold season ahead. She had sewn baby clothes from fine linens and soft Damascus cottons; and spent hours in the garden under moon and stars – praying, in her way, as Mia now knew. But despite her studied attitude of calm, Mia also knew that her heart was gripped with a terrible fear for Porphyrius. A week had passed since the letter had arrived, and there had been no further news.

'If he is ill,' she asked Mia and Jacquetta, 'who will know to reach me here with news of it?'

'His mother would be told, Agnesca,' Jacquetta answered. 'And she will understand how to find you. She sent on his letter in good faith. I think she cannot be a bad woman.'

'She has always been kind to me,' she nodded. 'But, Jacquetta, do they know even how to reach her?'

'He will direct any message himself to inform both of you, if he were sick and recovering somewhere along the Via Romea.' Jacquetta put an arm around Signora Toscano. 'Besides which, we are acquainted with many of the people who offer hospitality as we do, most of the way along the route to Rome itself. Together we are a network of help and care, giving direction to each other; and he would need only to mention my name for a message to reach us.'

'If he is well enough to do so,' came her answer.

'He is not ill, *la raggia*. He will be home soon.'

Mia spoke purposefully, and addressed her friend with the special name she had awarded her so many months ago, the name that equated her with rays of golden light. It spoke of her confidence, her conviction that everything would turn out as it should.

Signora Toscano kissed Mia's cheek, fully aware of what she was conveying. She had to stay strong, Mia was telling her, and full of faith that her own strength of will would bring her husband home unscathed. She smiled at both women, and nodded.

'Yes, you're right.' She tried to look encouraged. 'Yet, he is a long time coming home to me.'

'The road has been a challenge this time,' Mia said. 'And that is all.'

But on the following day, a pilgrim arrived from the north and spoke of difficulty finding lodgings there because of rumours of a mysterious illness reported by sailors in the port of Genoa.

'A boatload of men, dead or dying, Monna,' he told Aunt Jacquetta. 'It is said the disease chased the sailors from the Genoese trading port of Kaffa, in the east. The afflicted bore hideous swellings, which burst with a putrid black blood – a horrible stench that no man near them could bear. Death comes to those who catch the sickness in hours, or at most a few days. It is a punishment from God; and it cannot be outrun.'

Just a day later two travellers, a father and son, journeying from the opposite direction, returning from the Holy Land, told the women of an unknown illness that had visited the port of Alexandria. The spokesman was the older man, sensible and measured in his speech, Mia decided. She did not believe he was given to repetitions of the same exaggerated rumour as the pilgrim who had arrived yesterday with tales of horror from the north that defied common sense.

'I have heard that Cyprus may also be suffering from this, *signora*,' he answered to Jacquetta's careful questions. 'And no man can name the disease. Some men have said that the astrological signs indicate malady because of a conjunction among the planets.'

'Yet others,' his son added, 'believe it is because there are eruptions in the volcano on Sicily, and that it poisons the air.'

Agnesca Toscano heard all of this, and retreated into herself. She didn't share her thoughts with Mia or Jacquetta, refused to scoff at the reports or to ask for further lurid details. But after more than an hour spent lost in thought in the garden she had made with Mia, she sought them both out at the house. It took a little care to separate them from Loredana and Chiara and Alba, and from the pilgrims lodging there, but eventually she managed to get them on their own in the music room. She closed the door behind them for privacy.

'Whatever is the truth about Porphyrius, this news of illness is something we should take seriously,' she said to them. 'We have travellers coming and going from the villa, Jacquetta, and we have no real idea of what this sickness is or how far it might spread. It may be wise to separate the travellers from us all – until we know they are not ill.'

Jacquetta listened to her carefully. She had come to respect Signora Toscano for her ability to heal wounds and treat maladies, more perhaps than even the monks of the nearby abbey. But separating pilgrims from the main house and, ultimately, the abbey for the Church's statutory forty days had not been seriously imposed in time outside her memory. Nor did they yet know the extent of this. It had been talked of in a port or two, but that was a long way from here; and Jacquetta thought it greatly overstated by men delighting in any excuse for apocalyptic rhetoric about God smiting a sinning world. On the other hand, it was true that the first news of it had come from Porphyrius, who was a man with a reasoning head. Some kind of unnamed illness was appearing in the seaports.

'If it is as the father and son have told us – something coming from foul air or vapours – will it help us to separate travellers, Agnesca?' she asked.

'I don't know,' she answered her honestly. 'I have never heard of any illness like this they describe. But my governess would be cautious from habit about any report of growing numbers of people suffering disease. She learned from her father – and taught me – to keep everything as clean as possible to avoid contagions. She believed the plagues of Israel were averted from the faithful through the use of hyssop plant at the doorways and in the houses. Through similar means she kept me from a dozen childhood illnesses. I think we should at least satisfy ourselves that those travelling to us from other parts come without sign of infection.'

'Do you suggest we should turn pilgrims away?' Mia asked her.

'On the contrary, Mia,' she said, 'we must offer the same respite your aunt always gives. But we also have a duty of care to those who live here at the villa, and in the *borgo* and the village of Palazzetto, to prevent them from getting ill if we can.'

'You have a duty to your child, *la raggia*,' Mia answered her firmly. 'Don't put yourself in the way of any stricken visitors.'

'I agree with Mia, Agnesca,' Jacquetta said. 'But we should also exercise good judgement here and be thankful that no one is ill as yet. I wonder at the stories we've heard, and can't help thinking there is much

181

superstitious nonsense being reported. "A punishment sent by God", indeed. However, I see sense in our taking extra steps to keep the villa clean and insisting that guests bathe.'

'So then,' Signora Toscano suggested, 'let us strew the rooms with all the herbs I am familiar with for countering malady; and let us prepare the garden rooms for guests who arrive from the places we've heard have witnessed this illness. That will be Genoa and Sicily and the southern Mediterranean lands; in all likelihood also Constantinople. A quarantine of forty days may be excessive, if it is true that men have died quickly. But perhaps for a week, we might keep them comfortably away from the villa and the workers' cottages, and away from the monks at the abbey in their tightly closed community.'

This settled between them, Jacquetta spent the next two days supervising an exacting preparation of the separate quarters opposite the stables in the garden. These rooms had fireplaces and a small cooking area that had once been allotted for the precise purposes of quarantine, but had come to be adapted for only occasional use by surplus guests in the summer months when the roads were driest and safest for travel. Signora Toscano dedicated considerable thought to the choice of herbs to rake into the fresh rushes, both there and in the main house. She asked Mia to make one last batch of soap. This time, she recommended using a mix of thyme and lavender to scent and fortify it, rather than the more luxurious iris they preferred for their skin, and she instructed Mia to mix in some alum.

Every hanging was cleaned, rugs were beaten, bedding was aired and changed, and the floors were swept twice a day. Mia thought her friend might collapse from the arduous work in such high temperatures: tomorrow would be the last day of the month, but the heat was still considerable. Signora Toscano was now very obviously pregnant, and Mia was worried. But she seemed determined to supervise the preparations herself; and besides, she admitted to her dear friends, it took her mind a little off the non-appearance of her husband.

The next day, on All Saints' Eve, Mia watched Aunt Jacquetta's horse disappear along the lane towards the abbey in the early afternoon. She had decided to visit Abbot Angelo and consult with him and Fra Silvestro about the talk concerning this strange affliction, and to learn what they had heard. But a few moments later Mia caught the sound of the horse again – or horses, possibly. Had her aunt met Abbot Angelo on the way here? She looked out of her window in confusion to see whether Aunt Jacquetta had forgotten something or returned.

What she saw, however, was neither the red mare nor the slight frame of her aunt.

She called urgently down the stairs to Signora Toscano, who was resting in the room below her own. In a moment both young women were at the front door, running across the courtyard, breathless at the stables.

A strong, upright figure swung down from his horse and came towards them.

'I am perfectly well,' Porphyrius said quietly.

He met his wife where the deep shadow and blinding light collided just outside the stone-arched stable entrance, and threw his arms around her with a mixture of passion and tenderness. He squinted over her shoulder and saw Mia, who was following closely behind. He quickly extended an arm and folded it around her too, pleased to see her affection for him. Obvious relief at his return had overcome her usual reticence.

'I am well, truly,' he reassured them both. 'But, Agnesca,' he said looking into his wife's shining face, 'my friend needs your help.'

He gently unwound himself from her and stepped back into the gloom, where Mia was just able to confirm the shape of the second horse she'd thought she heard. She shaded her eyes to adjust from light to darkness and watched Porphyrius give his attention to a young man only a short distance away. Mia saw that he was sitting almost motionless on his horse at an empty stall.

She, too, stepped inside the arched door with curiosity and watched Porphyrius cross the space between them. Before he had quite reached the horse the figure slumped forward suddenly and slid from the saddle, but Porphyrius managed to get his arms under him and soften his fall.

Mia now rushed forward instinctively to help, but she was completely unprepared for what she saw: a young man, perhaps twenty years of age, with a cloud of soft light brown hair in curls, damp at the brow-line, and his forehead beaded with sweat. But what made her recoil involuntarily was a hideous lump on his neck, which turned the appearance of someone almost angelic into someone to be feared. She knew: he had the disease.

23

Claus attracted Maddie's interest immediately. If his demeanour hadn't been enough to earn her approval, his actions would have. He had a wonderful energy and enthusiasm, like Jeanette's, but he also had a winning expression, which she would later think of as a sort of Nordic Santa Claus's twinkle. It was directed at everyone, but it had first announced itself to Maddie when she'd watched him for just ten minutes with Vincent.

Tired as he must have been, he forwent breakfast and instead raced his laughing son to a corner of the garden where a trampoline had been carefully sunk to lawn level and then hedged in to make it both safe and pleasing to the eye. Maddie – and Eleanore, running behind them – had joined in the game, following to see the father lift his boy tenderly onto the surface, then roll him back and forth over the black canvas circle in the sunshine, with tickles and cuddles, and then bounce gently right next to him, careful not to overweight his side and crush the toddler. This was a delicate matter, for Claus was tall and physical, and the trampoline, though strong enough, was made for children. Yet they bounced in perfect synergy – Claus demonstrating a tiger's strength, but with a lamb's gentleness.

After half an hour – not nearly enough to tire Vincent – all three walked together to the house and rejoined Jeanette and Søren, who were deep in animated discussion about Milo and Peter's artwork in the dining room. The French windows were opened to the rose garden. Claus lifted Vincent onto his shoulders and concentrated on the effect of

184

the painted walls. After a moment or two, the eyes communicated approval.

'It looks great,' he said, in a pleasing and lightly lilting accent. 'I think it makes this section of the dining area look bigger. And he's perfectly captured the colours in the lemon trees.'

Jeanette was pleased about this, but her own eyes – more china blue than Claus's – indicated mild disagreement.

'Yeah, I know. But Søren and I were just thinking it would be nice if the trees on each wall showed the different seasons – maybe one with fruit, but not all the same. Otherwise it may as well be a transfer – and it's been hand-painted, so we should see the variations.'

Claus smiled at his wife, and Maddie could tell it was an expression he'd had ample scope to practise over the years. It was admiring, and yet resigned. He addressed his response to Søren, who was grinning.

'This means my darling wife will want them to paint at least three of the frescos out, and start all over again,' Claus said, 'and I wouldn't know where to put myself if she was happy first time.' He hugged Jeanette. 'But, Madeline,' he turned to her, 'what do you think of the job she's done with the house?'

'I think your darling wife is rather good at all this,' she smiled back at him, 'so maybe it's a wise man who lets her have her way.'

'My thoughts exactly,' he answered with his Santa Claus face, and Maddie confirmed her liking of him all over again.

Jeanette was delighted with carrying the point so easily.

'Come on,' she said. 'We've had a late start, missed breakfast completely and it's long past twelve. Maddie and I cooked up a feast for your dinner last night, and we have the whole place to ourselves today, so it's only for you two to decide whether we should picnic on your missed dinner beside the pool, or in the sunshine of the rose garden, or in the shade of the loggia.'

Claus gestured to Søren and Maddie to make the choice.

After a prompt, Søren suggested, 'Well, the loggia, if that's all right? If I see it enough maybe I can take the view away with me when I have to leave.'

'*Kan du lide hvad du ser?*' Jeanette asked her guest with an interesting smile.

'*Alt er smukt,*' was the laughing answer.

Maddie understood through her expression – and Søren's reaction –

that she was obviously pleased with his response to her beautiful Valle Serena. While Jeanette led Maddie into the kitchen to organise the food, Claus took the opportunity to walk Søren and Vincent around the gardens close to the house, just as Jeanette had first done when Maddie arrived.

'He has a very good eye,' Jeanette said to Maddie as she pulled dishes from the refrigerator.

'It agrees with yours?' Maddie teased.

Jeanette's eyes laughed. 'No, it's not just that. He notices everything. He's been looking around the house with me for, what, an hour? As soon as he saw the view, and looked back at the house, he told me he was sure it had been here since Roman times – probably a villa farm. And he might be right.'

'What makes him think so?' Maddie asked, busy with a salad dressing.

'He pointed out the defensive position, the command of the valley, the shape of the plot; he noticed some reused travertine stone, which he says is very old. But he also asked me something fascinating.'

Jeanette paused, thinking about its implications; and Maddie looked at her impatiently.

'I told him we'd had to look for water; that there didn't seem to be an old well to guide us, or anything. He said that if the house were Roman, there'd have been a cistern under it keeping it cool in summer, but collecting rain from the roof in the wet months to give them a constant supply of water. And you know, Maddie, there is – or was – now I think of it. We found what we thought was a cellar when we dug underneath, to underpin the foundations; and one day we hope to build a proper industrial kitchen in the cool down there – if Borgo becomes a hotel with a busy restaurant. But I think Søren's right about it being a cistern. I just never realised before.'

'What continuous history, Jeanette, in this house,' Maddie said. 'And you feel it, too. You feel part of its survival – even comfort that it's still here, having sheltered so many people, the pilgrims and those whose lives were here. They had emotions and troubles, came with hopeful hearts and minds, searching for something – for hundreds of years. It's very special, quite humbling. And for me, it puts my own suffering a little in perspective.'

Jeanette looked at Maddie, and nodded slowly. This was the first real confidence she'd shared with her; and she felt Maddie might be getting close to her real self again – strong enough to think over and analyse what she'd been through. She walked the few spaces between them, and hugged her with feeling.

'Your own suffering is real enough, Maddie,' she said. 'It's personal, and it hurts, and it's everything in the world to the one going through it. You're allowed to feel it. You must feel it. The important thing is whether it gives you compassion for others, or indifference to life itself. And I think I know which of those is more natural in your character.'

Maddie, feeling a lump in her throat, accepted and returned the hug; and she thought, for some reason, of Neva.

'Yes,' she answered. 'And now I'm going to lay the table before my emotions catch up with me.'

You'll heal, Jeanette thought, as soon as you allow them to catch up with you; but she didn't say this to Maddie, who'd had realisation enough today. So, she simply smiled at her in her usual way and passed her some silverware and napkins.

Søren had left Claus and Vincent watching carp in the large pond beside the infinity pool, and bounded up the steps to rejoin Maddie and Jeanette in the kitchen.

'What can I do?' he asked Jeanette.

She grinned, and pointed to the armoire. 'Five plates, and the child's bowl in there for Vincent,' she said. 'He and Justina will eat at least some pasta with us. And I leave to you whether you bring the larger glasses, for some Chianti? Or there's some delicious chilled Vernaccia from San Gimignano, if you're in the mood for white.'

Twenty minutes later they were sipping the Vernaccia in the cool space of the arcaded terrace. They passed dishes from one end of the table to the other and back again; and in a rainbow of accents and with considerable energy, they covered half a dozen topics in swift succession. Claus spoke briefly of the beginning of his love affair with Italy, when he'd been a ski instructor in the Dolomites years before. Maddie could easily recognise that man in the fit Claus sitting opposite her. Then Jeanette explained how he and she had met in London – set up by friends who knew how much they both loved Italy. 'Claus was coming out of a difficult marriage break-up; and I was getting over losing someone very dear to me,' she said. Maddie looked at her, and wondered why she hadn't asked any of these things since she'd arrived. Justina also mentioned her love for Italy, and explained she'd learned Italian at university in Lithuania because she loved the art so much. She was thrilled to get a job here that allowed her to practise it, she said. And Søren simply enthused about Borgo: the location, the atmosphere, the scent of lemons, and especially Jeanette's choice of Gustavian-style interiors, which he thought fitted in perfectly with such a classical Italian house. It worked uniquely with the light here, he suggested, which revealed the myriad subtleties in the creams and whites, silvers and greys and chalk blues, and the gilt accents of the furniture and lighting.

'It reminds me,' he said, 'of my grandmother's house in Copenhagen. As does the bust of your very Danish lady down there,' he added, indicating a small marble sculpture resting on the table at one end of the loggia. 'Will you tell me about her?'

Jeanette sipped some wine, and grinned. This woman was not a beauty; in fact, she had a rather severe look on her face, even slightly disapproving of something. But she had been with Jeanette for years, and mattered to her hugely. She was interested that Søren had picked her out.

'When I lived in Copenhagen – an old apartment I rented in a house on Store Kongensgade for about a year – I watched her every day and every night. She was outside in the garden alone, often in the rain; and I wasn't happy about that. I had so much thinking of my own to do, and over time she became quite close to me. I kept an eye on her, and,' she said almost self-consciously, 'when it was getting near the time to move out, I broached the subject of her with the landlord. I told him it wasn't right that she was left out in the cold. "Absolutely not," he said to me, "no way am I giving her to you, just forget it." So I let it go. But a few weeks later, when I'd packed my things and had the removal truck outside, he came up to me. "I think you've left something behind," he said. And he put her in my hands.'

Jeanette's face was animated and full of good humour, but she looked closely at Søren and wondered what he'd make of her sentimental tale – her unusual identification with an inanimate lady. But his expression was very involved – and her own careful eye studied his nose and sensitive jaw line; his shining dark hair, combed back from the forehead, and the light hazel eyes not often associated with Scandinavian men. He was not stereotypical, she thought. He was a thinker, with a mild nature; and he had a poet's dreamy eyes. He'd get it exactly.

Søren looked at the bust, dominating her shady end of the terrace. Then he smiled back at Jeanette. 'And now she's safe from the wind and the weather, in the land where the lemon trees bloom.'

The heat became hazy over the valley, and the afternoon slipped away with the bottle or two of chilled wine in the cool of the terrace. Vincent and Justina left them to play, but the talk between them all had scarcely begun. Claus asked Maddie about her work, and the law in San Francisco. It struck her how far away it all seemed, looking out from where she sat right now. But all three of her listeners heard her tale of the people she represented, the wrong that was done to them, Maddie's role in gathering proof of negligence on the part of their employer, assembling a case. No one spoke for a long time, until finally Jeanette asked a sensible question.

'Why don't they just admit there's a problem, and make it safe now?'

'They can't see it,' Søren answered. 'They're not really looking.'

Maddie nodded at him. 'Yes. I think that's the simple answer.'

She'd thought how wonderful it was, and how freeing, to sit here with new friends and talk like this. She'd confided in no one at home; and the strain – on top of her personal life – often made her feel worn. Here were three empathetic, intelligent people, and they understood quite clearly what was wrong. If only she could get that across to Pierce.

'Enough of me,' she said now, and swallowed the last of her wine. 'One question for Søren; and one promise honoured from you please, Jeanette?'

'Only ask,' he answered her.

'Obviously you're Danish, like Jeanette and Claus; and I'm gratefully aware you've all been speaking for hours in English, for my sake. But,' she looked down at the table and shook her head, 'will you explain the mystery of how you come to speak English with the vowels of a public school boy?'

Søren laughed. 'Oh! Not quite a public school boy, I think. But it's not even interesting. Why don't we scoot straight to Jeanette's promise, which sounds much more intriguing?'

'No, come on,' Jeanette interposed. 'I'm interested, too.'

Søren nodded. 'OK – quick as I can make it. My father is a professor at the university in Copenhagen. He was very culturally informed, so I had a childhood with lots of trips to the cities and galleries across northern Europe – Prague, Berlin, Paris, Vienna. I was very familiar with "high art", I guess, and having an opinion on all the great painters and music masters. Not so many beach holidays, though.'

Maddie leaned her chin on her hand, and nodded. She could partly identify with this, and yet Søren's version of a not dissimilar upbringing to her own sounded immensely glamorous to her, with its cast of famous European cities.

'My mother works in the health sector, but she paints in her spare time. Her father – my grandfather Frederik – was a serious artist; but he was also a bit of a gypsy, and not very responsible to his family. He left them, and went to live in Australia when she was a little girl. He sent wonderful letters, but never money. My mum suffered for that. Perhaps that's the reason her painting is a hobby, and she doesn't risk more with it.'

'Then, she's always hoping you might follow your father into the security of academic life,' Jeanette grinned sympathetically.

'You're exactly right,' he answered. 'But when I finished school, the gypsy gene must have claimed me. I applied to do architecture in London, because I thought my choices would be my own if I studied away from home. I was longing to do something that allowed me to express myself, instead of rating others. When I got to London without a safety net and met people from so many cultures, I began to know myself better. I started trusting my creative impulses, and stopped worrying about stressing my mother over them. I did my degree at the Bartlett, which was an amazing experience; and by the time I'd done a Master's degree I never thought about going back.'

'But you still have a little boat moored in Denmark, you told me, which pleases me very much,' Claus added enthusiastically. He twinkled at Maddie. 'You can trust a man who sails, Madeline. He'll always be a good man in a storm.'

Maddie half smiled and looked at Claus, thinking it perhaps a very odd, and yet also a very perceptive, thing to say.

She turned back again to Søren. 'Yet, you design gardens and not buildings now?'

'I like getting my hands dirty,' Søren answered. 'But, now, come on, what about this promise of Jeanette's?'

Jeanette moved to the loom chair near the edge of the terrace and lit a cigarette. 'Maddie, will you excuse me while I bring these guys up to speed in Danish?'

Maddie nodded, and Jeanette told Søren very quickly about the building of the rose garden, the excavation for the wall, and the fact that they'd found some bodies while they were digging. She explained about the authorities being called, and the choice of whether to contact a homicide squad or archaeology.

'Archaeology, surely,' Søren said in English, 'not just because of the age of the villa, but also because you said you used to have a church here a long time ago.'

'Well, you're right and wrong,' she agreed, 'because it turned out it was definitely a job for the archaeologists and anthropologists – and not a police matter. But I don't think it's to do with the old church. We're not even sure where that was.'

Claus interrupted, 'I think you said they're giving the bones back to us soon?'

'They finished the testing,' she replied, and nodded to him. 'And I do have something unusual to tell you. You remember, Claus, we found two of the bodies with their arms extended towards each other, as though they were lovers holding hands.'

'They had matching chains around their necks, and we wondered if they'd had a suicide pact,' he said with a smile that didn't quite match the seriousness of the statement. 'Were we right?'

Maddie had been playing with her hair while they spoke in Danish, twisting the heavy curls up into a cool chignon; but she ceased that now and leaned closer to Jeanette.

'They examined three distinct bodies, and have dated all to the medieval period,' Jeanette continued. 'They say the radio carbon dating would place them somewhere between about twelve fifty and fourteen twenty. And if it's as late as fourteen-something, Søren, it can't be to do with the church. That came down in twelve fifty or 'sixty.'

'Pilgrims, then?' Søren asked. 'Did they die here, miles away from their home?'

Jeanette shook her head. 'The teeth were analysed and they all had a local Tuscan diet, probably middle class because they can trace fish and meat proteins whereas vegetable was more typical for lower classes. And, the strontium from the water shows it was Tuscan, too.'

Everyone inclined his or her head towards her; and Maddie asked: 'Jeanette, who were they?'

'The metal object they took away near one of the bodies turned out to be a crossbow bolt – which most probably caused the death. And,' she added, her lovely blue eyes widening, 'they were all women!'

24

ALL SAINTS' EVE 1347, SANTO PIETRO IN CELLOLE, TUSCANY

'He was well. His spirits were high and he was in good humour when we reached Rome. That was five days ago.'

Porphyrius lifted his companion's body onto the prepared bed in the stable-yard guest rooms. Mia thought there seemed no weight to it from the way he picked him up like a child, though the young man was tall enough and had strong shoulders.

'We've heard stories about such swellings,' she said to Porphyrius. 'But I never imagined anything as grotesque as this.'

'He awoke with it only today,' was his answer.

Agnesca Toscano, having placed pillows carefully under the sick man's head, was looking closely at his face. She touched his forehead and then examined the lump. Loosening the clothing around his throat, she discovered that there were three of these ugly protrusions, the worst about the size of a small egg.

'He is dangerously hot to the touch,' she said to both of them.

Mia nodded, and disappeared out of the garden room door.

Porphyrius looked at his wife anxiously. 'This fever came on two, or maybe three, days ago; certainly he was ill when we reached San Quirico – though he was dazed and not himself when we left Bolsena. It made the journey slow from there. He's been shaking so violently today that I didn't think he'd keep his saddle. And for two hot days together he lost everything in his stomach. He's had no appetite, but even water wouldn't stay down today.'

'Who is he, Porphyrius?' she asked him.

'It is Gennaro, Agnesca,' he answered softly. 'I have spoken to you of him many times. We were close from our childhood, and it was he who encouraged me through all our troubles – when I confided to him my feelings for you. He had problems enough of his own, God knows, but still he had wise words to offer me about not giving up – even though your family were so set against us.'

'Yes, I remember,' she answered. 'His family were forced to leave Volterra some years ago.' She was divided between appreciation for her husband's loyalty to a friend, and concern that he had been closely quartered with someone as ill as this poor man for any number of days. 'How did you come to be travelling with him?'

'Chance, Agnesca,' he said. 'I'd been waiting without much hope of a sail from Messina, after panic set in at the port, and boats were diverted from it. You cannot imagine the disarray. Somehow I got back to the mainland, only because I travelled a day ahead of the worst news of the sickness, but after that everything – all movement – was halted. It was pure fortune that Gennaro was travelling a day or two behind me. He already had passage on a small ship to Salerno. Lucky for me that ship came from Sicily to the Calabrian port to drop off travellers who'd been stranded, and they paid heavily for the privilege of being ferried. He found me at the port in Reggio, where I was looking for a vessel towards Naples or Ostia. It was an answer to my prayers that he was able to persuade the crew to take me along. I'd have been caught there, forced to take the dangerous route overland, if he hadn't appeared.'

His wife's face relaxed into her usual smile. 'Then I'm grateful he found you, truly. But, I don't know what he may have brought on us all.'

'I have faith in you as a healer,' he said, touching her hair reassuringly.

'This may be beyond my skill, Porphyrius.'

Mia reappeared at the door carrying a small wooden pail and a ladle, with some strips of old linen.

'It is cool, *la raggia*,' she said. 'I drew water directly from the cistern. And I've picked feverfew from the unicorn garden.'

'That's well thought of, Mia, and so like you,' her friend answered. 'Let's bruise the herb and steep it, then try to get him to swallow some. Perhaps it may halt the fever.'

'I asked Chiara to bring hot water for that purpose,' Mia added, 'and she's coming directly.'

Porphyrius leaped to take the bucket from her, setting it on a stool next to his friend.

'Let us cool his body, Mia,' Signora Toscano answered. 'That is my first worry. I don't know about the huge blisters, but let's begin my reducing the sweating, if we can.'

Porphyrius helped his wife undo the fastenings of his friend's doublet, and unlace the elegant shirt; and with care, she and Mia blotted wet cloths across his chest and face. Mia was immediately aware of the fire in his skin, and thought any man with such a fever would hardly survive the next hour. She remembered her aunt nursing a youth once, with a similar burning heat ravaging his body. He had quickly slipped away into delirium, and never woken. Porphyrius's friend, however, seemed to get relief from the cool fabric. His shivering lessened. Soon his teeth chattered less, and he breathed more easily; but he winced and jerked his body when Mia passed the cloth under his armpit. She thought she had unintentionally applied too much pressure. Lifting the arm gently she discovered another lump, larger than those on his neck.

'Are you able to lance them, Agnesca?' Porphyrius suggested. 'He complained so much of the pain in his neck earlier today, and also of extreme aching in his limbs. He doubted he could make the ride, and urged me to go on home to you without him.'

'I don't know what is inside the swellings,' she answered, 'but I doubt it is pus. I am no doctor, and know nothing of the art of restoring the humours. Perhaps it may weaken him to meddle with them, while his fever is so dangerous. I think it better to leave them for now, and watch him; but I'd like to get feverfew into his stomach. It may counter the fever and aches you speak of.'

Porphyrius supported the body while the two women continued applying cool compresses to Gennaro's face, now carefully avoiding the tender areas around his collar and under-arms. Signora Toscano asked Mia to raise the leather coverings that served as glazing on the two windows in the room, allowing some air movement across his dampened body. A moment later Chiara arrived with a jug of steaming water, and Mia immediately folded and bruised the herb into it. Soon she was dipping the ladle in and bringing it to his lips, encouraging him to drink. He sputtered, but some liquid went down.

195

Agnesca now sent her husband for bark from the willows that bordered the river below the villa, and when he returned a quarter of an hour later this was added to the warm water to strengthen the tea. All three sat, the women laying fresh compresses against his skin, then dosing him with the tisane made up of bark and tiny feverfew flowers. Half an hour passed, and his chattering teeth calmed; then an hour more and his fever had abated significantly. After a further hour his bruised eyelids had opened just enough for him to communicate that the light from the windows was troubling him. Mia darkened the room again, and the young man sank into an exhausted sleep just as Jacquetta came to find them in the garden room.

'It is wonderful to see you, Porphyrius,' she said with great feeling. 'Though I never doubted you would come home safely to us.'

The small group had moved to the cooking area to allow the sick man some quiet. Jacquetta listened to the report from Porphyrius, which she thought was full of sense and restraint, unlike the gossip she had heard from the men on the road. Yet it worried her, too. Whatever it was, this malady no man could give a name to was here with them now at Santo Pietro in Cellole.

'The men who have informed us about it mentioned the rapidity of its onset, Porphyrius,' she said. 'Yet you are taking us through many days with your story of your friend. The fever began two or three days ago?'

'We didn't dally from the south, Jacquetta,' he answered. 'I knew Agnesca would be worried, and I was wild to be home. The ship had a good breeze and we found horses freely in Salerno, where there is no talk of sickness at all. I urged us on. I thought I had simply pushed him too hard, and he was fatigued. That was until the fever became more serious, and he retched up his food. And then these lumps appeared today. These were all that men spoke of in Messina – swollen buboes that burst with rancid blood.'

His wife was trying to track the time of the illness. 'You are saying Gennaro was in Messina little more than a week ago?' she asked.

'No. It must have been ten or eleven days,' Porphyrius answered her. 'I had been in Reggio for two, and was in Messina two or three days before him.'

Jacquetta counted on her fingers, and seemed puzzled. 'There was no sign of malady until the fever?'

'Let us say that a week out of Sicily he was feverish,' he answered, thinking deeply. 'And within a day or so it had become more violent. At this same time he complained of sickness to the stomach, lost his appetite and all he had eaten. Perhaps it was the day before yesterday that I noticed he seemed unaware of me. I spoke, but he made no answer. He looked faint, and I worried he would fall from his horse. He was oblivious of the route home, so I took his reins and led him like a child, which made us slower these days past than we had been through all the days before.'

'The pilgrims from the north spoke of people sickening in Genoa within the hour,' Mia said.

'Then perhaps your friend has a different illness, Porphyrius,' Jacquetta said with studied calm.

'Yet,' Agnesca countered, 'the lumps are the focus of the travellers' tales, and he has them.'

What to do next seemed of utmost importance. Each of them recognised that time was significant, and that treating the illness – whatever it was – would be more effective if they were quick. Agnesca Toscano was also trying to decide whether they could yet consider Porphyrius past all danger.

'What can you tell us about him?' she asked her husband. 'Has he always been strong and in good health? The fever has attacked him for two or three days, which is very hard on the heart. But he is trying to hold on.'

Porphyrius seized his wife's hand and squeezed it lovingly. 'He is strong in both his body and mind,' he answered her. 'He has been healthy every hour of his life, to my knowledge. He was trained from childhood to handle a sword, and he is equally competent with a crossbow or reading Latin; for he is a Volterran nobleman's son, Agnesca.'

Porphyrius looked at Jacquetta. 'I think he has kinship with you, Jacquetta – or at least with Mia,' he said quietly.

All three women responded to this statement with facial expressions that replaced the need for speech. All wanted information as to whose son Gennaro was.

'Have I not understood the implication, Jacquetta – I am sorry if I have presumed too much – that Mia is the natural daughter of Bishop Ranuccio?' Porphyrius asked in a tone that showed all the discretion he could convey.

Jacquetta and Mia replied to this with disparate expressions: the one wreathed in riddles, and the other in deep fascination.

'And if that is so, then Gennaro is her cousin,' Porphyrius smiled gently. 'He, too, is an Allegretti – the nephew of the exiled bishop.'

25

TUESDAY 19 JUNE 2007, BORGO SANTO PIETRO
AND SIENA

S øren's turn in the kitchen on Tuesday morning had resulted in
some American-style pancakes, served with bacon on the side and
a spoonful of maple syrup he'd found in Jeanette's kitchen of
plenty. They were cooked in Maddie's honour, and if she were honest
they were a little heavy, but the gesture was sweet and it made her laugh.
She had already conceded at dinner the night before that the delicious
local Chianti wines had stolen her heart – despite her loyalty to the
Napa – and she was quickly acquiring a Tuscan palate after little more
than a week at Borgo. So she was humoured in all the right ways when
Søren spoke up about the pleasures of breakfast in her part of the
world.

'It was a boiled egg and cold cuts, in my childhood,' he said. 'America
does breakfast like nowhere on earth.'

As they'd poured out the last of the coffee on the terrace he'd asked
if she might enjoy a lift into Siena. He had an arrangement to spend the
morning in the university library and to visit the Orto Botanico
dell'Università di Siena. This was the city's historic botanical gardens,
the perfect place to research plants that thrived here in the medieval
period and to seek inspiration for the garden design. Then maybe they
could have lunch? She had quickly said 'yes', and rushed up to her room
for a sunhat and some loafers so as to walk comfortably on the cobbles.
But at half-past nine, Maddie made the decision to jettison the sunhat
and found herself instead with her hair stuffed into an old cloth cap of

199

Claus's, flying down the sun-dappled SS441 past the abbey of San Galgano, with Søren at the wheel.

'You're on the wrong side!' she'd shouted, laughing into the wind as they pulled out from the feeder road.

Fortunately there was no traffic at all, and he'd laughed back at her, completely calm. 'Don't worry! I'll soon get the hang of it.'

The convertible Mini was perfect for the winding Tuscan roads between Palazzetto and Siena. Maddie glanced sideways at him and watched his sunglasses catch the changing light through the trees. Now that his brain was safely in left-hand drive, she felt comfortable sitting beside him as he handled the little machine around the bends; and it was just noisy enough with the wind and the road surface that she could look at everything and think of nothing, feeling no pressure to talk.

Maddie knew that Søren had been invited to Borgo for the weekend for Jeanette to consider giving her approval of him as the architect for the new garden; it was a 'getting to know you' opportunity with a clear understanding that nothing was yet decided. But over the three days minds must have been made up firmly. Jeanette seemed delighted and very sure he was the right person. Claus had asked Søren if he could stay on for a few more days to research local plants and consider an authentic design, then to come up with ideas they could discuss and get a rough costing for the project.

After lunch on Sunday Maddie had excused herself from the party, saying she had to send some emails, but she watched the other three vanish off from the house – deep in a Danish conversation – towards the wilderness of the undeveloped area of the property. She saw that Søren was armed with measuring tapes and a camera, and also a rawhide leather saddle bag, which was beautifully cared for, with a fine patina of age. She wondered if that bag contained clues about his entire life.

Maddie had completed her email duties and, now in complete solitude, was happy to occupy one of the big cane chairs and glance at an English newspaper Søren had brought from London. She put the paper to one side and gazed out over the hills, the 'crete', as locals called them. Across the distances to the far horizon she'd wondered about the remains of what looked like an ancient castle, rising out of the primordial forest. The colours of the valley had a muted tone from the moisture left by the spring rains, which softened the effect of the light even on a dazzling mid-June day. She felt close to the landscape; and this, in a way, she couldn't explain. She compared it with her response to the light in her native California; by contrast its starker sunlight often intruded into her thoughts and senses, although she loved it, too. But here, the landscape fed her thoughts, seemed to be part of her mind. It was quite different.

While she'd been lost in these considerations the surveying party had returned in animated conversation, still in Danish, from which they switched effortlessly to English as Maddie came into view. Jeanette mentioned coffee, and in five minutes had squeezed back through the terrace doors with a tray.

'Søren believes,' Jeanette had told her, 'that there were several developed areas around the house in the past. When we came, most of it had reverted to rough green waste. But we've been looking at some "landscape archaeology".'

Maddie had looked at him questioningly.

'I think there were several spaces allocated for gardens around the house. They always had a purpose, not just for growing things to eat or to look pretty. Most gardens had a much deeper meaning. There are traces of boundary lines around some areas, and that's related to the concept of a "Paradise", which came directly from the Persians. It's their word, and was a kind of hunting park of beauty and plenty enclosed by walls – fashionable, but also full of religious significance in large medieval estates.'

'An enchanted garden,' Jeanette had said in a dreamy way. 'There are local stories that there had always been something distinctive and even mystical about this place, and the people who lived here. One old woman in the village told me that the plague had swept across Europe in the late thirteen forties, killing more than half the population in both Volterra and Siena; but it spared the people here at Borgo.'

'Maybe this valley was like the Vale of Health in London,' Søren had suggested. 'The plague never came there either. No rats and no fleas!'

'No,' Jeanette answered him. 'It was different here. Stories tell of someone like a magus who lived here, who just kept the plague away. But maybe they're just old wives' tales.'

Maddie noticed the town sign for the familiar-sounding 'Sovicille' as they passed along the SS73, when quite suddenly the sun flashed across the windscreen and made her blink with the saturation of light. The car turned a sharp bend into the narrow gorge filled with a surprisingly rapid torrent, given the fact that it was summer; and on the right of the road, a strange isolated bridge came into view.

'Oh,' she said, and laid her hand on Søren's arm. 'Can we stop here for a moment? Can you pull over anywhere?'

Even with the surface noise there was a tone in Maddie's voice that made Søren react quickly, and he swung the car off the road onto the verge. The bridge, with a poignant single arch and no side supports, crossed the river, which the sign said was the Torrenta Rosia.

Søren was nodding. 'Jeanette mentioned we'd pass this,' he said. 'I think it's called the Ponte della Pia. She said it was an important crossing on the ancient road that connected Siena and the Merse Valley with the Maremma, during the Middle Ages. I think she said it dates from the thirteenth century, but it looks sort of Roman.'

Maddie hardly heard him. Her mood was deeply affected by the simple structure. The shape was evocative. Hardly usable, it somehow maintained a slim hold on either side of the chasm through some kind of mystical means.

'Can we walk across it?' she asked.

Søren's expression was a mixture of doubt and respect for her adventurousness, but her response to the bridge interested him. He glanced at her footwear, and entered into the spirit of things.

'Sure, why not?' He reached behind the seat, pulled a camera and a pocket guide to Tuscany out of his bag, and then sprang from the car.

Maddie had opened and closed her car door quietly, almost as if it didn't belong in such a scene. She leaned against the vehicle for a moment and just gazed at the bridge. She heard Søren's voice, as he was reading extracts from the book.

'It was Roman,' he said; 'but was rebuilt in medieval times. It only became impassable to traffic like this after the Germans took their tanks across it in 'forty-four, and destroyed the struts. A legend connected with it says that, on moonless nights, the silhouette of a woman often appears. A white veil covers her face, and she walks across the bridge without her feet touching the ground. She's been seen by locals time after time, and for hundreds of years. They say it's the ghost of Pia de Tolomei.'

'Who was she?' asked Maddie.

'A Sienese noblewoman, who seems to have met her death in an entirely different location,' he read on. 'But she crossed here on her way from Siena to a miserable marriage, and only her husband knows the secret, according to Dante, of how she died.'

Maddie smiled sadly. 'That's the kind of story that touches my sister,' she said. 'Medieval women almost buried alive in the stonework.'

Søren grinned. 'She's not married?'

Maddie shook her head. 'This world is so old,' she said.

'Older than your world, do you mean?'

Søren watched her carefully. He'd been immersed in the pleasure of looking into her face since he'd first seen her: the fabulous, impossible hair that would never belong to a prom queen; the long quattrocento neck and exquisite almond-shaped eyes, which possibly failed to excite her school friends, but would haunt an onlooker for half a millennium watching from a gilded frame.

'Don't you see,' he said gently, 'that this is part of you? Certainly as much as twelve-lane highways, or endless lines of SUVs. Maybe you've had it trained out of you. But we've all survived from a tiny handful of ancestors, no matter where we live now; and you still have a tantalisingly clear lineage from people who can't have lived too far from here, probably right about the time the bridge was repaired.'

Maddie nodded. She carefully climbed up to the stone curve at one end of the bridge, taking his offered hand to steady herself. The river wasn't deep below; it provoked no sense of fear for her, even though the bridge was relatively narrow and seemed precarious without a rail. There was an odd dipping sensation at one end – the bridge literally fell away at the opposite side. More than fear, she had a sensation of sadness from it. Yet Søren's story of Pia didn't quite chime with her. It's not about ghosts or unhappy marriages in the past, she thought. That was Barbara's domain, rather than hers. But she couldn't shake off something visceral: perhaps a feeling of compassion – for whom, she didn't know. It's not about Pia herself, she thought, but it does concern piety. This was her translation of the Italian word *pia* – the pious ones. She took a few steps forward, but couldn't bring herself to go far. Emotions, rather than anxiety, prevented her; and Søren, who was behind her and ready to cross, held out a hand instead to help her back. He seemed to understand, and asked her nothing.

He took time framing a few photographs, and she watched and waited. But it was not until they were back in the car and she'd clicked home the seat belt that Maddie's emotional response to the bridge stilled itself. They didn't speak until the car passed through the small hamlet of Rosia when, at lower speed, there was comparatively little road noise.

'I watched you the other day, before we spoke,' he said, and changed into a lower gear. 'You were counting the rings on the building in the chapel at Montesiepi, I think. What did it tell you? I made it twenty-four white and twenty-four red rings.'

Maddie pushed her aviators back and hid her eyes. 'You were watching me?'

'I like looking at things, and at people.'

For some reason this pleased Maddie, though it might easily have done the opposite. She recognised he was a person to look carefully. The corners of her mouth conceded a smile.

'What did it tell me?' she mused. 'I hadn't settled it; but my math concurs with yours. Jeanette told me there is an idea that the Templar Knights might have built the chapel for one of their own. Templars owned the nearby Castle of Frosini, and were involved with the abbey, if you believe local legend. So, maybe Galgano was one of them. They used sacred numbers, and I was thinking of the significance of twelve apostles, twelve tribes of Israel. Didn't Jacob have twelve sons? The chapel might have its origin there. Do you think it's intentional?'

Søren picked up his speed a little, but answered her with something she found surprising. His tone was not emphatic, but invited discussion.

'There are the twelve months of the year, and the zodiac, of course, which seems to be the Babylonian source of twelve as a sacred number in the heavens for most of antiquity. What about the twelve cities of the Etruscan league? They passed on the idea to the Romans of the number twelve being connected with rulership, and law. There were twelve tables of Roman law. Or,' he almost seemed to be thinking aloud, 'even the seven cycles of twelve years which marked an Etruscan's life span. That gave their elders eighty-four years of life, and after that they believed a man was no longer able to comprehend the advice of the gods.' He paused and seemed amused. 'It was more generous than the three score years and ten of the Bible.'

Maddie looked at him. 'These Etruscans,' she said, 'they keep turning up at the moment. I never thought a thing about them before. But yes, that shows respect for age, don't you think?' She hesitated only for a moment and teased him a little. 'So what did *you* see at Montesiepi – apart from me?'

'It reminded me of Etrusco-Romano shapes of shrines and tombs, and also the pantheon, which I spent a week studying and sketching when I was a student. So, I wonder if the core could be a much older, perhaps pre-Christian site, which was reworked? I thought it beautiful, and effective.'

'Yes. So did I,' she answered softly.

They kept within their own thoughts, Maddie looking straight ahead, lost in her private impressions, Søren following signs that promised an invisible Siena; until about ten minutes down the road he suddenly laughed as the car breasted a hill. They looked across to the two hills on which the old city was built.

'Now, I see it,' he said. 'It's like the reward for a quest.'

Maddie nodded slowly, emerging from a dream. 'And it's impressive,' she said.

The little car shot over the brow, and the panorama spread out below them about four kilometres away. The city, with its spires and palazzos of ancient red brick and tiles, stood out clearly from the area of urban sprawl, mainly to the west.

Maddie remembered the trip to Venice with Christopher, which brought her first independent and adult contact with Italy; but Venice was a kind of fairy-tale world. Before her now was a strange juxtaposition of old and new, set into the surrounding hills. It had a totally different vibrancy, and it made her excited and also a little nervous.

Søren did a few quick turns and lane changes, then took the south exit marked 'Porta Tufi'.

'Finding a space for the car in Siena is a challenge,' he said. 'So watch out for the blue signs with "P" for parking Il Campo.'

'OK,' she agreed. 'But I thought this was your first time here?'

'It is, but Claus gave me excellent advice,' he said. 'Let's hope we can follow it.'

Søren manoeuvred the Mini through the streets leading to the edge of the old town, and Maddie watched with fascination as the population went about its business. She loved the stylish girls on their scooters, zooming through the traffic. Despite the warning of the traffic exclusion zone they drove through the old city gates as Claus had instructed, and the scene became even richer. The incongruity of priests in their robes contrasted with businessmen in suits. Old women wearing their shawls even in summer were in harmony with the buildings, yet somehow displaced by the modernity of the life surrounding them. Everyone seemed in ardent conversation with someone else, whether moving purposefully through a throng or pausing by the wayside. Here and there groups of tourists stood out like odd islands in a river of people that washed around them.

'There!' Maddie laughed. 'It's a "P" Il Campo! Quick, right turn.'

But Søren was caught watching the people, too, and looked the wrong way.

'Turn, turn!' she shrieked in fun, and put her hand on the steering wheel.

Several people on the pavement laughed and waved them in the right direction. To her own surprise, Maddie waved back at them. Søren found the turn between a bendy-bus and an elderly lady on a Vespa, and darted into the narrow street, also laughing. There was an air of chaos and elegance about it all, and what made the scene extraordinary was the whirl of activity set against the background of wonderful medieval brick buildings. The clash of ancient and modern was part of this life, and Maddie reflected on what her companion had said earlier. People lived here in the middle of at least a thousand years of visible history, every one of them on a cellphone or listening to an iPod, and didn't seem to find any of it incongruous.

'I suppose you're right,' she said to him suddenly. 'We all come from the same beginnings; but this is a long way from the streets of my home.'

He nodded. 'It's very different from Copenhagen, too. But I love all the differences.' He swung the car into the parking area and grinned. 'We've arrived.'

Claus's information had been excellent. Even though cars were banned from the old town, 'P' Il Campo was well located and somehow popped up close to the heart of the old city. The Duomo and the University of Siena, with all its various departments, were a short walk away, as was the Campo itself, the most theatrical setting for the world-famous horse race, the Palio delle Contrades.

Søren picked up his saddle bag from the back seat as they set out from the parking area.

'I'd love a coffee first, but I'll be rudely late if I stop. I'll be about two hours, but the search might take me to the Pinacoteca Nazionale di Siena, which has a large collection of documents as well. How would it be if we meet up for lunch somewhere around one thirty? By then most of the staff will be away, and everything closes for two hours in the summer. I can start again later, if I'm still looking for inspiration.'

'Sounds good,' Maddie answered, freeing her hair from the cap and tucking it into her bag. 'Shall I try to book a place? I could text you, and meet you there. Give me your cell number. Jeanette loaned me her *Michelin* and told me it's absolutely reliable for food.'

'I love a woman who knows where to eat,' he laughed. 'Just send word and I'll find you.' He scribbled his number on a notepad which he'd taken from the saddle bag. 'What will you do?' he asked as he handed the page to her, almost sorry he wasn't going with her.

'*Vado a perdermi tra i fantasmi del passato*,' she answered mysteriously.

He looked at her, unsure how to translate this. His solid tourist Italian didn't cover much about '*fantasmi*', but he could see she had more than enough language to survive.

'Have fun,' he said, and followed his own path towards the university. He was thinking deeply as he walked and repeated to himself, '*Fantasmi del passato*.' Then a penny dropped, and he smiled. Yes, he thought; spirits of the past. You'll be quite at home among those.

It was still early in the day, yet the summer tourist lines were getting longer by the minute outside the Duomo, even though the cluster of buildings hadn't yet opened their doors. Maddie decided to buy her combined entrance ticket anyway, and joined the queue. While she waited she looked up restaurants in the red Michelin. She made a call and then texted Søren as she walked forward to buy her tickets:

Osteria Le Logge, Via del Porrione 33. Shall we try our luck? Have requested outside table – look for me 13:30, a block from the Campo. Table in name of 'Moretti'. A presto, M.

As she finished a voice beside her said, '*Prego, Signorina*.' She showed her ticket at the door of the great medieval church and stepped into another world.

It took a few seconds for her eyes to adjust to the low light level on the floor of the cathedral. Sunshine through the exquisite rose window at the end of the nave drew her eye immediately upwards, as it was designed to do, and the black and white marble pillars dramatically heightened the impact. Maddie thought of herself as an agnostic, a follower of no particular faith, but she found the effect dazzling and inspiring. As she wandered around the vast interior of the church, crowds of tourists gathered in clusters at points of interest, with tour guides or without them. Like flocks of sheep, she thought, grazing on a visual feast.

For Maddie in her wandering, the guide book gave her all the information she felt she needed. She was happy to pick up on what interested her rather than join a group, although sometimes it was fun to stand on the periphery of a tour to hear what the tour guide said. Circulating like this she realised that the vast floor was largely covered with matting. Only one section seemed to be open for view today, roped off to prevent tourist damage by the mass of humanity. She eavesdropped on one guided group to learn that when one could see the world-famous floor in its entirety, it was patterned with fifty-six mosaic panels, depicting Old Testament themes. It was only fully opened a few weeks of the year.

Maddie moved towards the open section. This was policed by pairs of robed clerics, engaged in their own conversations. Now and then one of them would shoo an invader off the mosaic, raise a finger to his mouth to remind them to be silent in a church, or speak briefly and softly to a tourist to answer a question. As she approached the exposed area she could see a powerfully inlaid figure of a robed man, his right hand outstretched, pointing towards an inscribed tablet. In the other hand, the figure held a document. She thought of the importance – then and now, in her own life – of the written word, the weight that was to be given to something legally recorded. Two figures of lesser rank were paying homage to the focal character, while attempting to read the paper he held.

Maddie gazed down at the panel and dimly recognised a mosaic of one of her father's conversation points from antiquity, a person he said had formulated the idea of monotheism at the time of Moses. She spoke to one of a pair of clerics standing by the ropes. 'Is this the sage Hermes Trismegistus?' she asked in English.

One of the men nodded indolently, turning away and folding his arms over the front of his cassock. Maddie found his dismissive and disinterested demeanour affronted her a little. She looked at the figure on the floor in all its glory: Hermes Trismegistus, Maddie remembered, had fascinated the medieval world greatly with the rediscovery of his texts from Egyptian times that were said to pre-date Moses. His writings included certain doctrines that were surely unconventional for the time, such as his concerns with conjuring spirits; and he was the guiding light behind the practice of alchemy. Yet here he was in the middle of this very Christian cathedral, a thoroughly pagan figure.

Maddie found she'd expressed this last view aloud, for she suddenly had an unlooked for answer.

'No, *signorina*, he was a very early prophet who predicted the coming of Christ, like the sybilla of Cumae. He is respected as a teacher.'

This was spoken by the younger curate, who then turned to watch the crowd milling beside his companion.

'Oh,' Maddie grinned. She felt bold and said – as if to herself, but clearly enough to be heard – 'Yes, I see. You mean in the same way that the Muslims regard Christ as a prophet, because they believe he predicted the coming of Muhammad and the rise of Islam?'

The pair turned and stared at her, considering a reply, but Maddie walked slowly away leaving the question to hang in the light from the stained-glass windows. She hadn't meant to be rude; but it frustrated her that so many belief systems selected from the facts exactly as much as they wanted to support their own case. Legitimate discussion about any remainder was always undesirable. This thought – despite the glorious setting – took her to Pierce Gray's ethos, and his inability to judge whether Stormtree's victims might have a legitimate case. Everyone, Maddie thought, has his or her own blinkers on. And I surely must too, she admitted.

Maddie passed her hours without count at the Piccolomini library and the museum, fascinated by everything and yet lost in her own thoughts. She felt vaguely discomforted to be enjoying her own time and not thinking too deeply about how much she missed Christopher being there. She still felt the empty space beside her, and her mind strayed to him at intervals, but she was beginning to remember who she'd been herself before she'd met him. It was odd, but not altogether unwelcome. The deep pain was real, but she began to see that she was somehow surviving it.

The heat and light hit her like a wall as she reached the door. Stepping from the building, she pulled on her glasses and checked her watch. It was now well after one so she headed in the direction of the restaurant, passing the magnificent Palazzo Pubblico with her neck craning high to take in the elegant tower. Then she came to the other side of the Palazzo and, with a little glance at her guide map, found the shy Via del Porrione.

The trattoria was beginning to fill up as Maddie arrived, but a table out the front was empty and she wondered if it might hers. A young man came to seat her and, at mention of the name 'Moretti', waved her to the table with the word, '*Signorina*'. His smile was for her short skirt and good legs, and he asked if she had come to the city to study. She decided to put a stop to her being treated like a tourist, and answered in her best Italian.

'*Sono qui in vacanza da San Francisco. Sto con un' amica che ha una casa graziosa in Val di Merse.*'

The waiter gave Maddie a look of genuine admiration, and smiled. '*Lei parla molto bene l'italiano, persino con accento toscano!*'

Maddie was caught off guard by this – not just the praise for her language, but especially the comment that her Italian sounded regional.

'*Grazie daverro, questo è un grande complimento. So che a Siena si parla il miglior italiano.*'

Yes, the boy answered her. It was true that the Sienese and Tuscans generally were known for speaking the best Italian and using proper grammar, with all its different tenses. It was because of Dante; he had made the vernacular language the national language. And her pronunciation, he said, was properly Tuscan – the way she had said '*casa*' with almost an 'h' at the front, like '*hasa*'. This, he smiled, was typical. She might have been born in Siena.

The patron of the restaurant now caught the waiter's eye with his own raised eyebrows. It was busy, and he was dallying with a pretty woman. The boy hastily asked Maddie what she would like to drink while she was waiting for her friend. She asked for a dry white wine and acqua '*con gas*' and settled back at the table to wait for Søren. She pulled out her phone just to check if he'd sent any message, as she'd turned it off in the cathedral. The phone beeped and there was indeed a text, but it wasn't from Søren. Instead, she found a note from Tyler hoping she was well and enjoying the food. He reported in a sentence that he'd been to see Neva in Maddie's absence, to video her so the court could see she was confined to bed. Neva had asked him to send something to Maddie, and this was attached.

I'll say more, when more's to say. T for Tyler, he signed off.

Maddie wondered whether the technology would work internationally, but she clicked the video link, shaded the screen with her hand, and soon saw Neva in her hospital bed. How strange, she thought, when I am here in the sunshine in Siena. Neva was propped on pillows, but Maddie smiled, seeing how she habitually carried herself as though she were a serene noble lady, rather than a sick patient with a tumour. Her hands were extended out of the frame, and she was trying to coax someone into the picture with her. She looked thinner than before, Maddie saw with a shock, but her eyes were bright and she was laughing. After a mock tussle she pulled a young boy, with a mop of black hair, onto the bed beside her.

'Hello, Madeline, in your Italy! I know you are seeing your ancestors, and we are thinking of you, hoping you are healing and getting much better.'

Maddie felt a strange shudder at the oddness of that coming from Neva, the selflessness of her greeting; but she hadn't time to analyse her response before she heard Neva again.

'This is my son, Aguila. You have Italian, so you know this word, and he truly is my eagle, with the sharpest eye,' she said, stroking the boy's hair. 'He can see everything – things others never see. Once his heart is fixed he will be perfect.'

Maddie smiled at Neva's pride. It was true that the boy was exquisite-looking, with his fine slender nose and eyes like deep pools. Seeing him brought home the innocence of the Stormtree victims; reminded her that the child had a small heart defect, which was arguably related to his mother's work at Storm. The sadness was outweighed, for now, by the strength of his mother.

'Now this,' Neva continued from the tiny screen, and pulling on her other hand, 'is . . .'

A basso profundo could be heard near her. 'Is this for the lady who knows the secret of the snows?'

Neva replied, 'Yes, Papa!' Then she gave an enormous heave with another burst of laughter. A man probably in his late fifties was drawn into the picture on the other side of the bed. Maddie tilted the phone again for better shade, and she saw a hoary face strangely like Neva's young and very beautiful one, but wrinkled and weathered. It was a face, she thought, that appeared to have seen a thousand sorrows in as many years, and yet still knew joy. Right now, it showed joy.

'This grumpy old Indian,' Neva announced, 'is my father who prefers not to have his picture taken, for fear the camera might steal a piece of his soul. It is an old and intermittent superstition of his people; but though he always says he doesn't believe it, Miss Madeline, he adds that you cannot be too careful. As it is to say hello to you, he has agreed to take the risk. This is an honour, really, but you have earned his respect already, and that is not easy to do.'

Maddie smiled, and noticed that Neva also laughed. Now she held them both tightly to her fragile body, and Maddie thought again how much strength there was in those meagre pounds of humanity.

'This is my family,' Neva said. 'And we all have made promises. I know you will be true to yours. I wanted to remind you,' Neva added softly, 'that I will certainly keep mine too.'

She pulled at her family, and they all waved and shouted their farewells; then the frame went to black.

Maddie closed her eyes for a moment. The two realities crossed: the lovely pattern of the ancient brickwork of the *osteria*, the overhanging geraniums from the window above, the antique lanterns attached to the wall by showy iron brackets, the sunshine streaming into filtered shade outside the restaurant. The power and majesty of the buildings surrounding her stood for longevity, grace, survival. And then there was Neva, near her cypress tree, confined to a bed thousands of miles away. Life didn't seem fair. All Maddie could do was to marvel at Neva's own grace and calm under duress, which she did deeply. Then, Maddie opened her eyes again and drank in the loveliness of her immediate setting. A cool breeze found her forehead, like a kiss in the heat, which had seemed dry and rather still today even though the outside tables were in partial shade. Maddie shivered – not from being cold, but as though a nerve had been touched.

'Someone walk on your grave?' Søren's rather musical voice came from behind her.

'*Certo*,' came her reply. It was a light response to a possibly conventional remark, but she felt he was closer to the truth than that. She altered her expression to a welcome. 'How was your morning?'

Maddie noticed he was carrying a very large scroll, which looked like a picture wrapped in brown paper with a rubber band around it. He dropped his saddle bag into a spare chair, rested the scroll on top of it, then peeked inside the restaurant enthusiastically. In a moment he seated himself opposite her, and seemed in excellent spirits.

'Great choice,' he said. 'It looks as though this was a chemist's shop in some previous century. Wonderful cabinets.'

But before he could answer her about his morning the waiter arrived with Maddie's wine and a bottle of water, and looked at Søren for his drinks order.

'*Signor?*'

'*Lo stesso, per favore,*' he answered. '*Vino bianco – ma non troppo. Sono la guida.*'

Maddie was pleased with this. Whether people drank and then got behind the wheel of a car had achieved enormous importance for her since January. She raised a slow smile and leaned her head, waiting for him to tell her why he was in such an obviously happy mood. He understood, and tapped the scroll.

'What is that?' Maddie asked with some curiosity.

'Wait. You'll see. Should we order some food first? This may commandeer quite a lot of our lunch.'

Maddie nodded. She passed him one of the handwritten menus in front of her, which she'd barely glanced at. 'Let's give our attention to this for a moment. Everything here is supposed to be out of this world, especially the seafood.'

When the waiter returned with Søren's drink he paused to give them the specials. He recommended '*branzino marinato alle pesche*' for the *signorina*, and 'sea bass with peaches' – the same dish delivered in English – for the signore. This brought smiles from both parties, and Søren – well aware of the compliment being paid to Maddie – happily consented to the choice. He ventured in Italian about side dishes, however, and a feast including *fagioli bianchi* – Maddie's beloved white beans – and a salad of pear and pecorino cheese for starters, was settled on.

'*Salute,*' Maddie said to him as the waiter left. She raised her wine glass.

Søren replied in kind. 'I doubt you could have found a lovelier setting,' he added.

'*Dimmi,*' she said grinning. She pointed at the roll.

'Brilliant morning at the university,' he began. 'Wonderful people

213

gave me an amazing tour of the Botanical Gardens. When I finished with the research fellow there he made a phone call and sent me to someone at the Pinacoteca Nazionale. She was a fascinating elderly lady, immaculately groomed and not at all academic, an archivist for the medieval collections.'

'She sounds like my grandmother,' Maddie said. 'So, did she give you this?'

Søren put both hands up gently. 'Cart before horse,' he laughed, and resumed in his own way. 'She was very interested in what I asked her. We talked about Borgo Santo Pietro, and the abbey of San Galgano. She nodded the whole time, as though there was nothing more I needed to tell her. She took me to a vault full of boxes of recorded material from the abbey – a wealth of unexplored treasures. She found me gloves and a coffee, and left me. Within a quarter of an hour I had something intriguing.'

'Wait,' Maddie interrupted him. 'The papers from the abbey are here?'

Søren nodded. 'Under the section for the See of Siena; although, originally, the abbey was in the Diocese of Volterra. There are hundreds of documents that haven't been catalogued into the main collection. Money and manpower is the problem, which is exciting for the local Ph.D. students.

'But,' he continued after refilling their water glasses, 'my helpful *signora* told me a riveting story about bands of armed brigands who pillaged the countryside around Siena during the last half of the *Trecento*, for many years. Because of them, church records and some valuables were brought into the towns for safety. She believed the abbey was sacked and the farms and houses looted around this time, and according to her version, the abbey never recovered from what they did to it.'

'That's why it's roofless to this day?' Maddie asked.

Søren gave her a sad smile. 'She believes so. And of course, Jeanette and Claus's villa was a near neighbour, so they must have suffered too. Anyhow,' he picked up the scroll and slipped off the rubber band, 'look what I found!'

Søren now invited Maddie to take one side of the document while he unrolled it. She suddenly saw before them a facsimile reproduction of what looked like a page from an illuminated manuscript, but it was a single sheet of surprising size.

'Oh!' she said, sounding almost English with the syllable. She was holding one side of an exquisite medieval rendering of a garden, in the style of a monastic illumination.

There was an overarching golden dome that immediately seized the eye, the heavens below starred in gold and faïence blue. Along one side of the picture there was a rendering of a bright golden sun detailed in what might have been gold leaf on the original; and on the opposite side was a silver-leaf moon. The former had the face of a young man and the latter a young woman, both set within the gilded forms.

Maddie exhaled, unable to speak. It was beautiful, and seemed deeply personal. Her eyes slowly scanned the details of sixteen Roman-numbered sections of the minutely chronicled plantings in the garden itself. In one area there were trees and rills; in another, planted sections rediated around what looked like a flourishing mulberry tree with a pair of doves, or possibly lovebirds, in its branches. Near this, in a kind of neighbouring orchard, Maddie studied groves of trees depicted with differing fruits and shapes, growing alongside a curling path of travertine; and at the foot of one these – a tree bearing small red fruits like apples – she noticed a reclining unicorn.

'Do you think it was a Madonna's garden?' she asked Søren without lifting her eyes from the sheet.

'I thought so,' he answered her. 'But when I looked again, I noticed other details that make me wonder. There are astrological signs on the plan, but I know the monks used lunar planting for their gardens, so maybe that's no surprise.'

Maddie looked closely in the area where Søren pointed; she found it overawing to consider she was looking at miniatures of the faces of people who must actually have been alive five or six hundred years ago. The sky around the sun was graded from brilliant white through azure to a midnight blue around the moon, giving an effect of the passage from day to night, and in between the night and day skies, in the twilight area of dusk, there were seven stars with planetary symbols inscribed below them.

'I think they may be the Pleiades,' Maddie told Søren thoughtfully.

He smiled slowly, and agreed. 'The hen and chicks,' he said. 'That's what we call them in Scandinavia. But my favourite is this portrait of the face of the wind puffing out her cheeks, surrounded with her curls of hair.' His finger skipped again. 'This is not the usual depiction of wind, which is masculine. It has the fresh face of a young girl with her hair streaming out. It's more of a cool breeze in a tranquil garden, just enough for pollination by wind.'

Maddie looked carefully and saw what delighted him. It did seem different, and she felt that this wind seemed happy presiding over the garden in place of compass points, or even the face of God.

'It's astonishing,' she said quietly. 'Is it the garden from the abbey?'

'Our *signora* feels it may be one illumination in a lost series of the gardens of San Galgano. She says the colours are typical for work of the thirteenth or early fourteenth century, and that they may have come here while the abbey was under threat in the thirteen sixties or 'seventies. But,' he said, shaking his head a little, 'while I think the workmanship is very good, it's a little immature. It might have been done by a novice – perhaps an exercise before he was allowed to work on one of the Holy Books. And,' he added with an expression of secrecy, 'I can't help but feel that there's just an element of something pagan about it. Maybe he was a doubting novice!'

Maddie laughed. 'Why not?' she said. 'Surely not everyone who joined holy orders was a hundred per cent willing. And yes, I agree, the sun and moon have an aura about them.'

'A perfect starting point for Jeanette's garden of a little bit of alchemy,' Søren said.

The starters arrived, and Søren carefully rolled up the illumination. As Maddie picked up her fork the breeze moved her hair, and he looked at her closely.

'Just now, you look like the figure of the wind.'

Maddie tossed her mane of black curls back off her shoulder. 'Because of this?' she asked. 'It was the bane of my life when I was growing up. Can you imagine the problems I had in a world of *Baywatch* blondes? And who was I to be strong enough to be different? My sister's hair is straight and beautifully cut around her petite, lovely face. Why was I the black sheep? Sure, when I came to Europe some people started to see me in another light, and I suppose now I quite like my hair. But I still feel it's a mess most of the time, and I'll never be immaculately groomed like my grandmother or your *signora* this morning.'

Søren reached out tentatively and touched her hair. 'Your hair is fabulous. Why would you want to look like a grandmother?'

She smiled self-consciously. She could remember a similar conversation with Christopher once. 'OK,' she answered him, teasing, 'so my hair's great. But I can find too much at fault with the rest of me!'

Søren laughed aloud. 'Are you fishing for my own appraisal?' He looked at her as if sizing up a painting.

'I'm not sure,' she replied. 'The pear and pecorino are good. Shall we stay safe and talk about the food?'

'Not now! You've invited me to enjoy the pleasure of looking carefully at you.'

He kept to himself that he would happily have given her the highest marks for her figure, her light olive skin and her nicely toned legs. But her head and shoulders were captivating, and he paused for a moment, considering what to say. He sensed that she wasn't at ease with compliments.

'I think you'd be appreciated by anyone, Maddie. There's nothing at all wrong with the rest of you. Your eyes … well, they don't belong to any lady I've ever seen. Not in our own time, anyway. And you're right about the pear and pecorino,' he added.

Maddie looked at him and saw that, though he looked serious, his eyes were smiling. 'What do you mean?' she asked, her curiosity piqued. What he'd said was caught up for her with her feelings about this place. She felt as though she belonged to it in a way she'd never belonged in New York or San Francisco, as much as she loved both.

'Your eyes are close to those spirits you wanted to slip in amongst this morning,' he said to her. 'They're a quite remarkable shape. Reversed almonds, more like a Persian goddess than an Italian or American beauty. But then, the art from Siena was very strongly influenced by the Byzantine – much more than Florence's art was. You fit in right here,' he said to her.

'Reversed almonds?' Maddie asked. She might have sounded flirtatious to anyone else, but she trusted that somehow Søren – whose life was art – recognised something about her that she couldn't quite get hold of herself, something that had become important to her now.

He rested the cutlery on the plate and unbuckled his saddle bag. 'I'll show you what I mean,' he said.

He placed a few items from the top of the bag, including a phone and a digital camera wrapped in chamois leather, on to the table. A small worn book emerged and caught Maddie's eye. She picked it up and saw it was an old hardcover volume of Keats, which made her smile for reasons she couldn't decide on. She asked him nothing about it, though, and waited until he finally produced a draughtsman's pen and a little sketchbook filled with drawings. He turned quickly and precisely to an empty page, opposite a detail Maddie observed of Vincent's face and the flowers and stone work on the terrace at Borgo. She was pleased by the quickly and effectively executed little line drawings.

Søren now finished his pear salad, tidied his knife and fork and wiped his hands. He placed the sketchbook between them and, with his left hand, drew a pair of almond-shaped eyes under sensuous lids in a face that reminded Maddie at once of a Leonardo or a Raphael drawing. It was reminiscent in spirit of a framed copy of one such – a study for an annunciation – which she had in her apartment.

'These are Florentine eyes,' he said. 'Wonderful – they look something like this.' He quickly sketched in the hair and the features of a female face that wasn't far from Maddie's. She laughed. But then he did another sketch, revising the first, and this time he made the wider part of the eye on the outside of the face so that the almond narrowed nearer the bridge of the nose. 'You see,' he smiled humorously. 'This is your face – full of intelligence and sensitivity, with eyes that have watched the world closely for a millennium or two. The effect is very unusual; and the life of the sitter will never be ordinary.'

The waiter came to clear the plates with the word, '*Buono?*'

As they nodded their enjoyment of the dish, he leaned across to look at Søren's hasty handiwork. He glanced from the sketch to Maddie, and back again. '*Si, è veramente la bella signorina,*' he said, smiling at Maddie. '*Bella come la Madonna,*' he added, and took the empty starter plates away.

'*Come il vento,*' Søren said. 'Like the wind.'

26

All Saints' Day 1347, Santo Pietro in Cellole

In the second chamber of the stable-yard guest rooms Porphyrius slept deeply. It had already been laid with linens for temporary accommodation and here, in the narrow space beside him, his wife was curled up too. Despite all the precautions of quarantine she would not be separated from him. What was the point, she argued, when she had already been closely exposed to the fever anyhow? But it seemed best, everyone agreed, that her husband should be quartered here for the present until they could decide if he might be past all danger of the illness.

Mia – who realised she was also now at risk – remained behind as well. She checked on the sleeping couple, added fresh brands to the fire and pulled the quilt over them both. At least she had prevailed in keeping her friend from Gennaro's bedside. As soon as he had fallen into a deep sleep, she had insisted on sitting with him herself. With only weeks to go to the birth of her child, Agnesca Toscano needed proper rest and calm – not that she'd get much of either on the slim bed beside her husband – but at least Mia would fill in as Gennaro's nurse. She had instructions and knew what to look for, and her thrill at learning of a new relative outweighed her fear of his sickness. She had been appalled by the malefic appearance of the swellings, especially in light of what she had heard of them; but she was able to look past the physical and be deeply touched by Porphyrius' friendship with him, and their loyalty to one another. She was restless to find herself suddenly so close to a relative, someone she had never met nor heard her aunt speak of. This had opened a door,

219

and Mia would wait for the moment when there was an opportunity for Aunt Jacquetta to explain more about her father and her mother, along with other family who must still be in Volterra. She would finally learn the circumstances of her birth. From tonight's disclosures, she at last understood that she was the exiled bishop's daughter after all. From the whisperings of servants she had imagined as much for many years; but Porphyrius had brought everyone's guesses into the open and soon she would know the truth. She didn't feel shame about it now, and believed she was ready to confront the past and the reason for her being named after the church's most famous penitent.

In this immediate moment, however, in the quiet slow hours before dawn, she wanted to give her whole attention to nursing her cousin. She was not prepared to find him after all these years, only to lose him on the same night. In both the old calendar of the Romans and that of the Mother Church this was a holy day, a magical day when the saints and the angels watched the living and the dead. She would give every ounce of her faith and her energy to keep Gennaro Allegretti firmly on this side of the line, with the living. She heard the wind at the shuttered window and icy rain borne on it, pattering against the roof, testing their shelter in the summer garden rooms. But she felt calm sitting by him, watching him. Her private thoughts were excellent company.

An hour ago he'd broken into a sweat again, thrown off his covers and sat up to vomit the negligible contents of his stomach. Only bile came out, and Mia soothed him back onto the pillow with a cloth of cold water on his face and a cooking spoon full of willow tea. He'd struggled a little, but she'd beaten his resistance. Now he dozed again, and she sat at his head and watched him. Oddly, she wasn't tired. How could she sleep with so many ideas racing in her head? He was a few years older than she, with brown-gold hair quite unlike the colour of hers, but curls resembling her own. He was handsome, she thought, though he was pallid and sweaty and dishevelled with the illness. He was her family, though, and a loyal friend to Porphyrius who described him as gentle and intelligent – 'a man entirely without rancour'. Mia thought it remarkable that he was here with her now, under her care. Like *la raggia* and Porphyrius, he had come unknowing to their door. She didn't doubt he would soon belong there, but the first step was to keep him breathing, and Mia understood the gravity of his illness. She would take each hour and fight for that; if he was well enough at dawn, that would be the time to think of the hours till noon.

But at dawn he was not so well. His body went into a kind of spasm, and jerked violently. The fever returned with added virility and he vomited again. In her chair Mia roused herself from the lightest of sleep and moved quickly to the pail of water, taking up cloths to begin again the round of sponging him down and then trying to get the tisane of willow bark and feverfew into his stomach. She peeled back the covers and started on his chest, but as she got closer to his neck she saw that the swellings had changed their appearance. The largest of them had grown again in size and was itself sweating. She checked under his arm: there, the bubo had grown to the size of a crab apple, and it too was redder in colour and sweating noticeably. She put her hand to his brow and withdrew it immediately. His skin was scorching.

Mia thought of the young man who had died under her aunt's care with the fever claiming him. She ran to the sleeping pair in the next room and reluctantly woke them.

'The fever is very much worse,' she whispered. 'I don't know how to break it. Even the swellings have a fever of their own, and I think we may lose him.'

Agnesca was quickly on her feet, and Porphyrius awoke from her movement. Both followed Mia back to the sick man and found him tossing and writhing on the bed in obvious pain.

'Mia, you'll be faster than me,' Agnesca said to her. 'Can you run to the house and ask your aunt – or Alba, if she's awake – for the animal skin she uses to wrap around new lambs when they lose their mother?'

Mia couldn't make the leap to understand what she was thinking, but she slipped through the door and out into the cold grey light. It was some time before she reappeared with Jacquetta and the enormous tanned hide from a Chianina bull.

'You're going to use it to wrap him in cool water,' Jacquetta said in a voice husky from lack of sleep. 'But, wouldn't it be easier to get him into the tub?'

'I'm not sure he could sit up safely in it; and I'd prefer to lay him down fully,' Agnesca answered. 'I thought we could stretch the skin over a frame and then fill it with cold water, so that he's quite submerged.'

'Agnesca!' Jacquetta said with gravity. 'The shock may stop his heart.'

'It may,' Agnesca answered. 'But if we don't try, the fever will kill him first.'

She pulled a shawl around her shoulders and left the warmth of the stable rooms for the chill morning. Mia stayed with her patient and began swabbing him again, rather ineffectively, with the wet linens. Porphyrius and Jacquetta meanwhile stretched the skin across a frame hastily made from split logs and iron posts brought to the threshold by Cesaré. These were left over from harvest, but what had only been asked to bear the weight of the olives was now required to support a man in a pool of cold water. Nevertheless, in a half-hour they had constructed something solid enough, and water was brought across from the house in deep barrels placed by the stable doors.

Agnesca returned from the garden. She was carrying a stalk and root of Jacquetta's favourite plant – that with the nodding bells of perfect white colour, and a delicious fragrance that legend told had lured the nightingale from the hedges into the shadiest woods to find her mate. It had so many names, one of which was 'common lily' and another 'valley flowers'; but Jacquetta preferred 'Our Lady's tears' because this beautiful plant was the jewel of every Mary-garden.

Jacquetta put a hand in to test the water, and shuddered. Nevertheless Porphyrius lifted his friend, stripped to his bare skin, into the bath. But the water was truly freezing, and he convulsed as soon as his body touched the surface. He flinched and trembled and flailed, sending water cascading over the side and almost drowning Porphyrius; but Porphyrius somehow held on to his friend and kept him in the chilly water in spite of every ounce of his friend's strength being set against him. Poor Gennaro shook unremittingly, and was sick to his stomach again and again, producing little more than a dry retch. Eventually his strength seemed sapped, and he fell back into the bath exhausted.

After perhaps twenty or thirty minutes of one of the most distressing treatments Mia had ever watched, Agnesca brought thick linen to wrap and dry him in, and he was laid back upon the bed. But Jacquetta's warning struck Mia now. He looked deathly pale, and she couldn't prevent her quiet tears from streaming down her face.

Agnesca crossed into the joining room, returning with bread from last night's supper table. She tore a piece off, and into this she put a tiny sliver of the plant stalk and some of the crushed root. Talking to him as though to a child, she cradled the man's head and opened his mouth, feeding him a little of the bread and herb, massaging his jaw and throat, encouraging him to chew. It seemed hardly enough to keep a bird from starving; and he was almost unaware. But a minute later she was satisfied that something had gone down.

'When the face is pale, raise the tail,' she spoke almost to herself. She placed a bolster under Gennaro's feet, then consulted the anxious faces of the others. 'It's very hard on the heart,' she agreed, 'but the fever will break, I believe; and we must hope that Gennaro and the valley flowers can do the rest.'

Mia looked dolefully at her friend. They had planted the lily flowers between lady's lace and Solomon's seal in their white garden. *La raggia* had told her that the three together – watched over by a pair of doves they'd housed in the small dovecote next to the mulberry – would bring love into Mia's life. Right now, though, Mia decided she would happily abandon any thought of finding a sweetheart if only her cousin would live.

Gennaro – wherever he may have been inside his head – could never know how closely he was watched by four good souls. An hour later he still hadn't moved, but Agnesca checked his chest and felt his heart still beating, his breath still coming softly through slightly parted teeth. Jacquetta, having carefully maintained a little distance from their intern, came and went. She brought some breakfast back with her for all of them, and they ate without much appetite, and watched. Another hour passed and Agnesca felt she could say that the fever might have gone. Then, close to noon, Gennaro woke. He was very far from well, but he was alive.

Agnesca and Mia studied him carefully. He still seemed dazed, yet his eyes focused and he was aware of his discomforts, the wish for warmth from the cover, the dry mouth that made him look for water, the groaning at the pit of his stomach from a lack of food, the pain in his joints that made him look so miserable. He was weak, yet he managed to communicate these things; and a light broth was prepared for him in the next room, with just a few spoonfuls meeting his wants. Then he fell back exhausted again.

Porphyrius sat by him while Mia slept and his wife made notes about what was happening to him, and what she had tried. When he stirred she spooned a little liquid down his throat, then watched him sink again into a sleep that might have been mistaken by a careless nurse for death.

While his breath during the highest point of the fever had been rasping and laboured, it was now barely perceptible. This, she believed, was owing to the medicine of the plant. It was the first time she had dared to use it, for its actions were reputed to be strong, but she'd been taught by Donna Calogera that the little white bell flowers and stalk of the plant slowed down the disturbed action of a man's heart when it was weak, at the same time strengthening the heart's power. It was irritating to the stomach, so taking on some food was vital. But she hoped she had met this need, and waited to see if she had dosed him highly enough to bring him through the fever bath. Time would tell.

For many hours, Gennaro slept. His row of doctors stayed close to him, but there was no change. In the late afternoon Porphyrius sat at the refectory table to write a letter to his family – then hesitated, not yet knowing what to report. At six, Alba knocked and told them she was leaving something at the door for them all to eat. At eight they heard the bells from the abbey drifting across the fields, marking another office for All Saints' Day; and a little later, when Jacquetta joined them, they talked about Gennaro and the ill luck that had followed the Allegretti family since the Belforti had sent them into exile from Volterra.

Mia listened quietly while they discussed the feud that had divided Volterra and much of Tuscany – the complex relations between the Guelphs and Ghibellines. For more than forty years the Pope had been in exile in Avignon; and his supporters – the Guelphs, who had been dominant in Volterra since Mia's grandmother's time, and supplied the city with a bishop of their party – had lost sway twenty-some years before when the Pope's appointed man went into open feud with the *comune*, the government of the people and city elders. The fierce rivalry between two of the most powerful families had erupted when an Allegretti bishop had replaced the Belforti candidate; but this had been reversed again when Mia was a child living with her mother. The Allegretti, Mia learned, had owned some of the most prestigious property in the city, including the wonderful palace and tower that fronted onto the main public piazza. But this was seized from them by Ottaviano Belforte when he drove Bishop Ranuccio from his office, and the Allegretti from the town.

'I don't understand how he was able to do that,' Mia said hesitantly. She looked to her aunt for explanation, but was secretly hoping this might also encourage her to talk about Mia's mother and her relationship with the bishop. However, it was Porphyrius who answered her.

'Ottaviano Belforte waited his time,' he said quietly. 'If ever a man wanted a signoria – to be lord of the city – Ottaviano was that man. His sister had married into the Allegretti in an effort to make peace between them, but Guelph and Ghibelline politics can't be so easily mollified, and he came to hate them all the more as their star rose and the Belforti waned. His brother had been bishop, Mia, as perhaps you know – and he was a bad one at that, a man who tried to make deals with other cities by selling off Volterra's assets in an effort to hold onto his own power. He was denied the income that came to the bishop through the privileges from the Emperor, so he tried to take back the episcopal castles and other landholdings that had come to the *comune* in the intervening years. His only hope of succeeding was with the aid of Florence, which was Guelph; but the townspeople were furious and deposed Ottaviano's brother, then insulted the man still further when his nephew was confirmed as the new bishop.'

'His nephew?' she asked.

'Ranuccio's mother was that same sister of Ottaviano,' Porphyrius answered. 'And, as uncle to the new bishop appointed at his brother's demise, Ottaviano's jealousy knew no bounds. He privately plotted revenge on Gennaro's family for twenty long years, and lusted for the lifestyle of a prince himself. It was he who eventually persuaded the people against Ranuccio, promising them freedom from the power of the bishops once and for all. But he gave them instead a tyrant – for that is what he has been – and he has effectively curtailed the voices of the populace these seven years past.'

'Oh, and he had the power, Mia,' Agnesca added, looking at her with something like private pain in her eyes. 'The skill of his own company of crossbowmen was famed throughout Tuscany for their prowess in tournaments. Volterra's citizens knew he had won every June competition on the meadows in front of the church of San Giusto. He had very little trouble in seizing power in the town.'

'His son, Paolo,' Jacquetta smiled wryly, 'was married to a noble lady – way above the Belforti in status – a few years ago. She was a member of the Aldobrandeschi family from Santa Fiora; and he was so delighted by his triumph in securing such a wife for his son, that he held a banquet to trumpet the occasion to the four winds. For fifteen days feasting took place in the Piazza dei Priori, and the ambassadors of Florence and Pisa, and Siena and Lucca, were in attendance. But this was not enough for Ottaviano; so he brought also all the premier lords of Lombardy, and the Visconti of Milan, and the sons of Mastino della Scala. Yet the occasion ended on a sour note when his sons quarrelled. One of them speaks hardly at all to his father or to his brothers now.'

'But the son with the glittering marriage is being groomed by his father to follow him as lord of Volterra, when the time comes,' Porphyrius said. 'If it is possible to imagine, the temper of the son is more implacable than that of the father, and his reckoning not as nimble. There will be trouble for the town when Paolo is in charge. He is known as "Bocchino" – the little mouthpiece – for he is only a conduit for his father's words and ambitions.'

'What happened to Bishop Ranuccio?'

Mia had a little courage, and wanted an answer to this pressing question, which had occupied her mind for some time. Around her neck she had worn – perhaps since she was six or seven, and her mother had died – a golden coin. It was minted by the Volterran government with Ranuccio's face struck on it. It was not uncommon for citizens to wear money in this way on a chain, as much for practicality as for prosperity. But Mia wore hers out of feeling for the man she had called her 'patron' or 'guardian', and who she could now feel even more strongly about as her father.

'Where is he now, if not in Volterra?' she asked again.

'He was in Berignone with his family,' Porphyrius told her. 'But Ottaviano laid siege to the castle for weeks when Gennaro was twelve or thirteen years old; and they suffered terribly. Ottaviano couldn't quite manage to kill Bishop Ranuccio, but he banished him from Volterra and then excommunicated him – using his son, Filippo, as bishop-appointee, to pronounce judgement.'

His wife looked up suddenly. 'And it was the same father who imprisoned me in the tower, the same son who passed sentence of heresy upon me,' she almost whispered.

Imprisoned, Mia thought, and looked over at her friend. She'd never heard that before, and knew only of *la raggia* being held in her family home. Did she mean she had also been held in the prison tower in the city itself? But after a moment, when no more was said and nothing asked on this score, Mia left it and pursued a different question.

'They've all been living at the castle of Berignone, then, the Allegretti family?' she asked him.

Jacquetta looked at Mia and smiled ruefully, knowing why this was so important to her. But she wasn't ready to tell a whole story yet, or here.

'The Pope eventually made Ottaviano rescind the exile, Mia,' she answered her niece before Porphyrius could do so. 'The others returned to live in diminished circumstances in Volterra three or four years ago, I believe. But the bishop didn't want to move back to the city. For the sake of security I have never spoken of his whereabouts to a soul, yet I have every trust in all of you here; so I will tell you that he is in Montalcino for now.'

Mia smiled at her in amazement. Montalcino was not so far from Santo Pietro in Cellole – indeed, it was on the Via Romea-Francigena. Her lips shaped to ask another question, but her aunt shook her head.

'That is all I will say about this tonight.' She looked at Mia firmly, and pointedly changed the subject. 'Will you look to Gennaro, and see if he is resting peacefully?'

Mia wanted much more; but she realised that her aunt was fixed on this decision for the present, and also that they hadn't checked her cousin for some time, having disappeared into a conversation that completely absorbed Mia. She nodded dutifully and got to her feet, Agnesca rising with her, and the two of them entered the adjoining chamber where Gennaro lay sleeping.

What Mia saw made her cry out involuntarily, and brought the other two from the kitchen area.

Set within his pale face, Gennaro's eyes were rimmed black and looked bruised; but the fearful sight was at his throat. The smaller lumps had swollen to the size of lemons; and the bigger one, which had earlier started to suppurate, had burst. The smell was absolutely appalling, and Mia put her hand up to cover her mouth and nose. From the enormous blister dark blood had oozed out – black, in colour – and Mia could see that a greenish froth, like spittle, was also visible in it.

Agnesca checked herself, almost prompted to vomit because of the putrid odour, but she also put her hand over her mouth and then gently lifted his arm, where the other large swelling had nestled. Sure enough, it too had burst and spewed out the same viscous horror of black blood and green pus. She had no idea what to do to treat this, but felt that it was better to do the wrong thing, than to sit idle and offer nothing.

Jacquetta was still keeping a distance from Gennaro to allow her to come and go, she hoped, in adequate safety between the villa and the stable apartments. But the smell affected her too, and she looked at Agnesca with urgency.

'I know nothing of blood-letting, or the balance of the humours,' Agnesca said, answering the look. 'I am only an empiric, and go by what has worked previously. But this is foreign to me, and I cannot guess what my governess would have done for this poor man.'

Jacquetta nodded sympathetically. She'd never seen anything like this either, and it was clear that blood-letting would be unnecessary as the illness was already effecting this step. But, she wondered, what would she do to dress topically such an ugly wound? She had only seen something so raw, so foul, on an infected gash her mare suffered after being gored by a boar last winter. That she had dressed with honey, straight from the hive …

'Honey!' she spoke aloud to Agnesca. 'It is new, untouched by anyone yet, harvested from the apiary only a week or so ago.'

Agnesca looked at her gratefully. 'Excellent. Yes. Let's apply it on a poultice of very clean winding linen; but, Jacquetta, I think we might use soft leather gloves to handle him?'

Jacquetta understood, and agreed. She disappeared from the chamber to bring what was needed from the house, and was back in so little time that Mia knew she must have run. She also carried a pair of silver pomanders, which Mia's nose instantly recognised: these were her aunt's favourites, kept for her private bedchamber. They were filled with autumn harvested pomegranate and exotic peppercorns, ground orris root, and shavings of frankincense and cedar wood. The smell was a welcome relief to the pungent odour in the room.

Jacquetta gave Agnesca one pair of the delicate leather gloves she had brought, and started to put on the other pair. Mia, however, stopped her.

'We need you as go-between,' she said sensibly. 'I am not afraid of the office.'

Jacquetta handed her niece the gloves. It was brave, but it was also both selfless and mature, and she was proud of Mia.

On these two open wounds Agnesca used no water, instead applying a poultice saturated in the honey directly onto the sores. The honey smelled strongly herbal, from the rosemary and lavender that was planted near the beehives; and she hoped, prayed, trusted that this might be enough to start some kind of cure and stop the bleeding. Gennaro winced pathetically each time he was touched, and drew his head away from the candlelight that the two women had brought over to see what they were doing. The light was clearly hurting him, and his limbs had become so painful that he seemed tortured if moved at all. But he succumbed, and in an hour they had dressed not only the open sores, but also the unbroken lumps. These had grown to such a size that Agnesca thought they must soon burst also.

When this was done Gennaro took down a little more herbal tincture, in a desperate bid to keep his fever at bay; then, he was allowed to sleep – which he now seemed to want to do more than anything else.

'Please, nothing more,' Agnesca whispered. Then she snuffed all but one of the candles and sat with the others to watch their patient into the midnight hours.

27

orning sunshine washed the fourteenth-century statues of two saints – a lady and a man. They overlooked the freshly dug grave from their post on the garden wall, slanting long shadows across the area. Four figures stood motionless in silent thought, their own shadows following those of the saints. After a moment each took a handful of rose petals from a basket held by a young boy and sprinkled some into the open grave; and with these last rites finished and their respects paid, the five turned away in quietude. A pair of workmen began to back-fill the soil, replacing the turf. It must have echoed a scene in this same place, some centuries before.

After the National Archaeological Department had dated the bones and conveyed the message that 'the remains found in the garden at Borgo Santo Pietro are of no interest to us', they had unceremoniously returned them to the villa in a recycled cardboard box. Jeannette was slightly bemused, but felt it was proper that the bones should be reinterred with some solemnity. After twenty-four hours in a state of gentle sanctuary – during which they had lain in state in the old bakehouse with only votives and roses for company – they had been taken back to their sleeping place of so many years. The graves had been dug and the skeletons positioned as near as possible to the way they had been found. The first pair lay with their hands almost touching in a single plot, and close to this the third woman was placed, but without the crossbow bolt.

Jeanette had suggested she might rest without further pain if it were taken away from her.

The five mourners included Claus, as he had returned from London late the night before and had asked to be present, and Vincent, who seemed to understand the dignity of the occasion surprisingly well. And when all five walked slowly back towards the main house, Jeanette poured out glasses of local wine to mark the occasion and drink a toast to the departed, and gave Vincent some juice.

'Thank you for being here,' she said. 'I believe the bones can rest well again now. One of the statues watching over them is St Peter, and that seems appropriate.'

Søren suddenly tilted his head, and looked at Jeanette. 'I didn't think of it till now, but the dedication to Santo Pietro here may have some association with sacred rock. That's interesting, with the famous sword in the stone just a little further around the river bend.'

Jeanette grinned. 'The house was built on rock. Maybe there's something special about the properties of the stone.'

She turned to Maddie, whose thoughts she knew were still at the graveside. Jeanette had noticed that Maddie seemed to find the occasion very moving. Perhaps, she pondered, it was strangely personal for her. She considered Maddie might have spent months thinking about death, because of her fiancé.

'Who do you think these three women were?' she quizzed Maddie. 'Has your research turned up anything definite about the people who lived here?'

Jeanette had set Maddie the challenge of researching the two coins that were found with the bones. Though at first glance they'd all assumed the pendants must be some kind of pilgrims' medals, they had discovered on closer inspection that regular, minted coins were in fact suspended from the chains found with the pair who were lying together. Each woman had obviously worn it at burial, but the chains supported two different coins. One had a seated figure on it, with an inscription, and was in fairly good condition. The other – which Maddie had originally felt would be similar, though more worn, and silver rather than gold – turned out, to her surprise, to be much older, and quite at odds with a medieval burial.

With the aid of a magnifying glass from Søren's portable 'office' in the saddle bag, she'd examined this older coin closely. A light and careful clean showed it had a double-headed man on it, each of his faces gazing in opposite directions. This almost stopped Maddie in her tracks. Surely it was Janus; and was it the twin of the coin sent to her by Pierce when she'd arrived? When she compared them side by side, she realised she was absolutely right. It struck her immediately that, whether she liked it or not, Pierce Gray was oddly linked to them all here, and it amazed as much as unnerved her.

Maddie's own double-headed Janus coin had a provenance that placed it as minted in Volterra. She assumed, but couldn't be certain, that it's 'twin' might also be from there. This seemed confirmed when the second coin was researched – which she did by aid of the internet and, not getting very far that way, with another phone call to a museum in Siena. As for the third coin in gold, with the robed, seated figure engraved on it, Maddie spent hours scrutinising an inscription and eventually persuaded herself that it might have said *Allegretti, Vescovo Volaterra* on it. If this were right, each of the coins led her to one place.

Here was a city she'd felt no interest in – no personal connection with. It was not as famed as Florence or Siena; not as personal to her family history as Lucca. But the women in the grave had suddenly become personal to her, and she felt a restless urge to find out who these people were, and what tied them to this imposing medieval walled city. For two days she lost herself on the terrace and read every guidebook to Tuscany Jeanette possessed, even making Søren interrupt his garden drawings to translate a few pages for her that were in some older Danish travel literature of Claus's. When she'd exhausted this stream of information she sorted through all kinds of entries on Volterra from the internet: some from reliable academics, a little from the tourist information office, still more from myths and travellers' blogs, and probably some uninformed opinions as well.

She became fascinated, however, and shared what she'd learned with Søren while he marked out planting areas in the garden plots. The oldest gates to the city, she told him, were Etruscan, which she knew would interest him. The Porta all'Arco was the most ancient and famous city gate, built several hundred years before the time of Christ with three weighty stone heads gazing down from it to the passer beneath. The features of each head were worn and now unidentifiable, and there was a controversy as to what was carved there: were they traitors' heads, to serve as a warning? Or the city's gods? No matter how badly weathered it might be, Maddie conjectured that one of the heads must surely belong to Janus. The Romans had borrowed him from the Etruscan god Ani, and with his two faces he was the first god, Ianus, god of the skies, of beginnings and endings, of the past and the future; Ianus even embraced Iana, and was both male and female. Two-faced Janus was master of all gates and doorways; and he gave his name to the month of January, gateway to the year.

Further reading finally dug up the name of a bishop from the fourteenth century called 'Allegretti', and Maddie felt she'd found the probable candidate for the head on the coin. His dates accorded well enough with the bone dating, and placed the people in the grave somewhere around the middle of that century.

All of this Maddie imparted with great enthusiasm to the group after the burial ceremony, over breakfast in the rose garden. Jeanette hardly seemed surprised and informed her that the house had been at one time under the control of the Bishops of Volterra – she hadn't thought to mention it before.

'It came to the diocese of Siena only around fourteen hundred, I think,' she said happily as she cut up an orange for Vincent.

Maddie looked at her astonished, and feeling a little silly. She wondered why she hadn't simply asked her hostess about links between the house and Volterra, instead of spending so much time lost in research to find out.

'Well,' she laughed almost at herself, 'it's made me very determined to visit Volterra before I leave you – even if that means I can't get up to Lucca.'

'You could use my car,' Claus suggested to her; 'but I have a meeting with the bank in Siena later today, and with the mayor's office in Chiusdino in about half an hour. Maybe Sunday. Or Jeanette could drive you early next week?' And with that, he smiled at Maddie and excused himself from the group.

Søren seemed lost in thought, and picked up his saddle bag to walk in the same direction as Claus. 'What a pity for us all not to go. But, take the Mini, if you'd like to. I don't need it today.' Then he turned to Jeanette. 'I've got an hour's work to do, and if you're free after that maybe you could find me in the garden so we can go over a few things *in situ*?'

She nodded enthusiastically, and he headed off with his camera and sketchbook along the old pilgrims' path towards the area they'd set aside for her medieval garden. He would be returning to London on Monday with Claus, leaving Jeanette and Maddie alone again, and she was thinking how she'd miss his company.

Justina came to collect Vincent, and the two women moved out of the sun in the rose garden under the shade of the loggia, with cups in hand.

'I think he's a very cool guy,' Jeanette remarked to Maddie.

Maddie smiled and nodded. This was a term of endearment she'd heard Jeanette use more than once for artistic people she really liked, and felt easy with. 'Yes,' she said thoughtfully. But actually, Maddie was thinking, she could almost describe him better as belonging to the opposite end of the temperature range if she were inclined to notice at all. 'It makes you wonder why there is no Mrs Søren,' she said in a lazy way.

'Well, the long-time girlfriend departed almost a year ago, he told me,' Jeanette answered her. She kept a smile a little to herself. 'But it's not my story to tell, so you should ask him about it.'

Maddie's expression showed she'd registered this, and was at least slightly interested.

But Jeanette gave her no time for questions and said, 'I'm going to collect the last of the furnishing fabric that needs dyeing, so I can finish off the covers and the drapes for the Rinaldo suite – the big bedroom on the ground floor. I'd love you to give me a hand when you're ready, so you might see it completed before you fly home next week. An hour should do it.'

'Great. Of course I will! Give me ten to shoot up to the room and do my ablutions, then I'll find you in the bakery.'

Just as Maddie fitted her key into the lock, under the inscription 'Via del Pellegrino', she could hear her phone beeping from inside. She came quickly into the room and sat on the stone lintel at the window, touching the cellphone into life. A text read: *Have two tickets for Opera – Puccini Festival Lucca, early July. Join me? I think we're on a promise. P.G.*

Pierce Gray! Maddie thought. You are out there. What's on your mind? What do you want from me? And, how did you come to send me an Etruscan coin whose twin turns up in a medieval grave below my window – by chance exhumed seven hundred years later, exactly where I am?

Maddie had never really considered it before, but didn't think she'd ever had a sense of 'destiny' about any events that happened to her. She believed firmly that life offered both opportunities and tests, and you made of them what you would. No divine force was responsible; nothing was 'meant'. She'd won a place at Columbia because she'd worked hard for it; had applied for two terms in Oxford, not because they might open her world to a Christopher, but because foreign study would strengthen her curriculum vitae. Friends had called it 'fate', but she'd always dismissed such ideas as human folly grown out of a need to feel that we were not truly alone in this world. But now she started to wonder if there could be some patterns after all – if there might be a path that lay before you; that you controlled much less than you imagined. She had no schematic belief system: no sense of religion, no feelings about predestination, no superstitious ideas that rituals would attract or avert any special outcome. Yet, others' footsteps she knew she'd walked in here made her feel far more connected to the past, more sensitive to those who'd been here before her. And patterns – well, coincidences – seemed to lie dormant in the landscape, along with the ghosts and shadows and skeletons in the ground.

Maddie left the room again with her brain filtering crosscurrents of thought. She used the back steps to bring her straight into the front courtyard, which was closer to the old bakehouse where Jeanette would be starting work. Opening the doors, she noticed how warm the room was, and saw that the gas fires under the dyeing vats were beginning to bring the colour to a boil and produce a little steam. She'd learned that the trick was to get the dye hot enough to take, but not to ruin the cloth. Jeanette was evaluating the temperature for the right moment as Maddie approached.

She looked up and wiped her brow with the back of a dye-stained rubber glove, and noticed at once that the colour Maddie had taken on in her short stay at Borgo seemed to have vanished. She was pallid and drawn.

'You look like you've seen a ghost. Has something happened?' Jeanette asked her solicitously.

Maddie smiled at her friend. She was constantly amazed at how Jeanette's thoughts seemed to chime so closely with her own, even though she seldom expressed what she was thinking to anyone. 'A ghost? Yes, in a way. I had a text from the man who sent me the coin, when I first arrived. It's kind of complicated, and I'm not sure how to deal with him,' she replied.

Jeanette immersed a length of curtain fabric into one of the vats, and Maddie quickly donned some gloves and came nearer to lend a hand.

'He is the head of the company we are in the suit with, and he's just invited me to the Puccini Festival in Lucca early next month.'

'That's a little weird, isn't it? The man you're fighting in law? But it also could be wonderful,' Jeanette said pragmatically. 'You're very welcome to stay longer here, if you want. I'll be sad to lose you when you go.'

Maddie nodded, knowing her hostess truly meant this. And what a blissful escape it was to be here with her – with them all – in this utter paradise that so richly reflected the sunshine and gentleness of Jeanette's personality. 'Thank you,' she said, putting a gloved hand around her waist. 'Staying is hugely tempting, although my boss might not be as relaxed about it as you are. But,' Maddie tried to voice her conflicted emotions, 'I don't know what to make of this man, Jeanette – of my role with him. He may be carrying a torch for me because I refused him once, when I was younger. A little later on that same day we survived a boating accident together, when the balmy California weather changed dramatically, in half an hour. The wind came up so suddenly, and violently, and his yacht almost capsized. I can't really remember the details, but for sure we nearly drowned.' Maddie looked into Jeanette's china-blue eyes, and took a long breath. 'It was a strange thing we came through together: somehow dividing, but also uniting us. I've never told my parents – never told anyone.'

Jeanette only nodded, and listened.

'I'm also aware that, in the present situation with the lawsuit, he's possibly just trying to use me,' Maddie confided. 'He might want inside information, though I'm alert to that. Or, he might be grooming me as a go-between – and in that role, maybe I could make a difference. But my feelings about the smooth Mr Gray are so ambivalent. In my mind, the people at home – the victims of his company's working conditions – are mixed up with my feelings about that car full of drunks in Oxford, which killed Christopher. In each instance there was no good reason for what happened. They made an error for which they refuse to take responsibility; and they can't even bring themselves to say they're sorry.'

Jeanette nodded sympathetically. She was sensitive to the importance of these very private expressions of both Maddie's grief and her anxiety.

'Yes,' she said gently, 'and with your Christopher, you know the pain it has brought with only one family and his friends hurting so deeply from it. The lawsuit touches many families. The suffering is drawn out and uncertain, and a lot of money and moral principle is at stake.'

Jeanette turned from her vat, took off the gloves and hugged Maddie. She looked at her pale face. 'It takes strength to care; and energy to fight for what's right. You have that.'

'Do I?' Maddie answered in almost a whisper. 'I'm not sure any more. Before I came here, I thought I would never feel anything again. I thought I would just put one foot in front of the other, do what was required of me, and let the days pass. But this place, the centuries of pilgrims, the hopes of so many, all of you here now; you've made me remember who I am; but I don't yet know if I have the courage to invest my emotions too deeply, and speak out. I don't want to care too much and then get hurt by a bad outcome.'

'I'm very sure that you know what you have to do. Though, how do you make the blind see? That may need something close to a miracle.' Jeanette snuffed the flame under the vats to let them cool and steep for a while, and then took her friend's hand. 'Come on, let's go and find Søren.'

The two women set off from the medieval *forno* across the courtyard, past the ancient olive tree and along the old path that was once the pilgrims' road.

'The word "*pellegrino*" in Italian meant more than a pilgrim, did you know?' Jeanette was holding Maddie's hand as they strolled down the pathway. And when she shook her head, not understanding, Jeanette explained: 'The word meant a foreigner – and a traveller. Pilgrimage took you to the inspirational sources of faith and miracles, but it also allowed you to break free from the limits of your personal world.' She smiled. 'We're all pilgrims here, you see.'

'*Hic locus est,*' Maddie answered in a slightly dreamy voice. 'The magic of place.'

Maddie and Jeanette spotted Søren seated on a groundsheet, with his back against an oval-shaped stone in an area of wildflowers. He had the print of the medieval garden unrolled in front of him neatly held down with four round stones, one at each corner. When he'd come back from Siena with the illumination, Jeanette and Claus had been transported by what he had found. The drawing contained all the elements that Jeanette had been looking for, and they couldn't believe their luck that such a garden had probably flourished at the abbey, just a mile or so away. It was a perfect fit for Borgo, and in her opinion all that was needed was to translate the medieval blueprint into a workable present-day construct. Søren was confident he could do this, although Claus had jokingly suggested that the realisation of a golden heaven would unfortunately be beyond his budget. Søren agreed that, at Borgo, they might have to settle for a gold firmament painted in by the Tuscan sun, and that the beautifully wrought moon and wind would also have to be provided by God, 'Unless,' he had said, 'Maddie wants the job.'

'Can we translate all the other elements?' Claus had asked him.

'We can do, and find, everything else I think – except maybe for the unicorn. They're in short supply.' But here, Claus had the last word, warning the architect that his wife had a strange way of sourcing the most extraordinary things for Borgo.

Maddie was thinking about this earlier conversation as she approached the seated figure from across the rough meadow, with Jeanette beside her. She whispered an observation: that everything around Søren had a kind of symmetry. His camera, a large rolled measuring tape, and beside these his weathered copy of Keats' poetry, his sketchbook – all seemed to Maddie to have been casually placed as though for a magazine shoot. There was a delicious aesthetic to his 'chaos'. His eyes seemed to be closed, and his drawing pen was tucked behind one ear. A bottle of water was propped in the shadow of the stone. Jeanette smiled and enjoyed the vision with her for a moment.

A light wind sprang up, heralding their approach to Søren, who felt the breeze on his cheek and turned in their direction. 'I've been waiting for you,' he called nonchalantly, and opened one eye fully.

'Do we disturb your inspiration?' Jeannette sang out as they came close to him. 'You look so comfortable.'

The pages of his sketchbook fluttered, like the passage of time indicated by a turning calendar in a film. He reached forwards to close it, and said, 'You always bring a breeze with you, Maddie. Do you think you can control the wind?'

Maddie stared at him, and was almost impolite. 'No one can,' she replied crossly. She didn't know why, but the idea troubled her.

Søren smiled without offence and indicated the rug. 'Come and sit, please.' He moved some items for them. 'I was drinking in the smell and trying to imagine how the garden might once have been – how it will be again – before I try to draw it.'

Jeanette looked at him closely. 'You're right. How can we make a better world, unless we can first imagine one?'

'You've done that here,' Maddie said to her. 'You've imagined it, and also brought it into being.'

Jeanette was deeply touched by this, knowing what it meant coming from Maddie. She'd been so damaged when she'd arrived. But she decided to alter the subject quickly, so as not to ruin the beauty of the moment.

'Thinking of the wind, Søren, if you manage to get to Volterra, you must make a short excursion. A friend of mine who is a writer told me a story about a place called the Casa al Vento just outside the town. It's a farmhouse and a cottage built out of medieval ruins. The legend says a woman lived there who could indeed control the wind.'

Søren grinned, and Maddie stared at Jeanette. But Jeanette herself just smiled enigmatically and started speaking to Søren in Danish about the garden layout. They pointed at various areas and got to their feet briefly to check the perspective and pace out one part of the ground. Maddie listened, enjoying the lyrical rhythm of the language, until her thoughts were broken by the sudden flapping of wings of a dove just above her. It landed a metre or two away on the stone that had supported Søren. The sudden movement made Maddie jump.

Jeanette noticed her reaction and came back, switching to English again. 'Don't worry. It's checking if we've got some food with us. The doves were here when we came, and the house itself was full of them. The locals told me they're lucky – in love, and life, and business. Anyway, I'm happy they stay.'

'I'm sure Italians have this close feeling about birds because of a much older Etruscan belief,' Søren said. 'For them, and for the Romans after them, the movement of birds foretold the future. They called it "augury", and though it's come to mean prophecy of a general kind now, it was originally specific to birds.'

'I've heard that,' Maddie said. 'From my father, I think. "Not a whit, we defy augury" – isn't that what Hamlet says? And then something about a sparrow?' She smiled mischievously and wrinkled her nose at him.

'He was a Dane,' Jeanette laughed.

Søren sat down again, facing Maddie. He was taken completely by surprise. 'Yes, Maddie. It's about having faith in your destiny. Whatever is to come will come – now, or later. "There is a special providence in the fall of a sparrow," Hamlet tells Horatio.' He smiled at her. 'According to St Matthew, we should "fear not them which kill the body, but are not able to kill the soul."' Søren seemed serious for a moment, and added, 'Whatever your spiritual worldview it's a strong philosophy, don't you think?'

Maddie had no idea how to answer this: she had been struggling to have faith in the most basic ideas – even the kindness of people – for months on end. But she was thinking that her father would enjoy Søren: plants and poetry, she said to herself.

Jeanette's thoughts raced in another direction. 'That reminds me of the Etruscan tombs in Volterra,' she said. 'Maddie, you want to go, so why not take the afternoon off? You could both go, and then you can buy something for dinner on the way back, which will save me a trip into Siena with Claus this afternoon.'

'Perfect,' Søren agreed. 'I'll cook tonight – and I'll drive you in the Mini, Maddie.'

'Oh, no, you won't,' Maddie teased. 'You can come, since you're offering me your car, but I'll drive. Danish or not, you're used to driving on the wrong side of the road now.'

Jeanette rose with them, laughing. 'No *frikadeller* for dinner, Søren. Let's stay Italian!'

Volterra stood high on its hill, wreathed in sunlight. The ramparts of the old town rose forbiddingly above the winding road, and unmoving fluffy white thunderheads hung in the heat haze above them. It was early afternoon, and the stillness had a stark beauty.

Søren's little Mini, roof down, and with Maddie at the wheel, dextrously manoeuvred the dangerous hairpins leading to the city approaches. Maddie squinted, following signs, and drove with beginner's luck into a copiously spaced underground car park just below the great Etruscan walls. Unsure whether to bring sunglasses or umbrellas – and deciding on both – the pair walked out of the main entrance rather than climbing the internal stairs to the town square above. The path took them instead alongside the modern road into town, and up a ramp towards the massive defensive walls.

Less than a hundred metres' walking brought them to the impressive stones that had tantalised Maddie from guidebooks and internet pages: the suggestive Porta all'Arco. The so-called arched gate was inserted into the city wall at an angle to the road, clearly designed so the overhanging wall gave excellent defence from the castellation above. The structure exuded an aura that was palpable to Maddie: it seemed to her that the gate was aware of the passage of people and events that had moved through it over time. Here it had stood since the fourth century BC, little changed by renovation; and the fanciful personification she accorded it seemed justified by the stone heads adorning it, worn by the passage of wind and time.

Maddie, for the second time today, felt the past was present on the periphery of her existence.

'You feel it too, don't you?' Søren's soft voice joined her own mood.

They stood at a little distance from each other, contemplating the gate and the street leading uphill to the town centre beyond.

Maddie had almost lost her voice. She felt overcome with new sensations. 'I don't think I can walk through it,' she said in a small voice.

Søren watched her carefully. '*Déjà vu?*' he asked.

'No . . . I don't know. It's never happened to me before.' Maddie could almost feel her hair rise, and felt fear – or emotion. She ran her hand over her head.

Søren laid his hand gently on her shoulder. 'Maybe you just feel for the people who have walked in and out, for so many centuries. For sure it's a powerful, evocative structure. Anyway, it's nice, I think. You've reacted to something.'

For Maddie, as suddenly as the sensations started they seemed to stop, as if whatever had 'walked over her grave' had vanished again in the bright sunlight.

'Well, it's over now!' she said, winding her heavy hair off her neck into a self-securing knot. She moved forwards again, but as they passed from the heat into the gloom of the old gate, the temperature dropped appreciably. Maddie felt her spirits sink a little as well, and was annoyed with herself. But once she'd emerged from the shadow, her emotions lifted again.

Søren quietly observed these mood shifts in her, and smiled to himself. As he saw it, she was getting closer to feelings that he understood she'd kept at bay to survive the pain of the last six months. Something was allowing her to be touched by the world around her again.

At the top of the incline the road divided, and a right turn down a narrow lane and a left into another brought them into the Piazza dei Priori, the magnificent, medieval town square. On their left was the Palazzo Priori, which Maddie had read was the oldest town hall in Italy, if not Europe. Tucked away further along down the south side of the magnificent piazza, with its mellow, crenulated and turreted buildings, was the sign for the tourist office.

'Information, or coffee first?' Søren queried as they walked across the space.

Maddie smiled, feeling suddenly like a schoolgirl who has an unexpected day off. 'Oh, information first, then museum, with coffee in between, if you can't hold out longer?'

They pushed open the glass doors of the tourist centre, and Maddie smiled at a young woman behind the desk. She opened in her best Italian. '*Buon giorno*. We're looking for a place called the Casa al Vento – do you know it? – which is supposed to be in the countryside somewhere near here.'

'That is a very unusual request,' was the answer. 'I don't know, but my associates may.'

She turned to her two male colleagues and put the question to them; and a three-way conversation ensued which Søren interpreted as, 'if you call so and so, he knows every inch of the hills, he'll know if it exists.' Then a number was procured, followed by a phone call, which developed into a search for a map from the inner sanctum of a second office, rather than one of the usual offerings on the tourist stands in half a dozen languages. Everyone stood around talking until a printer on the other side of the room spat out a copy of the precious Ordnance Survey map, and the young woman – who introduced herself now as Eva – smiled at them both and took out a yellow Magic Marker.

'*Allora*,' she said energetically, and made a ring on the page. Eva looked at Maddie, and then carefully at Søren. 'I don't have Scandinavian languages,' she said, 'so I do it in English. Many years ago, *mille ottocento e settanta* – eighteen hundred and seventy, perhaps – an American named Leland wrote a book which was called *Aradia*. It was something about Italian witchcraft, and one of the stories in it was called "The House of the Wind". He was supposed to have been given information by an

242

Italian *strega*, or witch, called Maddalena. You see,' she laughed, 'we had witches here in Volterra long before the vampires.'

Eva's colleague spoke to her in Italian for a moment, and Eva paraphrased the pith of what was said.

'*Ah, sì.* You know the Leland story, it is about this young woman who was condemned to death by her family for disobeying them. She wanted to marry, and they wanted her to be a nun.'

'The law permitted them to put her to death for that?' Maddie asked, stunned.

'Yes, in that day a woman had no rights at all, as long as she was within the family. The father, the Church, the town rulers – they decided everything that happens to women then.' Eva nodded. 'It's good we live now, yes? But, do you know this book?'

'I think we've heard indirectly about it,' Maddie answered.

'Well,' Eva continued, 'according to Leland, the night before she was to die she is said to have been allowed into her garden where she prayed to her goddess, Diana, who she preferred to the Church. You can still find the Porta Diana on the other side of town . . .' She broke off for a second and made another circle on one of the tourist maps. 'It's one of our ancient gates from Etruscan and Roman times, which led to the temple. So now, the story tells that Diana answered her with a whirlwind, which came up out of the *balze* and completely destroyed the house and everyone in it except for her. And no one knows what happened to her after that – only that she escaped with her lover.'

'You don't believe the story?' Søren asked.

Eva laughed, and her hands gestured without need for translation – *who knows?* 'There is no written evidence about this woman, to say any of it happened. An Englishman called Hutton researched a lot, and he found nothing. Here in Volterra we've looked a little bit too, but there are no records of a trial or a baptism, no marriage papers. Only in the early part of the fifteenth century, there is a story of a woman tried for witchcraft; and she says that one of her spells to find out if someone was innocent of a crime was to put them into prison and see if a whirlwind would come and free them. So, that could hint at something earlier; but otherwise, it's as if she didn't exist. And maybe she didn't.'

'But the myth does,' Maddie said thoughtfully.

Eva nodded with a serene smile, and as another couple came into the office she looked up and spoke to them. 'I'll be with you in one minute,' she said in German.

Turning back to Maddie and Søren, she held out the map. 'I know this place, but I didn't know its name. It's a wonderful location. The building that is there now is not very old. It is divided in two parts, but it is built from very old cut stone.' Turning the map towards them, she said, 'Follow this road, and when you leave town drive slowly or you will miss it. There is a modern house just before it, and it's up on a promontory that looks down both sides of the valley and back up to the town. Good luck!'

'Thank you so much,' Maddie said. 'Oh, and we want to look at the Guarnacci Museum first. Can you show us on the map where it is?'

'Sì, certo,' Eva answered. She circled the town plan again and plotted them a route by foot. 'If you are stopping for a late lunch, Osteria dei Poeti is very nice, and the coffee is good. Close to the Guarnacci, here.' She made two marks.

'Thank you,' Søren said.

'You are welcome!' And then she turned her complete attention to the German couple.

Søren and Maddie soon found the restaurant, where they tucked themselves inside away from the uncertain weather. They ordered a quick course of truffle pasta, and once the business of ordering was over Maddie's mind returned to the experience in the tourist office.

'How did Eva know those people were German?' Maddie asked Søren, looking quite bemused by the whole experience.

'How did she know we wanted coffee?' His hazel eyes twinkled. 'But, I would answer you that in this case the giveaway was the vintage Baedeker guidebook and perhaps the proper walking sandals.'

Maddie grinned and shook her head. 'But she knew you were Scandinavian, and you're not even blond!'

'Very true,' he laughed, 'which shows that she is wiser than to deal in stereotypes.'

'Or that Volterra is still full of nice witches,' Maddie joked.

Less than an hour later they stood in front of the Guarnacci, a fine palace of uncertain years converted into an extraordinary collection of Etruscan and Roman antiquities by an avid eighteenth-century collector who'd had the marvellous good fortune to live there. A cold wind had

come up, whistling along the narrow street, and the sky darkened – as
Maddie thought it often must here – with the earlier threat of rain now
seeming a reality. They were pleased to reach the entrance and, once
indoors, they obtained a guidebook each and one for Jeanette as well.
This informed them that the palazzo had been given to the citizens of
the town of Volterra by Mario Guarnacci, in the year 1761. The noble
abbot, it reported, had foresight enough to collect and donate a vast
number of Etruscan grave artefacts and other items, along with fifty
thousand books, to the *comune*. This had prevented their dispersal to
unscrupulous collectors, and now formed a large part of Volterra's
cultural heritage.

Knowing of one especially resonant piece of sculpture that was
somewhere in the building, Maddie asked a question in Italian and
received an answer and pointed finger, which made them bypass for now
the outstanding funerary urns on the ground floor, and make straight for
the next floor.

As they walked up the broad stairs to the floor above – under the
watchful eye of a larger-than-life painting of the same noble abbot – they
passed a guard at the top of the stairs whom Maddie quizzed, and he
nodded.

Maddie, however, seemed confused and looked at the floor sign,
which was marked '*Piano 1*'.

'This is the second floor,' she said to Søren.

'No, in all of Europe this is the first floor,' he replied, amused. 'The
first floor is first above the ground level, and ground is "*terra*". We're in
the right place.'

Maddie challenged him, saying that the old world was very backwards
as logic dictated that 'one' must be where you start, so they had climbed
to the second floor; and his response was that the Arabs had shown them
zero, centuries ago. This light-hearted debate continued humorously
until Maddie found herself in a darkened room, where all the objects
were individually spotlighted. It had sneaked up on Maddie so
unexpectedly that she gasped, her eye pulled to a showcase that contained
a terracotta cinerary urn decorated with a remarkably lifelike depiction
of a wrinkled husband and wife. Maddie brought her hand up to her
mouth: she'd seen the image in books and found it more evocative in the
flesh, so to speak, than anything could have prepared her for. A couple
in late age, lined and almost breathing, looking as if their lives and souls

had been tied together from the first to the last. The inscription said only 'Urn of the married couple, second century BC'. Maddie could see the true-to-life faces of two people who must have kissed, eaten together, threatened and cajoled one another for any number of years on earth and in eternity after. Husband and wife gazed into each other's faces as though they'd never tired of a single expression. Maddie wanted to cry, though she had no idea if it was for something personal, which she felt she'd lost, or for some kind of fellow feeling with the people who'd lived here and passed under that same gate when its stone was newly hewn.

She felt at sea again, and watched Søren for a moment to place herself back in the present. Then a sense of security was restored. She felt grounded again standing next to him, watching that familiar way in which his eyes came to life and seemed to drink in every detail of the object that so obviously pleased him – as though he were preparing to draw it later, and live the experience again. She smiled to herself and turned away, her emotions quite calm, until she suddenly spotted the object she'd come looking for. Her heart almost stopped beating.

There it was, in the background behind the terracotta figures, bathed in its own spotlight on the opposite side of the main room. She took hold of a somewhat startled Søren, and pulled him along towards the object. 'Meet the "Shadow of the Evening",' she spoke reverently.

The 'Ombra de la Sera' – surely the world's most celebrated former fire poker – stood isolated in its own alcove. The perfect face of a small boy stared from his Plexiglas case at them; but the body was elongated as if drawn out by the angle of the fading light. It reminded Maddie of the shadows over the graves at Borgo that morning.

Søren looked at the miniature face and slender body of the young boy wrought in iron. With a long breath of admiration, he said, 'It is exquisite. The idea is completely fulfilled by the execution of the work. If it is a votive figure, it's as though it just stretched upward to the gods. How do you know about this, Maddie?'

'Until a few months ago, I didn't. On my birthday last month, my grandmother had this obsession about me finding my family, and she showed me a postcard that my great-great-grandmother, Maria Pia, had sent to her daughter in San Francisco around eighteen seventy. She must have been right here in Volterra, looking at this just as we do now.'

'"*A la Recherche du Temps Perdu*",' Søren said. 'The finding of times forgotten helps us to know something more about who we are.'

He took her arm and they wandered towards the top of the stairs, passing the guard again. Suddenly the whole building shook under their feet, as thunder rumbled beneath them. It seemed to come from somewhere deep inside the earth – the very rock the town was perched on – and almost instantly there was a second deafening thunderclap and a lightning flash, which gave them a jolt.

'My God!' Maddie exclaimed. 'It feels as though the building must collapse.'

'It's all right, *Signorina.*' The stair guard touched her arm and spoke in Italian. 'It is not the end of the world. It happens often on very hot days, when a little rain flushes the streets. The Etruscans loved it. They had a reputation in the ancient world of being able to throw thunder around. Julius Caesar was very respectful of them.'

Søren understood him and laughed. 'I'm not surprised.'

The rumbling continued – *piano* and *forte* – while they spent another hour looking at the collection. Maddie carried the boy's face with her in her head; and Søren found an object of his own that sent his thoughts into a world of speculation. He pointed out to Maddie a large, oval-shaped stone which the guide explained was a *cippus*, or grave-marker. There were several, some spherical and surmounting a plinth, and others more conical in shape. He was drawn by one that was carved like a pine cone – what might in England be called an acorn or a pineapple, and seen so often at the gates of eighteenth-century houses. But for Søren, it looked like nothing so much as the worn oval stone in Jeanette's garden against which he had been sitting that morning. What is your story? he wondered.

It was after four, and if they were to make Eva and Jeanette's suggested stop and still buy provisions for dinner, it was time they were away.

'Shall we head for the House of the Wind?' Søren asked his companion.

'I'd like that,' she answered.

Maddie steered the Mini west towards a remarkable sky of pinkish light and a line of dark purple clouds, brooding to one side of the lowering sun. It was a dramatic collision of night and day in one place in the sky. Søren navigated them along a ridge that gave expansive views to the north and the south, over vast ploughed farm fields to one side and a lunar landscape, that the locals called the '*balze*', or crags, to the other.

They thought they had gone too far; and then, not far enough: when suddenly on a bend, the silhouette of a building on a promontory stood out against the apocalyptic skyline. Søren pointed, and Maddie quickly turned off the road into an open area on the opposite side from the dwelling.

'The location fits,' Søren said, running round to open the driver's door for Maddie; 'but this building would need a lot of architectural investigation to give up its secrets. It could be medieval at its core. It's been much altered, and isn't at all beautiful now.'

'No,' Maddie said a little shyly. 'The feeling of this place, though: that's surreal.'

They crossed the road and found the cottage: a ruin, of a sort, built close by a thoroughly modern farmhouse, with which it shared a wall. Maddie wanted assurances and found a woman in the garden next door. A few simple words of Italian clarified that this was indeed the 'Casa al Vento'.

On the ground level were several doors, many long barred up, Maddie thought; and there was a window with an ancient iron-work grille, and a very new extension, and outside a stairway leading up to a first floor, probably the oldest part of an original rough stone build, Søren believed. A pile of uncut wood was heaped on one side of the yard, and the place had a feeling of abandonment.

Maddie felt the return of that earlier sensation of fear, and moved over to sit quietly on the stairs. As Eva had promised, the view up to Volterra was just as it might have been from Etruscan times, certainly since the Middle Ages. The story seemed to touch her – a girl entrapped by family and religion and society. There was no room to think differently in a world of forced conformity. But to be willing to die, because you couldn't live the way others wanted you to? It was exactly what Christian history would never record – a pagan martyr. Maddie shuddered.

'What of the girl, and her love? Did they really escape with the wind, and find a happy ending? Or were they crushed by the social engine and just cancelled from history?' For some reason, Maddie thought of Neva, and Marilu, and even of Christopher.

Søren came and sat beside her on the stair, putting a warm hand on her back, and she turned to face him. He was nodding at her, smiling softly.

'And they are gone – ay, ages long ago
These lovers fled away into the storm.'

Maddie looked up at him, and from her wonderful almond eyes tears sprang without warning. They streamed down her face, though she could not say why.

Søren opened his arms and folded her into them: and on a ridge between soft fields and stark cliffs, under a sky of darkness and light on a day that seemed to straddle a divide, she wept as she had not been able to before.

28

Yesterday there had been a succession of light, frequent snowfalls, which had gradually softened the stark winter landscape. Further flurries had continued intermittently throughout the day today. At around four o'clock, however, as the afternoon light had faded and it was time to light the candles, the weather had also improved. A clear, cold evening had been crowned with a brilliant moon, Siena gold in colour and close to a full orb. This bathed the countryside in light, perfect for hunting; and it was for this reason, Mia thought, that she could now hear the owl circling outside, with its strange three-note call that was almost human. The repetitious sounds cut across the last bell for compline at the abbey, which had an eerie effect. Bird cry often unnerved her, always commanded her respect; and she looked over at Porphyrius.

He was fully aware of her anxiety, and smiled at her as he reached across to feed the fire with another log. It was a studied gesture of calm, an attempt to take his mind off the waiting and communicate a normalcy he didn't feel. Nevertheless he answered Mia's strained look in a light voice.

'It's not a cry of alarm. The owl is simply using that call to drive its prey out of the cover,' he said to her, 'hoping to startle a rabbit or a small rodent into the moonlight. It must have gone to bed hungry last night because of the snow.'

Mia nodded; but the explanation didn't offer any consolation. Everyone knew that owls were associated with the weather; and witches;

250

and birth, death and sickness. Truly, Mia thought, at least three of those things were appropriate in the present circumstance; and she wished the creature would be silent or hunt nearer to the abbey.

'Owls are also friends to wisdom,' said the gentle voice on her left. 'It's a good omen. Any other hunting bird is male, but the owl is a messenger from the wisest of goddesses, offering salutations from Diana the huntress, according to Virgil.'

Mia smiled and nodded. Actually, yes, she thought; that is the most reassuring idea, and equally fitting. '*Ave Maria, stella Diana*', she and Agnesca would sing together. Diana was for her friend what the Virgin was for Mia. 'You're right, Gennaro,' she said. 'And *la raggia* is worthy of such a messenger.'

Just as this thought settled in her mind, though, another loud scream came down the stairwell from the chamber above, altering the mood of the three people gathered in front of the fire in the hallway room. Porphyrius squeezed his hands together and stood up again, wondering what he could usefully do. Mia had no notion how to comfort him. She'd never been present for a woman brought to childbed, and beyond the talk of servants she had no experience to offer him about what was likely happening now, what was still to come. It had been hours since the pains had started; that was all she knew. The day had darkened, the weather improved, the house become quiet, the servants kept busy with their own duties. Mia had been asked only to sweep the room and provide it with fresh rushes and bedstraw, then to place a clean coverlet on Agnesca's bed. From that point only Aunt Jacquetta and Alba had gone above, with Cesaré appearing just once at the door with hot water. Porphyrius was exiled from the room altogether – sent down to the hall to wait with Mia and Gennaro to pray or hope or think what thoughts he may until the women and Mother Nature had done their work and his child was born.

Loredana came to them and laid out some bread, olives and a small flagon of wine on the side table. She lifted this nearer to where all three sat.

'No doubt you've small appetite for a full supper, Master Porphyrius,' she said. 'It's wise to eat something, though, for you may have some hours to go.' She said this casting her eyes in the direction of the scream.

'Thank you, Loredana,' Mia replied.

She knew this was good advice, and also that because of her own preoccupation with Agnesca's labour she'd quite forgotten to arrange some supper for Gennaro, who was still recovering his strength and needed to eat. He was vastly improved in appearance these last two weeks, but he was still thin and weak from his battle with the illness, and neither Aunt Jacquetta nor Porphyrius would hear of him trying to sit his horse for the long miles back to Volterra yet.

'Shall I bring some cuts of cold meat, Maria, at least for you and Signor Allegretti? And then I'll be off to bed, for I'm no more use to anyone tonight,' she added.

'Do, please,' she said. 'Perhaps a truckle of cheese too, Loredana. We might be hungry eventually, when things move quicker upstairs.'

Loredana nodded, but her look was wholly unconvinced. She was no midwife, but she knew there was some distance to go as the screams were not yet close enough together to suggest the end was in sight. And as she'd supposed, when she returned later with prepared meat and a small wheel of cheese from the storeroom, nothing further had been heard above stairs.

'You might go and unlock the chest in your bedchamber, Master Porphyrius, if you wish to be of some help,' she grinned at him. 'And you, Maria Maddalena, the best office you could perform for your friends is to run down to your garden and untie the cord you girls knotted under the doves' house. Nothing works better to open the womb and hasten a birth.'

Mia blushed. She didn't know anyone was aware of this knot, intricately tied into a flax rope handmade by *la raggia* and Mia herself to bring strong magic into their garden. Agnesca had told her that such a knot was reckoned by their ancestors to tie up the wind; it should be unbound only when a breeze was wanted. But, she confided to Mia, it was much more effective for love magic. It would bring her a husband if they left it there, guarded by the lovebirds.

Mia looked at Loredana and tried to appear good-humoured, but dismissive. 'You surely don't believe it will make any difference to do such things.'

'Yet, it is always done if a birth goes on for a long time, Maria,' she answered, and left the room, bidding them all good night.

Mia and Gennaro picked at some of the food, but Porphyrius couldn't be tempted. He drank a goblet of wine, and changed his sitting position a few times, otherwise moving only to tend to the fire or open the front door into the courtyard for air. After another hour had passed this way, however, he became restless and stressed – a state Mia had never seen in him. He was always a model of calm, in every testing situation.

'Don't fear for her, Porphyrius,' she said to him. 'Aunt Jacquetta has experience as a midwife. To my certain knowledge she has delivered four babies on her own here at the villa, and two of those were before their dates, yet survived. She has also helped with others in the village.'

'It is his happy privilege to worry, Maria Maddalena,' Gennaro answered her.

The smile he offered her expressed many complex emotions, not all of which she could read.

'He is the most blessed of men,' he added, keeping other thoughts to himself and leaving Mia to wonder on his meaning.

It was some time later when Mia heard another piercing scream, and then her name called from the top of the landing. She had dozed off to the sound of the owl, her head cradled awkwardly against her hand and the corner of the settle. She was stiff, but she quickly sprang up the stairs towards her aunt, leaving both men behind, acutely aware of the concern etched on each face.

'We have been this great time because the child is in the womb the wrong way around for birthing,' Jacquetta explained to her.

She came through the doorway of the pretty room, which Cesaré had named after the *bella pellegrina*, and her eyes adjusted to the relative darkness. Only one candle and the small fire were aglow. Yet she noticed the moon came in at the window and gave radiance to the room, and it seemed beautiful. She saw Agnesca sitting at the end of the bed looking like a ghost – and yet quite in control of her mind and physical senses.

'I need you to take hold of her hand, Mia, while Alba and I try to turn the child,' Jacquetta told her.

Mia swallowed: she had heard only morbid tales from travellers about babies in a footling position in the womb. Some of them had come from sad women on pilgrimage, hoping to be blessed with other healthy children. This was the thing most feared by birthing mothers and midwives – and in extreme cases, a surgeon might be called on to cut the foetus from the mother and try to save her, if nothing more could be done. She shivered unconsciously, and thought of the dreaded owl.

Agnesca drew back and leaned against the bed-head, where Mia plumped a feather pillow for her. 'Don't look like that, Mia,' she said to her. 'The morning will dawn bright, with good news for us all yet.'

Mia tried to smile for her friend; but when Aunt Jacquetta nodded and Agnesca braced herself, it was she who needed to hold onto Agnesca's hand, rather than the reverse. As her aunt pushed down on her belly Agnesca gasped and let out a desperate, stifled scream that made Mia's heart break.

'Don't mind me,' she said apologetically to Jacquetta. 'I know you do only what you must: and I can take it. The sound is not of my volition.'

'Another go, Agnesca,' Jacquetta answered. 'The child moved a little, and I must keep the pressure going to encourage the motion.'

But Mia could see the look in her aunt's eyes and knew it was a mixture of sorrow for the pain it was causing Agnesca, and anxiety that there was considerable danger. When the pressing started again and she felt her friend's powerful grip on her own hand, almost bruising the skin, Mia wanted to run away. She would have borne the pain herself, but hated seeing another having to endure such agony. This thought sharpened when a third attempt to press the child into the right position – and the pain it caused Agnesca – still failed to bring results.

Mia looked at the poor woman's face, shining with perspiration and leached of its usual colour and light. She knew Agnesca was not yet nineteen years on this earth, but now she looked harrowed, and might be any age. She glanced at Alba, who stared blankly back at her. Even Aunt Jacquetta's face lacked its characteristic surety. She was biting her lip without realising she did so. Mia couldn't bear it, and felt useless and stupid. She thought of Loredana, and then of *la raggia*. Could it help, truly, to unfasten the knot? But perhaps it might, if Agnesca thought it would. She whispered into her friend's ear, and then excused herself from the room, promising her aunt she would return in haste.

Mia's feet covered the stairs faster than they ever had, and she passed the quizzical looks of Gennaro and Porphyrius in the hallway without pausing to answer them. She heaved open the door, and was out into the cold night without a wrap; out across the soft crunch of the packed snow without pattens to protect her slippers; out beneath the trees that lined the pilgrims' road and played host to the owl, whose call now echoed in her ears. But fear would be a luxury.

When she reached the garden she felt energised to be out in the air, beneath the beautiful moon. She needed no lamp as she found the ancient, egg-shaped stone under the mulberry tree, and prised it to one side. Here she took up the flaxen rope she had woven into a thick cord during the summer months with *la raggia*. With her friend in pain and in need of a breeze, or a miracle, her fingers teased the knot free. She cared nothing for a husband or a lover, but would give anything for her friend and for those she loved. She reverently placed the loosened rope in front of the stone again, in a way she thought might have become Agnesca; and after this she whispered a few words of her own to the Archangel Michael, who had once been so close to her home, a mile away where the shrine to Galgano was built. This was for herself, for her own belief, and it belonged with her certainty that unicorns were true and could be found in her garden on the right day. Mia – quite changed in her outlook – then retreated to the house with steps as light as a fawn's.

A finger held suspended to Porphyrius as she passed him warned him not to ask questions yet; and in a moment she was back at her friend's bedside looking at least flushed from the exercise.

'Push down again, Aunt Jacquetta,' she said in an unwavering voice, 'for there is nothing now to impede the birth of the child.'

Agnesca smiled wanly, and agreed to the idea that they should try coaxing the baby into birth position once more. She gritted her teeth without expression and nodded at the women.

Downstairs the fire had all but gone out, and the two men looked dazed, confused, exhausted. But within half an hour of Mia's appearance, disappearance and reappearance, they heard screams that suggested to Porphyrius that his wife must be in terrible danger; then further screams that told him not only that she still lived, but that they must have held to hope and be trying something new; and finally, things were silent again.

When Maria Maddalena opened the door of the chamber he shared with his wife, she could see Porphyrius's body was slumped, his face turned towards the fire. Gennaro's, she saw, was turned upwards to her and ashen – more so, if possible, than the face of the woman she had just left. She came down the stairs much more slowly than before.

Gennaro tracked her movement. He saw that she was carrying a bundle, inert and quiet. He hesitated before placing a hand on his friend's shoulder to alert him, and then he saw the young girl's eyes. He recognised a look of fatigue and distress, because he had watched that face nursing him through the fight of his life just weeks ago when they had journeyed to heaven and hell together – and every place between the two, he'd thought at the time. Tonight, as before, her lovely features expressed eventual triumph; and Gennaro touched Porphyrius's arm with vitality.

Mia was by this time at the bottom of the stair, and managed a tired smile. It was not yet dawn but couldn't have been long from it, and she spoke to Porphyrius in her soft voice.

'It is the morning of the feast day of St Agnes, just as it was when you first came to us a year ago,' she said to him. 'I know it is also your friend's birthday, and that he takes his name from this month.'

Mia looked at Gennaro. She knew she had been instrumental in helping him to reach his birthday after an illness that might easily have taken him to God. Then she moved towards Porphyrius, and placed the tiny linen-wrapped child in his arms.

'In the early hours of this same day, as fate would have it, your wife has presented you with a son, Porphyrius,' she said. 'She has asked me to invite you to be his godfather, Gennaro, for she says she will have you or no other. To you,' she turned back to the awestruck father, 'she asks that you take him now to her bed, and introduce your son to her by the name you will give to your first boy.'

The owl, however, had neither moved on nor requited his appetite; and within a few hours Mia would have cause to connect this date forever with the hunting bird, and all of those events which it was said to presage.

PART THREE

29

23 June 2007, Pisa to San Francisco

From the half-consciousness of desultory dreams Maddie's stomach lurched, and she felt movement around her; a general shuffling, followed by a sound of metallic abrasiveness. She struggled to orientate herself through a haze of fatigue, in a world strangely without light.

'We've just started encountering some turbulence. The pilot has turned on the seat belt sign, and the toilets will temporarily be out of use. Please return to your seat and fasten your seat belt. Thank you.'

I remember, Maddie thought. Her brain began to clear a little. In her dream she'd been sitting at the grand piano in the almost-completed music room at Borgo Santo Pietro, her fingers revising a forgotten passage of Beethoven.

The fully laden United Airways flight, outward bound from London to San Francisco International, had another seven hours to go before she'd be free from the overly cologned individual sleeping in the seat beside her. She'd been up twelve hours already and had almost entirely missed her sleep from the night before. Everything since her shower at sunrise was a surreal sequence of actions and strange faces. She'd been forced to leave Borgo with Gori to catch the only scheduled flight from Pisa to Heathrow that might make the tight ongoing connection. Between dreams and reality, she stalled the sense of foreboding as to what might lie ahead. There were no cardinal points she could relate to in the here and now; she was adrift.

She moved her body, kept her eyes closed, and assembled fragments

259

of the return from Volterra through the strange lunar landscape and then the rich, breathtaking hills of the Colle Val d'Elsa. She saw the row of pines standing sentinel along the driveway at Jeanette's, and recalled she had bathed in the beautiful claw-foot tub, and then put on a pretty dress. She'd taken a peacock-blue pashmina and selected her purse from the drawers inside the antique dove-grey wardrobe; picked up the keys for the Mini, to give back to Søren . . . Yes. That's when she'd made a mistake. She'd put her phone into the bag instead of leaving it in the room to charge. Why did she do that? She could have left it longer, and gone downstairs without it.

In her mind she retraced her move down those twisting stairs, in silence, just smiling, just curious about who was down there. She looked along the hallway towards the kitchen, then turned back to find the door to the music room open and inviting – saw Jeanette had set a bottle of champagne to chill in an ice bucket, the glasses for four placed beside it. Claus was showering after his sticky day in Siena, Jeanette was dressing, Søren was cooking; and she was previous for drinks.

Passing the large mirror she was a blur of white and peacock fabrics and dark curls entering a domain of ambers and golds as she passed the table with the drinks and placed her bag and pashmina on one of the comfortable chairs. She smiled to herself: 'Do I dare?' and she seated herself at the grand piano, and placed her hands on the case. It had such an evocative smell, and reminded her of her great-grandmother Mimi's instrument, which was now at her father's house. She lifted the cover and looked at the keys.

It was with feelings she couldn't articulate that she very slowly shaped a scale which leaped along the keyboard, then followed it back down with a more confident arpeggio. Her right hand drifted into a familiar four-note phrase finishing with a staccato note, a piece of music her hands seemed to be searching for. She was rusty and loosened her fingers again to repeat the shape, then tentatively started a Beethoven sonata. She knew several from memory but this one was complex and had kept her after school, demanding meticulous practice, burrowing into her summer beach weekends until she had it etched in her mind and hands; and even when she'd conquered the technical requirements, she remembered how she'd struggled to find a convincing interpretation.

Was this part of her dream? Did it really happen?

Maddie repositioned her head on the synthetic airline pillow and saw her fingers begin more confidently with the first notes. Allegretto, D minor. Was it a day, or a year ago? How far back did it take her, to the pressure from her teacher to study music and forget law? And for how many months had she not even lifted the lid of her upright? But here on this day a deeper urge had taken over, and her heart was otherwhere. Her eyes were unseeing, but her fingers explored the keys to unlock the notes as though she were seventeen again. She felt exultant and hungry for that lost piece of herself that seemed to be everywhere around her, if she were willing to look. And just as in other heightened moments in the past, the music swept the world away with fast-flowing passages that jumped from serene beauty to restlessness.

As she was in full flight Søren had appeared in the room like a child compelled to the kitchen when cakes come from the oven. Her brain was with her fingers, yet she registered his expression and his face. He'd looked relaxed, she remembered thinking, in fresh trousers and a pressed white shirt. And she'd been pleased when he'd sat without disturbing her. Søren had a reverence for the moment, she'd thought.

She pushed the sleeping shades off her eyes.

A stewardess noticed Maddie was wakeful and offered her a glass of water as she prowled through the cabin checking seat belts. Maddie took it from the tray with a tired smile and sipped some, doing her best to concentrate.

'"*Der Sturm*",' Søren had said softly to her when she'd executed the fabulous falling chromatic scale to finish the sonata movement. He was shaking his head in surprise. Unspoken words seemed to be resonating in the room along with the last chords.

She nodded. '"The Tempest"? Yes. My father says it was inspired by the play. It was his favourite sonata, so I guess I learned it for him.'

'You're very good,' he'd answered. 'Can I bribe you for more, with champagne?'

He moved from his position on the sofa, but in the quiet after the music a beeping sound became apparent, emanating from Maddie's handbag. Søren hesitated, and then handed it to her.

'Is it important?' he wondered. He smiled rather regretfully, feeling it had broken the spell. 'Can you leave it?'

Maddie looked at the message, and shook her head.

'No. I'd better take this.' She rose and explained to him, 'I have to make a personal call. Keep a glass cold for me?'

He nodded, and she took her phone and headed out of the room. A wave of uncertainty washed over her. 'If I'm gone a little while,' she turned back to say to him, 'would you ask everyone to go ahead and eat without me? This could just be five minutes; or it may take some time.'

Maddie imagined every possible disaster that could have brought about a message like this from Samantha, a woman not given to overreaction. She took a deep breath as her thoughts turned away from Søren – now seated alone in the music room – towards her home; and in the main hall she paused. But she didn't, for some reason, automatically step to the right and climb the stairs to her room. Instead her feet took her to the left of the music room, and she swung open the massive door of the villa and headed out into the warm June night on the longest day of the year. She crossed the courtyard and started down the drive towards a grassy knoll, with a bench set upon it. She had looked at it a dozen times but never stopped to survey the scene from it. Now, however, she stepped over the low box hedge, which divided that area of garden from the pebbled pathways, and she started to climb the hillock. Suddenly a black silhouette rose from the darker space in front of her.

'Oh,' she exhaled in a passing moment of alarm; but in another second she realised it was only Eleanore, the Shar Pei, whose dark-mouthed ancestors had for centuries guarded the Forbidden City from trespassers and evil spirits alike. The wrinkly dog snuffled, recognising Maddie, and took a few steps towards her.

Maddie bent and gave her a hug. Some days before, Jeanette had told her the sad story of why Eleanore could so often be found on this mound, sitting alone at midday or in the early evening.

'Balthasar was her mate, and her elder – almost my child, before I had Vincent,' Jeanette had said. 'He tried to rescue her from a scrap with a wild boar, maybe a year ago, but died later of his wounds. We buried him up there on the hill, because he'd sat by my side through wind and rain while we laid out every garden, and repaired every wall. Eleanore grieved so much I thought her heart would break. For months she just refused to move from the spot where he was, but eventually she seemed to get better and joined in with the rest of us again. I thought if she could get over that she could deal with anything. Still,' Jeanette had added wistfully, 'even now, when something worries her, she returns to the place and spends hours up there on her own. I guess we know very little about how animals feel.'

Eleanore now moved up the hill with Maddie, and the dog took up a position on her haunches next to the bench as Maddie dropped onto the seat, and kept her hand on the dog's sandy head.

'Do you have worries of your own?' she asked. 'Or are you here now for me?'

Eleanore turned her head to look at Maddie and the two of them sat together for a while, listening to an owl somewhere in the trees and watching the lights of Chiusdino twinkling in the middle distance.

'Well, I'm glad to have your company, whatever the reason,' Maddie confided to the dog as she studied the text on her phone and read it through carefully a second time.

Have a problem which could become very serious. We all believe you are best equipped to affect a resolution – if at all possible. Time is vital. How soon could you be back? Call me at home as soon as you get this – no matter the time. Must talk urgently. Thanks, Samantha

This was followed by Samantha's private number, as she often worked from home on a Friday afternoon in summer. Maddie input the digits and waited for it to connect. She heard the US ringtone only for a beat or two before Samantha's voice came on. The 'hello' was crisp enough to tell Maddie she had been waiting for her call, and was stressed.

'Our plaintiffs are dropping out. No explanation at all! We've had more than twenty calls this week – one from your girl in Jose – and they're all ready to drop the case. Exactly *why*, is the question. No one wants to talk to us about it, Maddie. They're all scared of something. Can you break through the ring of silence, do you think?'

Maddie's brain had swirled with a dozen quick ideas: buy-offs, out-of-court offers. Or maybe there was something more sinister going on. 'I'll come,' she answered simply.

'I knew you would,' Samantha replied.

She followed this with a succinct account of how Jacinta would organise the flight arrangements, connections, and surplus fares if required. Maddie should watch her phone or emails, she said, for a complete itinerary over the next few hours.

'She'll ring every airline if she has to,' Samantha said with dry humour. 'It's part of her penance for being caught with Mr Hugo – which tale I think you've heard? No amount of overtime seems beyond her willingness at the moment,' she laughed, 'so if you're unclear what's happening at bedtime, be prepared to check your data during the night. She'll be trying to get you out early tomorrow your time.'

Maddie had folded her phone to end the call, and Eleanore turned her head quizzically to watch her.

'Ladies and gentlemen, the seat belt sign has now been switched off. Please feel free to move about the cabin again, and we will shortly be passing through with drinks before we serve the meal.'

In irritation, Maddie pulled her mask further down over her eyes to try returning to her dream. It must have been about eight in the evening British time, though they had left the airport some hours earlier, and where they were now – what time zone they were flying through – held little interest for her. She wanted no food. She'd not wanted to leave Borgo, not at the time Samantha's message had come through, anyhow. She hadn't been ready; but she hadn't protested. She felt emotionally torn between two worlds.

She remembered she had sat a long time on the knoll, watching the crescent moon rising in a sky that was still not dark. The moon shape was a hammock, as her father used to say when she was young: you could imagine the Man snoozing up there, arms folded behind his head, one leg dangling down, surveying earth from his privileged vantage point. Then, as these thoughts made her mouth turn upwards at the edges, Eleanore had stirred; and out of the twilight the figure of Søren had come, carrying her pashmina and two glasses. He approached without speaking, draped the shawl around her and slipped into the empty space beside her on the bench.

'You've been a long time,' he said after a moment, looking away to Chiusdino with Maddie and the dog. He felt her shiver in the cool air, and put an arm easily around her. 'I thought you'd like this,' and he offered her the champagne.

Maddie took the glass and leaned her head slowly to the right, until it found his shoulder. She rested it there, and waited a minute or two before she told him, 'I have to go back. My people need me.'

'We thought it might be something like that, but we'll miss you,' he said gently.

'There's a crisis brewing in the law case, and my boss thinks I can make a difference. I'm not ready to go yet, Søren. But I said I would.'

'You don't have to explain, Maddie,' he assured her.

'Because Samantha thinks the people we represent might talk to me, and tell me why they're suddenly nervous about the suit,' she added, as though she either hadn't heard him or needed to talk about it.

Søren looked down at her leaning her head against him; and even at such an odd angle in the in-between light, she could see his grin. She thought she knew what it meant – that someone, somewhere, was working very hard to undermine their confidence in the strength of the case – and that this someone had got to them.

Eleanore put her head on Maddie's lap, and Søren reached over and ruffled her ears.

'You want to believe this man, their boss, has some basic goodness – some integrity. But he may not, Maddie,' he posited.

'He's had an open window while I haven't been there,' she replied almost bitterly, 'and I think he's been playing our clients off against us. I agree, he's not the intrinsically moral man he tries to persuade me he is. And I'm a fool. I hoped he could be honourable,' she said flatly.

'We select what to believe, Maddie,' he said, 'and remain deaf to contradictions.'

She waited, feeling she could hear his mind working towards something more, and after a while, he spoke again.

'Do you know,' his tone altered subtly, 'I once lived with someone who I thought was one thing, but turned out to be another. She was warm; she had a good mind, and was very pretty. But in the end she was only interested in the beautiful things that money could buy. She fell in love with a man she thought would be a corporate architect, who would take high-paying jobs and give her a chic home in a London mews somewhere in SW3. But I failed her in that, and bought an unpromising-looking warehouse in Southwark. I wanted an adventure, with no safety rail. We realised we were very different, and couldn't make each other happy.'

Maddie lifted her head and looked at him. She thought, in this neat sketch, there might be the trace of a tale of deeper hurt.

'What happened to her?' she asked quietly.

'Oh,' he smiled, 'she works in the City. She has an architecture degree, but she buys futures instead of designing them now. She'll end up with what she wants, and I wish her well in that.'

'Do you miss her?'

'No. Not any more.' He looked at Maddie's face, and smiled at her. 'Will you come and eat something? I made a good dinner, and we've waited for you.'

'Yes, the Danish meatballs.' Maddie managed a laugh, knowing he'd gone to much more trouble than this. 'No, I'm sure you did, and thank you all for the courtesy. But I suddenly have a lot to arrange to be able to leave here early tomorrow. Send my apologies to the cook?'

'No,' he mouthed good-humouredly. 'Do you need a ride to Pisa?'

But Maddie didn't want to think about that just now. 'I'm not good at airport goodbyes,' she answered. She wasn't, either. She'd had one too many of them with Christopher, and dreaded any more.

She stood up to stretch her legs, looking away along the drive. 'If our clients want to drop the lawsuit and settle privately – probably for next to nothing – what can I say to change their minds?' She was almost thinking aloud. 'I'd been deluding myself that there might be some words I could find for Pierce, to get him to see what they suffer. But now I realise, he wouldn't even hear me out.'

Søren got to his feet and took a pace forward to stand beside her. He took hold of her hand, which was cool to the touch, and he covered it with his warmer one.

'Remember what Boccaccio says, Maddie,' he told her with calm assurance. 'More than any other thing, language has the power to alter the outcome of events.'

She faced him under an indigo sky. Very gently, she reached out and drew his face to hers, and she kissed him. He tasted of sweet and spices – something like peppercorns and raspberries, as though he'd been cooking with them – and she lingered over the kiss, enjoying its tenderness. It was just half a breath away from absolute passion, and she realised the moment hovered between them. It could take whatever direction it may with just one gentle push from one of them or the other. Søren was on the point of saying something, but she answered him before his words could find a voice.

'You'll see me again,' she said, 'and in the meantime, you have a friend in San Francisco.'

It was late, though the night was still not completely dark, and he reclaimed her hand. They sprang lightly down the hill towards the villa, and Eleanore trotted after them.

30

Consulting her recently adjusted wristwatch, Maddie learned it was just gone five in the afternoon local time as she shuffled her way along the untidy line of passport control.

She spotted Barbara – or rather, she couldn't miss her – waving like a palm frond in a hurricane, with a helium-filled balloon tied around her wrist and some flowers in her embrace.

'I've only been away for a couple of weeks,' Maddie said in a slightly embarrassed voice as they hugged.

Barbara took control of the trolley and gave her the balloon to hold.

'Yes, but I've missed you,' she told her truthfully. She gave her sister a quick once-over and noted she'd gained a little weight, and a touch of sun. 'You look great! I thought you might be bored, not being in a city. Was it the Tuscan food – or some other reason?'

Maddie smiled and breathed in and out in such a way that it could have been taken for exhaustion, or something more enigmatic; Barbara couldn't decide which.

'No, I wasn't at all bored. There was sunshine, and an infinity pool, and a backcloth painted by the gods. It was extraordinary,' she answered sincerely. 'Jeanette's place is a paradise. But I'm so tired now I can't think straight. Let me tell you about it when I've recovered. I have to work tomorrow, so can you just get me home?'

'You have to work Sunday?' Barbara asked.

Maddie nodded. 'That's half the reason for the unscheduled return – to be able to go down to Jose on a weekend.'

'Wow. Mom will be disappointed. She's already started cooking for you.' Barbara looked at her sister and smiled ironically, understanding she might be relieved to be spared Sunday lunch going over the entrails. 'Anyway, you might be better off staying up as long as you can, and sleeping later.'

They moved out of the terminal to Barbara's Nissan, and loaded Maddie's bags. Barbara whizzed off through the airport traffic, heading towards the city.

'How is everyone?' Maddie felt as though she had been away for much longer, and that she was adrift from their lives here.

'Same as usual,' Barbara grinned. 'The routines remain, and I'm happy with that. But something's changed with you, I think. You seem different – in a good way. What a shame you had to come away early.'

Maddie's head moved up and down in an unusual, slightly exaggerated manner. She felt as though she should be enjoying the end of a late supper on the loggia, overlooking the Valle Serena. 'I know. There's a problem with some of our clients jumping ship from this huge lawsuit, with no apparent reason. Samantha thinks I can find out why.'

Barbara's laugh contained a slightly wicked note. 'I'm sure Mr Gray has nothing to do with that?'

'Your guess is as good as mine,' Maddie answered. 'But in fairness, I don't know until I've talked to a few people. For sure, Stormtree must be at the bottom of it.'

Maddie looked at her sister, suddenly reminded of a question that had been plaguing her for days.

'That Etruscan artefact you were asked to source, Bee. Was it for him – for Pierce?'

Barbara's head said 'yes' slightly nervously. Even to her sister, she wasn't supposed to disclose details like that. But she was curious as to how Maddie had made the guess, and asked her why.

'Can you tell me what you found for him? Because, I saw some fabulous Etruscan art on my break and I've become interested.' Maddie had no idea why she didn't want to tell Barbara about the gift.

'I shouldn't,' Barbara's eyebrows rose, 'but you'll enjoy the joke. I found him a coin with a Janus head on it – about two hundred years BC, and in lovely condition. I couldn't resist finding an object with such tailor-made symbolism.'

Maddie's head tilted in question. 'The god of beginnings and endings?'

'Oh,' Barbara replied, 'no, I didn't know that. I was amused about him being two-faced.'

Maddie only nodded.

'He was going to head off to Italy next week,' Barbara was still saying, 'to visit some wineries in Chianti. All of a sudden he was talking nothing but "Brunello", at every meeting. But then I heard he's just changed his mind, and cancelled everything. He's more than two-faced. He's positively schizophrenic.'

'He's not going?' But she caught herself and the revelation; she didn't want to explain why she knew about his plans, about Lucca and the opera, or any of these things. She wanted – though she wasn't sure why – to maintain a level of secrecy about Pierce. 'Samantha also mentioned he'd be away,' Maddie tried to cover her tracks.

'Well,' Barbara said in a tone she habitually used when talking about Pierce Gray, 'maybe he was giving himself an alibi, if he were suspected of anything underhand with your clients. Better to be out of town, perhaps, and plead ignorance?'

'That may be exactly right,' Maddie answered, considering her sister as shrewd a judge of character as ever. But she wanted to stop talking about Pierce. In her own mental space it was late evening in Borgo, under a perfect night of stars, with a view suspended in front of the villa of the lights of medieval Chiusdino. And, she thought now in a lonely way, the conversation tonight was probably in Danish. Her mind wandered from this to what must have seemed a non sequitur to Barbara.

'Did you know Nonna's friend isn't Italian at all?' she asked tiredly.

Her sister looked at her, not quite sure what she was saying, and shook her head.

'She's Danish,' Maddie said. 'They're all Danish. They're lovely.'

Whatever they said for the rest of the journey, Maddie was still thinking this a couple of hours later as she heaved her washing into the machine and pushed the button, then took a coffee out onto the balcony and sat down. All her plants were in perfect condition. Nonna Isabella, she thought to herself, and blessed the woman from the depths of her heart.

'Yes, I think you might have saved me,' she whispered as she looked out over the city in the early light, 'inviting me to become a pilgrim. And that's something I never would have expected.'

The sun rose at a quarter to six on Sunday morning, and Maddie – still living in a strange timescape – was up a moment or two behind it. Barbara had stocked her sister's fridge with some unusual treasures, so Maddie helped herself to a fresh fruit smoothie and took it out onto the balcony. She looked down towards the sea. The air smelled salty, and she knew it was going to be a beautiful day – hot, perhaps.

In the early morning sky above her head she recognised a pair of turkey vultures, as they soared into the western part of her view. They must have been on a sortie from the Presidio, looking for breakfast, and she thought how beautiful the great birds were in flight. On the ground they were rather sinister in their dark brown or almost black plumage. Their bald heads and red, jowly faces were accented by short hooked tearing beaks of a clean ivory colour, and the overall effect was fearful. They were always searching the ground for carrion. She smiled to herself and wondered, what augury is this? She watched them circle and glide over the air effortlessly, with next to no wing movement. She wished it were really possible to read the future from their patterns in the sky.

Now wide awake at such an hour she started to unpack properly and get some home chores underway, moving last night's washing load into the drier and starting over again. She set up her Vaio in its home spot and sent Jeanette an email, saying she'd arrived without incident and apologising again for leaving without fulfilling her promise to take them all to dinner at La Suvera, the luxury hotel and restaurant, which had once been the Pope's residence, not many miles from Borgo. 'I'll come back just to do it,' she wrote, missing everyone there; and she made a mental note to send flowers as soon as Jimena opened tomorrow.

She downloaded her photos of the trip, mostly of Borgo itself and especially of her beautiful pilgrim's room, which she selected as her wallpaper. She wanted the reminder not only of its tranquillity, but also of the sense of proportion it had gifted her. She had sat there in so many lights – silent dawns, cheerful noons and moody sunsets – lost in consideration of her loss and deep sadness. Countless visitors over the centuries had brought their troubles to the villa. They'd also brought their hopes, and a belief in the chance of miracles. She envied them, but she also felt she'd learned something from them.

She checked her latest email from Jacinta to find out about her schedule for today and what would spill into next week. Sure enough, there was a long attachment listing all of the grey-area plaintiffs in the litigation – those who had resigned the suit, and those who were hedging – along with their addresses. Jacinta added that she had phoned Marilu and Neva, as she had been asked to do, and that they were expecting Maddie somewhere between ten and noon this morning. Maddie smiled at the many hours of work this hinted Jacinta had put in, and it almost redeemed her, she felt, for a lapse in judgement as to her lunch companion.

Marilu and Neva would indeed be a great starting point to learn what had scared away so many of their clients. It was almost impossible to imagine that Marilu would give up her fight against Stormtree for anything. Anger at them was what sustained her, and Maddie was sure she'd stand firm. But Neva: that worried Maddie. Was she seriously thinking of resigning the case? Neva's tenacity was directed not so much at anger against Stormtree as at a sense of what was fair, and what would ensure her son's survival if he were to need ongoing medical care. She'd made Maddie a promise to live long enough to see it go to court. Could anyone undermine that?

She took these thoughts into the shower and, at around nine, was turning the key in the door of her Cougar. It was covered in salt and seagull droppings, but this time she wasn't consciously looking for a message. Instead she was relieved that the engine started right away. She decided she'd pass the car automat before heading south for San Jose on the freeway, and dug in her bag for her sunglasses. Unzipping the case, Søren's cellphone number – scribbled that day in Siena – popped out, and she smiled as she carefully stowed it again and zipped it tightly back in. She could imagine him right now in Jeanette's garden, with his sketchbook and measuring tapes, before he and Claus left to go back to London tomorrow. She was missing something, not to be there with everyone. She clicked home her belt and pulled away from the steeply sloping kerb. 'Well, holiday over,' she said aloud to the rear-vision mirror, 'and now you've got an important job to do.'

The car radio gave enough local news for her to feel she'd caught up, and she quickly reached the airport road, which swept past on her left. Thoughts of her day out with Pierce to Seattle intruded on pleasanter ones and made her disgruntled and rather annoyed. She was suddenly dreading whatever was to be uncovered in San Jose, but she was there too soon for those thoughts to overwhelm her generally good spirits, and in no time she was driving straight into Marilu's driveway as the gates had been left open for her. She closed her car door respectfully, as it was still rather early on a Sunday, and she noticed Marilu had stepped onto the porch and was waiting for her. Her hair, Maddie thought, seemed a little thinner than before – the telltale sign of renewed chemotherapy.

For her part the lady of the house was surprised by the young woman she saw walking towards her, with cool white jeans and a lemon-sorbet top that set off her light tan. This was the Madeline Moretti she first remembered meeting, not the one who had come last time to the house. She was pleased, and said so.

'*Hola, Madeline. Qué tal?*' Marilu greeted her.

'*Mejor que antes,*' she answered: better than before.

'Yes. I see that.' Marilu kissed her cheeks, and extended an arm to invite her into the house. 'I'm so happy you look well and stronger, because we're going to need your strength.'

'Are you still ready for the battle ahead?' Maddie asked her, partly to encourage her to talk and at the same time aware that she might be feeling tired and unwell again.

But the feisty older woman nodded and closed the screen door behind her guest. 'Oh, I hope so, yes. But the battle lines have changed.'

Marilu gestured with her hand at a beautiful cymbidium orchid, champagne in colour, which was on the table. She thanked Maddie for sending it, and Maddie remembered that this must have been Jimena's choice for Pierce's June bouquet to Maddie. The lovely long stems had obviously pleased Marilu, and Maddie decided it was a good omen in some way – a better use of Pierce's funds, albeit that he was unaware himself of the generous act.

Marilu gave Maddie a cool drink rather than coffee today; then she relived the event of four days ago.

'I was just finishing off my hair, Madeline, when I heard a car pull up in front of the gates. I was on my way out to make a hospital visit, but I glanced out of the front window. The car was not one I recognised, and I felt immediately concerned.

'I could see a man, not very tall, and with a reddish colouring – both his hair and his complexion. He wore a light suit, but he was not a man to do well in the heat – I thought that immediately. He climbed out of a slinky black Porsche and started unlatching my gates, and I remember thinking that the car was worth more than this house. He seemed very posed when he pushed a pair of those gangster sunglasses up onto the top of his head, and looked up towards the house.'

Maddie was taken by surprise. It definitely didn't sound like Pierce; but the hair colouring threw her a clue.

'He took a handkerchief from his top pocket,' Marilu continued, 'and wiped his forehead. Well, Miss Madeline, the outside temperature was already around eighty degrees, even though it was not yet half-past nine in the morning. I thought to myself, this person does not take well to California. He's a newcomer, from some cooler place.'

Maddie nodded, with a show of amusement.

'I watched him tip the driver's seat forward, and he took out a very thin leather briefcase. Then he closed his door, with a big popping sound for the lock and alarms flashing, and he started going at my gate again. I could see a big gold-strapped fancy watch and a fraternity ring on his finger, trying to undo an old-fashioned lock on my gate, and for all his obvious money he didn't know how a gate like mine worked. But he was wearing his money, you know, Miss Madeline.'

Maddie loved the picture of the man unable to get in at the gate. She thought she knew who he was, and it amused her that Janus wasn't on his side that day.

'The word "yanqui" came to mind. Someone from a different part of the country, but still a proud citizen of the United States! My friends come from everywhere, Madeline, of all colours and religions, and I make a point of getting on with everyone. But I'm a sound judge of character, too, and this particular person? I knew I had taken against him. And so I changed my word to "gringo". You know, what this means for us is not very nice – an arrogant white Anglo who wants something, more or less.

'Madeline, I went out onto my porch and locked the security door behind me. The man pulled his glasses back down so I couldn't see his eyes. "Maria Luisa!" he stated. He did not ask, Miss Maddie. "It is Señora Moreno," I corrected him; and I walked towards the iron gate with the key for the lock, but I didn't open it for him.

'"A friend is picking me up to take me to the hospital,"' I said to him, very politely. "Can I help you?"

273

'Then he started at me with a speech, Miss Madeline. "I represent Stormtree Components, and we want to talk to you. We have a financial problem, and we are considering withdrawing our ongoing financial support from the employees who are involved in litigation against us."'

'Oh, my,' Maddie breathed.

'He stopped me in my tracks with that, Madeline. Just as I unlocked the gate, and came out onto the path, I looked into his glasses. I could feel the eyes behind the dark lenses, almost smiling with superiority. I scented the man behind the lenses, a weak man, sweating. *No tiene corazón*, I thought, he's got no heart. But I smiled at him. I knew only the car and suit separated him from me; but this *hombre* wanted to forget that. Maybe a generation or two ago, his people had had to fight the rats in a tenement some place in a foreign land.

'But in the strict law of survival, Señorita Maddie, if his people have somehow found enough will and money to get on a boat and come to America, you have to respect this. And his family must have found the way to give him an education. But I stayed behind to help my family survive; and I felt this man would never do that. No matter what cost to others, this person would not give up an inch of what he had won; and I almost felt sorry for him at that moment. It is the worst thing in life, I think, to have no soul.'

'Yes, Marilu,' Maddie nodded. She smiled at her. 'Did he say any more to you about pulling away your medical funds?'

'*Sí, Maddie*. He was very clear. "If you withdraw your complaint, the company would not have to do this," he told me. "We could go on supporting your insurance deductible and other expenses."'

'I need to look into their liability, Marilu,' Maddie said, balancing anger with a strong sense of feeling for the woman. 'I'd be very surprised if this threat is valid – if they can really just withdraw support for your medical bills.'

'I understand, Madeline,' she answered. 'But it is very scary for me – probably for everyone. I know this is like a game of poker, and you don't give anything away to the people you're fighting, but my heart had sunk into my shoes. The smile just froze on my face. Lucky for me, my friend's Buick pulled off the main road and beeped for me, and I told him, "That's my ride." Then I thought quickly, and asked, "Have you got a business card, *Señor*?"

'"Yes, ma'am!" he answered me, and he flashed through his wallet to hand me one. He told me to call as soon as I can. And I nodded at him, Madeline, but I ran for my friend's car, and when I opened the door I just said, "*Hijo de la chingada madre.*" I sat inside my friend's car and crossed myself. I said, "I have just met the devil." And then I pulled out my cell and called you, Señorita Maddie.

'But, what am I going to do?' Marilu continued. She stood up and crossed the room. 'That was three days ago, and I have not called him back. I want to tell him to go to hell, but I am sure he can afford every comfort in hell, and I cannot afford my own hospital bills.'

Marilu picked up a business card from the corner of her mirror, and handed it to Maddie. The words on the card failed to surprise her: 'Gordon J. Hugo, Attorney-at-law'.

'Your description of him left me in no doubt,' Maddie smiled grimly. 'Anyway, now we know for sure. I'd like to keep this, if I may? And I'll phone you tomorrow from my office, when I've had a chance to check the legality of what they're doing.'

Maddie hugged Marilu as she left her on the porch. 'Don't worry yet,' she assured her. 'They certainly can't move that quickly, and, for what it's worth, I really believe this is scare tactics. I think we have them worried.'

'I'll stand strong, Señorita Maddie.' Marilu tried to smile. 'But call me when you're sure of our position.'

Three days earlier the corridors of the Mater Misericordiae Hospital had echoed to the footsteps of Gordon Hugo. He was familiar with the place long before his firm had been retained by Stormtree. Hugo had, as a young lawyer, sought out accident casualties and other possible injury victims to see what work could be turned from this place. For him there was no real mileage in this, because he wanted big money and a higher standing; but his solid law degree from a small Midwest university hadn't made him a front runner for a job in one of the established East Coast firms. For this reason he had come west straight after law school and gone into business with a fraternity buddy whose father was a judge. Dwight's well-placed family friends had pointed work in their direction, and the pair had worked hard. After years of their just covering the ground, a high-profile win for a small insurance company against a nuisance suit had launched something of a meteoric upward curve in the firm's fortunes, culminating in a multimillion-dollar retainer from Stormtree.

Gordon Hugo liked Pierce Gray. He admired his daring, copied his style. He thought him straightforward and pioneer in spirit – and he knew that Gray always wanted to win. This was honest of him, Hugo felt, because everybody really wanted to win, and those who denied it were deceiving themselves. In Washington, DC, and in Maine and Massachusetts, Stormtree naturally used the old-established firms with their WASP networks of lobbyists and contacts. But here in California, where things could be done in a different way, Hugo's style suited Stormtree's needs well.

He knew the company started by Pierce's father in the eighties had only just survived the 'dot com' collapse, and the young Gray had taken it over from his father in the early nineties. Pierce, though, had pushed hard. He anticipated future trends in the market well, and the firm's growth had mushroomed nicely. Both Gray and Hugo had also enjoyed the politics of the period since the millennium, and the company's success had presented Pierce with more funds to invest in his wine-making, now that he'd inherited the Napa property from his grandfather. Why have a dog and bark? he'd asked Hugo; so Hugo's firm could do all the barking for him and leave Pierce more time to tend his grapes.

The strategy that Dwight and Gordon had worked out for Stormtree was cynically simple, but surprisingly effective. Delay, and delay, and then delay some more. By then, hopefully most of the problems would go away or irritable foes would have lost heart or funds to fight them with. Hugo had not, however, quite allowed for Harden Hammond Cohen's tenacity. As it looked increasingly as though the cases would go to hearings, the second-tier plan was to put as much pressure as possible on the opposition to reduce the number of claimants. That way, if some piece of evidence made things truly uncomfortable for Stormtree, they could probably afford to settle on the court-house steps. Winning would be great, but was never as important as the best deal.

The Moreno woman had been a cakewalk, Hugo thought, and he'd felt certain he would hear from her within days. She wasn't going to lose her house over a few medical bills, and she was smart enough to see sense. That was five cases that looked good for him, but now his attention had turned to the Walker girl. He had a feeling she might be more difficult. After all, she wasn't going to need hospitalisation for much longer, and he knew she had a child who was a part of her case for the future. She might want to go the distance.

At about half-past eleven on Sunday morning, Neva's face lit up as Maddie entered her hospital room. Aguila and Wyman Walker sat on either side of her bed, and Maddie smiled at all of them without appearing to notice the worsening bruise on Neva's arm courtesy of the long months of hosting the drip.

'Ah, welcome, Maddie,' Neva beamed at her. 'You look well. Maybe just a little tired. You've had a long trip to come to us today.' Neva took the newcomer's hand and chafed it, and then she became thoughtful for a moment. 'I'm sorry we've pulled you away from the people you were so happy with; but selfishly, we are glad to see you.'

'No, I've come back only a few days early, Neva,' Maddie said rather shyly. 'This is much more important than my holiday.'

'On the contrary, Maddie,' Neva said, 'your trip was to get back your soul; and that is the only important thing.'

Then her tone changed to one of light-hearted happiness. 'This is my father, Wyman, and my son, Aguila. You've met them both, of course, wherever you were.'

Maddie said hello to Neva's son, and then smiled and shook the hand of Neva's father. He was a strongly built man, in a denim shirt and jeans, and a fine silver-buckle belt inset with turquoises. Maddie noticed he was wearing cowboy boots, and she felt his presence very powerfully in the room. Somehow, it was exactly the kind of reassurance Maddie herself was looking for.

'Hello,' he answered. 'You are the lady who knows about snow,' he said again. 'It's an honour to meet you.'

'My father has a story to tell you about Mr Hugo,' Neva said to Maddie. 'He has no shadow, and we believe that means he has no spirit.'

Maddie settled herself in a chair and waited for Neva's father. He didn't hurry, took a moment to put his mind in the right place, and then he began a tale that was to follow Maddie for the many miles of her return to San Francisco, and the many long hours of her restless night.

'The man's shoes could be heard along the hospital corridor for a long time, before he walked into this room.

'"I need to have a word with Neva Walker," he spoke.

'He appeared surprised, perhaps, by what he saw. He looked me up and down, and then I got to my feet.

'"Hello, I am Neva's father. Can I help you?" I asked.

'He wasn't pleased with this, but I pointed to my daughter in the bed.

'"She is asleep. Please don't wake her," I said.

'We moved towards the door. It took much of my will to make him see he must go out.

'"We can speak outside," I told him.

'Mr Hugo was a man who had never been up close to an Indian. He did not know how to respond. The poor Mexicans, and the black population – they are part of his world. Even they are pretty much interchangeable, I think, as far as he is concerned. But here he was with a man who is not very tall. He was not on dry ground, and he offered a level of respect just because my people are not familiar to him. He began his speech to me, and he was nervous.

'"I am Gordon J. Hugo," he said. "I represent Stormtree Components. I must talk with Neva about the mounting costs of her care."

'I stared at him with no expression to tell him my thoughts.

'"You see, the Company cannot afford to continue paying for the rising costs of her medical bills, in the light of the impending legal case," he said.

'I stood very still, and looked at him. It might have been for some time.

'"Mr Hugo, I am a hauler of timber. I drive a truck. I don't make a lot of money," I said. "But I read a lot of newspapers. Didn't I read that Stormtree Components will show an eleven per cent increase in their profits in this quarter? The total was several hundred million dollars."

'The man's face was very pink. He said nothing, so I spoke again.

'"Can you explain to a simple trucker why a company like this cannot afford the medicine for my daughter and my grandson?" I asked.

'But still he gave me no words, Madeline.

'I said, "Mr Hugo. Do you understand what an Indian giver is?"

'Now, Mr Hugo looked more comfortable. He was sure he knew exactly what this means.

'"Someone who gives a gift, and then demands it back," he answered me.

'"This is as I thought," I said. "But it's you who does not understand.

If an Indian gives a gift it is given with a good heart, and it has an obligation that goes with it. An Indian's gift is not a piece of property," I said. "It is not a thing, or a profit. It is something deeper, a token of respect and peace for everyone to enjoy. Once it has been enjoyed it should be returned to the giver, or passed to another who can enjoy it. It is not for a shelf, like a trophy. It is not for banking, like a profit. That is what an Indian's gift is."

'Mr Hugo had nothing to say. He was swinging his briefcase, like a schoolboy. He moved his weight from one leg to the other, and he looked down the corridor. Having just arrived, I think he wanted to go.

'"My daughter has given your company the gift of her being," I said. "She has given her loyalty. She has worked with Mr Gray's company for many years, and in return they have crippled and depleted her and poisoned my grandson."

'Now, the pink one spoke. "You cannot prove that," he said to me.

'"No. But we both know it's true," I said.

'Mr Hugo had no more words for me, Madeline.

'"I'll come back another day, when she is awake," he only said.

'And then he took his wet face back down the hallway. I watched him go, and noticed how he passed through the light and shade. I wasted my words. He is not a man to know about gifts and obligations.'

'No,' Maddie answered him, very quietly. 'For Gordon Hugo, people live and people die, and there is no more. He is the son of Scottish Protestant immigrants to this country, and I think he understands success as a sign that God smiles on you. But a friend just reminded me that language has the power to influence the outcome of events, Mr Walker. I don't believe your words were wasted.'

31

Early in the morning on Holy Agnes' Day a small group of men
bearing their pilgrim's staff and hat made their way along the
road toward Galgano's shrine, and the residents of the villa of
Santo Pietro took themselves to bed for a few hours of sleep. For some
time under Jacquetta's roof a tree of silence flourished, and bore the
fruits of peace. Porphyrius and his wife and child slept in blissful
exhaustion in their room with the view to the north and west, over the
ice-whitened pilgrims' road; and even Jacquetta had retired to her suite
of rooms facing across the Valle Serena, leaving the running of the house
to Loredana and Chiara, who had each enjoyed some part of a night's
sleep. When Mia had climbed the narrow stair to her bedchamber under
the eaves, a greyish light had just been breaking to announce the new
day and more expected snowfall; and the monks' bell had called them to
lauds. But as she closed her eyelids, she could still hear the owl somewhere
in the trees below her window.

Before midday she woke to gentle knocking on her door, and
reluctantly left the warmth of her bed to attend to it. Chiara had brought
warm water, and instruction from her aunt that she was to wash and
make ready for the service of sext at noon in the abbey. They had missed
the earlier service for the holy day in the village, but would be permitted
to stand at the rear of the monks' church and join silently with the lay
brothers in their worship before they had their lunch and retired to their

280

dormitory for a siesta. She must arrange her hair quickly and not dally, Loredana insisted.

So perhaps it was a little after three in the afternoon on Agnes' Day – when they had eaten a little, and retired to the fire in the music room – that Aunt Jacquetta vanished and then reappeared with a *scarsella*, a purse used by couriers for letters and packets. This was put into Gennaro's hands.

'I'm so sorry,' Jacquetta said to him. 'It was given me yesterday, by a messenger who had travelled from Pisa. Agnesca's labour took it from my mind until this moment.'

He smiled his thanks to her and unfastened the bag, which contained a waterproof canvas bound with string. As he pulled this covering aside, Mia and her aunt both sighed appreciatively. Gennaro was holding a finely wrought flat wooden object, roughly square and about the length of a forearm. It had been silver-gilded, and over-painted at the centre and each corner with figures and symbols. Mia came to sit on the settle beside Gennaro to look more closely, and saw that it was carved with a symmetric pattern of rills and stops. At the centre a water mill was depicted; and each corner showed the cardinal points, the elements, and the face of each of the four winds. It was dazzlingly beautiful, but she was at a loss to understand its purpose. She looked at him with a puzzled expression.

'It is a board for playing *Il Mulino*,' he said to her, 'and I have never seen one as fine.'

'I don't know this game,' she said, looking from Gennaro to her aunt. She felt ashamed, as though this lack of knowledge meant she was an ignorant country girl.

'Then it's time you learned how to play,' he said, and turned to Jacquetta for her benediction.

'Yes, why not?' came Jacquetta's answer, along with an expression that blended a smile with something more secret. 'It is the game my French grandmother called *Merrelles*, and she always said that every girl should learn to play it.'

Gennaro grinned at her, making Mia feel they enjoyed some private joke between them. But she would not be allowed to share it, she thought, as he turned back without further explanation and gave his attention once again to the contents of the *scarsella*, and to a parchment contained within it. This was a letter comprised of several sheets of paper folded in three, closed with a small cord which passed through holes at the edges, and sealed at each end. Breaking the seal, he unfolded and began to read a beautifully written page which, as he told both ladies, contained salutations for the anniversary of his birth on this date, twenty-one years before.

He then returned to the body of the script, and Mia felt he should be accorded some privacy. She got to her feet and, having made him a sweet chestnut cake the day before, wondered if now might be the appropriate time for them to cut into it. She'd hoped to wait for Porphyrius and *la raggia*, to emphasise the point that it had suddenly become a day of double celebration for both births. However, they were still resting upstairs with the baby, and she would certainly not disturb them. She whispered to her aunt that they ought not to forgo some recognition of Gennaro's special day much longer, and suggested that the receipt of this gift was a good prompt. Jacquetta nodded her agreement, but as Mia started towards the pantry room to bring the cake Gennaro placed his hand on her arm.

'My letter contains within it another, Maria Maddalena,' he said. He held out a folded sheet, with a separate seal. 'And it is for you.'

'But, who can it be from?' she asked him.

Certainly she knew who it might be from; who she wanted it to be from. Her brain had been occupied night and day – since Gennaro's arrival had opened the way for a half-voiced conversation about her family – with wanting to learn the truth of her existence and identity, the reason for the loss of her mother and her coming here to her aunt. A flood of questions would not be compressed into clear thoughts now, but the imperative to know flushed her cheeks and made them burn. For Mia it was as though Gennaro and her aunt already knew her secrets, and could grant or refuse her wish for ever with the delivery of that letter.

But watching Gennaro's eyes she read them as kind, and they encouraged her.

'Yes, Maria,' he said.

He looked at the pretty girl, dressed in simple elegance for the holy day. Her hair was braided and fastened up with ribbons, and her pale green kirtle was cinched at the waist, revealing her feminine shape. She seemed young, and hopeful, and nubile; but also infinitely vulnerable. Whatever news it would deliver once opened, he knew this was what she waited on. No caution would hold her impatience at bay.

'It *is* from my uncle.'

Mia took the letter carefully from him, as though it would burst into flame with the heat of her fingers if she handled it wrongly. She looked at her aunt, but whether for approval or shared pleasure – or even an explanation as to why such a thing was directed through Gennaro – she couldn't say.

'I'll save it for later, then,' she said. 'I must see to the chestnut cake.'

'Mia!' Jacquetta cried. 'You've been waiting on that correspondence for weeks past count. Open it, for Our Lady's sake, and I shall bring the cake.'

Jacquetta left the room and Gennaro nodded at Mia, who took her sealed paper to a chair nearer the fire. She turned it over and read the name – her name. She was aware of the irony: to have waited so long for nothing else, and to sit unable to break the seal. But it delivered a verdict, and she was suddenly very unsure about whether she could find the courage to confront the tide of emotions it must surely bring with it.

She had sat with it for some time when Gennaro smiled, and addressed her.

'Maria. It can say nothing that will alter the feelings your friends have for you. It can say nothing you must apologise for. Yet, might it put your mind at rest, and settle your uncertainties?'

Mia studied Gennaro's expression. She wasn't sure why it was that these words carried so much meaning for her, but it helped her put her fears aside, and she slit through the seal with her thumb and unbound the cord. Her eyes drank in the black ink of the script, and she was immediately aware of the relatively few lines, the paucity of words. It confused her, and she read slowly.

Distinguished Maria Maddalena,

I greet you well on the eve of this holy day. Jacquetta calls me to mind that I have a duty of family business to convey to you, now that you have attained an age of understanding. I am sensible of this, and upon the honesty I owe you. Yet herein I mean to be brief, or otherwise I must write you a whole Psalter.

I come to Villa Santo Pietro in Cellole, where I shall speak with you.

On that occasion I shall bring your gift for Epiphany. You may understand that it is only business, which lately brings me to Pisa, that prevents me from coming to you now; and expect my visit upon any day, perhaps even within the se'nnight, when matters that urged me here to this city have been concluded.

With these few lines I thank you, also, for your part in the recovery of my nephew; whom I understand came to you with death upon him. I learn from him directly of the part you played in restoring his health.

I leave you in God's hands, and come as soon as my journey may allow;

Ranuccio, Vescovo, Volterra

Mia sat in silent contemplation. When she looked up she noticed her aunt had come back into the room with cake for Gennaro, and a subtle curiosity aimed at Mia herself. But she didn't know what to answer her, and instead put the letter into her aunt's hands.

Jacquetta read through it twice before she offered an opinion.

'There is too much for him to say in a letter, Mia. His coming here to you is the wisest and kindest act. We will prepare his chamber for him.'

A week later the house was still quiet, with only a handful of pilgrims on the road in the winter weather. Mia tried hard not to look impatient for her visitor. She passed her time making vinegar, reading her lessons, and happily sitting with Luccio, Agnesca's beautiful child, whom his father had named in honour of his birth on the night of such a bright moon, at the moment of the first light of day. She managed her winter chores, kept the rooms fresh with new strewing herbs each morning, and sat in taper-light on the long evenings with Gennaro, who was teaching her how to play the game of *Il Mulino*. She soon learned the strategy of getting three of her pebbles – dark or light in colour – into a row by taking one move at a time, only in straight lines, and only one space with each move. Then she could capture any piece of Gennaro's from the board until he had fewer than three left, and could make no row of his own. After losing the game more than a dozen times at the start of the week, she'd managed to win one by the end; but she smiled when

Porphyrius took a turn in her chair and the game between the two of them proceeded at such a pace she couldn't follow all the moves. She realised her cousin must be letting her win.

She'd come to know him better, to laugh at the seriousness of their competitions, to admire the sense he spoke about so many things, and to share his enjoyment of good company and friends. His nature was very gentle; his opinions always on the side of moderation, and kindliness, and patience with others. This, she knew, was a studied position he had come to through his family's severe adversity. They had been a family who had enjoyed every privilege, and then lost nearly all of them. Yet he always made her laugh – was less serious than Porphyrius. She couldn't deny that these days passed in pleasure. However, no visitor came for her.

As the last days of January turned into those of February and they observed Candlemas, Gennaro offered some reasons for his uncle's non-appearance.

'The roads from Pisa will be slow, Maria, in the winter weather, and perhaps his business drags.'

She nodded. It was certainly probable that the 'matters that urged' him to Pisa weren't concluded, but the weather was not a reason. The snow was light or nearly absent, and anyone who really wished to pass along the roads, and knew them well, could surely do so.

At the end of the first week of February, they had to watch Gennaro go. He declared himself fit to travel, and no longer content to be an encumbrance upon them. Jacquetta tried to detain him a little longer: his company was a delight, and she saw how he had grown in Mia's affections, even if her niece was unaware. But he felt he should be back and working, and wanted funds to repay her kindness properly and some news of his family, having spent weeks away from them. Jacquetta understood.

'You'll see me again,' he said to her, 'for among other things I must do, I wish to arrange a gift for my godson. And in the meantime, you have a friend in Volterra – should you need one.'

Jacquetta proved to be right, however. His departure was a terrible loss for Mia, who supposed she missed his presence because he was the first person she had come to think of as her family, outside of her bond with Aunt Jacquetta. Or perhaps it was just that *la raggia* and Porphyrius were so caught up with their new child, and in this season there was less to consume Mia in the world within her own doors. The garden slept under a sprinkling of snow; the path to the abbey was too icy to negotiate without an important reason to go there; and pilgrims were fewer in number. With all these half-reasons for her apathy, the worst was her longing to see Bishop Ranuccio. But less than a week later, she had news.

The palfrey's tread belonged to a friend. Agnesca had been putting her son into his cradle when she saw a rider approach along the familiar path in the early afternoon. She called to Porphyrius, who was on his way to the threshing barn; and in a few more minutes Jacquetta was mulling ale in front of the kitchen fire for the young man who had left them only days before.

'You never made it to Volterra?' Jacquetta asked him, concerned about his health.

Gennaro shook his head. 'I was never going there. My road always took me west and north, towards Pisa.'

Jacquetta's face was suffused with wonder at what this revelation implied. 'To find out what has happened with Bishop Ranuccio. Why didn't I understand this was your purpose in leaving us? And yet I am not really surprised, Gennaro.'

'Of course,' he answered. 'He couldn't know how much importance this has assumed for Maria Maddalena. But we do. I needed to tell him. Nevertheless,' he sighed, 'I didn't get to Pisa.'

She set the hot drinks on a tray and ushered both Gennaro and Porphyrius into the solar where the fire was lit, to give them privacy. Mia was in the bakehouse with Alba, and Jacquetta wanted time to hear Gennaro out before they called her to the house; but having settled the baby, Agnesca joined them as they were sitting down.

'I am happy to see you, but something is wrong,' she said to Gennaro, kissing him on each cheek. 'You're unwell again?'

'No,' he said emphatically. 'You're a fine doctor, and I am in good health. But there is trouble with others.'

'Is it the sickness?' Agnesca asked.

Her pretty face had gained lustre since the birth of her child three weeks before, and Gennaro had been thinking how lovely she looked again; but it just as suddenly paled as she voiced this question. He nodded solemnly, and began his tale.

His journey as ambassador for Mia had taken him from the villa to the west along the ancient Massetana Road, to avoid the icier pass through the more mountainous Val d'Elsa. He had then struck north, finding lodging with friends in Pomerance who were still loyal to his uncle and the Allegretti family, though Ottaviano had claimed the bishop's castle there for his son. A second long day on his horse brought him to Montecatini in the Cecina Valley, where he thought his troubles behind him after he'd managed to stay without incident in a town so well reputed as a stronghold of the Belforti. But the next day the going was slow, with more snowfall, and he could make it only as far as Ponsacco, though he'd hoped to travel the whole distance to Pisa. At an inn he learned news, from a Florentine merchant, of an illness that was sweeping through the coastal city. The merchant had been unable to enter Pisa to pick up his goods at the port, and had returned to Ponsacco with an empty cart to regale an awestruck crowd with tales of a pestilence so virulent that anyone unfortunate enough to even speak to the afflicted could not evade death.

'It is thought that the disease made its way to Pisa from Sardinia or Elba,' Gennaro told them, 'perhaps aboard galleys much like the one Porphyrius and I took passage on to Salerno. Sailors seem to have unloaded the catastrophe along with their spices and cloth. Since the middle of January it has been making its murderous way through the small city. There is talk of some coughing blood from their insides; but from his report of fever, and blackening buboes, and people collapsing in the street too exhausted to get up again, I believe without doubt that it is the same fearful malady I had. I only wonder tenfold at the miracle of my escape.'

From a long habit of being without a voice, Mia was a quiet human being, and she had reached the door of the solar without anyone noticing her approach. She had heard this last speech from Gennaro's own lips, and it took away her joy at seeing him there, and made her shudder. It was as though he were living afresh the horrors of his own illness, and she moved towards him haltingly. Before he could rise to greet her, she kneeled in front of him at his chair by the fire and squeezed his hands, then laid her cheek on them.

'Is my father . . . ?' she started to ask him.

'Maria,' he answered her, 'I don't know if he is well or ill; but travel to or from the city may be quite impossible for the present. I could not even write to him, for no man would undertake the errand of playing messenger into Pisa.'

Jacquetta was profoundly worried about Ranuccio, for whom she cared deeply, and the further implications of the reports from Pisa.

'We must hope he is unaffected, make enquiries as best we can, and tighten our vigilance here, just as Agnesca first urged us to do when the illness arose from the south, and Porphyrius and Gennaro were tangled in it. Pilgrims come and go, and *Carnevale* has just begun. If the weather is mild the house will fill, so we must implement those same careful measures Agnesca advised weeks ago.'

'I wonder if Gennaro may be safe from reinfection, now that he has survived it?' Agnesca suggested tentatively. 'Report of others sickening immediately run contrary to our experience here with Gennaro. Indeed, Porphyrius for some reason did not sicken at all.'

'Yet we can take nothing for granted, Agnesca,' Jacquetta answered. 'We have collective stories of this pestilence in the southern ports of the Mediterranean, in Genoa and Pisa. Whatever unleashed it, it is loose and on the prowl.'

'And will follow the ports,' Porphyrius said.

Agnesca agreed. Discussion between them decided Jacquetta to reimplement quarantine in the garden rooms for guests – which they had largely dispensed with in the period following Christmas because the quarters were not really warm, and there had been no more talk of illness. Additionally Agnesca felt that personal cleanliness and control of the numbers of people coming and going should be a priority, and that the farm dogs should be kept away from the villa in spite of Mia's affection for them. This might give them some chance of restricting the winter dirt and dust, and fending off whatever it was.

Gennaro smiled grimly. 'Do you think I've forgotten the horror of the baths you subjected me to, or the misery of Maria washing my hair with some foul-smelling stuff, when I hated touch of any kind and was freezing cold?'

Agnesca looked at him without apology. 'Your head was full of lice, Gennaro; and the baths may have saved your life,' she replied.

'When you travel to the seaports, Agnesca,' he said wryly, 'lice and fleas and, yes, sometimes even rats are your bedmates. Few hostelries are as scrupulously cleaned, or as comfortable, as Villa Santo Pietro.'

Porphyrius looked furtively at his wife, and then said something Mia would never forget.

'From the days of her imprisonment in the priors' tower in Volterra, she has a horror of vermin. Rats and fleas were her companions at that time, and she has been fastidious about excluding them from every chamber, and from our clothing, in every way possible, every day since. That is why she always smells of crushed pepper and lavender.'

'The prison tower! Agnesca!' Mia cried, using Porphyrius's now familiar name for his wife on a very rare occasion herself.

'This is not a tale I wish to tell today, Mia,' her friend answered firmly. 'I'll save it for a night when we, perhaps, are so full of mirth that we can indulge one of woe. But for now let us prepare the stable rooms afresh; and Gennaro might be willing to try other means for news of the bishop?'

Gennaro had a hand on Mia's head, but looked up at this request from his friend's wife. 'I'll think of an alternate way to get through to Pisa,' he said.

By the middle of the next week, however, when Gennaro had written a host of letters bound for the west from the comfort of the villa, a message arrived from the opposite direction. This time it was directed to Jacquetta, a short sealed note that afforded only a few lines.

Arrived at Montalcino a fortnight ago, but illness has since struck my household. We are many of us blighted with a strange infirmity. However, God willing, I make my way to you forthwith.
R. Allegretti

Two days later – before Carnival had given way to Lent – the small party arrived. There was no ceremony, no trail of attendants. No confident and still handsome bishop rode at a smooth gait in front of his brightly caparisoned retinue. Two men, each astride a rouncy, accompanied a litter borne by a horse and rider at front and back. Jacquetta had never seen the bishop travel this way – not in any cavalcade, for ceremony or show. He was a proud horseman and an agile hunter. At a glance she knew that the worst was not only possible, but certain.

The exiled bishop's servants were lodged in the stable rooms in line with their protocol, but Jacquetta couldn't bring herself to impose the same strictures on her much-loved Ranuccio. He was clearly ill, and suffering. She thought, in a sober moment, that he was not long for this world, but she banished Agnesca from any role of caring for him, knowing it exposed both her and her child to danger. She insisted on nursing him herself, whatever the cost, and installed him in his own comfortable room on the ground floor of the villa, overlooking the knot garden. This room, Mia remembered, had long stood empty – ready for no guest but him, unless a king should call. Jacquetta imposed a kind of cordon, separating it from activity throughout the rest of the household, limiting movement between it and every other chamber. But outside this room Mia now took up a vigil, waiting to see or speak with its occupant, passionately offering up orisons to the angel of mercy for his recovery and health.

Jacquetta, meanwhile, consulted with Agnesca. The bishop had arrived with severe fever and had been vomiting the contents of his stomach for many days. He had boils over several parts of his body: in his neck and underarms, like Gennaro, but also in his groin, which she had defied modesty to see and treat. She knew the lumps were likely to burst but, unlike his younger nephew who had shown remarkable resilience, she doubted the older man could endure the treatment of an ice bath to bring down his fever. She was holding everything at bay with honey poultices and a tea made of thyme and feverfew, but even this he could not keep down.

'He is worsening at such a rate,' she spoke through an almost-closed door to Agnesca. 'The lumps are dark in hue, already the size of apples, and livid purplish spots are breaking out everywhere on his skin. For two days I have tried everything I watched you do, and I have no notion what more to try for him.'

'It is a more pugnacious case, perhaps, than Gennaro's,' she answered. 'Jacquetta, I will come to him if you ask me?'

But she knew her hostess would never allow the young mother to the sick man's bedside, and this was exactly Jacquetta's answer.

'Then I believe the only thing to do,' Agnesca advised her, 'is to send Gennaro in with him, to sit with him, and offer companionship. I hope he is past further contagion himself. From what you describe, I think we must make the bishop comfortable, if possible, but it may be wise to send for your Abbot Angelo if he would desire absolution?'

Jacquetta was upright and dignified from habit in any circumstance, but she slumped against Agnesca's door at hearing this. The younger woman opened it and put all other considerations aside to comfort her friend and long-time protector. Her arms enveloped Jacquetta.

'Why do you think, Agnesca, that I have been unable to turn this around?'

'I think that he is an older man, Jacquetta, and perhaps we came to it too late for treatment.'

Jacquetta sighed, and gratefully accepted the embrace from her friend. After a moment she added, 'And, Mia?'

'If he is as unconnected to the world as Gennaro was, then it falls to you to tell Mia his story.'

Late that night Jacquetta followed Agnesca's advice and sent for Abbot Angelo. Mia's eyes were swollen with tears when, near midnight, he entered the bishop's immaculate chamber which, in spite of every costly strewing herb and pomander, had the unmistakable stench of death. There he sat with Gennaro and Jacquetta for hours. Unlike the night of little Luccio's birth, when the owl had warned of trouble with the birth and hinted at an unhappy fate connected with Ranuccio's letter, there was no sound outside. Mia remained at her post on a chair by his door. With stinging eyelids she watched the abbot leave again in the hushed hours of the night; and at some time after that Agnesca, who got up briefly to see to her son, came down the stairs to join her. She pulled a second chair to her side and sat, holding her hand.

At dawn, Gennaro opened the door into the hall.

'If you are willing to risk coming in,' he said in a husky voice to Mia, 'he is cognisant, and would like to see you.'

It was fortunate for Mia that her repulsion to the horrible sights and smells of the buboes had already been blunted after nursing Gennaro for so many days. For here was the face of the man she most wanted to see. His eyes were yellow and staring; the burst sores had a choking odour; and his face was so misshapen and red and swollen that it was impossible to imagine how it must have been before. On the rare occasions when Jacquetta had spoken of the bishop – when a gift had arrived for Mia, or news had come about him – she had always described him as handsome, and wise, and a man with kindly eyes. It was this likeness that Mia had recognised in Gennaro after his recovery.

Now, however, the man trying so hard to focus on Mia's features was at some distance from the description the girl had cherished of him. She had never consciously stared death in the face, but she knew she did so now.

He beckoned her over, and spoke in a voice made up only of breath. It sent a chill through her, reminding her bizarrely of the sounds her mother had made at her death, like gurgling blood on cold steel.

'I have left it too late, Maria.'

His staccato words were high enough in volume for her ear alone.

'Arrangements I have made for you will be to your liking, I trust. If they are not,' he went on with difficulty, 'do not adhere to them. You are accorded a free hand to do what you wish – with your aunt's advice.'

Gennaro came over to him and raised him on his pillow, to help him voice these words; then he stepped away from the bed to give Mia a final moment of unhallowed intimacy with the man.

'Your aunt and Abbot Angelo can tell you everything you need to know, but from my lips, you must learn a single thing.'

He grasped her hand, and though the proximity to a man in such a pitiful human condition – vile-smelling and hideous to look upon – would have beaten any other person, Mia held his hand tightly and returned the pressure.

'Your mother was the sweetest soul in my world,' he said in a final effort to communicate with her. 'Yet, I was never her lover, Maria. Your guardian I am, and have always been. But I am not your father.'

Mia's eyes widened, and she heard her heart beating in her ears. She looked at the poor man, and felt he must be speaking in a kind of delirium. Surely this was false.

'I am the father of your heart,' he rasped out. 'The father of your flesh, however, is the man who stole your mother's virtue and made her unmarriageable.'

Mia looked him in the eye.

'Who, Your Grace?' she asked quietly.

His answer came without volume, but Mia was in no doubt about the word that shaped on his lips.

'Ottaviano.'

32

25 JUNE 2007, SAN FRANCISCO

I t was no surprise for Maddie to see a blanket of low fog from her
bedroom window at seven in the morning in summer. What was
odd was that it only covered the buildings in her view to the height
of about the third floors. The fog left her in sunshine, while those below
her were shrouded in mist. The taller blocks protruding out of the layer
of cloud gave a surreal effect to the landscape below. It was a reminder
that, in San Francisco, you could never tell what would happen next, as
far as the weather was concerned.

This morning Maddie felt like walking into work. She needed to
think about the impact of what she had found out on her Sunday visits,
before confronting the rest of the office. She was deeply upset – though
not shocked – by what she regarded as a complete lack of morality on
the part of Gordon Hugo. She needed to qualify her own attitude to
these actions in a non-emotional way, and also clear her head of so many
other things that were still whirling around in her thoughts before she
got to work. Part of it, she supposed, was jet lag, and a good walk would
help sweep that away.

She set out for the office in warm sunshine. It was as she started her
descent toward the Embarcadero that the fog began to close around her.
It made her feel as though she'd passed into another time as it thickened
with her every footstep down the hill. The outline of cars and pedestrians
blurred, and the sounds of traffic muted. When she came round the
corner near her office, the fog was quite heavy along the shoreline by the
bay. Through the gloom she noticed a florist's van passing the curve of

293

her building, which reminded her to stop by Jimena's and organise some flowers for Jeanette on her way home.

The weather today recalled to mind her feelings of five months ago, when she'd returned to work after Chris's death. Then, she'd felt the depressing effect of the fog had followed her right to the office door and wrapped her in a shroud, dulling her to the world. Today the fog seemed neither so depressing nor personal, and it abandoned her at the street entrance. She laughed at herself, deciding her thoughts were taking an oblique direction. She wondered if it were the combined effect of Søren's joke about her 'being' the wind, and Neva's father saying she understood about the snow? If we are happy, she thought, we notice the sunshine, and when we are low in spirits the rain has more impact on our consciousness. We give it our own significance; and that is all there is to it.

She pushed through the glass office doors to a smiling Teresa, who looked like she'd had a weekend at the beach.

'Hey, Maddie, you look great,' Teresa said with marked sincerity. 'Even with the Italian food, I'm thinking, you've hardly put on a pound! How can that be?'

'Oh, yes, more than a pound,' Maddie smiled, 'but that's not the worst thing that could happen. Is everyone in already?'

Teresa nodded. 'Samantha wants "the key players", as she puts it, in the bull ring as soon as possible. She's not so easy-going this morning,' she added, 'so please go straight in.' Teresa gave her an extra big 'glad you're back' sort of smile, and then trilled, 'Harden Hammond Cohen,' into a phone.

Samantha had indeed suffered a sense of humour failure when Maddie had phoned her with the findings of her weekend visits. Not only had she spoken with Neva and Marilu but also three other front-running clients who were prevaricating about the suit, and five more who had suddenly pulled out of the fight without explanation. Samantha's justifiable sense of outrage was now permeating the entire crew as Maddie join them in the bull ring.

As she entered, Charles and Tyler were sorting through a pile of law books open on the table in front of them. Charles tapped one with his finger: 'I've checked *Cornell University Law School* – in the volume *The Book of American Legal Ethics* – and looking at the section on *California Rules of Professional Conduct* I'd say Stormtree's lawyers have stalked out onto very thin ice. But, they've not quite broken through into the freezing waters of total misconduct yet.'

'Hi, Maddie,' Tyler said, looking up. 'Nice tan!'

Charles grinned at her. 'I don't suppose you brought us back any Chianti?'

Maddie shook her head. 'You can't carry alcohol in your cabin luggage if you have to change planes,' she explained. 'But I thought of you, Charles. You'd have loved the wine – and the white truffles!' She quickly put her work brain into gear, and sat down. 'What were you saying about the legality of Gordon Hugo's pressure tactics?'

'Well, perhaps you can tell us exactly what you understood he's said to these people. It would clarify the position we can take,' he answered.

Maddie looked at the alert faces of Charlotte, Yamuna and Daisy; then at the young and good-looking David Cohen, who'd joined them today; at Marni, in the corner; and finally at Samantha, who was doing her best not to say what she so obviously felt about their opposition lawyers.

'Yes, Maddie,' she sighed. 'Give us a summing up, if you would.'

Maddie took a deep breath, and for the next half-hour recalled in minute detail what she had been told by everyone she had spoken to, referring to her notes for exact wording when necessary. Her mind was clear, and she conveyed the information with power and emotion – particularly as she recalled the report from the Walkers. When she finished, Samantha and the team gave her a little round of applause.

'Thank you; and welcome back,' Samantha said. Her tone meant that Maddie was 'back' from more than just Tuscany. 'I thought they might be relieved to unload it all on a good listener.'

Charles had been following Maddie attentively with one ear while reading from a book in front of him. He now said, 'The words that spring to mind include "witness intimidation", "overreaching", "harassment", and varying forms of "vexatious conduct". But,' he said, taking his glasses off, 'it may be hard to prove intent. They'll certainly deny that there was any such purpose behind their actions.'

Charlotte had been listening to Maddie's report, shaking her head from time to time in disbelief. She said with irritation, 'So, Hugo will take the position – for public consumption – that he was acting on Stormtree's instruction in the best interests of everyone. He'll plead it was a movement in the direction towards a bona fide attempt to discuss, and hopefully conclude, matters more swiftly for the people concerned.'

'Of course,' David Cohen said with a cynical smile, 'this was not a formal offer of settlement. So he'd claim it wasn't necessary to notify us of his actions. If Stormtree was going to make such an offer he would naturally put it in writing, in due course. And he would be very sorry if we felt he'd gone behind our backs.'

Tyler's frustration bubbled over. 'Meanwhile, back in Gotham City, The Joker is terrorising the entire population. The tactics have been very effective, and several people have been scared off about losing their medical, and actually resigned the case.'

'Quite right,' Samantha said. 'We must stop this. Fortunately we know how he's approached them, thanks to Maddie, but he's succeeded in undermining their confidence and scaring them witless.' She looked directly at Charles. 'You and I should draft a strongly worded "cease and desist" letter, implying that if they continue on their present course we'll have to register a formal complaint with the Bar Association, asking to have Gordon Hugo suspended pending a formal misconduct hearing.'

'With a view to having him debarred in the longer term,' Charles added. 'That should give him food for thought.'

'But I don't understand,' Daisy sighed. 'You have the upper hand here; so why wound him when you could kill him off entirely?'

'Don't tempt me. I would love to really go after him,' Samantha admitted, 'but if Charles is right, and we fail to prove intent, the whole situation could just waste time and bear no fruit. With a warning I think he'll pull back, because he won't risk being suspended for persisting. We have to chase down other quarry. Maddie, I think you have some politic hours ahead to smooth the feathers of our ruffled plaintiffs, and encourage those who have dropped out to reconsider.'

Tyler raised his head from a page he'd been scanning. 'What is the legal position with cutting off their medical insurance? Are they allowed to do that?'

David Cohen was a specialist in this kind of field, and shook his head vigorously. 'Almost certainly they can't terminate their responsibility for the cover of the bills,' he said. 'The exact wording of the workers' compensation package in their employment contracts would clarify, but if they're fairly standard Stormtree can't just walk away. However, what Gordon's firm knows is that they could conceivably withdraw cover in the immediate future, and make the victims appeal to have it reinstated.'

'This wastes time in the lives of sick people,' Charles added, 'and leaves them exposed in the meantime, not knowing how to afford their medical care. It's rough tactics.'

Chatter broke out, but Samantha held up her hand.

'I have a little window of good news,' she smiled. 'I spoke with the toxicologist on Friday, and he's almost finished his preliminary report from the critical illness records. He's ready for the next phase, but already makes two key points. The first is that, in his opinion – from the medical records in the data base – there is little question that something in the clean rooms has been making people sick, or killing them slowly for years.'

Samantha consulted her notes to a chorus of cheers from Tyler, Charlotte and Yamuna.

'Do they know we're getting this information right now?' Maddie asked Samantha quietly. 'Is that why Stormtree is trying to fight their corner another way?'

Samantha raised her eyebrows at Maddie. 'That's something to consider; you mean we might have a leak of information. Would it be at our end, or at theirs? It's interesting, and might be worth looking into. But it's just as likely that they understand what we can deduce from their records – simply because they know we have them now.'

Several faces looked mildly disconcerted, and even for Maddie the notion of Jacinta having some role claimed her thoughts for a moment. But that was probably unfair, she decided, and Samantha was likely right that Stormtree were just nervous of what Harden Hammand Cohen would learn from the database.

'But his second point,' Samantha resumed, 'suggests Stormtree are culpable in the extreme. If his conjecture is right, he believes he can prove that the cumulative effect of inhalation of small amounts of carcinogens over long periods has the same effect as a heavy intake over a much shorter time span. It just takes longer to poison the individual, and the symptoms may not be as obvious.'

'This is why there is nothing on the medical records we examined earlier about symptoms of poisoning?' Charlotte queried.

'Yes,' Samantha answered. 'You get ill, but it takes longer to show. The professional's hypothesis is that, although the toxins in the air in the clean rooms hover around the legally allowable level for industry, these are still appreciably higher levels than those allowed for public exposure in normal Health and Safety requirements.'

'His point being,' David asked, 'that he thinks no one has taken into account the cumulative effect?'

Samantha nodded.

Everyone stared. This, if demonstrable, was the major breakthrough they'd been hoping for.

Charles now went back over Maddie's previous thought. 'Of course, Stormtree has the same information available to them that we do; so it could be right to assume this is why they're attempting to interfere with the clients. They can see a potential problem looming, and are looking to circumvent it.'

'And yet,' said Maddie, 'I can see how it could be part of their general strategy. Pierce Gray is bright enough to try for a cheap settlement, if he thinks his company might be found in the wrong. The tactic has already reduced the number of claimants. But he equally has to answer to his shareholders, and they'd hate the notoriety involved if their investment were proved to be killing children. That argument will come up in court, and while they love their dividends, they won't want to risk their reputations.'

'True,' Charles agreed.

'There's more,' Samantha smiled wryly. 'Anybody who's squeamish might want to cover their ears. The toxicologist warns that he may have to kill a lot of lab rats to prove his point, but it could take as much as six or seven months to complete the controlled studies that will stand up in court. We've been pushing for a trial date, so we can't suddenly pull back. This means we've got to support these tests financially.'

'So, no cake this Christmas,' Charles said to her. But his words offered support, rather than regret.

'If we win,' Samantha answered, 'I promise everyone will share. Charles, we have a letter to write. Thanks, everyone.'

There was a general clamour around the table as Charles and Samantha left the room, and Tyler was immediately effusive in his enthusiasm.

'We've got them,' he almost shouted.

But while everyone was fairly sanguine in their expressions, it was Yamuna who asked, 'What happens if we lose? The firm could go broke!'

Marni Van Roon had sat quietly at the table to the left of David

Cohen, without audible expression or engagement. Now she commented, 'Yes. You still have to satisfy twelve men.'

This put a slight damper on the occasion, and everyone scattered off to their work places, realising they were a long way from the winning post.

Maddie was lost in thought about whether Stormtree could possibly have been privy to their toxicologist's initial findings, but when she opened her office door her heart almost stopped. On her desk, wrapped in plain Cellophane, and in the same distinctive ceramic pot she'd first seen it in, was Christopher's white orchid. It was perfectly restored to health, and three feet tall at least. A few delicate flowers were open, but a dozen more along each of the spikes were still plump buds. On the little card, which Maddie found tucked into the wrapping, were the words: 'Paloma. I promised I would make her well, and here she is to welcome you home. Jimena x'.

Maddie flopped into her chair. She stared at the exquisite cream flowers in front of her, not knowing whether to weep or sing. The orchid had appeared like this on the first day of her new job, and looked almost as well when she'd closed the door on it for her week off in January, to welcome Chris for his holiday. With the fog and now the orchid, the morning reminded her of Groundhog Day. It was as though she'd been living a liminal existence, and something had just floated her over that line with a breath of hope. But suddenly someone, or something, seemed to have wound the clock back to the time when everything was perfect, full of promise and without pain. She was the young girl going about her silent preparations for the much anticipated vision of the man she loved. For months the clock had stopped while her life hung in suspension. Now, the clock seemed to have started again, and while she couldn't take away any of the trauma she'd suffered, she seemed to be slowly moving again.

She'd walked out of the door and onto a flight to Borgo Santo Pietro; and then she'd reappeared to find Christopher's orchid restored. Maddie pinched herself, because she was – she'd have said – the most rational creature in the world, but something unexpected had happened. She thought of Janus, the god of doors and gateways, past and future; and she wondered, how did this appear on my desk at this precise moment, when Jimena surely couldn't have known I was back?

Maddie studied the orchid for a long time – she lost count of the minutes – as if to anchor its beauty very clearly in her mind. Then she made a decision. She lovingly picked up Paloma and carried her to the front desk, where she carefully placed the plant next to Teresa.

Teresa looked at the orchid with enormous brown eyes and smiled at her, unsure of what she was doing. 'It's the most beautiful one I've ever seen, Maddie,' she said. 'There must be thirty buds waiting to open.'

Maddie knew that Teresa had broken her heart over her role in 'killing' the orchid all those months ago. She'd felt almost superstitious about it, and could hardly look Maddie in the eye for some time.

'This is that same orchid we thought we'd lost, Teresa,' she said. 'Someone breathed love back into it for me, and for the moment I think it wants to be right here next to you, in a place where everyone can enjoy it,' Maddie said.

Teresa's eyes filled with tears, and she came from behind the desk to hug Maddie. 'Thank you,' was all she could say for a moment, and then: 'It will be beautiful here until you want to take it home. I promise I will look after it properly this time.'

Maddie smiled and squeezed her. 'Just out of curiosity,' she wondered, 'when did it come?'

'It arrived from Floritas this morning, just minutes after you went into your meeting. The delivery man said he was called Enrique, and to say hello to you. He told me in Spanish that his sister knew you were back, and insisted he bring the orchid here first thing, before all other deliveries. It wasn't on his run, so I offered him a five-dollar tip, but he wouldn't take it.'

Maddie nodded, and started back towards her office, but then turned and spoke again. 'She's called Paloma, by the way, because her colour is like that of the dove.'

'And the dove is the bird of the Maria Maddalena,' Teresa replied.

'I didn't know,' Maddie said quietly.

It was a little before the official end of the working day, but Maddie felt it would be acceptable for her to leave as they'd all started so early. She'd called Marilu, Neva and the other claimants she'd visited to tell them not to panic about the medical insurance, and Samantha and Charles had completed their missive to Gordon Hugo's firm. Samantha needed some air, it seemed, and had headed off to see her sister, indicating that

Maddie could get home to finish her unpacking if she wanted to.

It was in a mood of strange reverie that her footsteps took her along to Market Street, with sunshine rather than fog in her mind. She knew exactly where she was headed. Past Montgomery to Third Street, she craved that little shrine in the city that never failed to lift her spirits, even when she was feeling oppressed. Today she was in an unusual mood, and wanted to breathe in the scent of Jimena's lilacs and irises.

Seeing the proprietor herself outside the front door of her bower of delights, she waved and smiled at her. These gestures were immediately responded to in kind, but as Maddie came to within a yard of the doorstep Jimena turned the 'Open' sign round to say 'Closed', and pulled the blind. Maddie was confused until the door was suddenly flung open and Jimena grabbed her by the hand, tugging her into the shop and pushing the door firmly closed again behind her. Now she gave Maddie an enormous hug.

'I close specially, right now that you are here. You can tell me all the news.' Holding her client at arm's length, Jimena grinned at her. 'You look all new. Something has happened in Italy.'

Maddie wasn't ready for a conversation about the contradictions she was experiencing over endings and possible beginnings. She still felt the loss of Christopher with raw power, though she admitted to herself that she was not in the least blind to her nascent attraction for Søren. But Jimena seemed to have the powers of someone blessed with subtle vision and empathy.

Maddie smiled at Jimena. 'Yes, I had a smothering weight upon me, and Italy – all the people I met there, and the place itself – have started to lift it off me again. They say the Archangel Michael appeared centuries ago in the valley where I stayed, and that miracles have happened down the centuries there. I don't know if I believe in that, Jimena; but when it comes to Paloma? That's a miracle. How could you know I was back? To get that beautiful orchid into my office today – I can't explain how it's affected me. Thank you so much for saving her.'

'Miracles, no! Well, maybe a little one,' she answered. 'You need to believe. You remember I told you I had put her with some friendly plants that would help her to recover. I don't know why, but I do know if I can get the right plants together and say a little prayer it seems to make them happy, and they grow much better together.'

At the back of Maddie's mind, she remembered her father talking

301

about 'allelopathy'. Magic or science? she asked herself. She looked around the shop and wondered if there was a 'people allelopathy', too. She thought Jeanette would call it the Borgo effect: everything seemed so alive and wonderful there, as though there was some alchemy at work between the people and the place.

'Jimena, I want to send some flowers to the friends I stayed with in Italy. I know they can't come from your shop, but do you know how to find just the right agent at the other end?'

'I don't know what's best, or what is available, Señorita Maddie, but I will make some phone calls and maybe talk on the net with some friends, and see what I can find. How much do you want to spend?'

'No budget, Jimena. They saved my life a little bit! Spend whatever is necessary to find something special for them,' Maddie said. 'Jeanette loves flowers. I wonder . . . if you can find something that wouldn't be out of place in a unicorn's garden?' Maddie said this a little self-consciously, and almost as an afterthought.

'*Seguro*, certainly,' was the answer. 'You mean some very natural flowers. I'm not sure I can find pomegranate blossom at this time of the year, which would be traditional, but maybe some irises, which represent the Virgin and the city of Florence, I believe. I will find you something magical for your people,' Jimena enthused.

Maddie was astonished by Jimena's suggestion. The idea that there was anything 'traditional', when it came to unicorn flowers, was not at all what she'd expected to hear. Smiling, though, she opened her wallet for her credit cards.

Jimena put her hand out to stop her. 'Don't worry, I'll tell you how much it is when you come in next time. I will do it tonight from home; the flowers should be there on Wednesday.'

'What about the orchid?' Maddie asked. 'You must let me give you something for that – you invested so much time.'

'*Nada*.' Jimena shook her head. 'That was to help you mend your heart. It was a *regalo*, a present from me and from your Chris, whom I know you will never forget, even when it is time to think about other things. Take the best from everything that you have been lucky enough to have, but be willing to go past the pain eventually, and let go of it.'

Maddie nodded pensively, and then asked, 'How did you know I was coming back today?'

'Maddie,' Jimena answered her instead, 'you have a fear that something bad might happen, if you want it too much. *Querida*, you must have some faith, and the strength to try for what you want. Hope is more important than anything else for us after heartbreaks. And you were not rejected, Maddie, you were really loved. If love were enough by itself, you would still have your Chris. But you can't wait for something to happen to you, in your life. You have to be willing to go out and make something happen.'

This was almost too much for Maddie today, and she diverted the words back to her own question. 'Come on, Jimena, please tell me. I am beginning to think you are a woman with a sixth sense,' She tried to laugh as Jimena prodded her gently out of the shop.

'I am a woman with a sixth sense, Señorita Maddie,' she laughed. 'Of course I am. But in this case there is not so much mystery. Mr Gray told me.'

33

24 February 1348, San Galgano, Tuscany

Two elegant, near-black Spanish horses picked their way along the icy path of the pilgrims' road as it wound towards the abbey of San Galgano. In harness behind them was the small carriage that bore the body of Ranuccio Allegretti, Bishop of Volterra.

Although light snowfall through the night had made the ground more difficult to pass over on foot, a dedicated cortège of mourners walked behind the funeral cart just as the sun was lowering. Jacquetta and Gennaro were in front, with Porphyrius accompanying Agnesca and Mia just a few steps behind, and Cesaré and two of the members of the bishop's household completing the group on foot at the rear. Other retainers were quarantined in the stable-yard rooms, and little Luccio also remained at the villa in the care of Alba.

Not a word was spoken between the small company, and Mia had said hardly a word in the three days since the bishop had died. She felt unable to lift her head from the ground. She could have explained this because her eyes were fixed on where she placed her pattens on the slippery road; but if she were truthful, it would be better recognised as a response to despair. She'd been on the verge of coming to terms with her real self, as though unveiling the past might transform her future. Now, she felt a horror of knowing, a dread of learning anything more about how she came to be the daughter of the man who was the enemy of her family, 'the tyrant of Volterra', as so many called him. It chilled Mia to consider herself physically related to such a man, and the knowledge that she was so had set off a string of ugly possibilities as to why her mother

304

was murdered by one of the town guard. Everything that seemed hopeful had been erased, and full explanations were likely to be denied to her. She'd waited years for an audience with the man who was her guardian – a father to her in every sense except, as it turned out, physically. Now the chance had come too late, and she would never know him.

As they followed the curving sweep of the road, Mia thought with sadness that her unicorns were lost to her. She would never see them now, in the woods between her home and the abbey. She knew that unicorns only appeared to the worthy, to the virtuous, or perhaps to someone who was chosen. That could never be her now; and her sense of being able to bear whatever lay ahead was sullied, her strength diminished. She understood exactly why she had been named after the sinning Magdalene. A lifetime of obedience and piety would have to be her goal; a sense of duty to all others must dominate her thoughts for the rest of her days. Her spirits would improve eventually, she didn't doubt, and she'd have moments of private joy, but the truth of who and what she was could never now be undone. However kind others might be, she would struggle to live with this alien part of herself and the recognition that she was Ottaviano Belforte's illegitimate child.

These thoughts pressed in on her to such an extent that she hadn't noticed everyone had stopped moving forwards. The horses had slowed in front, and she was suddenly aware of whispering. She wondered if one of the horses had thrown a shoe, or a wheel had embedded itself in a drift of snow on the bend.

'Look up, Mia!'

It was *la raggia*'s voice. She had taken a step towards her and held her arm, pointing upwards and asking Mia's eyes to follow.

Mia slowly raised her head. At first she was aware only of the light. It was a little past three in the afternoon, and on a winter's day like this it would be getting darker within the hour. Yet Mia noticed the world seemed very bright around her, with a rosy light reflecting on the snow as she looked towards the abbey through the trees ahead. She looked into Agnesca's face, which seemed flushed, and she followed her pointed finger back over her shoulder towards the villa, from where they'd come. Turning fully around, Mia saw the sun in a white-orange ball of intense brightness just lowering towards the horizon. But the sight that drew all eyes was what was to be seen on either side of it. To left and right, at the same height as the sun, there were two more suns, each almost as intense and radiant and lovely as the sun itself. All three appeared behind the thin mauve cloud that hovered between earth and sky; and a great halo – easily visible to them all – arced from the orange ball at one side to the orange ball at the other. It created a beautiful ring around the shining orb in the centre. But which is the true sun? Mia wondered.

'Aristotle mentions two mock suns rising with the real sun, and lasting all that day till sunset,' Gennaro said in a voice that echoed Mia's incredulity. Like everyone else he was rooted to the spot and unable to take his eyes from the apparition.

'I have heard it is an ill omen, or that the weather will change – that a storm will come,' one of the bishop's men pronounced in a voice betraying alarm.

'But I think,' Agnesca said in a softer pitch, directed to Mia, 'that it is a sign that your Holy Trinity is watching over the bishop; and that the past, the present and the future are all one.' She squeezed her friend's arm. 'It is a good sign, Mia. Something is ending, but paves the way for something radiant to begin.'

Mia smiled at Agnesca. She had said nothing of her doubts, her self-torture and her pain; yet always Agnesca showed extraordinary compassion towards Mia and awareness of what preoccupied her. She pressed her arm, and turned again to look at the three shining suns, shielding her eyes from the brightness with her hand. They were beautiful indeed, guarding the approach to the Valle Serena, and she felt blessed to see them. But the strangest thing for Mia was this vision on this day, of all days. Today was 24 February in the year 1348, and it would occur twice. Tomorrow was leap day, when the date would be the same; and here there were three suns watching the last appearance on earth of this man of the Church. Mia felt they stood outside time, in a place where neither calendar nor physical measure of the world could be relied upon, and though she didn't quite understand the sign, she had utter faith that it meant something very important.

'It is Janus for you, *la raggia*,' she whispered. 'This apparition is the lord of the skies who looks behind, and ahead; the guardian of beginnings and endings.'

Agnesca nodded, and added, 'I wonder if his lady will appear in the night sky?'

Then the group moved off slowly again behind the horses, taking their route towards the abbey.

* * *

At half-past three on 24 February, the body of Ranuccio of Volterra was interred, with great solemnity, at the abbey of San Galgano. Here, at the end of a life marked with exile and political tumult, was the locus of peace where he had desired to be. The simple grace of the building made an eloquent backdrop to the sober mourners. Though she had never been seen in church by any of the residents of Villa Santo Pietro, Agnese Toscano joined with her friends out of respect for a man she hardly knew, but who meant so much to those she did. All were grouped together with the bearded *conversi* in the lay brothers' choir within the nave. Segregated in their own stalls the choral monks sang a full requiem and Nunc Dimittis to free Ranuccio from the ties that had bound him to this world. Throughout the funerary rites the eerie light from the three setting suns lit the rose window at the western end of the church, and cast long shadows into the nave. Mia, though her heart was breaking, felt moved by the melodic beauty of the chant and the ethereal light, and believed St Michael the Archangel had announced his presence to them all and was watching, ready to carry the soul of the bishop to heaven.

One hour later the trio of suns were fading into a blood-red horizon.

Jacquetta, along with Mia and Gennaro, sat in front of the fire in the guesthouse waiting for Abbot Angelo to come to them as he had promised. He had been present for part of the funeral office but left during the *Pie Jesu Domine*, which Jacquetta had thought extraordinary. Ranuccio was a benefactor to the abbey and a friend of the abbot, and his departure during the service of mourning for the bishop concerned her.

Agnesca and Porphyrius had remained standing for some time by the window, wishing to show courtesy to the abbot, but they were equally anxious to get back to Luccio. At last they excused themselves from their friends. Porphyrius helped his wife into her cloak as they stepped from the guesthouse to follow the path back home before the light was gone; but as they reached the porter's gate they heard a single bell chiming urgently from the campanile. This preceded a rush of feet from where they had just come. Each face consulted the other, and without words they turned on their heels and ran back to the guesthouse, which separated all visitors from those consecrated to life at the abbey.

Agnesca lifted the latch delicately and pushed the door in time to hear the prior talking with Jacquetta. An outside witness may not have thought his news too troubling: the abbot was unwell, he was brought low with a fever, he felt lightness in his head and needed his bed. He had respectfully asked that his guests might leave him for a day or two without taking offence. In winter such ailments were common, but he sent apology for the discourteous timing.

The party from Villa Santo Pietro, however, looked at one another with more awareness than the prior.

'I know it is beyond every norm in your abbey, Prior Lodovico,' Jacquetta said politely, 'for women to enter your cloisters or the dormitories, or to stay overnight except in time of pure peril. But Abbot Angelo may have the illness that killed Bishop Ranuccio; and if you were wise and flexible, it would be in the interest of all the brothers to allow Signora Toscano or me admittance to the abbot to assess him.'

The prior was aghast. They had their own surgeons. There were strict rules prohibiting the movement of women within the monastery, and he could still recall a time when women were not permitted into the church even for prayer, and never allowed to partake of meat in the abbey. Abbot Angelo accepted change and made concession to Jacquetta and the other noble ladies near the abbey's estates; in general he allowed women access to the church. There was a line, however, and it should not be crossed. These sentiments Prior Lodovico related to Jacquetta, all the while addressing Gennaro equally, as though appealing to his common sense would carry the day. Jacquetta, however, would not be dissuaded. She argued gently for what would best aid the abbot – what might ensure, in fact, the health of every monk and lay brother if she were right that the abbot had contracted the pestilence of the seaports. She reminded the prior of their meeting some months earlier about this disease; that they'd agreed exceptional measures might be necessary to counter it. In the end she prevailed, and while the remaining mourners returned to Villa Santo Pietro, she and Agnesca were both shown to the abbot's house.

Thus on the eve of the leap day and the day of the three blood suns, the abbey witnessed the visit of two women beyond the precinct and into the private apartments of its abbot.

No one knew for certain how or why the abbot had caught the disease. Agnesca theorised it must have been passed through his visit with the dying bishop or one of the sick retainers – perhaps via the breath. But in this case, she wondered, why had they not all been struck in the same way?

The testimony of one of the physician monks, Fra Melani, interested her very much. He related the oddity that he had only the day before given the abbot a salve for a particularly angry-looking insect bite. Abbot Angelo had complained it was abnormally itchy and swollen. As it was not high summer, when the marshy fields below the abbey gave them trouble with mosquitoes, the abbot believed he had been bitten by something after opening a package of precious cloths which Bishop Ranuccio had put in his care on the night he lay dying. These were silks obtained in Pisa and were to form the basis of Maria Maddalena's dowry and wedding clothes, and also provide three further dowries for poorer girls in neighbouring Chiusdino and Monticiano. Nobles and the clergy acted as such benefactors so that young women without money could marry. Ranuccio, too unwell to fulfil the role, had left the responsibility of finding worthy beneficiaries to the abbot. What struck Fra Melani was that he had applied the salve to an area close to where the pustules had now appeared at the abbot's elbow.

Jacquetta and Agnesca could advise little to the brothers about cleanliness in the monastery: their quarters were almost as stringently prepared as those at Villa Santo Pietro. But the two women did their best to treat the abbot's fever, fortify his heart with the tonic and dress the swellings as they had done successfully with Gennaro, and unsuccessfully with Bishop Ranuccio. Against their own expectations they also succeeded in persuading the prior and Fra Melani to quarantine the abbot's house.

Over the course of a week they shared the task of nursing him with the two physician monks who would not leave, tracking back and forth themselves to the guesthouse to sleep – to satisfy decorum – and allowing Agnesca to feed Luccio morning and night. Eventually the abbot showed signs of a slow recovery. His strength seemed completely sapped, so in the second week Agnesca astonished the brothers by demanding that the observations of Lent, which they had just entered, should be set aside for the recovering Abbot Angelo. She insisted he needed more than vegetable broth to recover from the exhaustion she had also observed in Gennaro; and though the prior and the cellarer were mortified, they eventually agreed.

Two weeks from the day of three suns, the abbot was thought to be out of danger. The four bells tolled gratefully from the campanile, and Agnesca left the abbey to go back to her husband and son at the villa.

APRIL 1348, SAN GALGANO, TUSCANY

The last week of March had been mild, fulfilling an ancient lore that if the early part of the month was as gentle as the lamb, the end would be lion-like – and vice versa.

Gennaro had taken his easy cheerfulness away and left for Volterra early in the month, with family business to settle after the death of his uncle. There was no time to miss him, however, as pilgrims came in their numbers to lodge at the villa in the days leading up to Holy Week. Travellers were on the roads, despite talk of the fearful illness that was gripping coastal towns from the north of Italy to the south, and which was now in Marseilles. Tradesmen and citizens alike were falling prey to a creeping sickness: disease had stormed the gates of the proud cities of Lucca and Bologna, and been unloaded from merchants' carts into Modena and Pistoia. The roads were alive with rumour that a pestilence so morbid had broken out in Venice that mothers had abandoned their children and wives their husbands, that piles of the dead lay in ditches, and that the illness was translated through breath and sight. But what could journey-makers do, if they were already on the road?

Jacquetta and her household sharpened their precautions. They quarantined guests in the stable rooms and converted two further apartments, which normally housed servants, who were now moved into the attic of the villa next to Mia. They drew baths for every guest on arrival and insisted they use the harsher soda-based soaps to wash; and they changed the bedding and added hyssop to the cedar shavings on the floors as though they were expecting all the nobles of Europe to arrive at their door.

On the day before Holy Thursday – which occurred late this year – the morning arrived like full spring, every tree proliferating with buds; and in an extraordinary gesture Abbot Angelo sent one of the lay brothers to Jacquetta's home to ask for the company of that lady and Maria Maddalena; and of Porphyrius Toscano and the accused heretic, the lady Agnese, his wife, at the guesthouse of the abbey tomorrow to dine with him and mark the end of Lent. Perhaps Jacquetta alone understood what this invitation embraced: a gesture of utter tolerance and kindness from

310

a man who knew he owed his life partly to the accused young woman from Volterra.

When they arrived just after noon on Holy Thursday, the abbey bells tolled across the Valle Serena ending the office of sext, and calling the brothers to the refectory. The gate arches and door to the visitors' house were hung with white blossom from the pear and apricot trees.

'The Emperor Hadrian's splendid tomb on the banks of the Tiber,' Abbot Angelo told them as he welcomed them through that door, 'supported a miracle eight hundred years ago. In a scene witnessed by crowds in Rome the Archangel Michael appeared before them, dancing in wheels of light and flame on the roof of the mausoleum. He was observed to sheath his sword and bring grace to Rome, ending the terrible Plague of Justinian, which had killed almost half the population. The building was renamed that day as the Castel Sant' Angelo,' he said.

The abbot stopped the lay brother waiting at one side of the chamber and brought the wine himself, carried on a tray from the refectory table. He gestured for his guests to sit before the large fire – too hot for the day – and as Mia took her goblet she lifted her eyes to make contact with Abbot Angelo, who stood before her. She thought he looked tired, but decidedly alive; and there was humour in his smile.

'I seem to have been equally honoured,' he continued in a tone that intrigued Mia, 'with a visitation of three suns and the appearance of two local saints to ensure my own recovery.'

He lifted a simple chalice of wine from the tray and passed it with his own hands to Agnesca, then said to her, 'Welcome; and my thanks.'

The implication was not lost on Agnesca.

Mia smiled to herself as their first course was carried to the table. What the *conversi* had called 'a feast dish' was plain boiled fowl without spice or sauce, garnished only with medlar jelly and a few root vegetables as accompaniment. How strongly this recalled her aunt's report of dishes being served in the Cistercians' refectory completely unadorned. Mia thought with wonder of the great lands they owned, the abbot's vineyard, which supplied the wine they drank now, the fields they tilled and the mills of iron and water that brought them prosperity from the outside world. The monks' horses were esteemed and sold to nobles and gentlefolk throughout the land; and their cattle – the handsome white Chianina reared here in the hills around Siena – were famous beyond

311

the Italian peninsula. Yet, the brothers seemed to prefer to live abstemiously. Mia would long after remember the relative splendour of her aunt's table – the delicious food prepared by Loredana and Alba – in comparison to dining with such a landlord as the abbot of San Galgano. But it was the Cistercians' way, and showed no lack of generosity on his part.

As the lay brothers began to clear the trestle of the poultry plates the door opened again, and Mia found herself smiling involuntarily. A much-cherished face appeared.

'Forgive me, Your Grace. The weather is so fair I thought to have an easy journey from Volterra.'

Dressed in finer clothes than Mia had ever seen him in, Gennaro came to the abbot and bowed his head, then turned to Jacquetta to excuse himself for interrupting when their meal was begun. He kissed Agnesca and Mia discreetly, and water was brought for him to wash. He took a place opposite the abbot at the other end of the trestle.

'I left at daybreak, and my progress was rapid until I came to Casole,' he said, taking a small portion of the poultry that was offered him before it had left the table. 'But it was there that I learned the mortality has come to Florence, where it has been devastating. They were wary of all travellers in the Val d'Elsa for that reason; but from my friend I learned that the illness may also have reached into San Gimignano.'

'Then it cannot be long away from Volterra, or indeed Siena,' Jacquetta said softly. 'What can be done to halt it?'

'And what unnamed horror is it?' Gennaro asked. 'It is as though we stand on the edge of a great abyss.'

A whole fish enclosed in pastry had come to the table, and everyone waited while it was cut and served by the lay brothers.

'It is hard to comprehend.' Abbot Angelo spoke after they had left the room. 'If it is a wrath sent upon us by God, which Abbot Claudio in Pisa advises – and with which the prior agrees – then do we suffer for our individual sins, or a collective sinfulness? Why would Ranuccio, a good man, pay with his life for the godlessness of a population – if this is truly the cause – when I am spared?'

Agnesca was fascinated by the idea that God was angry with his people, and punishing them. It tore at every irreverent bone in her body. She had never had sympathy with a god she couldn't see and saw no evidence to believe in; a god whom she refused to praise if he truly did all that was laid to him, who treated women indifferently. If all people were his children and created by him, she struggled to understand why he was negligent towards so many. No parent with such favouritism would be praised by a single soul.

Though a woman speaking her opinions at a host's table was unheard of, she felt emboldened to pursue this with the abbot.

'Is it through false worship then, Your Grace,' she asked gently, 'or faithlessness – as the Bible recounts when the Philistines were beset with plagues of mice and tumours – that whole cities seem to suffer now? Or is it some as yet unidentified fault at the heart of Christendom? Because for myself, I do not believe that disease is a trial sent by God to test human faith, or a punishment for deviant behaviour. I was taught by a healer who tried to observe patients, and who rejected any supernatural causes of illness.'

Abbot Angelo looked at his pretty adversary. Signora Toscano held considerable interest for him, as he was aware of the mystique surrounding her; and he vividly recalled his conversation with Jacquetta a year ago, which he knew concerned her. He had never knowingly entertained anyone whose theology was so at odds with his own – or whose sense of God was completely absent, by all report – but he was drawn to her loveliness, her honesty and intelligence, as well as her gentleness and considerable strength of purpose. He lacked sympathy for a social system that allowed parents to thrust on their children a spiritual devotion they were too weak-willed to impose on themselves. Cistercian houses never admitted children. And he had long wondered why canon law's dictates that two people could choose one another for husband and wife should be so flagrantly overturned by civic custom and the partisan jealousies of families? In this he thought she had suffered wrongly.

As to her choice of religion, if God had appointed her as his healer how could he, Angelo, second-guess Divine Will? If she had begged for rescue from imprisonment and torture in the name of Our Lord, he thought, and the winds had risen and answered her, we would chant her praises and declare her another Agnes or Barbara.

'Perhaps we are not as right, as we believe,' he answered her at last, 'and our worldview is neither more perfect, nor less heretical, that that of the East, which we staunchly condemn. We have closed our mental world since men have gone on Crusade, and need reminding of humility. Who can know the divine mind? For if ours represents the last bastion of true faith, how should we understand God's anger directed so clearly against us?'

Agnesca was quite silenced by his honest doubts and willingness to question. She had been embittered for some time that those who tried to bend her to Christian doctrine – her parents and the priests and state of Volterra – had threatened and tormented her. Their message of Christ's love was filtered through promises of pain and death if she didn't obey. There had been no language but hatred, and the certainty of their position Agnesca had found overwhelming. But the abbot might – like Mia and Jacquetta – offer an example of those whose religion encouraged acts of kindness, rather than divisiveness.

Fruit was served to follow the salmon, and when the clatter of dishes being removed had quieted, Agnesca thought to say something in reply to the abbot; but instead, he spoke.

'As a measure of respect for you, Monna Agnese,' he began tentatively, 'would you allow me to perform a marriage rite for you and Signor Toscano?'

Every face at the table looked at him. Mia put down her stewed pear and glanced from Agnesca to Porphyrius and back again. This was a consideration each of them had privately wondered about, but no one had voiced.

'For I feel sure,' the abbot added with tact, 'that no priest or notary in Volterra felt able to disregard the state and your parents' wishes, to formalise your private vows?'

A tear just started to form in the corner of Signora Toscano's eye. This was an offer to make her promises with Porphyrius legally binding – and she would like to do that for him. Almost imperceptibly she nodded her head at him. Yes: she would allow him!

In languid afternoon sunshine on Holy Thursday, Agnesca – carrying an armful of blue irises picked where they had been teeming in the abbey gardens – climbed the hill with Porphyrius and their friends to the tiny chapel of San Galgano above. If this seemed a concession to propriety, she noted to herself that the little hermitage had everything in common with an Etruscan temple, which suited her religion perfectly; and with Jacquetta and Mia as her witnesses and Gennaro acting for Porphyrius, the abbot blessed their union in a short service of marriage. Gennaro, who had been secretly prepared for the possibility, produced a ring, which he had brought from Volterra. Then Porphyrius kissed his beautiful bride. At the conclusion of the simple service the couple walked out onto the grassy terrace and were showered with blossom from the abbot's orchard by Jacquetta and Mia.

Agnesca beamed at Mia – the nearest to a sister she had in the world – and reverently handed her the irises.

'I assure you,' she said, 'that you are next.'

Her friend's apparent certainty made Mia blush. But neither woman knew that what would transpire at the abbey over the next hour would send them on a journey that would change their lives and relationship for years to come.

34

6–7 SEPTEMBER 2007, OXFORD, ENGLAND

From the train, patches of mist could be seen suspended in pockets between the swathes of oak and beech, just turning gold and russet. Maddie thought it quite as lovely, if not as dramatic, as the first breath of fall in New England. But the late afternoon was still bathed in sunlight as she stepped onto the platform at Oxford railway station.

Samantha had given her a quick pass to allow her back to England for the hearing at Oxford Crown Court and the sentencing of the driver who'd killed Christopher. She was more than happy to grant Maddie these few extra days which, she hoped, would help her get a little nearer to closure on Chris's death. But it was also a way of repaying her the days she'd lost from her Italian holiday. The information Maddie had garnered from their clients had enabled the firm to handcuff Stormtree's lawyers from further witness intimidation, and Gordon Hugo had slunk away without a whimper. Maddie was also due considerable credit for her efforts, along with Tyler's, in securing almost all of the clients Hugo had frightened away and getting them back on board for the suit. It was a job well done.

Harriet Taylor had emailed Maddie that the hearing in England was set for 7 September in Oxford. From January to September was a longer wait than usual but one of the passengers in the drunk driver's car who'd been badly hurt in the crash was now sufficiently recovered, and could attend court. This hearing was the moment for the judge to determine what the sentence should be for the drunk driver, and the presence of a second victim was helpful. Her message had ended saying that the

Taylors hoped the accused would spend a large amount of his young life behind bars, but nothing could replace their son.

Maddie knew she was making the trip partly to support Chris's parents, as they had asked if she could be there. However, as her taxi took her along the familiar lanes she realised she, too, had ghosts to lay. As she watched the colleges and mellow golden buildings of the ancient city pass by her window, her mind revisited the pleasures of her time spent here. She smiled to herself, recalling the snowfall that had been the prompt to her first meeting with Chris. If Neva knew the story, Maddie was sure she would have told her that she'd ordered up the snow on purpose. But thinking about it, she felt that the whole enchantment of her wonderful Oxford 'bubble' had been confined to a period of relatively little actual time.

It had been a time of such intensity, of joy and laughter. It was a combination of hard work and hard play, and everything English had seemed enchanting. In January she had come to Oxford on the exchange course, and in February her life seemed to be complete with the meeting of Chris. It was such a brief time: a true fairy tale, but with a twisted ending. She still had no idea how the heroine would come out; but she did understand that, without negating the validity of her feelings for Chris, she had been swept off her feet and then along on a tide of romantic events. She had finished here just over a year ago, but she felt she had grown very much older in the time since she'd left. That seemed in part a good thing, and in other ways very sad; but it was true that pain had changed her, had made her wonder whether every young woman simply 'deserved' a fairy tale in her life. She thought of what Jimena had said about not waiting for things to come to you, but to go out and *make* something happen. As the Georgian-looking façade of Worcester College flashed by on her left, and then the Edwardian edifice of the Randolph loomed into view on her right, she considered afresh the strangely appealing idea that it was now time for her to take charge of her own destiny. She felt she might not have done that enough in the past.

She recalled the literal thrill of her anticipated reunion with Chris in San Francisco, which sadly never was to be. But this surreal city had been their place; and, she thought, perhaps their ghosts were still here somewhere, along with countless others whose lives had been touched or shaped by Oxford. She felt Chris's absence acutely as she watched first Brasenose, and then Queen's, flash past the taxi window. What a brief moment of time it had been; how nonchalant she'd been about it. It almost made her heart break wishing she could turn back the clock, but she knew absolutely that she couldn't, and that what would define her life was what she chose to do now – what came next.

The taxi turned into a lane off the High Street, sparing her the possibility of a glimpse of Chris's college by the bridge. Instead the rattle of the tyres on the cobbled surface of the lane suddenly jolted her back into the here and now, and deposited her at the back door of the Old Bank where the reception area was. She paid the fare and walked up the steps of the outdoor terrace, with its benches and patio heaters, towards the desk.

Through glass patio doors along the way she could see Quod, the restaurant that formed part of the hotel. She remembered it well. It was a stretch to eat here on a student budget, but the food was consistent and good, and the atmosphere was airy and comfortable. She and Chris had begun their evening many a time here before going on to dance late into the night. She also remembered with crystal clarity sitting here in her ball gown for breakfast on a June morning just over a year ago, close to the end of her time at Oxford, when she and Chris were among the so-called 'survivors' – having made it to sunrise – of her own college's ball.

Today the restaurant was almost vacant at teatime. In another month it would be teeming with undergraduates and their parents, but this seemed the moment between the tourists and Oxford's term-time residents, and Maddie smiled at what looked like one solitary academic – perhaps here for a conference or late summer school – making notes with the remains of an afternoon tea in the expanse of the empty dining room.

Maddie checked in and took her bag up the old staircase to her room on the first floor. She hung up her suit for court in the morning, and then opened the window at the front of the building. Looking out across the High, her eyes fastened on St Mary's University Church, and then ranged beyond to the spires and roofs of the Radcliffe Camera and the Bodleian. How strange it was to be here on her own, in these extraordinary circumstances, with a hearing that would once again bring home the loss of her love at ten in the morning. Someone to have a drink with would have been nice – but everyone had already gone down. She had exchanged emails with a friend from New College who was doing post-grad, but she hadn't come up yet. She'd texted Jeanette before setting out for England just to see if she might be in London for a swift hello, or lunch, during her short visit, but she and Claus were still in Italy. She'd called Søren briefly, but he, too, was still away and getting his hands dirty, as he liked to say. He'd be returning to London soon, but the times didn't quite match. Sad to miss her friends, she'd arranged her trip to be as purposeful as possible rather than stretching it across the weekend. At least that accorded her a day at home to recover before work on Monday. She would meet Christopher's parents outside the Oxford Combined Court centre at half-past nine tomorrow, as they were going to drive up in the morning.

Maddie sighed, and took herself in hand. She decided that, after more than sixteen hours of travel, she badly wanted a shower. But a little later, when she came back into the room wrapped only in a towel, she made the mistake of lying down for a minute. Her next awareness was that she was cold, and it was almost dark in the room. After a brief pause to marshal her thoughts, she switched on the bedside light. Her watch was still on San Francisco time, which she'd elected to do to lessen the impact of the jet lag until her return. She calculated it was about eight in the evening here. Wrapping the towel back around her she pulled open her bag and extracted a stylish pair of leather running shoes with enough support to deflect Oxford's cobbles, then a light cashmere sweater, a pair of jeans, and an Abercrombie gilet.

The lamplight colour of the streets was beautiful under the autumn evening sky as she left the hotel by the door onto the High Street and walked directly across to the lane beside the church. She considered the idea that Madeline Moretti was setting forth into a brief but important journey back to her past self. Through Radcliffe Square and on into Catte Street, Chris's ghost seemed to be quite near to her. Maddie wanted his company, believing it necessary to subject herself to the painful awareness that he would always be there with her and never again be there with her. She craved the rawness of this emotional trauma, perhaps so that she could shape some kind of ending from it.

A short turn took her into New College Lane under the Bridge of Sighs, which had been her home for months, and she remembered the loveliness of the lilac hedge in spring. But now, in autumn, there were no flowers. Further up the lane she vanished into a narrow passageway which took her to the Turf Tavern, where she'd eaten so many times with Chris. She walked a familiar path remembering how the thirteenth-century ale house had been the go-to place for Chris and his medical friends. She'd thought it funny that they'd wait there, with one beer at most, until the moment when a rugby match would end and send them scrambling off together to find someone who needed stitching at the hospital. They worked hard, were always eager to watch treatments and see injuries, and they were competitive with each other and drank and partied harder than anyone else at the university.

Maddie thought walking inside tonight that she wasn't naturally a pub girl, although the quaint old place had an undeniable charm. They used to drink here because a pitcher of Margarita was only fourteen pounds – less than other places – so for old times' sake she ordered a Margarita and some bar food. She took her drink to a table on her own and waited for her food. Independent as she was in her own town, she was strangely overcome with apprehension here, not least because she was travelling and didn't belong to anybody. Tonight seemed a test. None of her early life or education had equipped her to deal with the sense of being truly adrift. Now she could see she was regaining strength and beginning to want things again: the right outcome for the Stormtree claimants, the achievement of some work she could be proud of, some adventures in new places, and yes, even some companionship with a lover in good time. Isabella's gift of the trip to Jeanette and Claus had given her just the objectivity she needed, and brought her back from the abyss. But she was still a fledgeling, with some miles to go.

By the time the food arrived Maddie had lost her appetite. She tipped the waitress and thanked her, then left without touching her food or finishing her drink. She walked out of the Turf into the moonless Oxford night, with a beautiful star-studded sky above her. Maddie had always loved to walk in Oxford. Later at night, after a certain hour, it became a ghost town with few cars and even fewer people. In this moment and mood she began to revisit her old haunts. She walked past the shuttered gates of the great colleges, the libraries and museums that housed centuries of knowledge; then she passed by the debating society building, called the Oxford Union, where she'd first met Chris; then along the river and the backs. She heard a dozen bells chime the hours, and her memories flooded around her. The walking seemed to settle her state of being. She needed to visit every place that she had known and loved, wanting to implant the images indelibly in her mind to remember every detail. She understood without telling herself that she was trying to pack these memories away to take them into the future with her.

She was obviously functioning on California time when she finally put her head on the pillow at around three thirty in the morning, and her wake-up call had come around too early at seven thirty. Maddie had to fight her way out of a complex dream involving herself, Pierce Gray and something to do with water. The dream had made her anxious, and she sat up in bed almost in tears. Desperately, she tried to place the dream in relationship to something that had actually happened. It was something she had tried to suppress – details she had almost blotted out of her mind. She sipped some water from the bedside table in a half-dream, and then the reality flooded back. She started piecing together the details of an event she'd been dreaming about in Chris's town, though it belonged to a time long before.

It had happened when she was nineteen. She and Pierce Gray had just put to sea on board his Santana sailboat. They had left from the San Francisco Yacht Club at Belvedere Cove. In her mind she couldn't remember why she was there; and she squeezed her brain for information. Then she could see the idyllic day, gentle, with unusually little breeze for the bay. Over drinks at the Berkeley campus she had learned there was to be a small party on Pierce's boat; and she'd accepted the invitation to prove her independence to herself. Her mother had been arguing that she was too young to study away from home – too young to know her own mind. Pierce had invited her to a party of swish 'grown-ups', and she'd decided to be a sophisticate and go, just to prove she could cut it with the *beau monde*. As it turned out, Pierce was her only companion.

Maddie's dream had unleashed her recall of events in minute detail – events she'd tried to shut the door on for six years. She'd remembered it in broad strokes: but now, she could see exactly the sequence of events on that day.

They had set out on a short cruise of the bay, and as they cleared the moorings and left the harbour Pierce had put his mariner's cap on her head and given her the tiller. He had plucked champagne from the fridge in the cabin and brought out two glasses, saying they should enjoy themselves, apologising that no one else had been free at the last minute. He'd sat beside her, opened the bottle and poured. Maddie knew enough to see she'd been set up, and had felt trapped by the circumstances, but she was unsure what to do.

After a quarter of an hour Pierce might have moved a little closer in topping up her glass – she didn't exactly recall what he'd said to her. She did remember the clear innuendo, her anger and embarrassment, and she'd moved away from Pierce at the helm to give him back the tiller. She'd got up and walked towards the cabin door where she turned to face him in the stern, trying to think what words to use to communicate her disdain, and to shame him into feeling he wasn't acting as a gentleman. She thought she was going to explode in a tirade against him, but as the words started to come she became aware of a spectacular – seemingly innocuous – spray of water on the bay right behind Pierce's head. It was driven by the wind, and it danced across the surface of the bay towards them as if conjured by an illusionist's hand.

It looked breathtaking, and in spite of her rising anger her expression changed to such an extent that Pierce's curiosity was piqued. He looked back and followed her eyes. The plume of sea-spray moved with increasing pace towards them, and as much as Pierce had exclaimed at the wonder of it, just as abruptly his demeanour changed to one of concern, and then naked fear.

He yelled to her over the rising sound of the wind: 'Hold on tight, Maddie. We're going to be hit!'

It was only seconds later. They were enveloped in a swirling wall of water, rising almost to half the height of the mast. It was as if the boat had been taken in a giant's fist and spun violently, the sails ripping like tissue paper. Maddie had screamed; and even now, at the length of years, she could remember the sensation of screaming mutely, with no sound coming out. It felt as if they were being lifted out of the sea, and a second later the force of the wind reversed, slamming the boat downward and driving it almost beneath the waves. A dark green wall of sea water cascaded over the stern. Pierce cried out and clutched desperately at a handrail on the side of the cockpit to keep from being flung overboard. The rudder was ripped from its fastening, and the tiller snapped like match wood. Maddie heard herself scream again – a hollow sound in her ears – as she, too, clung to the rail on the cabin roof. She was sure they would sink, sure they couldn't swim in the eddying waters that had turned from beautiful to brutal in five minutes. Then, in another moment of adrenalin overload, the wind and spray vanished.

The whole episode had lasted only minutes. Maddie knew certainly that another such minute would have seen the boat disintegrate around them, and they would have sunk without trace. The cockpit and cabin were swamped. The rudder dangled from its broken fitting, and the sails were in tatters. The main electrics had shorted, the radio and navigation equipment smashed, and the back-up motor had been drowned.

Pierce had reacted quickly, she remembered, once he had recovered from the shock. He pulled a distress rocket and life jackets from one of the water-soaked lockers, and helped her into a jacket nimbly before firing off the flare. He'd then plunged into the cabin, and Maddie had heard him floundering for a few minutes until he emerged holding his cellphone, with a nervous smile on his face. It had been safe with his keys in a little net hanging above the water level, and had somehow survived the deluge. He spoke on the phone for a minute and then was quite comforting, putting an arm around her chastely and assuring her help was coming. The boat seemed to be stable, although the water was over their knees, but the sails overhead were a mass of shreds, and the aluminium boom was bent like a hairpin.

'We've got to get the sails down, quickly,' Pierce had suddenly barked, 'because the next gust of wind could pull the whole boat under.'

Something instinctive had made Maddie reply, 'There won't be another gust.'

Maddie pulled the bedclothes over her again in the hotel room, remembering clearly how hard they'd fought to get the spent sails down. After what had seemed an eternity a Coast Guard helicopter had swooped in just above them. Moments later they spotted two high-speed rescue craft on the horizon, and as the boats came alongside the helicopter turned away.

She remembered the smooth transfer to one of the boats, the blankets thrown around them, the sprint across the water back to the Yacht Club. She could taste the sea salt as she relived in her mind the arrival at the club, dock-side. A man whom she hadn't recognised took charge of her almost as soon as she got her feet ashore, ushering her to the ladies' changing rooms at the club and directing her to have a shower. He'd arranged to have her provided with towels and some dry clothes from the club shop. Only after she'd changed and warmed up, and drunk a little coffee, had he asked her if she was well enough to drive. After her assurances he'd escorted her to her car, made sure she could focus, and told her to go home and rest. He suggested it might be better, to avoid unwanted publicity and panic, not to tell anyone about the event. That was when she'd looked at him properly, realising it was Pierce's reputation he was protecting rather than her state of shock or wellbeing. She should never have been left to drive herself home in the shaken condition she was in; but Pierce in a boat with a leggy nineteen-year-old might not look so good for the man who was pictured wherever he went.

'Oh my God,' Maddie suddenly said aloud to herself, emerging from under the quilt. She shook her hair out and stared unseeing up into the ancient ceiling mouldings of her Oxford room. 'It was him. It was Gordon Hugo! He was right – we'd met before.'

Maddie got up now and put on a bathrobe, shuddering involuntarily at the realisation. She could recall perfectly the morning paper of the next day reporting, 'Famous entrepreneur, Mr Pierce Gray, with a single crew member was rescued unhurt from his Santana 22 when it almost capsized after being hit by a freak waterspout.' The paper recounted that there was no known reason why these phenomena occur. Scientists suggested they arise out of unique circumstances combined with some unexpected outside factor, which triggers them off. This meant Mr Gray and his 'crew member' had been extremely lucky.

Maddie sat back on the bed. The whole story was now sharp in her mind, but she couldn't understand why she'd been suppressing it for so long in her memory. Perhaps it was because, at the time, she'd felt responsible in some way; or embarrassed to have put herself in such a situation with Pierce.

A knock at the door was a relief, and told her that breakfast had arrived.

Mr Hugo, Maddie thought walking over to answer it, you were a small-time fixer then, and you're an even nastier, amoral little douche today. If I have anything to do with it, you will not get away with this stuff when people are being hurt.

At shortly before ten, Maddie checked her watch again and realised she'd been waiting for almost half an hour in front of the court in St Aldates. From her vantage point on the street corner she watched Christopher's mother and father walk slowly towards her. She made no mention of the time as she embraced them, understanding that, much like her, they would rather be in any other place on the planet at this moment than where fate had brought them. They all understood the events of today could change nothing of what had been. To Maddie the couple looked sad, and much older, when she silently kissed them both; and minutes later all three seated themselves in the front row of the public gallery of Court Four.

They watched a young man in a wheelchair being pushed into the public area by a court official. He was accompanied by his family and a pretty young girl in tears. The wheelchair was placed in an aisle between the seating in front of the dock, and Edward Taylor commented – looking at the state of his twisted body – that he thought the young man might never walk again. Harriet added that he looked like a broken human being, and Maddie could see she was close to tears herself.

The boy looked over at the three of them and offered a nervous smile, which signalled to Maddie 'I have pain, too.' Yes, she thought, but you didn't stop your mate from driving, did you? Still, she realised, he had a right to be heard, and must have wanted to be in court for this moment. Two more families were also ushered in – families, she would learn, of the other boys in the car. All of these people want to be here at this hearing, she thought, when she heard the clerk's voice.

'All rise,' he called. 'Her Majesty's Crown Court is now in session.'

They stood as the judge in his wig and gown moved to his chair; and everyone was seated again. The clerk turned to the judge, quoting the case number. 'Your Honour, the matter of two charges, the one of "causing death by dangerous driving", and of "driving with excess alcohol",' and the clerk placed a folder in front of the judge.

Maddie listened, dazed, while she heard him speak of a pre-sentence report, and add that the defendant had pleaded guilty.

'Where is the defendant?' the judge asked.

He was in the cells.

'Have the defendant brought up,' the judge directed.

There seemed an endless pause, during which Maddie looked at the Taylors and then around the courtroom. The judge had opened the file in front of him and began to study the contents. Silence fell over the proceedings when the court bailiffs ushered in a neatly dressed young man in grey trousers and a clean white shirt, and accompanied him to the dock. The entire visitors' gallery turned as one to examine him. The young man stepped up and stared directly ahead of him with a blank expression. Maddie thought there was no trace of emotion in his blue eyes, and he was told to remain standing.

It had taken a second for the impact of the moment to strike. Maddie felt a blow to her stomach – a physical sensation of nausea and violence as if it were done to her. It had come quite out of the blue. Here in front of her was the man who had killed Christopher, a murderer, really; yet he seemed so ordinary she'd have passed him in the street without a glance. Someone along the row coughed nervously, she felt Harriet Taylor slump a little beside her, and the door to the public gallery quietly opened and closed behind her; but her concentration was fixed on the sullen boy in the dock. Maybe he was just scared? She wanted him to look at her so she could know what this person felt, what was inside his head about the night of the accident.

Why did you do this? she projected silently across the courtroom at him; but the boy in the dock refused even to make eye contact with her.

'State your name,' the judge asked.

'Jonathan Gilbert,' was the reply from the boy as he stood up.

'You may be seated.'

The judge looked at his papers while the clerk of the court read out details of the case, and on finishing the judge began to speak.

'Mr Gilbert. You have pleaded guilty to the charge of causing death by dangerous driving. Additionally you were two times the legal limit for alcohol consumption when you took the wheel of your car, with which you killed a completely innocent person and seriously injured your friend. Do you have any idea of the absolute ramification of your actions on the lives of others, many of whom are here in this courtroom today?'

Maddie watched him closely, but there was no sign of feeling or any expression on his face. *Come on*, she thought, *say something*; and she tried to will him to speak. It was to no avail.

The judge resumed. 'I see from the pre-sentence report that you have done well at your education. You have been in regular employment with a retail firm here in the city, ever since you left school. You also seem to come from a caring family background. However, the person compiling this assessment also notes that your favourite past time is – and I quote – "getting drunk on a Saturday night with your mates". She says you admit you make a habit of this.

'The writer also comments,' the judge continued, 'that when told about your victim's death, you said—' and here the judge paused to consult the papers – 'you said, and these are your words, "He's a posh university git who's had every advantage, and you think his life is worth more than mine".'

Maddie's eyes widened in amazement, and she watched the judge for a clue as to how this affected him. He'd seen and heard it all, however, she thought, and little could shock him.

'Is that what you said?' the judge spoke again. 'Is that what you think?'

There was no verbal response from the dock, but he nodded his head a little defiantly.

Maddie felt poor Harriet Taylor's discomfort beside her, and she took hold of Harriet's hand, which was cold. She could see a woman on the verge of breaking down, and wondered if perhaps she should take her outside. Harriet returned the pressure of Maddie's hand gratefully, and Maddie looked again at Jonathan Gilbert standing glibly in the dock. It dawned on her that either he was so affected by the events he was responsible for that he was in shock, or that he just refused to see Dr Christopher Taylor as a person. Maddie focused on the inscrutable face glaring back at the judge, and was taken aback by her own intuitive comprehension. It's true, she thought. He doesn't believe he has anything to say or apologise for. Is that Pierce's problem too? To people like them, is this no more than an unfortunate accident?

Edward Taylor moved in his seat as if to get up, and Maddie thought he was going to say something publicly; but when she looked in his eyes she saw that he was stunned, physically dispirited and mute for words.

The judge looked at the boy before him – for a boy was all he seemed to be.

'I can see no sign of remorse in you for the pain and suffering you have caused the family of Dr Taylor; or the families of your other victims. Though your learned counsel is right to remind me of your previously good character and your guilty plea, I find no mitigating circumstance for your actions. In the family's statements, I find people whose only son was taken from them for no reason, leaving them with a bleak and empty future with no more children and no grandchildren to look forward to. Neither will they enjoy the bond that began with the young woman who was to be their daughter-in-law.

'That young woman,' he said solemnly, 'whose statement of loss moved me to despair, has had her own life torn apart. I hope it is not beyond rebuilding.'

Maddie swallowed in the gallery.

'Mr Gilbert, do you have anything at all to say before I pass sentence?'

Maddie wished she could revile the boy, but he was so puny and unaccountable that his life seemed to have no weight. Nothing that could be sentenced upon him would make up for Chris, and no words coming from him could lessen the misery for the Taylors beside her, or her own. She noted for the first time that there might have been some awareness of the enormity of what he had done flickering on his face, but a second later she was sure he'd almost winked at his friend in the wheelchair as if to say, 'This will soon be over, and we'll laugh about it one day.'

Maddie watched the boy in the wheelchair lower his head and avert his eyes. He knew it was not going to be all right, and there'd never be anything funny about it. This physical response seemed to have more impact on Jonathan Gilbert than anything else that had transpired that day, and he mouthed the word, 'Sorry'. It was directed towards his friend, but not to anyone else in the courtroom.

'In sentencing you,' the judge intoned, 'I am limited by law to a maximum custodial term of fourteen years. However, I have to take into account that you have no previous convictions, and must discount your sentence because of your guilty plea. This Court therefore sentences you to five years in prison, with a concurrent sentence of five months for the second charge. You are banned from driving for the same period. Given that you have already served some time on remand, and given good behaviour while you are in gaol, you could be eligible for parole in less than two years. Given the attitude you have demonstrated here today, I will recommend that you are not considered for parole before a period of at least two years. I hope during your time in prison you will reflect on the people suffering daily as a result of your poor judgement, and learn to consider the ongoing effect of your actions.'

Maddie heard the judge finish and the clerk of the court tell everyone to rise. The court would adjourn before the next case. The judge left the courtroom, and the entire process had taken less than forty-five minutes.

Harriet Taylor stood up weakly and leaned on Maddie's arm. Maddie noticed she was ashen, and wondered if she was actually going to collapse.

'Madeline, thank you so much for coming all this way,' she said, 'and for such a terrible duty. You know we would have taken you to lunch, but I must ask you to forgive me. I just can't manage it. Edward,' she said, turning to her husband, 'will you please just take me home.'

Maddie was almost more distressed for the Taylors than she'd been for Chris. He was gone, past pain, and not in a wheelchair. His final hours had been spent doing a job he was passionate about. His parents, on the other hand, had to live without him until their last days, and they looked so lost to Maddie that she could only nod her understanding at them. She turned to follow them out along the row of seats, to a gangway that led to the exit. Her understanding extended itself to a new awareness. Her night wanderings, coupled with today's sentencing, had given her an end-point from which she could start to think of herself as an individual again, with a future; but this would not happen for the Taylors, and might take years for Aguila, and Wyman, and the circle of people around Marilu. She was buoyed by the idea that one good thing she might do was to give a poignant voice to those who suffer needless injustices and, as Søren had said, help to change the outcome of their events.

Then Maddie's mood altered in a moment. She spotted a familiar face quietly watching the unfolding events from the back of the court; on the bench next to him was a worn leather saddle bag. She smiled in disbelief.

Maddie excused herself from the Taylors for a minute. 'I've just seen a friend I need to speak to. Can I meet you on the way out, and walk with you to your car?'

Then she crossed over between the benches; and he spoke before she could.

'I thought you might want a friend in England in your corner,' he said surprisingly seriously. 'But you also might want to be alone right now.'

Maddie shook her head. 'It's wonderful to see you. And no,' she added gently, 'I've had enough "alone". I need about half an hour. Can you find Quod in the High, and get a table outside in the sunshine? I'll meet you there as soon as I can.'

'Of course. *Vado a perdermi tra i fantasmi del passato,*' he added. 'I'll see you when you come.'

Maddie smiled at him, in spite of her sadness. 'The ghosts here should be interesting company!' and she turned back to the exit, where she caught up with the Taylors as they were moving out of the main door of the courthouse.

Søren was sitting in the courtyard at Quod with his back to the building, his face tilted to catch a patch of sunlight. He had his dark glasses on the top of his head, and his eyes closed, when Maddie surprised him from behind. He got to his feet and kissed her on both cheeks, in his European greeting. Then, holding onto her hands for a second, he pulled out a chair for her.

'I've ordered a coffee for us. It won't be as good as Jeanette's,' he said.

'You're just a little bit of a miracle,' Maddie said incredulously. 'I didn't expect to see anyone while I was in England. I thought you were in Tuscany.'

'I was,' Søren said in his characteristically easy tone, 'but I left yesterday. It wouldn't have mattered desperately if you hadn't seen me, but I wanted to be here for you today. I flew in last night and drove up this morning.'

'It would have mattered to me,' she answered. 'I'm more than glad you came. I'm sorry I can't change my ticket, and I'm booked on a plane back home tonight from London in the early evening. I have to leave Oxford around three.'

Søren looked at Maddie's face and thought she'd been all around the world, both literally and metaphorically. The hearing, he was sure, had been an ordeal. 'Well, we have a few hours – and sunshine. Is there anything you would like to do? I'll buy you lunch, if you'd like?'

She nodded slowly. 'In fact, I'd enjoy that very much. I think I've eaten half a croissant since I left home.'

The coffees arrived, and Søren suggested they might eat at the Old Parsonage, on Banbury Road. 'We could sit outside in front of the ivy?'

'Ah, you do know this place a little!' Maddie answered. There was always going to be something more to learn about Søren, she thought. 'Yes, that's lovely: but there's another place I'd like to go on a day like this. It's ten minutes away – and you've got your car?'

He nodded. 'OK – that sounds good. And even though you don't like airport goodbyes, let me drive you to Heathrow after. It will save you time, and you're tired. It's on my way back to London.'

'Yes, I'd like that,' she agreed.

'I don't want to intrude on your grief,' he said softly, 'but, do you want to talk about any of this?'

'No,' she whispered. 'Not right now. Tell me instead about our garden.'

Søren thought she needed to talk about it, at least a little; but he respected her choice and didn't push. He took comfort in the fact that she'd said 'our garden'. It meant she'd left a part of herself at Jeanette's.

'There's very little hard construction left to do. All the herbal planting is complete in the main garden, and we need to see if it over-winters well, and how it grows in. Jeanette's a bit worried about the line of pomegranates I put in, because the wind destroyed the ones she planted before. But I've staked them well, and our fingers are crossed. I'll go back in early spring before the hotel opens, for the finishing touches.'

Maddie drank her coffee, and looked at Søren. She was pleased to see his sunshine on such a dark emotional day. They always talked easily together, and his presence was a release from the gloom that surrounded the Taylors. She empathised with their plight, but she was glad to be diverted from their devastated world.

Søren chatted on humorously about the Unicorn's Garden. 'Jeanette thought, on reflection, that the unicorns would be happier in a field environment if they come. We decided to leave the larger space like a meadow,' he grinned. 'I had a kind of labyrinth cut in patterns in the long grass, to make walkways for a unicorn.'

Maddie giggled. 'I see.'

Søren was happy to hear her laughter. 'It all got a bit out of hand when Jeanette said she wanted to leave the side gate open at night, so the unicorns could get in from the forest. Claus became a little over-heated about security, and told her that a wild boar would be a more likely visitor. So, they dropped the idea. Anyhow, no unicorns have taken up residence in the garden to date, but Jeanette and Vincent are scouring the horizon.'

'Are expectations high on that score?' Maddie was still laughing.

Søren's hazel-brown eyes smiled at her, and he gave her a look of shared confidence. '*Mezzo, mezzo*,' he said. 'Jeanette pointed out to

Claus that hope makes life worth living. She reminded him that their ruin had been rebuilt into a modest palace on hope alone; and she says it was Claus's confidence that made her commit to the work.'

'Jeanette is exactly the person to entice a unicorn to her – if one can ever be found,' Maddie answered him.

They both laughed, and Søren attracted a waiter's attention to pay the bill. Moments later they'd collected her bag from reception, which Søren carried to the parking lot at the rear of the hotel and restaurant. Maddie was not at all surprised, but suitably amused, to find they were walking towards an ice-blue Beetle cabriolet, with its roof down. There was a rose in a vase made for the dashboard.

'An English car in Italy, and a German car here,' she joked. 'Don't you find it a bit cold for the climate?'

He stowed her bag in the boot. 'Not at all,' he replied. 'I like the wind.'

Fifteen minutes later they pulled into the car park at the Trout Inn, on the upper Thames at Lower Wolvercote. Maddie spoke to the hostess at the door, who led them both across the slate floor to a table on the terrace, between the seventeenth-century free house and the river's edge. The sun was bright enough to put up the umbrella, and the setting idyllic with the river running only feet from the table.

Maddie was caught in a wash of emotions. The jet lag, the late night, added to her anxiety about her changing feelings towards Chris's memory. God, how she loved him; but he wasn't there. Her work was also revealing the depths to which people would go to protect their own interests, whether right or wrong; and the sulky Mr Gilbert in the dock this morning proved the world could be thoroughly indifferent to individual suffering. Somehow, she thought, you had to survive by finding a place where you could surround yourself with people who mattered, and make your own reality.

She put on her sunglasses and lifted her face into the warmth. Here she was with Søren, who'd been in Tuscany yesterday, just as she'd been in California. Now they were about to have lunch on the Thames, a few miles from Oxford. Life was really, at times, both unexpected and remarkable.

She heard Søren get up to order drinks from the bar, asking her what she'd like.

She pushed off her glasses again as she turned to answer him, and he saw a face full of mystery and emotion. He sat again.

'Can you tell me what's going through your mind?'

Maddie leaned on her arm and tried to talk to him, but she couldn't seem to express the complexity of what she was sifting through.

Søren gave her a moment, and then spoke himself.

'I have just witnessed a hearing that couldn't begin to address the death of someone you loved. I have watched you comfort that loved one's parents. You said in your last email that there's strong evidence a man your family respects is running a company involved in what is sometimes called the "silent murder" of its employees. Today we shared the awfulness of watching the person responsible for you losing the man you wanted to marry, distancing himself from his actions. It's a lot for one person to deal with.'

Maddie grabbed hold of Søren's hand, and felt surprisingly strong. She wasn't going to cry today – she knew that now – and she managed a small smile.

'I'm going to look ahead,' she said, 'which was impossible for me even a few months ago, when all I could do was survive a day at a time. Now, I'm looking forward to Jeanette opening Borgo next spring as a hotel; and to seeing your realisation of an alchemist's garden. I want to walk in a unicorn's labyrinth, in a place where a better world has been imagined.'

Søren nodded.

'And I think,' she added, smiling more naturally, 'that I'd like you to take me sailing in Denmark. I've never been to Scandinavia, and I haven't sailed for a few years. But I'd like to again now – at some point.'

Søren laughed. 'You remember about the boat!' he said. 'Well, I haven't taken it out in a while either. But of course, I'd love to take you – as soon as the Pleiades are in the sky.'

'The Hen and Chicks?' Maddie asked, with both humour and surprise.

He stood up to go for the drinks, but paused to answer her. 'Yes, the Seven Sisters. They're the time-keepers for the harvest, and also for sailors. When they reappear in the spring, we can go.'

35

END OF MAY 1348, VOLTERRA

At the bottom of the hill Agnesca shifted her weight back in her saddle and gently tugged on the reins for her jennet to halt. The bulk of Volterra rose above her, and she contemplated its enormity from under her eyelids, without daring to lift her head fully.

'I don't think I can,' she said, barely audibly.

The weight of the city seemed to bear down on her, and she felt unable to move. As a child she had thought it so beautiful – had been proud of its pale gold stones and its independence, its dominion over a land of rolling hills and lines of cypress trees, wheat-fields and pasture land that supported its people. Metals and salt, mined from the landscape around it, made it rich; and Volterrans had won a voice against the tyranny of the bishop-counts and over-reaching nobles with a government largely of the people, and a town hall built before any other in the land. When Agnesca was a child these qualities had thrilled her, and made her feel privileged to be one of its children. Now she felt only dispossessed, an 'accused'.

What was she doing here, on its doorstep? She adjusted Luccio's weight in the wrap secured against her body, and drew him closer to her. Then she turned to her husband.

'The breath will be choked out of me, if I go in.'

Porphyrius brought his horse alongside her. Her small gloved hands were gripping the reins tightly, and he covered them with his larger one. 'You have a powerfully worded letter of recommendation from the abbot, Agnesca, and Bishop Filippo needs support now from the mighty Abbey of San Galgano. Besides, you are not alone.'

Mia sat on the other side of her friend, and she too pulled her mare forward a step until she drew next to her. 'It's true, *la raggia*. Trust to the diplomacy of Abbot Angelo. He believes you should have the charges dropped against you, and his strong testimony to your character will carry enormous weight with men of law.'

Agnesca looked up at the walled town, the imposing battlements that had kept the commanding Roman army at bay for months before the time of Christ. She kept her eyes on this, rather than look at the faces of her own companions, when she answered them.

'Since I was here last the charges merely of heresy against me – more than enough for anyone to defend – have been dwarfed by a worse one. I am now accused of parricide; and the murder of one's parents carries an inescapable sentence.'

'Agnese,' Gennaro spoke up, trying to sound reassuring, 'you are not accused of trading in potions or poisons; and the charges of heresy were brought against you by your own aggrieved mother. As I understand it, no formal enquiry had yet taken place. The council of the podesta will pride themselves that they are able to distinguish between what is possible for you to have done, and what is fraudulent. I do not think they will be persuaded that you raised a storm to kill your mother and father. The abbot's letter pleads your case with great eloquence to Bishop Filippo; and as Porphyrius says, following the death of my uncle the new bishop relies upon allegiance from the powerful Cistercians.'

'I think just the opposite of you, Gennaro.' Agnesca shook her head slowly. 'Now that there is no longer an exiled, but still ordained, bishop living to oppose him, Filippo Belforte's power runs unchecked. He may do as he pleases, and he declared me guilty of heresy, subject to proper enquiry, before. Furthermore,' she said, concentrating on the impregnable walls above her, 'it is not Bishop Filippo who will choose my fate. Ottaviano wields the power, and he will decide what is to become of me. He will love to make an example of a wilful daughter who does not submit to the state's religious indoctrination. This is the same for him as a subversive citizen.'

'But if he takes arms against you,' Mia said, looking into Agnesca's bewildered eyes, 'I will accuse him publicly. I have a just grievance; and he must hear me.'

Agnesca looked at each face, her husband and friends, trying to console her. If she had been true to impulse she'd have turned her horse's head away, and ridden to safety with her child. But she saw a fleeting chance to regain her legal freedom, to stop living in semi-hiding, and give her child an honest life. She was more frightened than she could tell them, but she drew a long breath in, to the pit of her stomach, and agreed to climb the imposing hill.

Perhaps thirty paces from the great south-facing gate, however, which had watched travellers, traders and citizens come and go since the time of their furthest ancestors, Agnesca stopped again. She looked at the three stone heads of the city's ancient gods, looming in front of her.

'They wonder what I do,' she said in a strange voice, 'for the last time they beheld me, I was fleeing with Porphyrius.'

The riders paused in late May sunshine that was hot, despite the clouds moving rapidly overhead and blocking the sun at regular intervals, and drew close to her again. They listened to her speak, and Mia never forgot the words.

'I was brought through that gate to the podesta on a charge of filial disobedience, supposedly out of disrespect from a daughter towards her father, but my mother was my accuser. In piety, she said, she had conceived me; and to piety I must be pledged. Her only recognition of happiness was that her child should become a bride of Christ, and chant cold hymns to an invisible God. But my heart did not belong to God. I know nothing of what will become of us when we are dead – I have no certainty about where we go – but of this life I believe we should have the right to be happy in it, as far as we can; to treat others with respect and kindness, to live and make good account of ourselves now. If there is a God, there must also be a goddess – a mother, I hope, more loving than my own – and it is to her that I address my prayers. For me she is not Mary, Queen of Heaven, but the much older Ana, or Diana, the consort of the skies and lady of the hunt.

'My worst sin, though, was not my heresy – of which my mother at that time made no mention. It was that my heart was given to a man, and not to chastity. He was a kind man of a noble family, far better than my own, whom no parent with their child's happiness at heart could refuse as a son. He came duly to my father's house to ask permission for me, when I was fifteen; for within that year, I was to be sent to the nuns. My father might have been persuaded, for his pride saw a socially desirable match, and immortality through his grandchildren, but my mother was intractable.

'Not content to lock me in my room, she dragged me here, to the city. She brought me before the priests and the podesta, who would reason with me, she said, to understand my privilege and learn that I must submit to my parents' will and to the will of God. Such duty was owed by a daughter who was worthless in the world, she reminded me. To the prison in the Palazzo Pretorio I was brought – and thrown like a beggar into that very tower over which the stone figure of the boar reigns – the signal of our city's prosperity, its self-reliance, courage, and fearlessness. I thought it was to frighten me, to rid me of my stubbornness and make me cower into giving up my love. But Porphyrius alone can vouch for the ruthless system that was used to break me.

'I slept at first, for a night or two, on a stone floor in a room high up in the tower. It was small hardship, when you have strength of purpose; though I was hungry. But on the third night I was brought into an airless chamber lower in the building, where I shared my straw and the company of rats with other prisoners. One was a servant girl, an ex-slave who was brought before the *anziani* on a charge of attempting to bewitch her master. Not only that she was female, but that she was low-born and an outsider, spoke fiercely against her; and false accusations that she invoked the devil for her magic were laid upon her. Candles were tied to her fingers and set alight, so that they would burn with the wax. After three days like this she confessed, and spent a night of unspeakable suffering close to me in the prison tower. Her incantations had been only to dissuade her master from raping and beating her continually. But our justice is barbarism, and in the morning she was taken from the chamber to a room below, which served as a chapel. A trap-door in the floor was opened later that day, and we heard the tolling bell in the tower announce her execution. I learned that her body was discarded into the grim underwater beneath it.

'It took almost a week for Porphyrius to find me. Only after relentlessly pursuing me, using his wit like a felon and parting with many florins for information, he came to me with some bread and clean water and told me to look to Janus that night for help. I was moved back to my first chamber, and that night, under a cold bright moon, I indeed found my door open. Coins slipped to my gaoler were my key, but he would later tell that I had bewitched the lock!

'We fled on horseback through this very gate, with the porter counting his payment and the gods of our ancestors gazing after us. I swore I would never come before them again.'

Agnesca was quiet for some moments, looking ahead to the gateway with its portcullis and its porters, the stone gods watching her in their turn.

'I don't think I can go through it,' she said.

Mia had sat on her mare in silence, hardly noticing the stiffness in her bottom and lower back. She had wanted this story for months; to know what Agnesca had suffered, and thus to suffer it with her. Now she wished it could be untold, as it frightened her too. Her own memories of Volterra were equally tortured, and she wondered if their journey here was ill-advised after all.

'I thought,' she said quietly, 'that you had come to us from the prison of your parents' home, which you escaped on the night of the storm.'

'My mother sent the captain of the people after us; and after many months she recaptured me. It was then that they placed me under house arrest; and the morning that I met you at Villa Santo Pietro, Mia, I was to have been given back to the priests for torture and a full confession of my heresy. Instead of waking to a flogging, and to manners of torture too awful to breathe, I awoke to you and to Jacquetta, to your warmth and kindness, a new life and family.'

They had stopped and stood many minutes in the heat, with Agnesca shading her child's face. No one had come or gone – no traveller had passed or questioned them. The possibility of what might lie ahead inside the walls, however, was clear to each, and Gennaro was on the point of offering Agnesca escort if she wanted to return to Santo Pietro.

But she surprised everyone. Sitting up straight in her saddle, she said: 'Let us see, then, if the support of one very good churchman is enough to outweigh the enmity of a very bad one.'

Gennaro and Porphyrius were both still legitimate and high-profile Volterran citizens – and, in the case of the former, readily identifiable. Passing under the vast arch of the ancient gate, the group was waved through on this account, but not without a warning from one of the two porters.

'A great fever is laid upon the citizens of the town, and no one travels abroad, Signor Gennaro,' he said. 'For days without count now, many have sickened with the same malady that has caused utter destruction in Pistoia and in Florence. There, hundreds have died at the hands of this illness, which seems to strike where it will – whether through well-water or the touch of the afflicted from one to another, no man can say. Now it is here in our midst. The sick develop a boil on the thigh or an arm, and vomit blood after. For fear that the same will happen here as in Florence, no priest wishes to say the office for those who are dying, and some seem likely to die without receiving the last rites.

'Soon the citizens must carry their own dead to be buried, as in other parts of Tuscany where the churches have dug down pits deep to the water-table, and the poor who die in the night are bundled up and flung in. Then the gravediggers take up some earth and shovel it on them, preparing the way for the bodies of the next morning – with layers placed one upon another as one makes up lasagne with layers of pasta and cheese. This must come to us too, for it is said that few escape the horror of the mortality.'

The man stopped and looked at four faces, paying no attention in particular to Mia or Agnesca, wondering only why anyone would willingly enter.

Though the gloom and cold of the dense stonework had already unsettled her, these words chilled Mia to the bone. Every one of her party knew what this news meant; the journey to Volterra now seemed ill-fated.

'You should return to San Galgano,' Gennaro told the others. 'But I must go in, and see my family.'

'We'll all go,' Agnesca said firmly, and she seemed to Mia full of courage and determination, and entirely without fear. Following her lead, and to the disbelief of the porters, all the horses passed under the arch and through the gateway into the city.

Mia was immediately struck by the sounds in Volterra. She was unsurprised not to hear birdsong, which accompanied everything she did throughout the day at Villa Santo Pietro: she'd held a clear recollection of the din of the city when she was a little girl, in marked contrast to the relative hush of the woods and fields in the *contado*. But the shock in fact was the deathly silence all around her. That cacophony of vendors and carts on the cobbles, of conversation shouted in the street between friends, and the ring of industry from the coopers making barrels and the blacksmiths fitting horseshoes that she could still hear from her childhood had been quenched like a fire-poker plunged into water. There was, at most, a quiet hiss of steam: the faint trace of voices in further streets, a lone cart rumbling along an alley, a dog barking. It was unnerving and completely unnatural.

She was equally unprepared for the unmistakable stench of the illness that unfolded as she walked her horse through the cramped lanes. Windows were open in the hot weather, and the smell she knew issued from within. Here, however, it was stronger, and more intense, for the numbers of people outreached anything she had witnessed at home. Vomit rose in her throat and threatened to spill from her mouth, but she held it back with will alone. Surely, she thought, the porter was right, and death would take many here.

Gennaro and Porphyrius, she noticed, rode without attention to their horses, staring instead from side to side at what must have been a greatly changed view of their city. The streets were deserted, apart from one servant hurrying to a laundry house and a man carrying bread. Beside these isolated figures, only the corpses of a few animals were seen lying in a ditch, or in the shade of a house, where they must have crawled to die. Few shops were open, or stalls laid out. The city was unrecognisable.

They rode in silence to the town square, and here a decision had to be reached between them. Both men urgently wished to see their families to know how things stood, and if the worst had happened there. Agnesca, however, was concerned for the first time about taking Luccio into a confined space where the disease might already be seeded. She preferred to accompany Mia to see her father, on Mia's business, as directly as possible. Then, she hoped, her letter from Abbot Angelo would gain her admittance to Bishop Filippo to pursue her personal affairs. But Porphyrius was reluctant to let either of them make these visits without him.

Gennaro had most recently exchanged letters with his family and heard nothing of illness, so it was agreed that he would check on them briefly in their home close to the piazza, and then come to the others at Porphyrius's family home near San Michele church, where Agnesca had always been welcome. If all were well, he should see his friends within the hour.

He rejoined them again in the road running down to the church, however, in moments only. A servant was in sole possession of the

Allegretti town house, and the family had fled the sickness days ago, retiring to their farm estate on the road to Pomerance. Gennaro would go there when their business here was complete, but for now, there was no more to be done.

The boyhood home of Porphyrius's father had been the majestic Casa-Torre Toscano, and they trotted under its shadow on their right. After his father crossed the goodwill of the Belforte family while Ottaviano's brother, Ranieri, was bishop, he was excluded from the list of those who could hold public office in the town. Thinking it appropriate that they should move from the family's splendid and self-confident tower house, it was sold to the Rapucci family – to whom it now belonged – and Porphyrius's family had moved to a more modest dwelling further down the road on the other side of the church, where he was born. It was here that they tethered their horses, and rapped against the door.

It took some time for anyone to answer, but after a repeated and more demanding request of the lily-shaped knocker the familiar face of the steward, Ugolino, appeared – followed by expressions of amazement at the arrival of the prodigal son. The four travellers found themselves sitting in the large ground-floor room used for business by Porphyrius's father, Fortino. In minutes his mother was greeting her son.

Mia smiled at the small woman, with her dark hair twisted tidily and swept under a simple hood. She tried to look away, as if fascinated by the huge sacks of spices and goods from the East, to give the happy parent and her child some privacy. But soon she, too, was swept up into a welcoming embrace after Gennaro – who was clearly well known to the family – and then as quickly set aside for an exalted greeting to her son's lady and to the beautiful child who was her fair-haired grandson, who had slept all this time. The grandmother picked him up and cuddled him noisily. After the ghostly feeling of the city streets, the fluster and excitement at the Toscano house seemed reassuringly human, and Mia relaxed.

They were shown up to a sizeable chamber draped with hangings on the second floor, and refreshment was brought by Ugolino. Then Monna Elisabetta, Porphyrius's mother, told them all of the arrival of the 'great mortality' – as it was being called in Volterra – and of its impact on the city and their family.

'You'll not find your parents or sisters in town, Gennaro,' she said, 'for like most families with country houses, they have fled the sickness.

And your father and brother,' she addressed Porphyrius, 'have also halted in Lucca on their road from Marseilles. The mortality is there, too, but they are so far well and stay with friends in their villa outside the town. Why, dear children, why, do you choose this unholy time to come home?' she asked with some panic. 'I'd have come to meet my grandson on my own orders, and would have saved you the threat of visiting the city.'

'How many families are struck with the disease, Monna Elisabetta?' Agnesca asked her.

'As many perhaps as one in three,' she answered. Her words were barely exhaled, as if she thought that speaking so quietly would lessen the chance of tempting a greater number. 'And from what we hear from the doctors and priests, many will die. We have been fortunate not to sicken, but we have not left the house. Ugolino and I are alone here with only Pascuala as nurse-maid for your nieces, and the five of us live on what is in the store cupboard. We have ventured to but one shop for meat, and visited no friends.'

Porphyrius now explained to his mother more fully a story that his letters had merely glossed: of Gennaro's long and ghastly fight with the disease; of his eventual recovery under the care of Agnesca and Mia; and of his own escape from the creeping horror at the port of Messina months before. The poor woman's face went through a dozen contortions as the account moved through its various stages and cast of characters, until Mia thought her heart might give out when she realised her son might have contracted the illness in Sicily. In the context of report about Florence, and about what was happening at a frightening pace here in Volterra, they understood the miracle of their being untouched by death, excepting Bishop Ranuccio. But at the end of this tale, Signora Toscano asked again why they risked themselves now, when the unsparing disease was striking Volterra with such biblical intensity.

'Maria Maddalena,' Porphyrius told her, 'is the daughter of Signora Barbarina and the niece of Signorina Jacquetta, both of whom you will remember, *mia madre*. She comes on purpose to speak with Ottaviano. And Agnesca, too, carries a letter from the abbot of San Galgano abbey, whose life she also rescued from the mortality.' He entreats Bishop Filippo to pardon her and overturn her mother's accusations; and, he has married us.'

This was more than Monna Elisabetta Toscano could absorb in one breath! She deliberated a moment, taking each point in turn, starting first with the last mentioned detail. She sprang from her seat like a woman half her age and hugged her son again, and then her daughter even more forcefully than before, so that poor Luccio was squeezed between them, and cried for the first time.

'You have my blessing – which counts, I know, only for a mother's joy,' she said – 'but the more important assent will come from your father, and he will be neither unkind nor ungenerous to you both.'

Agnesca was deeply affected by this emotional response. Though Porphyrius's parents had been courteous to her at every meeting, she was still a woman of uncertain legal status, and entirely without a dowry. She could have been disowned for less, as many marriages were immediately annulled if a dowry went unpaid.

'Now then, for the rest, luck may be with you, Agnese.' Monna Elisabetta picked up from the other points. 'Having been confined to the house for days, I may not have the current news; but Pascuala learned from the butcher yesterday that the bishop still remains in the Palazzo Vescovile, as Church business detains him. Yet you, Maria,' she turned apologetically to Mia, 'will not have your chance. Ottaviano and his other sons, and wife, have certainly gone to Montecatini. At the first sight of peril they were away, and I have no idea when they may return. Excepting when he is surrounded by his crossbowmen, the lord of our city is not brave.'

Mia's body slumped, and she covered her face with her slender fingers. She was embarrassed by this show of emotions defeating her dignity before Signora Toscano, but she had hung on for weeks to know about her mother, and ask how Ottaviano could explain his act to her – his natural daughter. She had questions that her temerity persuaded her he would answer. Now, the journey here was wasted for her. She would pull herself upright for her friend, and go to the bishop, but in the present moment she could not be so selfless. She had lost her chance to look on her father, and say her piece.

Gennaro came over and kneeled beside her.

'Maria, Ottaviano is not your family,' he said, gently prising her hands from her face. 'That name belongs to those who fill that role, and that is your aunt and your friends, who love you. The understanding you are wanting can be given you, at least in part, by Jacquetta. She does not know all the details of the story, but she knows enough. I will come back with you to Chiusdino, and we will hear her together.'

Agnesca, sad as she was for Mia, couldn't stop a tiny smile from coming. Surely only you, Mia, she thought, could be so unaware of his feelings for you. But she intimated nothing of this and said instead something that was now pressing on her mind.

'Forgive me, then, but I should waste no time and ask an audience of Bishop Filippo now. My heart is not eager, and I have many fears about it, but it is what I have come for, and what I must finish in one way or another. Perhaps,' she tried to muster a little more hope, 'he may be more disposed towards me if his father is not here to direct him.'

Their affairs at Casa Toscano were concluded with some advice from Agnesca to her new mother about medicines for the mortality, should they be needed, and hints about the cleanliness of the house: 'For it is not certain what brings the illness, Monna Elisabetta,' she said, 'but it may be carried with – or worsened by – the bites of lice or mosquitoes, or even animal ticks and flees, which seem to become acutely inflamed. Keep the dogs on the lowest floors, and be liberal with your strewing herbs.'

The old bishop's palace had been at the city cathedral, abutting on the Piazza dei Priori; but as the people's *comune* had gradually increased their power and gained dominance in this centre of government, the bishops had relocated and built a new *castello* one hundred years before in the area of the old Etruscan and Roman acropolis.

Mia looked up at the imposing building, and felt very small. Its soaring tower was of great strength and some beauty; and a loggia ran along the front of the palace. Even from the outside, the chapel looked luxurious. She felt the splendour and the pomp of the Episcopal role that was being freshly asserted here, and it frightened her. She was a country girl of no birth and with no power; her arrogance of expecting that she had any call on these people suddenly evaporated.

It was Gennaro who led them all to the clerk of the house, and demanded admission. Despite more than a generation of family enmity with the Belforti, he carried the bishop's ring from his uncle and particular words for Filippo's ear alone. And indeed, it was on this basis that their horses were taken to be watered and cared for while they were admitted into the waiting hall of the Bishop of Volterra. Mia's head turned a half-circle as she scanned the vast expanse of stone that carried a pair of servants to the upper floors of the palace; she breathed in the lingering incense and watched the noiseless parade of clerics and other householders coming and going through the building. A silver-gilt chest, more elaborate than any she'd seen, dominated the seating area; and a large arras on the facing wall floated gently outwards and back as the front door was opened again. If everything outside were in chaos, the interior of her brother's realm looked as daunting and impenetrable as ever.

It was several minutes before a secretary came, robed, almost to Mia's disappointment, like any other cleric. He had instructions to bring Signor Allegretti only, and with a hand gesturing reassurance Gennaro left them and climbed the stone staircase to a world beyond their sight.

About a quarter of an hour passed, and only a man dressed in the black and white of a physician came from an outer room through this one, and disappeared into another hall. A bell chimed once in the clock tower for the half-hour – though half of which hour, Mia had lost track. The midday meal had long ago come and gone, so she thought it might be half-past two, but the bright light and long day's heat gave no indication. Agnesca fidgeted beside her for a moment, the baby stirring and resisting being quietened. She would take him somewhere to feed him, she said, and was at the point of asking a steward where she might be permitted to do so when Gennaro reappeared at the top of the stairway and came down to them, accompanied by a servant.

'He will see you both,' he said, in a tone of authority Mia had never heard him use before, 'Maria Maddalena, and Agnese. The servant will show you the way; and we, Porphyrius, shall wait.'

Agnesca's eyes widened, but Mia clutched her hand and nodded at her. She passed Luccio to his father, and together the two women followed the man who had just come down with Gennaro, back up the stairs.

As the carved door opened, Mia's jaw dropped. The bishop's chamber was hung with no space between the beautiful tapestries and silks, so thickly were they massed. A casement window, high and triple-arched with tiny glass, threw splashes of red light on her face and on the floor; and carvings of fruits and flowers decorated each pillar. It was a world away from the simple grace of the abbey church of her neighbours, and this was only his *studio*.

Bishop Filippo stood and offered them his ringed finger to kiss, and, remembering herself, Mia kneeled in front of him and brushed her lips against the stone. Agnesca bowed only from her place standing behind Mia, and let the bishop speak.

'You, then, are the child of the Capobianchi woman,' he said with exaggerated interest, looking at Mia as though she were a horse at market.

Through a veil of confusion, Mia couldn't answer. Was this her mother's family name? Her aunt had always called herself 'Jacquetta di Benedetto', which was her grandfather's given name; she had never heard the name he just used, and she tilted her head, unsure of her answer.

'The woman,' he continued in his own time, 'who first destroyed the morals and reputation of my predecessor, and then set her cap at my father.'

The pun on the family name annoyed Mia. It was true, she had not learned the whole story of her mother's unhappy history; but this, she knew, was certainly false. She remembered Bishop Ranuccio's last words to her, and her face reddened at the accusation implied by Filippo Belforte. Suddenly he seemed to her not a gracious prelate and nobleman who outranked her in every particular, but the lying son of a dishonourable father whom she had every reason to despise. She drew herself up to her full height.

'Though it is no wish of mine that it should be so, your father and mine are one and the same,' she said in her distinctively quiet but clear voice. It was a voice that, for all its softness, demanded to be heard – as though the listener had to adjust to its tone and pay full heed to the speaker.

With these few words out Mia experienced a rush of confidence and a sharp feeling of injustice, and they were followed by a stream.

'Bishop Ranuccio, God rest him,' she continued, 'gave me a full account on his deathbed, when his soul was in peril; and whether you know it, or will admit it, it was your father who spoiled my mother's only chances of happiness by fathering me on her. In doing this, he ruined my aunt's opportunities as well. It was his men, I know, who were guilty of her death: because, Filippo, I was there, and I saw.'

Mia was nervous, and breathed deeply as she spoke; but to those who heard her it sounded only like justified anger and emotion, and she was able to speak on unhindered.

'This woman who comes with me carries the goodwill of Bishop Ranuccio – who acted faithfully as my guardian for all the years of your father's misdeed, and in the absence of any restitution from him. She bears also a letter from Abbot Angelo of San Galgano, who is my aunt's neighbour and friend. Attend to her with proper dignity, as befits her right; give her the courtesy your office demands; and you will save me the need to make my grievance public. For even if your panel of elders is hand-picked by you, and you find my complaint wanting, yet the accusation of murder will be out, and tongues will wag and judge your father as they see fit.'

Filippo Belforte was silenced, and Agnesca had nothing to add; but no one was more stunned by her daring than Mia herself. No one sat, and no one moved. Mia could see the wheels of motion in her half-brother's mind and knew she had impacted upon him. He soon held out his hand.

'Give me the letter, Signora Toscano,' he said tonelessly.

Filippo Belforte sat at his desk and, without inviting his guests to be seated in front of him, read the lengthy discourse from the abbot of San Galgano. He sat for some time, bringing his hands together and cracking the bones in his knuckles, to Mia's distaste. She was ready to ask him if they might sit, when he looked up suddenly at Agnesca.

'The abbot argues that you are a saint, in a guise we are too flawed to recognise. He believes we cannot always understand God's will, and says He has spared you by His own hand.'

His eyes gave nothing away as he spoke, and Agnesca said nothing in reply to him, as no question had been put to her. With looks of subtle challenge they regarded each other for perhaps half a minute, until the bishop called a servant to him and spoke in a whisper to exclude Mia and Agnesca from hearing them. The servant left the room, and Bishop Filippo's eyes swept over the women.

'Sit!' Mia finally heard him say, in the tone of a command given to a dog.

It seemed endless, the time that they waited in absolute silence. Mia could have drawn the hunting scene on one of the tapestries from memory, for so long did she gaze at it. Eventually the servant reappeared carrying a deer-skin borse, which the bishop now opened. He withdrew documents from it and skimmed them, breathing out audibly, looking

347

back at one again, studying in detail the inserted note in the margin of another.

'Signora Lucini, your mother,' he finally spoke, 'seems to have made all the complaint against you. I see that no witness from among your neighbours could be found to speak against you, and that your father was silent. However,' he looked at her coldly, 'you escaped from your cell, and that is an offence against the State.'

'The State omitted to feed me,' Agnesca said flatly, 'and it is human instinct to eat and live freely, if possible. I obeyed the laws of nature.'

Bishop Filippo's lips curled up in a smile without warmth, but not without some amusement. He consulted once more the letter from Abbot Angelo, then tidied the papers and set them in front of him on the desk.

'I find that the Church had not yet enquired into your religious conscience,' he said, 'and that it was accusation only, brought by your mother, which forced me to proclaim you in danger of heresy, and a possible threat to the State. Furthermore,' he said in a weighty voice, 'a marginal note tells me that you were placed in the city prison at the request of your parents, to help you to understand your duty of obedience to them. This is not properly a Church or State offence. If an enquiry into parricide, however, or the conjuration of demons was ever brought against you, I would be powerless to help you.'

Now he looked at Mia, whose face was deeply concentrated on his. She thought afterwards, when recalling his expression, that it might possibly have said, 'This girl could be troublesome. This girl – as nothing as she is – will invoke sympathy, and we should muzzle her.' And Mia would not look away from him, as though she were being tested for her strength of will.

Agnesca and Mia watched Filippo Belforte, Bishop of Volterra, clench the papers in his hand and walk to a wall on the outside of the room beside a window, where a censer wafted perfumed smoke into the chamber. He took a taper from the shelf beneath it and lit that from a fine tallow candle in a wall sconce; then he slowly and deliberately crossed to a fireplace where no fire was lit today in hot May weather. In silence and some amazement, and even a little fear, they watched him burn every paper, every note, including the abbot's communication to him.

Agnese Lucini – whose full birth name Mia had only learned today, and which she would hear only that once – watched as her history crackled in the flame, the paper curling up the stone chimney. Both women watched as Agnese Lucini was expunged from history.

Filippo now stood above the seated figure of Agnesca and passed her the empty borse, which she took from him; but though the matter she had come about was rather spectacularly settled for her, his curiosity was not. He leered at her, and leaned down close to her body.

'Did you call upon your gods to raise the storm that set you free?' he asked quietly into her ear.

Agnesca recognised a fleeting moment of her own power. The documents had disappeared; but he still thought her a witch, and she frightened him. A mixture of amusement and pleasure provoked a half-smile, and she got to her feet before answering him.

'This city was founded on the ancient gods, who still watch from their sacred place above the gate. We live in houses built upon those of our ancestors, and the fabric of your palace is fashioned from stones that made their temples, their theatres and their halls of government. Perhaps those ancestors, sleeping in tombs below our ramparts, and surrounding us in their hills, yet hear us. And when our emotions are untethered and we cry in despair against what is not just, I wonder if they allow us to call – as they so famously did – on thunder, rain and wind?

'For every generation the ideas of its parents are at fault; every new age shows contempt for the beliefs that went before. But this age will come to be derided by those who follow us; and theirs, in their turn, will be supplanted in an unspecified time in the future. We love to be right: but who is certain that what has been forgotten has no worth? I believe my ancestors knew the song of the rain. Perhaps they heard me, or perhaps it was just a stormy night, and we live in a place blighted by the wind.'

Bishop Filippo's eyes examined hers while he thought how to answer. His question surprised Mia.

'Will I outrun the mortality? Shall I survive this?'

'Prophecy is against the law of our city, so I shall hazard a guess only. Keep your palace clear of vermin, and your household and servants clean, and you shall live.'

He heard her, and Mia saw relief as well as anger on his face before he lifted his right arm and pointed to the door.

'Go from here,' he told her in a voice of clear threat. 'Go not to any place that comes within the diocese of Volterra. Go not to any of our allies – neither to Pisa, nor to Florence. Take yourself to Siena, with whom we quarrel, if you will, or to Lucca; but come not this way again. If I hear of you in any part of Tuscany, I will bring charges against you myself, and bring all the force of my father's house, and that of my brothers, against you.'

Agnesca bowed at him, and grabbed Mia's hand; but at the door, she paused.

'You shall live, Filippo Belforte,' she said, 'but your father may be less fortunate. And your brother should beware the winds of change when they blow against him in this city.'

She bowed again, and they left.

36

THURSDAY 22 NOVEMBER 2007, SAN FRANCISCO

It was a tradition of the house, Enzo always said. At the end of the Thanksgiving feast, the host and guests should 'raise a glass to the memory of absent friends'.

The family, along with Tyler and Charlotte, whom Maddie had invited on the strict understanding that there would be no discussion of work, were among the gathering, which included Barbara and her best friend, Drew, and Nonna Isabella.

They all charged their glasses with one of Pierce Gray's lesser vines – not, as Professor Moretti advised them, the much-hyped Gray Lady – and everyone stood. Enzo's words carried their usual poignancy no less for having been said at so many Thanksgivings before: 'To absent friends', and the group repeated his toast, lifting their glasses and drinking.

Each reflected for a moment.

Maddie's first thoughts were of Christopher, and then his family; and although the Taylors didn't celebrate Thanksgiving, she knew they'd be looking ahead to a cheerless festive season – the first without their son. She uttered the closest thing to a prayer – at least, a benediction of hope for them – that she could; and then her mind turned to Borgo. She vividly conjured every face in her mind's eye: Jeanette, and Claus, and beautiful little Vincent; then she came finally to Søren, and she heard his distinctively musical voice, with almost the trace of an accent, speaking those last words when they'd parted in England. Her hopes were that spring might come early this year, and bring the Pleiades into clear sight in the Northern skies once more. Of course she knew the stars would come at their appointed time no matter what she hoped, but hope made her feel better able to face the world and the stresses of her work.

Her thoughts led her to a question she put to her father.

'Papa, do you think hope, and belief, are a part of our DNA?'

'That's a philosophical direction for Thanksgiving,' he said, not deeply surprised. 'I don't think hope and belief – or even faith – are quite the same thing. Hope is a kind of wish list of things we might want; I think hope gives the human animal the ability to face and overcome adversity.

'If we think of the illness and oppression people face today,' he added after a moment's thought, 'it is terrible; but then, think about medieval times, when hope was vital for survival. Yes, Maddie, I would say it was hope that has brought humanity to where it is today. So, without any scientific proof, you may be right that hope is an essential component of the human genome.'

Barbara groaned, largely as a matter of entertainment, but not only to be funny. 'Dad, don't let Maddie take you off on some flight of fancy. You'll bore the rest of us to death!'

Everyone laughed on cue, but Enzo continued with his ruminations in spite of Barbara's admonishment. Maddie had opened up something interesting for him.

'Belief and faith are a bit different, I think. Belief runs the gambit of possibilities from superstition, through belief in one's self, to a belief in God. Children believe in fairies and Santa Claus; many people believe in God and the person of a loving Jesus Christ who cares about them each individually. Scientists believe broadly in an indifferent universe.'

Tyler, Drew and Charlotte were now fully engaged in what Enzo was saying, and Tyler nodded at him. 'I'm a firm believer in positive thinking. It raised me – I could say it raised me up,' he said sincerely.

Enzo nodded at him with great consideration, and then addressed his younger daughter again. 'I am very sure that people in a pre-modern world believed utterly in the power of prayer, in the possibility of a better after-life, and even that life could be miraculous and improve their conditions at times – if they worded their petitions well. And I believe that believing in that belief sometimes actually made it true. It is this strange truth that is behind what medical men call the "placebo effect".'

He smiled at Barbara, whose expression of mild exasperation was a familiar friend. She was thinking, without doubt, that he was just about to get the bit between his teeth.

She quipped in her inimitable way: 'Now we will be going down the road of the metaphysical difficulties for the scientist to encompass the realities of God, creation and providence in such a way that it can sit with what they know to be true.'

Everyone laughed again, but Barbara thought she knew her father. To her surprise, however, Enzo kept his tone very light, and guests at table showed no inclination for him to finish when in fact he did.

'We live in a post-metaphysical age,' he said easily, 'and science has demonstrated that the world of life is not dependent upon, nor derived from, any other realm. What we know, or have learned, has altered our view of reality, and we cannot unlearn what we have learned. But we are very lucky, all of us sitting around this table. There is no compulsion to believe, and we are free to think and believe what we will. Though there are those – both here in America and around the world – who would have it otherwise. An excellent reason for our giving thanks, don't you agree?'

And glasses were raised again.

TUESDAY 25 DECEMBER 2007

Carol Moretti, in an apron and rubber gloves, stood at the sink in the kitchen at Wildcat Canyon washing up the last remnants of Christmas dinner. The two sisters – holding Williams-Sonoma tea towels, which had formed part of Maddie's blue-themed gift to her mother for the season – dried the best glasses and the silver, which Carol said should not go into the dishwasher. She handed them to the girls from the sink, and in the background the over-stuffed dishwasher groaned to itself as it ran its programme.

'Your dishwasher sounds like it's on its last legs,' Barbara commented as she took another glass. 'It sounds the way I feel – kind of over-full. But what a lovely Christmas feast,' she added, as they all quietly enjoyed each other's company. Barbara hugged her baby sister in particular, who looked so much better than she had a few months ago. But she still had the anniversary of Chris's death ahead to cope with.

Earlier in the day she had privately told Maddie that she had celebrated the Solstice this year with some pagan friends of Drew's, and had ended up in bed with a Druid – 'not to be confused with Drew,' she'd laughed. She was still more than a little worse for wear, but in excellent spirits.

'You know,' Carol said, giving Maddie the silver cake-slice to wipe, 'you both should have come to the midnight choral Mass at St Mary of the Assumption last night. It was wonderful. It just gets inside your soul and lifts you right out of banality. I think even your father was moved on this occasion. I know the cathedral is very modern, but it's quite awe-inspiring when it's filled with the music and those wonderful vapours of incense.'

'Dad took you to church last night, all the way into the city?' Barbara questioned. 'No one mentioned that at lunch.'

'Oh, there are a lot of things you don't know about your father,' Carol answered with a mild tone of victory. 'Yes, we took Isabella as well. Even a pair of old sceptics like your father and your grandmother sometimes find the atmosphere and the music almost unbearably moving. Last night was one of those times. It affected everyone deeply. Maybe it is in our DNA, as you put it, Maddie.'

TUESDAY 1 JANUARY 2008

Monday December 31 2007
Stormtree Components Inc
invites
Miss Madeline Moretti
to
New Year's Eve Celebrations
at the
San Francisco Yacht Club
RSVP

The invitation fell off her fridge as she opened it, hunting for orange juice. She wasn't feeling well at all.

A few days ago she had emailed Søren 'Happy Holidays'. He had answered her with a greeting for a Happy New Year and attached pictures of the Copenhagen Christmas Market, which was a fairy tale. The unequalled setting of the Tivoli was resplendent with lamps hung in trees, miniature villages with shops full of gifts, an enchanted lake to skate on and the whole scene finished with a light sprinkling of snow that drew on every connotation of Christmas she could imagine from her childhood to the present. It seemed wonderful to Maddie.

He had also sent a box of beautifully wrapped iris soaps from the pharmacy of Santa Maria Novella in Florence, which Jeanette had told him Maddie had very much wanted to buy, though she had been unable to visit the shop when her trip was cut short at the end. The package had arrived only on Friday, and the note in the box said: 'Perhaps not what I'd have chosen for you, but the near-violet scent is nice, and I'm glad if it's what you like. Søren x'.

'Ah! I wanted them for Nonna,' she'd said aloud to herself as she lifted the lid and breathed in the perfume. She was astonished, though, that he would go to such trouble.

His email said he had flown back to Denmark for the first time in years to have Christmas with his parents and brother and sister. He hinted that there was something in his relationship there he wanted to sort out with his mother. He had avoided it before, which was why he had stayed away so long; but he felt good now that he had done it. He thanked Maddie for her unknowing complicity, he wrote, as he felt it was she who had made him realise he must go.

Maddie thought she could guess something of what it might be about – connected with his wish for independence, which he had mentioned briefly that day on the loggia at Borgo. But the markets, and the man, seemed a very long way away.

Pierce Gray had phoned some days ago to ask why she hadn't called since her return from Italy, nor RSVP'd her invitation for New Year. She had been quite abrupt with him, stating that she was too busy trying to repair the damage done to the hearts and minds of her clients by one Gordon Hugo. His baboon, she actually told him, had gone feral. Pierce had been unusually silent on the phone for a moment, but had finally asked her to ring him when she had time as he would like to see her again and had a small gift for her. But Pierce's gifts were unsettling and not altogether welcome.

So she'd put off responding to his invitation, which she admitted now was a little rude. Instead, like many fellow Friscans, she had gone dancing and ended up absurdly drunk at a gay rave over in the Castro with Barbara and Drew. She had unexpectedly enjoyed herself, but the party had gone on until the early morning light, and she'd crawled into her bed only a few hours ago.

She picked up the invitation and looked at it while she drank her juice. She felt as though her head was unrelated to her body, but she sat for a minute trying to think. The gateway opens into a new year today, she reminded herself; and she set down her juice and the invitation, picked one of the soaps out of the box, and headed for the shower.

SATURDAY 5 JANUARY 2008

Isabella had invited Maddie to her house to celebrate the feast of the Epiphany on Saturday night. Maddie felt a little feasted out after the last month, but the celebration was a childhood memory that included the tale of a witch known as La Befana, a character she loved.

Italian legend was that La Befana was an old hag who had missed out when the three Wise Men were on their way to give their gifts to the newborn Christ. The Wise Men had stayed with her for a night on their way, but she had refused to go with them the next day. The story ran that she had had a change of heart, but it was too late and she had missed the party, and never met Jesus. To make up for her behaviour, La Befana was left to fly around the world on her broomstick during the night of 5 January, and fill the stockings with toys and sweets for good children and lumps of coal for the bad ones.

Maddie had never had coal, and as a child she saw no problem in reconciling this person with the Christmas story. She thought La Befana a more interesting character than Santa, and anyway, it meant she got a double dose of stocking presents. No one in the family had celebrated *Epifania* once Maddie had reached the age of nine, so she wondered what game Isabella was up to now.

Usually Isabella's was fun and not too far to walk home, Maddie considered, but it was very dark when Maddie pushed open the gate to Isabella's front garden at around seven in the evening. It creaked, and Nonna Isabella opened the front door before Maddie could touch the doorbell, just as usual.

When Maddie entered the sitting room, the white marble statue of Diana was wearing a pointed black witch's Hallowe'en hat. A stocking was hung around her neck. This was exactly as it had been from Maddie's early childhood, and she felt a touch of nostalgia.

Isabella gestured to Maddie to take the stocking; and oddly, Isabella seemed more excited than she was. She watched Maddie like a hawk, as if she were anticipating some special reaction.

Maddie took down the stocking and shook out a jeweller's box, tied with an old white ribbon. Maddie opened the box carefully and pulled the cotton that covered its contents away, and a smile warmed her face.

At this point Isabella could not contain herself any longer, and she blurted out, 'Since your birthday I've been tearing the house apart, looking for that. I finally found it in the back of a drawer last weekend. Is it beautiful?'

Maddie looked down on the large cameo brooch depicting a pair of doves lifting a garland of flowers in a lovers' knot between them. It was still pinned to the black silk ribbon that was in the photograph of her great-great-grandmother. She felt a tear moisten her eye, and then she nodded her head. Yes. It was beautiful.

'It's for you,' Isabella said. 'I knew that, when I first saw your face looking at the pictures on your birthday.'

Maddie looked at Nonna Isabella as if to ask a question, but no words came out.

'Oh, do I think Barbara should have it?' Isabella responded to the look. 'No, I don't. She'd never wear it – but I think you will. Barbara is too much like her namesake, St Barbara. If you mess with her too much, you get struck by lightning.'

Maddie thought this one of the oddest things Nonna had ever said, and she looked at her questioningly again.

'You know the story of St Barbara, the saint who would not die, even though they kept cutting her up? She seemed to grow back together each time. Finally her father got fed up and went to cut off her head, and as he swung the axe he was struck by lightning. I think of it every time your sister cuts your father off when he's talking. No,' she said again, 'this is for you. You are the one who is rooted in memory of the past. You feel it, like me – although you don't quite understand it.'

Maddie hugged her grandmother. She had to admit, looking at the cameo, that she had a strong sensation that she had seen its image some place before; and it was not in the picture of Grandmother Mimi.

SUNDAY 20 JANUARY 2008

The day had begun with soft rain.

There was no avoiding the calendar – no escape from the anniversary of tragedy, of her being catapulted without warning into heartbreak and then numbness. It was as though she had been, she thought now, thrown into deep water that was dark and impenetrable, chilling her to the bone, stopping her breath, lulling her into a sense of lifelessness and hopelessness, so that the struggle for her own survival seemed irrelevant. She hadn't wanted to die; but neither had she wanted to swim. She had lived for months, she saw now, in a kind of suspended animation. But the year had passed, and she was here.

In a very personal way she'd wanted to honour Christopher's life today, rather than concentrate on his death. She didn't want to be morbid, but she needed time to herself. Barbara had rung yesterday, worried that Maddie should not be alone; but Maddie insisted she was fine and only desired her solitude. She would light candles and permit herself some thoughts – thoughts she had closed the door on for most of the last year. She had told Barbara she would prefer a silent vigil.

With this in mind she spent the morning immersed in the pages of her Oxford photo album, reliving the moments in each frame with friends on the river; in a play on Merton College lawns; with Chris on May morning at Magdalen Bridge. Every memory was tender, and yet less immediate than the emotions she had invited in on that September evening before the hearing. Chris wasn't in the photos; but he was – would always be – with her in the lanes and buildings of their city, and in Venice, too. She still felt the loss, but it was by degrees less acute than even a few months ago.

Brutal as it was, Chris's death had forced her on a journey towards a whole, stand-alone state of being. The journey was far from complete – only beginning, in fact – but she saw herself increasingly as a pilgrim in the way Jeanette had described: seeking to break free from the limitations of her own world, and being scrubbed clean in the process.

But towards three o'clock, the memory of the phone call itself broke into her thoughts. She looked at the handset in the kitchen and heard Harriet Taylor's voice in her ear all over again. Her stomach tightened and she felt a rush of mild panic.

As slowly and calmly as she could, Maddie seated herself on a rug on the floor of her apartment, her computer open on the coffee table in front of her. She started trolling her collection of pictures of Borgo, looking for solace in the images. Vincent and his mother were laughing in the rose garden in one of them; her pilgrim's room beckoned her, with an unmade bed as though she'd just woken, in another; and she lingered over one of Søren she'd taken in three-quarter profile. The right side of his face always looked so finely drawn and handsome – almost annoyingly so. The left, she remembered, was not quite so perfectly executed by nature, and he was pleasingly mortal from that angle. Janus, she smiled to herself; and then she flicked to another frame, this time of the view of the Valle Serena from the loggia, with Jeanette's giant pots of lemon trees in the foreground. She could almost smell them in flower.

The pictures did what she asked of them and helped her find comfort in the thought that someone had cared, and tried to imagine a better world.

It was now five, and the rain, which had looked like clearing earlier, began again and made it dark a shade early. Maddie saw the time and stood up, finding her joints stiff. She stretched and decided a shower would help, and pass some time. Replacing the votives, she lit fresh candles and selected some Puccini on her sound system, keeping a respectful volume but pleased with the feelings the music immediately helped to release. About an hour later it was properly dark outside, though not really cold, yet, she was shaking a little. Perhaps she needed food, though she didn't feel hungry.

Mimi was singing as Maddie started towards her window with its view to the bay, and she hugged her arms around her upper body and shivered, looking at the rain falling and feeling much less brave than earlier in the day.

That was when she heard it. Softly, coming from behind her, someone was knocking on her door. There'd been no buzzer from the street, so it was a neighbour; was her music too loud? Or possibly Nonna or Barbara – both of whom had a key. Well, if it were Nonna or her sister they would be surprisingly welcome, she thought, and not the intrusion she'd imagined. She opened the door.

'Don't say anything,' he said, putting his fingers very gently over her lips in place of a kiss. 'I don't mean to break into your day; but, as mild as it is, I thought for you it must be one of the coldest of the year.'

Maddie's eyes streamed tears. She couldn't ask how he was here, or why he was here. She knew she had called him to her.

'It's only the opera – making me cry,' she managed to say to him.

'I know,' he said. And his arms wrapped around her.

37

END OF MAY 1348, VOLTERRA, TUSCANY

As they so often did, late on a day of prickling heat in summer, thunder clouds started to gather above the towers and rooftops of the city and a strong breeze picked up, forcing its way through the near-empty streets. Mia's only comfort was that it blew the terrible smell of the sickness in the other direction.

They were almost through the Etruscan gate when Mia stopped.

'You must come home at least for your belongings,' she cried to Agnesca, who was a horse-length in front of her.

Tears impeded her words. She was sheltering just inside the porch under the gods of the old city; but the wind coming around the face of the hill suddenly grabbed at the hood of her cloak and tugged at her long hair, freeing it after a moment from the loose ribbon that bound its thickness inadequately. Strands of long dark curls now escaped across her face, and the current of cold air scorched at the salt on her cheeks. She wished she could take things back to that lazy long-ago morning when they'd set out from Santo Pietro; it was impossible to understand that that was only yesterday.

'We arrived with next to nothing,' Agnesca struggled to answer, with emotion in her throat, too, 'so our possessions matter little to me. But we must leave from here, because he'll keep watch on Santo Pietro,' she had to almost shout into the wind, 'and that would bring calamity on all of you.' She sounded more resolved than she felt, but clung to the idea of being strong for Mia.

361

Mia really wept; it seemed like the freeing of tears that had been imprisoned since she'd left these gates as a child. Her voice then had been frozen, and she could tell no one her misery. Today she could make the necessary sounds, but they issued only as moans between a few clearer words.

Gennaro pulled his horse close to her and caught at her cloak, which mushroomed out to one side across her body. He helped bind it around her again so it gave some protection from the wind.

'We might wait the weather,' he said to everyone, 'for a storm is certainly coming. But you are right that it's safest to take different roads from here.'

Agnesca nodded, and was all of a sudden oddly calm. She turned her horse against the elements and faced Mia, taking a strong hold of her arm and forcing out a smile, which was entirely in keeping, Mia later thought, with the strength and radiance of her character.

'Today our roads divide us,' she agreed, 'but if you retie the knot in our garden under the doves, Mia, one day I promise it will bring me back to you.'

Agnesca's face was also wet with tears when she hugged her friend so tightly that the horses frightened one another, and Mia's stumbled. Gennaro lunged for the bridle to steady it, and he spoke briefly to Porphyrius in words which, to Mia, were lost on the wind.

Mia held her loose hair away from her face and watched Agnesca smile, and then pull her mare around again. But the moment was gone, and with Luccio wrapped inside his father's mantle like a cocooned silkworm, they struck off at a pace down the hill with the iron of the horses' shoes sparking and echoing off the stones behind them.

Mia cried out in pain, 'Where will you go, *la raggia*?' but the question came too late for an answer.

'Porphyrius has places, Maria, just as I do,' Gennaro told her, watching the riders passing out of view. He still held her reins firmly. 'And I should perhaps take you to my family in Pomerance, with the sky threatening. But the storm is local, I think,' he tried to soothe her, 'and if you can sit your horse and stay close by me we can make it home to Jacquetta by nightfall, with the hours of light still left to us.'

Mia's tears ran unchecked, but the word 'home' came out audibly, and he squeezed both of her hands, and nodded.

* * *

362

Jacquetta had sat embroidering by a pair of candles long into the evening. This was something rare for her – she was not a woman who liked to dedicate hours to needlework. This, she always said, was the preserve of gentlewomen who had no estate to run, no harvest to supervise, no accounts to write up at the end of each week, no guests to provender to. Today, however, these tasks were in hand, and she could find no further subterfuge to wait up. For this reason she had walked into the music room and set up the frame hours ago, and she had worked nearly two inches square of the pattern Mia had under-drawn for her, of a unicorn reclining in an orchard of pomegranates. Her eyes were getting tired in the low light, and she longed for bed, but she was anxious about Mia and Agnesca and knew that her mind would keep picking at the possibilities, whether she went to bed or not.

Alba brought in a beaker of wine and looked at her with the canny eye of a woman who had served one person since they were both young. At twenty-four, Alba was two years younger than her mistress; but in spite of the differences in money and birth between them, Alba had been closer to Jacquetta than custom decreed because of the adversity they'd shared, and it was not unusual for them to speak in some confidence about their private feelings.

She gave her the cup. As no one else was up, Jacquetta had taken her cap off, revealing the soft line of red-gold hair that was plucked back from her brow to accentuate her high aristocratic forehead. Alba thought she was still very pretty, with her neat figure and navy-blue eyes inherited from the French grandmother after whom she was named. Tonight, though, she looked tired and alone; and though Alba knew what worried her, she could offer only modest comfort of reassurances she didn't entirely feel.

'You wait up for them,' she said sympathetically, 'yet they may remain another evening in the city. Signor Gennaro's family have their town house in Volterra, and it is a long road home.'

Jacquetta raised her eyebrows, and her cheeks dimpled. Without lifting her concentration from her needlepoint, she answered, 'If that were uttered to kindle me back to spirits, Alba, it's a poor effort. We both know the road from Volterra is manageable enough at this time of year, under a clear moon. It is a matter of neither travel nor lodging.'

'Signora Toscano is the most self-possessed woman I ever met,' Alba smiled back optimistically. 'I think no harm will come to her. She has two men for protection; and either or both would give up their lives for her.'

Alba said this to persuade herself that the dangers of the city were less alarming than in Mia's mother's day. Then, there had been a strain of anarchy in the town while the Belforti established themselves in place of Gennaro's family. But three years after Mia had come to Santo Pietro, Walter de Brienne, the Duke of Athens, took up a brief reign as lord of the city at Florence's behest, and the Pontiff intervened to insist the Belforti abide by the laws and allow their enemies to live in Volterra peacefully – if not splendidly. Ottaviano honoured this grudgingly when he returned to power, and Alba chose to believe that the young bishop-elect would behave nobly – or at least non-aggressively.

'Abbot Angelo is a subtle debater,' Jacquetta said to Alba, 'but I am wary from habit in my expectations. Justice that is well-deserved is very often not meted out.'

It was after midnight when Jacquetta quit her embroidery, took her night taper and started up the stairs to her own quarters. But at the top of the landing outside Agnesca and Porphyrius's room she heard horses on the road below: perhaps not as many as four, she thought. She caught up her dress and turned heel, feeling both relief and disquiet. She felt it was Mia, but her reappearance at this hour might bode ill in some way. Had they ridden hard for home? It didn't suggest successful petitioners prolonging their pleasure. Or, perhaps the mortality was making many hosts nervous of strangers between here and Volterra.

She was at the heavy door, releasing the bolts and offering her taper to the darkness. The moon was still waxing and bright, though not whole; and at this hour there was no torch lit at the stables. Sharp-eared Cesaré, however, had dressed hurriedly and brought a lamp, and he now squeezed by Jacquetta to run to the aid of the late arrivals. Not many minutes later Jacquetta had used her taper to relight the sconces near the hall fireplace, and footsteps crossed the courtyard. She was at the door again, watching shadows move under the olive tree, until her arms were suddenly filled with her niece in tears, and a distraught Gennaro behind her.

'She has liberty, Mia,' Jacquetta told her niece after mulling wine in the kitchen and hearing a vivid account of the events that day. 'She must choose carefully where to live; but she is married, and no formal sentence hangs over her.'

'Nor hope of the restitution of her property,' Gennaro added with irony. 'Banishment means that the family land and home – whatever is left of it – falls to the Belforti. But yes, they have a future at least.'

'Banishment is not the worst that might have happened,' Jacquetta said wisely.

'But I'll never see her again,' Mia said without appetite for the bread in front of her. 'And we had no true goodbye.'

She looked at her aunt pathetically, and then decided something. The day could be no worse: she had been torn from the person she loved best in the world after Jacquetta; had revisited the scene of her childhood terror. The mortality had hung like a pall over the city and seemed to Mia to say that an apocalypse was being unleashed on the world, affecting greater numbers than the sickness that had come here. For a second time in her life, nothing was certain: her world lacked whatever security she had rebuilt here since she was abandoned as a little girl.

She put this to Jacquetta, and added: 'My half-brother abused the memory of my mother with hints I couldn't refute with certainty, though I bluffed to do so. He called her "the Capobianchi woman" – a name I have never heard you use. It is time I knew all, however awful it may be.'

'It is late,' Jacquetta cautioned, 'and it is a sad story for bedtime.'

Mia, though, was determined it must come now on this – one of the worst days she could remember. So, encouraged by a nod from the young man who had faithfully brought her niece home, Jacquetta agreed. 'I shall make it as brief as I may,' she added.

'We are indeed a branch of the Allegretti family,' she smiled softly, 'though it was in my great-grandmother's generation that we were close cousins. And your mother, Barbarina Capobianco, was the pride of our family. She was without question the beauty of the city – and I say this truthfully, with no jealousy. Her eyes were large almonds under heavy lids, and her hair was defined with deep rivulets of curls – rather like yours, though not as dark in colour. But her face, Mia, was sculpted by an angel. Her lips had the hue of an apricot, and her cheeks were defined but sensual. If she had a flaw it was that she knew her power over others, and sometimes used it to get her way. But this made her more fascinating to many men, and raised her price.

'Our father had high hopes of a magnificent match for her, and through careful plots and machinations he came in time to entice a son of the Aldobrandeschi family to offer for her. She was fourteen when the bargain was struck, and was to be a countess.

'But his ambitions soared too near the sun for Ottaviano. Such a powerful family of counts would have bolstered the Allegretti clan; and Ottaviano was implacable against them. On the eve of his becoming podesta in Bologna, he found an opening to damage everyone's hopes and wishes inalienably. Following her home from the church where she prayed on a stormy afternoon – when rain and wind had washed the streets clean of witnesses – he fell upon her and her servant with three of his men, all at arms, and both women were attacked, dragged to a grain store and raped. She was fifteen, Mia, exactly as you are now.

'My father would not see past his daughter's being spoiled, and questioned whether she had gone with the ambitious enemy of our house willingly. Such was his shame – and the injustice of family power – that he would not hear her defence. My mother's pleas were weak, for her aims, too, were thwarted, and the betrothal was annulled. Ottaviano had fled to Bologna, unable to answer any charge. But our father brought no charge, Mia, hating the notoriety of such a thing and knowing it would necessitate vendetta, for which he had no stomach. Many years later Ottaviano was to claim my sister had given up her virtue far too easily.

'Disowned by her father and gossiped about by the city, she would have been lost had it not been for Bishop Ranuccio, the highest-ranking member of the wider family. He loved your mother, Mia – in every good way. Refusing to be cowed by the opinion or talk of others he provided a house for her and for her servant, and looked after you. Of course, this played into Ottaviano's hands, and he was to spread rumour years later that she had become Bishop Ranuccio's lover now. Soon everyone decided you must be the bishop's daughter – and that Ottaviano's falsehoods were true: for who had courage to dispute the lord of the city, as he had become?

'The rest was but a little step. When he took power himself and exiled Ranuccio, he confiscated all of the Allegretti property – and wanted most vindictively to have your mother thrown out of the town house she had been given. He allowed his men free rein to remove her in any way possible: I had always believed she was accidentally killed in a scuffle, trying to hold onto her rights. It was only a year ago, when you spoke, that I learned the truth of what had happened inside the house that day.

'All I have left to tell you, Mia, is that I was determined you should come to us – to live under the protection of your grandparents' roof – but they would not hear of it. So you cannot imagine the pleasure of my defiance when I gave my family back their name, and called myself after my grandfather from that day. I brought you, and Loredana and her son, away with me to this house, which was given to me in trust for you by Bishop Ranuccio. And it has been our happiness ever since, don't you think?'

Tears were rolling down Mia's cheeks. No single part of the tale made her feel like this, but the whole: the grandfather who had turned his back on her mother and herself; the duplicity of Ottaviano; the reason for Loredana's life as a mother without a husband; the lack of compassion of others.

'This forced you to abandon your hopes of marrying – my mother's disgrace? And then you defied your father,' she said softly.

'It was my choice,' Jacquetta said boldly, 'and you're quite wrong. I had a love – and I'll say no more about him than that he was a member of the Rapucci family, who bought the Casa-Torre Toscano that used to belong to Porphyrius's family: this is why I knew much of his history. Our marriage was delayed because of the complications of my sister's life and the agreement on a dowry; but I was seventeen and getting ready to say my vows and move to his home, when your mother was killed. Without any feeling of loss, Mia, I chose you instead – and would again in a heartbeat.'

Mia's mouth opened as she searched for something to say, but she could find nothing. This was an impossible revelation! Her aunt had sacrificed her marriage solely to become Mia's mother. No clarification was needed: to assume responsibility for the illegitimate daughter of her sister put an end to her chance of marrying her suitor. However much her suitor may have cared for her aunt, custom among noble families would never have condoned it.

'You chose me,' was all she managed to say for some while, and she threw her arms around her aunt and buried her face against her bodice.

Then Mia straightened herself. 'You chose me,' she said again, 'and I choose you. I will follow you anywhere, Aunt Jacquetta, even to the grave. When it is my time I will be buried beside you, come what may.'

For only the second time since she had come to Villa Santo Pietro – the previous occasion being when Agnesca and Porphyrius had first arrived and the house was overflowing with guests – Mia slept that night beside her aunt in the large room overlooking the Valle Serena. Her emotions threatened to overwhelm her. She still felt the loss of Agnesca desperately, but her love for her aunt had also subtly deepened, if that were possible. Mia wondered if she would ever have the strength to do such a selfless thing and take on another woman's natural child rather than marry and have her own family. It was rather like entering holy orders, she thought; and the very opposite of what Agnesca had chosen.

Gennaro, meanwhile, had gone to his familiar room full of thought. He had sat listening in silence to Jacquetta's unfolding story. It accorded with much that he knew from Bishop Ranuccio, but hearing it from her lips he was affected by the strength of her character, to go against her father and mother for Mia's sake. And he was as moved by the fierceness of Mia's loyalty for her aunt. These two women were – and should rightly be – devoted to each other. But these thoughts also made him restless. For some time he had begun to think of himself as under a gentle enchantment – and if so, it was most willingly that he submitted to it. And so he now considered whether – and how – it may still be possible to ask a question that had been on his mind since the birth of tiny Luccio on St Agnes' Eve.

After a night entirely without sleep he walked over the abbot's fields at first light to the little rotunda where San Galgano lay buried. Here he sat, and contemplated, and prayed; and after some time he returned to the villa. He found Jacquetta alone with Giulietta, the laundry-maid, and after a quick enquiry he led Jacquetta by the hand to the bottom of the large estate, where Agnesca and Mia had planted their garden of healing and enchantment and knot-magic. There they found Mia sitting below the mulberry tree and the pair of doves.

'I have agonised all the night,' he said to both of them, 'and I respect you, Maria, for the feelings you voiced at the end of a long evening.'

He sat on the stone bench beside Mia, pulling Jacquetta gently down next to him. His full brown eyes were so full of feeling that both women wanted to do or say something to take away his pain.

'You are right in the pledge you made to your aunt,' he said, nodding to Mia. 'But, would you both put off the grave for a time,' he tried to laugh, looking from the niece to the aunt and back, 'and let me ask Mia if she will take my family name?'

Jacquetta had been waiting for this question since the games of *Il Mulino* in the winter. She merely put her small hand over his shoulder and smiled.

But Mia found that she received unexpected pleasure in hearing Gennaro call her by her familiar name, for the first time; and coming after two days of a flood of emotional revelations she was surprised by the force of those she felt now, for him. When had he come to be such a part of her happiness? she wondered.

Her aunt's gesture was the only blessing she wanted to make up her mind, and she smiled at Jacquetta as if they suddenly shared a secret.

'Yes,' they both said, and laughed.

'Yes, please,' Mia said alone; and she laced her fingers through his light brown curls and kissed his forehead.

38

LATE WINTER – EARLY SPRING 2008, SAN FRANCISCO

There was very little fog, and the morning quite perfect: but Maddie felt dazed as she strolled down the hill towards the water. She was still in her jeans and she would be late, but she needed to breathe the salty air which – if she were lucky – might be fragranced with frangipani. She had to try to clear her head and understand what had happened last night. The whole of last evening had seemed surreal; and if it were not for the presence of the flowers – the distinctive smell of violets in her apartment, which he'd said had a meaning – she'd say that none of it had happened, and that she'd been drugged or dreaming.

She stood watching a seagull wheel and someone swim for a few minutes; and she inhaled the ocean – not just its scent, but its vastness, which always made her feel alive and free. He had been like an apparition, almost an angel; but was this what she wanted? What he said to her, though: she understood its wisdom to her core.

Her breathing deepened and she took her cell out of her pocket. She needed to cheat, just a little bit. She phoned the office which, at just a shade past eight, was still on answering service; and she left a message for Teresa to let everyone know she would be in by midday. 'There is something I have to do,' she said, 'and I'll be out of contact for a couple of hours.'

She went by her apartment and dressed for the day. Only a damp towel hung over the wrong rail and the hand-tied bunch of roses and violets in a round glass vase told her she had really had a visitor. He'd

370

gone again, taking away the hazel-brown eyes that had watched over her all night, just under an hour ago.

Now she took the cable car over the hill, making her first call Jimena's shop. When she arrived the blind was still down and the Closed sign was up, but she knocked on the glass door as she could see Jimena's silhouette inside, with her back to the window. Jimena waved without looking up, as if to say, 'Go away – I'm not open,' but then she did look round, and grinned when she must have seen enough of Maddie's hair or profile to know who it was behind the knocking.

The door flew open just briefly enough to let Maddie in, and was then firmly closed again in a second.

'You look *curiosa* this morning, Señorita Maddie,' Jimena said, a little puzzled.

'I feel exactly that way,' she answered in an unusually deeper voice. 'I have to take some flowers to the cathedral, Jimena. I want to light a candle for Christopher, which I haven't done before now; because I came to understand during the night that I need to say goodbye to him. I didn't have a chance to do that, but I have to find some way to try. What flowers do you think would be the right choice for such a thing – to leave with the candle?'

Jimena was deeply moved by this. She knew Maddie wasn't religious, but what she said was poignant and true. He'd been taken from her with no chance for either one to breathe a goodbye, and there must have been so much left unsaid.

'Yes, Maddie, I understand,' she said softly. 'I think white roses are perfect to express a deep and lasting love – instead of red, for passion only. They also indicate something "secret" – which is right, isn't it? – because it is a private message you are leaving, for him alone. And they are said to be the original roses of paradise. I like them better than any colour.'

Jimena said this and started to carefully select a dozen white blooms from a display bunch. Maddie watched entranced as she picked the very best of the display, smelling one or two, and started to wrap them with clear Cellophane and a simple raffia tie.

'Jimena,' Maddie asked suddenly as she waited, 'do you know the meaning of a bouquet of violets and white roses?'

Jimena's hands stopped tying the raffia for a moment, and she raised her head to look at Maddie. It was impossibly hard to get violets at this time of the year in San Francisco; but she'd had some, a day or two ago. She smiled to herself. Ah, Señorita Maddie! I know you have an admirer, because on Saturday afternoon a man came to me for just such a bouquet. He had looked all over the city for the right flowers, and someone had told him I was the one who might have violets a little before the season. And he bought them all!

But none of this did she say, preferring to enjoy the knowledge quietly.

'White roses, as I said, are for deep love and also for secret or unspoken feelings,' she said, returning her hands to their labour with a discreet smile; 'and violets traditionally mean compassion and even watchfulness. I think that's right. Anyone who would choose these flowers together definitely has something to say,' Jimena said grinning.

She handed the rose blooms to Maddie, pleased that those she had sold with the violets had also been perfect but a little smaller, and still in bud. They married exquisitely with the violets, and the most important thing about them was that they had to have a strong scent, he had said. It was not always possible with commercially grown blooms, but Jimena's roses did have a perfume, and he'd been delighted with them.

'Twenty dollars plus tax for you, Señorita Maddie,' she said, refusing to take more though they were worth twice as much. She held the door for Maddie and added, 'I am pleased if someone brings you violets, Maddie; but where he would find them? That is a mystery,' and she smiled, very pleased with herself.

'Thank you,' Maddie answered, feeling a riddle in the remark.

Enzo Moretti was enjoying the fact that it was a sunny day in February – the last of the month, and a leap day to boot. Spring was almost upon them.

As he stood at his lab bench at the university he found himself humming parts of the superb polyphonic mass of Palestrina, which had given him so much pleasure at Christmas. His eyes were glued to his microscope as he watched the moving forms of the bacteria *Xylella fastidiosa* on a slide prepared by one of his students, as part of his study of Pierce's Disease. He smiled to himself, knowing that what he was looking at had its origins several million years ago; and he contrasted the incongruity with the belief system that had inspired the music that moved him so deeply – created just two thousand years ago.

He let his mind wander momentarily to pursue a long-running discussion he was having with himself. He always experienced a deep, personal impact from music and ecclesiastical architecture. He considered that he attempted to live by the ethical standards traditionally associated with Christianity, which appealed to him; but he could not bring himself to believe in the actual existence of the underlying metaphysical entities, never mind the hard-line faith that made so many people the least charitable in the world. A 'poetic' Christian is what he might call himself, he thought: a pilgrim to the beauty, but a fugitive from inflexible doctrine.

A phone rang in the adjoining room, disrupting his chain of thought. He heard one of his students pick it up.

'Professor, it's your daughter,' she said.

'Which one?' Enzo queried, not moving his head from the scope.

A moment's pause brought the answer.

'Madeline. She asks if she could come and see you here whenever you're free, but at some point today,' came the reply.

Enzo was suddenly worried. It was not like either of his daughters just to call and ask to see him at the college unless it was important. He lifted his head from the eye-piece.

'All right, then. Ask her if she can meet me in my office at twelve thirty for an in-house lunch. I'm free until two, and then I'm giving a lecture. Thank you, Miss Chang,' he added, and then he put his head back down to his work. His concentration, however, was gone.

Enzo's office was reasonably large and smelled of good coffee, courtesy of the princely appliance in one corner. Otherwise it was somewhat utilitarian, with few personal touches. Bookshelves lined the walls, from floor to ceiling; a large seminar table was placed with a dozen chairs for teaching and faculty meetings; and an informal seating area boasted a low table, with armchairs and a sofa. An iPod docking station – gifted him by Maddie – gave a small clue to one of his passions.

At precisely half-past noon Maddie's tousled head appeared around Enzo's door. She was carrying a large manila envelope, and entered the room a little nervously. This was the first time she had come to her father as an equal for professional advice, and she hoped she hadn't made an error of judgement. She knew she needed a second opinion, however.

Enzo rose from behind his desk and greeted her with a hug. He thought how exceptional and beautiful she looked today – how like an angel of the annunciation, almost, with her cloud of billowing curls and her face full of mystery and intelligence. She had grown up in a year, for all her grief; and he studied her carefully.

'You look "like a missioned spirit",' he smiled at her, and invited her to the sofa.

Maddie didn't recognise her father's quote, but she admired his perceptiveness.

'You're right, Papa,' she said. 'It's about work.' She held out the envelope she was carrying. 'This is a report on the scientific study my firm has commissioned. It is an analysis of a data base, and the records of a set of lab tests. The test work was done to support a hypothesis about toxic poisoning in the microchip industry.'

Her father looked at her without giving any thought away.

'This is important, Papa, and totally confidential. But I urgently need your advice and thoughts on it. It is personal – in some ways.'

Enzo raised his eyebrows in mock gravity, and her heart froze. She hoped he would take her seriously. But she smiled at him and put her finger on his lips before he could open his mouth, then she pushed the envelope into his hands.

'*Segreto!*' she conspired, and made him smile back. 'Now, I'm going to get us something for lunch from the deli Mom loves in town. We can talk when I get back, and you've had a chance to look at this.'

Then Maddie turned and left him; but half an hour later a wondrous spread of salamis, olives, and antipasti, breads and a bottle of San Pellegrino appeared on the seminar table, while Enzo was still slowly turning the pages of the report.

'Papa,' she said, 'let's eat something.'

She could see from her father's face that his mood had changed, and he was engrossed in what he was looking at. She also thought he seemed distressed by its contents.

'Yes,' he said, and he moved to pull out a chair at the table. 'How long has this been going on?'

'I've known about it since I joined the firm.' She poured him out some water. 'But as far as they are concerned, it's about six years prior to my arrival, I believe.'

Enzo considered for a moment before he spoke.

374

'As a scientist, I can tell you this material seems to have been very carefully and well prepared,' he began. 'It examines firstly a set of health records spanning twenty-five years, for all the workforce of an unnamed company. It isolates a particular cohort of workers by job function.'

Maddie drank some of the water, but her father ignored his glass and talked on.

'The report states that one cohort works within an environment that is filled with toxic chemicals. It lists the chemicals involved in detail and gives what is historically known about them from existing and proven scientific work: that these chemicals can make women miscarry, and that they are also identified as carcinogens that can cause long-term genetic defects in the first, and maybe the second, generations of offspring of the individuals who have been over-exposed to them.'

Maddie nodded.

'Secondly, there are a series of lab tests on rats over a period of seven months, which were concluded earlier this month, in which they have artificially tried to replicate, as far as possible, all the variations in the atmosphere of that work environment. There is also a control group, a cohort that exists in normal conditions.

'I would like to look at the material in more detail,' he said, 'but from what I can see here the experiments have been well run – though perhaps, it might be argued, it was not run for long enough to be one hundred per cent conclusive. The duration of the test should give at least seventy to eighty per cent accuracy, I would suggest.'

'I can leave them with you, Papa, if you want,' Maddie said as she listened to his comments. 'I'd be very grateful for your objective opinion.'

'What is fascinating is the comparison between the rat studies and the human health record of this undisclosed company. The health of the laboratory animals mimics almost exactly the health of the workers in every cohort – even including the control group. For an immediate opinion, I think it might have been possible to avoid the incidences of fatal illness if someone had spoken out, and the workers had been rotated out of the environment after a certain period to avoid the build-up of toxins. It makes me angry that people have suffered this fate probably unnecessarily.'

Maddie watched her father as he spoke. He looked concerned as he thought. Then he told her: 'Maddie, I realise as I get older that I have always been far less questioning about the world – outside of my science – than you or your sister. I was brought up with a different ethos, where the captains of industry were heroes and supposedly beyond reproach. Of course, I know that's silly. Balzac says that behind every great fortune, there is a great crime. But I, too, have my investment portfolio. I am looking to my dividends to pay for my old age. What is suggested in these documents, however, is a completely cavalier disregard for human beings, which may affect generations to come. The lack of thought and consideration demonstrated in this report is no better than the treatment of slaves in Europe a thousand years ago. It is morally unconscionable on human grounds and unjustifiable even in economic terms. Maddie,' he took a long breath, 'can you understand why this is happening?'

She looked at her father and simply shook her head.

'I assume this report has to do with a company like Stormtree – or one of their competitors. They are in for a hell of a wake-up call, looking at the information presented here. It could savage their share prices,' he said grimly.

'Thanks, Papa,' Maddie said tenderly. 'Now, please have lunch with me?'

The pair ate in silence for a while and Enzo made appropriate obeisance to the picnic spread she'd brought for them, but his appetite was affected by the information he'd digested. After a while Maddie said she would collect the report back from the house later so he could dwell on it. Then she smiled slightly sadly, and asked him a completely different question.

'As a poetical scientist,' she mused, 'or a scientific poet, I need you to give me some advice.'

'That sounds a nicer mission,' he said. 'How can I help?'

What followed surprised and pleased him.

'A friend of mine – someone I respect – drew it to my attention that I'd never been able to say goodbye to Christopher. I think I have begun to do that in an emotional sense, but I don't want to leave him behind altogether or try to pretend that he wasn't a part of our family,' she said seriously. 'I would like to plant a tree in the garden at home, and dedicate it to his memory. If you think that would be OK with you and Mom, I'd like you to tell me what would be a good choice.'

'Maddie,' he said, 'like Isabella and the pot of basil.' He stroked her hair.

'No, I don't feel maudlin, Papa,' she said. 'I won't weep and pine; but the tree would be strong and grow on quietly near us all.'

'Yes, of course. Your mother will agree too,' he nodded, 'and I understand. So . . . something a little out of the commonplace; an emblem of peace, perhaps. What should it be?' Enzo got up and crossed to the bookshelves, hunting down a volume, which he opened with satisfaction. 'Ah! Perfect. I wanted to check that it grows in zone six, and we're in luck. How about a *Davidia involucrata*?'

Maddie laughed. 'Oh, sure, let's have three of those,' she said as she started to pack up the lunch.

Enzo smiled too, then showed her a full-colour photograph.

'It's known as the dove tree because of its extraordinary, wavy flowers in May. They look like doves flying in the breeze. It's also known as the handkerchief tree – but that's more prosaic than doves, don't you think? I'm sure your mother would like it, and she'll be the one who's going to have to water it to get established.'

'It's beautiful, Papa,' Maddie almost cried. 'I don't know why that seems especially perfect. But,' she looked worried, 'will it survive? My heart would break if it died.'

'No, it should grow very well once it gets its roots down into the subsoil. It can stand up to our winters in the mountains. Zone six means cool temperate, and once it gets the feel of the earth your grandchildren will be able to climb in it. All the neighbours will come to look at it when the creamy flowers come out, you'll see.'

Maddie smiled and put the remains of the lunch into various carrier bags, then turned to give her father a quick kiss as he stood. With his old-fashioned manners he moved towards the door to open it for her; liberated as she was, it pleased her that her father remembered these courtesies.

She turned once more before she left him. 'Can you solve a riddle for me?' she asked. 'Is there any poetic significance to white roses and violets?'

'You're full of mysteries today, Maddie,' he grinned. 'My first thought is of Wordsworth's Lucy poems. "A violet by a mossy stone . . ." Something shy and hidden, but the more special for its being so private. Or Dorothy Parker calls violets "heaven's masterpieces", if I remember. But let me dwell on it. It's violets and roses together?'

She nodded as he held the door for her. 'Does Keats have anything to say on roses and violets?' she asked, knowing perfectly well that Keats was the bringer of the bouquet's poet of choice.

'I'm sure he must. Very good,' he said – answering something more than just the confirmation. 'I'll give it some thought, and I'll see you soon. I hope the work goes well.'

'Thanks, Papa.'

Maddie kissed him again, and was gone.

By the middle of March there was already a clear feeling of spring, but mist was still rising through the pines along the ridge behind Wild Cat Canyon. It was back-lit by the sun stretching long-fingered rays through the forest.

Maddie stood near the end of the family garden in light early shade, and she steadied the Dove Tree, which Jimena had found for her at a specialist nursery. She had just eased it from its large tub and carefully placed it in the hole her father had dug out for her. Enzo, down on his knees, was filling in the space around its roots with compost from a wheelbarrow, then he pushed himself onto his feet and picked up a watering can. He poured its contents around the stripling and put an arm around his younger daughter. It was a silent, contemplative moment; and they stood back to admire their work.

Everyone was away from the house, Barbara having taken Carol to Berkeley to shop. It offered Maddie a window of quietude, without comment or chatter from her mother or even from Barbara, who mightn't altogether understand.

'I hope it will bring you good memories over the years,' Enzo said, pulling Maddie to him, 'and I'm sorry we never met him.'

'Me too, Papa,' she answered with some strength. 'He was a truly good, kind, intelligent man; and he'll always be a little part of who I am.'

'Doves were used to send messages between the ancient oracular sites, Maddie,' Enzo told her gently, 'so let's believe Christopher can receive yours.'

She nodded and hugged her father, lost in a wash of thoughts. But she was far less distressed than she had imagined she would be.

They started the walk back to the house, and Enzo gave her a deeper hug. Then something flashed into his mind, and he faced his daughter with a warm smile. Maybe now was not the time to say it: but he'd thought of it now, so he followed his instinct.

'Before your mother and sister get home, let me tell you that the place for your violets and roses is surely in Keats, as you suggested,' he stated.

'Have you found something?' she asked gently.

'Something very fitting,' he answered with a nod. 'I remembered it the other day, and checked the exact wording. I put a copy of the poem in with your toxicology report, so don't forget to take them when you leave.'

'Thank you,' she said.

39

OCTOBER 1365, TUSCANY

In Siena's proud Palazzo Pubblico, Master Simone had painted the Virgin Mary enthroned in all her glory as heavenly patroness of the city and its *contado*. The countryside and smaller towns under her benevolent eye would enjoy the Queen of Heaven's special protection and favour; and she would inspire wise government among the authorities.

But the truth had, for the seventeen summers since their marriage, seemed very different for Mia and Gennaro.

The great mortality had made a cut so deep that no living witness could amply express the suffering. Across an idyllic countryside people had died in their thousands. Brothers and wives left sisters and husbands dying in their beds, promising to return with food and drink, but instead closing up the doors, never to do so. Children starved when their parents died, and the corpses of animals were heaped beside them. Close to eighty thousand people had died in Siena – and the scars were equally visible in the *contado*. Houses were deserted on the green sloping hills, tidy rows of trees and vines went unpruned, and the valleys, with their flowering pasturelands and carefully tended fields, became tangled and overgrown.

At Villa Santo Pietro they lost five pilgrims – until pilgrims almost ceased to come; then three of the farm-dwellers; and then death stepped inside the house, taking Giulietta, the laundry-maid. Every effort for cure was hopeless; unlike Gennaro, all bore the illness in their lungs and coughed blood before the evil goitres appeared. Pretty Giulietta had been eating her supper on Friday night, and was dead on Sunday morning.

But the residents of Santo Pietro were lucky to lose so few of their own. Volterra buried close to half of her citizens, including Gennaro's sister and a niece, and Ottaviano Belforte – just as Agnesca had foretold. An even worse toll affected their neighbours. In the abbey of San Galgano more than half of the monks and lay brothers were taken by the disease. The abbot's forge became indolent and his glass factory idle; monastery fields went unploughed, and many remembered the three blood suns on the day the abbot had first sickened.

During the early years of their marriage no certainty existed for Mia and Gennaro, other than the certainty of work. To this they were committed from morning till night, and with fewer left to help in the fields most work was done by those at Santo Pietro. As well as the shortage of labour, over several seasons the weather turned unkind, and crops suffered. For many summers there was less rather than more, and Mia lost two of her babies in the womb; but the small family survived. Jacquetta said that many were the ways of dying, but that they must find ways of living.

In the summer of the seventeenth year of their marriage the harvest had looked better. A balance of sunshine and spring rain supported rippling fields of grains; the movement of the corn and nutty spelt under the wind reminded Mia of her childhood. The grapes were also well set and the olive harvest promised to be better than in the two or three seasons before.

But in late summer an order came from Siena to the people of its rural hinterlands. Bands of mercenaries were once more in the *contado*, and in an effort to make their stay less comfortable all hay and straw was to be burned by government officials. Additionally, all stores of grains, wine, meat, poultry and even wood should be brought to the city for safe-keeping, otherwise it would be a lure for the lawless men who had, several times within a few years, brought the countryside to its knees. Two years earlier the much-feared 'Company of the Hat' had devastated the barely recovering territory by burning crops and houses, and kidnapping livestock and citizens so that they must be redeemed for florins if their owners and families wanted them back. Unpaid ransoms left unfed prisoners to die within a few months. The mercenary companies had plagued the land for twenty miles in every direction around Siena.

In the old kitchen at Villa Santo Pietro, Gennaro put his young son from his lap and read the order again. Most of the harvest was now in, and decisions were needed; but he shook his head unhappily.

'Imagine such a trail, stretching from here to the city!' he said with disbelief to Mia and Jacquetta. 'The transfer of long caravans of goods will trumpet an invitation to the *condottiere*. We provide a perfect opportunity for him and his soldiers in open air to swoop on us like jackals and steal the meat and provisions for their thousands of troops.'

Jacquetta's expression was strained. 'And if appointed men from Siena also burn our fodder now, how in heaven's name do we feed our livestock in winter?'

'We cannot disobey,' Mia said, catching her child's hand and giving him some cut apple. 'Besides which, you read in the order that they will waive the taxes on all goods at the gate. Our profit may be worth the journey.'

'Who are they, Papa – the *condottieri*?' came an uncertain voice from the herb drying room off the pantry.

Gennaro turned to answer Isabella, his younger daughter. She came to sit with her family at the trestle in the kitchen, lifting her baby brother onto her lap; and her father looked at her intelligent, almond eyes. Though she had been named for his mother, her eyes were those of his wife; he was reminded of lovely Mia, whom he had met at fourteen, just a year older than Isabella was now.

'They are unemployed soldiers looking for war,' he explained in a gentle voice. 'When the English King Edward sent his men home from their battles at Crécy and at Poitiers – with all the spoils they'd come for – hordes of his knights and their rank and file stayed behind in France looking for mischief and pay. Peace is not profitable for soldiers, Isabella,' he added.

'But we are not at war with England,' she said, confused.

'These men make war on us because they can,' he said. 'They have grown in number with fortune seekers from the Visconti family in Milan, and also from Germany; but the worst of them is the company of Englishmen. When I travelled some time ago to Avignon with silk and spices, I heard of the brutal raids of these men who fought as "The White Company", though now they ride under the banner of St George and the command of a knight named John Hawkwood, whom we call Giovanni Auto. At Arpajon in France, a thousand people fled from them in fear, taking refuge in the priory of the Benedictines. When they were trapped there the villagers offered to surrender to the army, but the chivalrous men preferred to set fire to the church and everyone inside it. All were burned to death, but for a hundred or so lucky souls who escaped the blaze. They lowered themselves from the church walls with ropes; but they could not cheat the English, who waited below and slaughtered every one as they reached the ground.'

'Please, Gennaro!' Mia cautioned. Honest as they were, such stories would make the children afraid.

'But, Papa,' Isabella pressed, 'why do they come to Tuscany?'

'The Italian states are a rich prize,' her father answered, 'for we are still relatively wealthy through trade. Yet even when all luxury items came to Europe through our merchants, and our granaries and wine stores were filled to capacity with the blessings of rain and sun, we hadn't the sense to assemble an army to defend our citizens properly. For decades instead we have fought ourselves – the Pope's party against the Emperor's, Florence against Siena, Pisa against Genoa. We have placed each other in a weak position, but seem unable to extricate ourselves again.'

'It is only money they want, Isabella,' Jacquetta said softly. She could see that Mia's second daughter – more curious and independent than her elder sister, Barbara, but also more imaginatively engaged – was affected by his words. 'They would not prosper by killing the farmers and villagers. They want to rob us, if they can, and demand that we buy back our safety with gold.'

'They would attack even us?' the child asked.

'Siena will make a treaty, Isabella,' Mia told her daughter. She stroked her hair, and tried to reassure her. 'The city needs the grains, the wine and oil we grow; they need the abbot's iron and horses, and our pigs, and timber from the forest. They will be bribed by the looting soldiers rather than lose their bread and taxes.'

Isabella was still turning this conversation over in her mind later that evening when, carrying her taper to her room under the eaves, she heard a pounding at the door and nearly jumped out of her skin. She retraced her steps to catch a glimpse of their visitor, and as Barbara was in the hall snuffing candles, it was she who opened the vast front door. Her mother and father came from the solar to join her while Isabella sat watching from the stair.

'Monna Maria,' the voice rose in the darkness, talking beyond Barbara, 'the abbot has sent me to warn you.'

It was a lay brother from the abbey, and Isabella saw her mother call him in to sit at the waning hall fire. The abbey bell could be heard through the open door, tolling urgently on the wind.

'We learn that the main party of the Company of St George, under Auto, are setting out along the Via Marittima from Frosini Castle, where they also leave some men,' the lay brother told them. 'The abbot believes they head for our abbey, to loot what they may, and take fresh horses. He advises you bring in your own animals as protection from theft and slaughter.'

'But our neighbours will seek sanctuary within your walls,' Gennaro said.

'Many have done so,' the lay brother answered, 'but Abbot Angelo believes it is better not to resist the marauders at the gate. We can fend off a few thieves, but not an entire army with our modest defences. Our pitiable resistance may only antagonise the soldiers, and double the strength of their reprisals. The abbot asks that we comply, as far as possible.'

'His logic is fair,' Gennaro agreed, 'but offers no safety for the villagers.'

'What shall we do, Gennaro?'

This was Jacquetta, who had come back into the hall from the room she now occupied along the passageway, once Bishop Ranuccio's. She had overheard the lay brother's fears about the futility of resistance.

'Will you take the children and servants, excepting for Cesaré, into the old cistern under the house?' he asked. 'And let us bring the estate workers in from their cottages for safety. We should keep our gate closed, but be ready to answer an intrusion. Mia and I will treat with them – and pay what we must.'

'Mia should mind the children and servants, and the residents of the *borgo*,' Jacquetta contradicted him. 'I will stay and face them with you.'

Mia argued only briefly with her aunt. She was five months into carrying another child, and knew Gennaro would quickly agree to her taking safety with the others.

'Whatever we do, it is too late to move the produce to Siena now,' Mia said.

But her husband didn't agree. 'We know that they move by night and sleep through the day,' he said. 'There may be a way to slip the goods past them.'

Mia gave him a chiding look, much unpractised in her sweet nature.

'Don't be a hero,' she said. 'They will pluck you off the road and demand a higher ransom than we can afford, after so many lean years. Be a father to your children, and that is hero enough.'

Gennaro understood his wife had lacked a father in every important sense – the mortality having taken first the one she loved, and then even the other she despised. She had known neither, and wanted more for her children. Yet, Gennaro argued, it was a risk worth taking; that his own life would be in little danger.

'It is money we need, Mia,' he insisted. 'They will take or burn our food and livestock anyway. Only florins will send them on their way.'

'Until another year,' Mia told him.

The neighbourhood of the little *borgo*, and the family of Gennaro and Mia, were to sleep that night – and two more – under the villa in the now disused cistern the Romans had built. It smelled damp but was perfectly sound. On that first night Gennaro left Jacquetta watchful at the house while he and Cesaré took the river track to the abbey. Together they studied all movements for some hours from a safe line of trees. In the hours after midnight the considerable army appeared to descend on San Galgano, taking over the complex of buildings for their own quarters. Besides sympathising with the abbot, Gennaro realised this put Villa Santo Pietro on their doorstep. He wondered how long they would stay, and when the army's bailiffs would appear at their own gate.

The following day Mia was up at first light – having slept an hour or two at most – and took her daughters, with Alba and Chiara, to the chestnut huts to bring in as much as they could. The nuts were still drying, but to leave them would make them vulnerable, and in the years of low grain yield they had come to rely on the chestnut flour for basic bread.

Before the sun had risen far, however, Gennaro came looking for his younger daughter for a special task.

Isabella had taken up the duty of raising her mother's doves in the sacred garden, and having tended them for years they were now many in number – still pure white and untainted. Every three or four years her father brought her a pair of baby birds to add to their own. These new additions were Barbary doves, with their distinctive dark ring collar contrasting with their white plumage. These Isabella was told to keep in their original pairs so that the males would resist fighting one another. They were housed in small cotes among the pomegranates, while the pure white birds that were born here remained in the centre of the main garden, close to the mulberry tree. Their droppings were used for fertiliser, certainly, but unlike the wood pigeons none of these birds was ever brought to table. This was because, as Isabella knew, they were precious to her mother. She had been told the doves were the device of Mary of Magdala, whose birthplace had provided the sacred white birds for the purification of the temples even before Jesus' time. And they were equally sacred to their ancestors, the Tuscii, who had lived in their hills centuries before the Romans. Isabella believed this was the reason her mother had chosen a pair of doves, linked by a garland of flowers, as her own emblem. Her father had given her a chest at their marriage, and a birthing tray when Isabella herself was born, with the tied doves depicted as the central motif. The birds, they told her, were a symbol of their love and 'the ties that bind'.

Isabella was unsure of the hour, as no bell had tolled from the campanile today. The height of the sun said it was early as she went with her father to a mission unknown. They sat in the orchard of pomegranate trees, and Gennaro now consulted his daughter.

'Which is the oldest and strongest pair?' he asked her.

Isabella looked unsure. The oldest pair had died, not many months apart from one another, perhaps two or three winters ago. But two other pairs had been with them since Isabella was small, and were now eight or nine years old at least. She told this to her father.

He nodded. 'Can you choose one of them?'

The child was full of curiosity but did as she was asked, returning with a bird nestled in each arm from a small dovecote. 'These two are best and wisest, I believe, Papa.'

Her father took two tiny squares of folded parchment from his tunic and some linen thread, then bound each one tightly and squeezed first the one, and then the other, into a pair of small pouches. Isabella watched with fascination as he tied each pouch, with the deftest handling, around a bird's neck. He soothed their feathers in one hand while he tested the security of the pack with the other. They seemed to leave little room for the bird to nod its neck up and down as they often did.

'Can they fly like that?' she asked him.

'Let us hope so,' he answered, and in seconds the birds were set free. Father and daughter watched them circle into the sky and, quite at odds with Isabella's expectations, they flew across to the west of the orchard's reach, and out of sight.

'Where do they go, Papa?'

'To their first home,' was his reply.

On the second day, everyone wondered why the unwanted visitors expected at their gate had not yet come. Alba suggested they count their blessings and continue to bring fruit and livestock to safety underneath the house. Mia, however, was convinced that silence might bode ill: that they were planning something much worse. So on the second night, while the occupants of the *borgo* and the main villa dozed, Gennaro took Loredana's son, Roberto, with him to watch the abbey once more. Concealed in darkness within the boughs of an oak, they could see no activity at all over the abbot's wall, and with everything quiet they considered whether the men had arrived only to lie low for a day or so, recovering their strength and health.

But on the third night, in the same place and at the same hour, Gennaro – accompanied once more by Cesaré – saw a frenzy of activity. Smoke rose from the chimneys of the forge and many horses – Gennaro reckoned in the hundreds, but less than a thousand – were being shod and groomed and prepared for what must be a sally.

Gennaro was stiff from the mist and cold when he returned to the villa before sunrise.

'They have ridden out – not the whole group, but some hundreds of riders and foot soldiers carrying lances,' he said. 'They leave as many knights and men-at-arms behind at the abbey, where they have set up camp. The ring of hoofs moved away east, past the Eremo of Galgano.'

'Then, where do they go?' Jacquetta asked.

Mia watched her aunt's face, full of cares at the possibility that Gennaro would try to use the daylight hours to load the farm carts and make a dash for Siena. But even in privacy away from Alba and the others, everyone seemed either too tired or too worried to speculate. After a minute or two Mia collected a rough shawl from the kitchen and draped it around her shoulders. Then she walked to the chest in the hallway, and withdrew the precious drawing of the garden design she had created with Agnesca years before. She rolled it carefully and tucked it under the shawl.

'Under the guise of asking for advice as to planting times I shall go to Fra Silvestro, and find out all I can,' she said emphatically, and she swept out of the door and joined the pilgrims' road before anyone could stop her.

A tired Gennaro was belatedly shocked into action and leaped up to follow her, but Jacquetta laid a hand on his arm to stay him at the door.

'Alone, she may succeed,' she said. 'Fra Silvestro has always been permitted to see Mia without contravening his vows, because for years they spoke only by sign. If she communicates with him in their old way he may tell her much, and quite privately.'

As she hoped, her niece was back without the illuminated drawing, but with the information they needed, unharmed and whole, within the hour. The soldiers were now sleeping with just a few men posted as sentry. She learned that the army had usurped the abbey – and even the bishop's house – for their own quarters, intending to stay a week or more. They were nursing some sick, and those who had left during the night were a splinter group making a raid on the abbey at Roccastrada, half a day to the south; but they had taken carts for plunder, which would slow them. Another sizeable group were still east of Siena – at the abbey of Berengaria, Fra Silvestro thought. The abbeys offered rich pickings and a perfect base from which to send out sorties to loot the villages. But it did mean that a relatively smaller force now occupied San Galgano.

'They say little of their plans, in order to exert more fear and speculation among their victims, but he is sure they will burn what is left in the fields when they go,' Mia told her husband and aunt, away from the children. 'Fra Silvestro shared with me their grim motto: that war without fire is like sausages without mustard, and the English will have their mustard.'

'Then I must run at once for the city with our goods,' Gennaro said in a flat tone that invited no contradiction.

Mia walked into an embrace, asking only consolation, and he hugged her tightly.

'While they sleep,' he said with quiet confidence, 'I will pack two carts only, to slow me less; and I will ask the farmer and his sons to ride with me, leaving Roberto and Cesaré here with you. I shall start now, to clear Frosini long before the sun lowers, and if I quarter the carts in the city to speed our return I'll be back in two days with the produce safely inside the city walls and most of our money banked in Siena. The rest I will bring as insurance for ourselves and the *borgo*.'

Mia wanted to complain and beg him to stay; but she knew he was right, and that it was senseless to quarrel. Her head believed that a man who could cheat Death would somehow evade the *condottieri* as well, but her heart felt very human objections.

Nevertheless, she toiled alongside everyone else to pack the lighter carts Gennaro normally used for trading spices with the most valuable goods from their estate, and by noon, he was ready to go.

In the clamour for departure and adjusting of the load it was Isabella alone who, at that moment, saw six horsemen coming through the gate, which Roberto must have opened for them. They moved at walking pace, and she caught her breath. She touched her father's arm, indicating approaching riders. As he shaded his eyes to see and straightened his body bravely, everyone else shivered in the sunshine.

'We were so close,' Gennaro said, taking a step forward in front of his family. Then he tipped his head a fraction. When the riders broke into a gentle trot towards them, his face gradually relaxed.

'Make sure to cover the wheels with cloth – to dull their noise on the roads!' a well-dressed man said at the front of the group, and then halted his horse.

'An old trick of yours I'd forgotten,' Gennaro grinned, and in a second he had helped one of the riders down from a horse.

Isabella was shocked to see, throwing back the heavy cowl of her cloak, a beautiful woman, with hair silver-gilt in colour and bound loosely with cord as if she were a young girl. She hugged Isabella's father and then, with shining face, strode past him to her mother. Mia's expression, Isabella now saw, communicated disbelief.

'You must have retied our knot,' the woman said, in a voice like a river; 'for we are come home.'

Isabella had never seen her mother weep as she did now. Her arms and body blended with the woman so they made one shape.

'To stay?' she asked.

The lady nodded.

Agnesca had welcomed home the doves bred by her own hand at the farm they had occupied in the Lucchese countryside for many years. Leaving their second son, Fortino, in charge there with his young wife, they had ridden hard for Chiusdino with their eldest and youngest and two servants, immediately after getting Gennaro's message. They had moved swiftly through the long night, leaving the Via Romea at San Gimignano to take the same winding back-roads around the hills from Volterra that they had used to come here for the first time, more than eighteen years before.

Isabella had gone unusually quiet, unable to take her eyes from the woman her mother called *la raggia*. She seemed first one thing, and then its opposite. Her aura of calm blended with a productive busyness; she talked only a little in a voice like music, yet was heeded by everyone for her sense when she spoke; and moonlight had surely coloured her hair while her eldest son's was closer to sunshine. Even Aunt Jacquetta seemed in awe of her.

'We will have many nights to talk after this, but go now,' Agnesca said to Gennaro and her own husband, 'and I would keep your number to as few as can manage the carts. That way you are less visible and make only a little noise.'

'Send your own particular prayers after us,' her husband said, embracing her as though they were newly in love.

Agnesca clutched Mia's hand as she answered him. 'If I did so, I would be praying that those few light clouds above us now would darken and become heavy over the next few hours, then burst towards nightfall. By that time you may be almost at the city, but wet roads will hamper large numbers of men and horses trying to travel fast along them.'

Porphyrius laughed, and waved, and they disappeared surprisingly quickly through the main gate, which Roberto closed behind them once more.

Isabella went to bed under the house that night with no expectation of sleep. One of the reasons was that her father was on the road somewhere between here and Siena, and she had no idea if they were safe; and another was that her mother was unhappy hearing the call of a bird in the night, which often distressed her. Isabella's mind also teemed with thoughts about the new arrivals: the beauty and character of her mother's friend, and the handsome face of her eldest son, Luccio, who was also her father's godson, as it turned out. Isabella had noticed his slender nose and olive-coloured eyes at once; so too had Barbara, however, so Isabella vowed to say nothing of her own interest in him.

But the worst impediment to sleep by far was the dripping sound inside the cistern. Though their father had diverted the drains that had gathered rain off the vast villa roof and dropped it into the cistern many years before, to lessen the damp in the house, there was always a steady drip of water in one area when it rained really hard. And tonight – hunting bird or no hunting bird – the rain was heavier than Isabella could remember in a long time.

After an hour, Signora Toscano sat up and spoke first to Mia, and then to everyone else.

'The weather will prevent them coming out on raids tonight,' she said. 'No fires will catch in the unharvested fields, and the roads will turn muddy and make travel treacherous. Let us sleep upstairs.'

So that night the farm workers and villagers went back to their beds, while Isabella and Barbara and little Ranuccio slept in their mother's, giving up their own shared space under the eaves to the sons of Signora Toscano. Agnesca herself opened the door to her old room, where Luccio had been born. Mia had reserved it from guests through all the years of her marriage, sweeping and cleaning and strewing it freshly each day, moving not a single item or piece of furniture. And for the first time in nights, everyone slept. When they woke, it was to a morning of continuing rain.

'You have a good nose for the weather, Agnesca,' Jacquetta quipped as she found them all breakfasting in the dining hall.

'It is well-timed,' she laughed, 'but if it continues too long it will work against us, forcing the soldiers to frustrated actions.'

Isabella desperately wanted to ask Signora Toscano what prayers she had used to such effect, but no one else seemed concerned, and she lost her opportunity when her mother spoke.

'Fra Silvestro told me the men have been drinking so heavily of the abbot's wine that they must be unfit for fighting for a week at least.'

'Unfit for battle, Mia,' Agnesca said, 'but they will brawl with fierce strength.'

Much later, in the early evening, Isabella walked out into the garden looking for her mother. She found her with Signora Toscano, sitting on a stone seat on the small hill within the grounds, not far from the villa.

It offered a good lookout over the row of work cottages, and the orchard and vines that led up from the gate; and at a slightly altered angle it also provided a clear view up to the town of Chiusdino, on the hill above. As Isabella approached them she could see they were watching something in the twilight sky.

Her mother held an arm open for her in invitation, and Isabella accepted it. After a moment, when her eyes had adjusted to the light, she could see what they saw. Something glowed on the horizon, and there was a faint smell of smoke on the wind. She realised it was a distant fire. Turning her head a little to the left and right, she understood it was not one, but possibly as many as a dozen.

'It is the villages of Luriano and Ciciano,' her mother said. 'The raids have begun.'

40

Maddie was almost choking on the swirling exhaust fumes from the passing traffic. She stood in the parking lot of the main court building on the corner of Market Street and St James in San Jose, and her eyes were stinging.

At eleven that morning she suspected the feeling of a series of fresh starts she'd experienced – which had encouraged her to smile recently – must be slipping away. Up to a point about an hour ago all had seemed wonderful. There had been a spirit of optimism in the office after she had told them of her father's comments on the toxicology tests and report, a genuine sense that the case might, after all, give them a better balance and result in a favourable outcome for the victims. But now fate seemed to be twisting events beyond anyone's control.

Maddie felt sick as she listened to Samantha talking to Charles on her cell. It was extremely difficult to comprehend what had just happened and, unusually for Samantha, she was almost shouting into the phone.

'That's right, Charles! The judge has just disallowed the tests and toxicology report and forbidden us to present jurors with what is our most compelling evidence.'

A second later the vocal was accompanied by extravagant hand gestures Charles would never see.

'We can use the corporate mortality files, but his reasoning is that the comparative study is not relevant. In Californian law, workers can only sue employers in special circumstances, such as "fraudulent concealment". We must prove this in each individual case, and the tests only show that

393

the environment is more likely to give workers cancer. They don't actually prove that any named individual *did* contract cancer from the clean rooms. It is the most illogical argument I can think of.'

Maddie watched Samantha, feeling desperate sympathy for her. Maddie herself had worked for months without weekends off on the compilation of the material, but Samantha's investment of time – and cash – was no longer simple to calculate.

'I know,' Samantha was saying in answer to some question from Charles, 'it is a very rigid interpretation of the law. But he won't budge, Charles. It's his opinion . . . and there is nothing we can do except to proceed. It prevents us using the general to establish the specific.'

Samantha finished with: 'Yes, we'll have to try the case with our hands tied behind our backs. He has set the trial date for two weeks from now, and there's no looking back.'

Adding to the strain of work as March slipped away, Maddie's personal state of being also felt a little traumatised. What lay ahead for her? She'd made some forward steps to place her personal life finally in a better perspective, specifically concerning Christopher. She understood that any chance for more than just survival – the possible happiness of building a future – was dependent on her ability to get past the pain. Chris had been a joy; pain must not be the last word on their relationship. She didn't have to pretend the sadness was less than it had been, or marginalise his enormous presence in her life; but she couldn't let his death cast a shadow over everything that came after it. She had to transmute the pain into strength and a deeper understanding about who she was, and the world she inhabited. The same, she realised, was true for every individual who suffered overwhelming loss and hurt.

Her emotional and physical appetites were returning. She was starting to feel hope about what might be allowed to happen with a real flesh-and-blood male, someone more than just a 'guardian angel'. She was still unsure how to make sense of Søren crossing the northern hemisphere to hold her for a night, chastely, while she was living through her vigil for Chris. It was extraordinary – almost unnerving; an expression of unusual empathy for another person. But, what did she want it to mean? Who could hold someone all night – a living, breathing, sentient person, in a highly tensed emotional state – without a hand straying somewhere more intimate, without crossing a line?

Yet, he had. Perhaps fortunately, the pressure of work at present permitted her little time for too many reflections, or any meaningful analysis.

As the month ran out, the Harden Hammond Cohen crew worked overtime to double-check that all the documents and evidence were properly logged on the court's complex case data base. The collection represented seven years of accumulated information and papers, some of it dating back ten years. The department of the Superior Court that dealt exclusively with the organisation of 'complex' cases moved into top gear, as the case was going to be a long haul. For Maddie this was the first time that she had been closely embroiled in a full trial. She felt the slight adrenalin rush of competitiveness, but, after hearing Samantha's phone conversation, all of this was mixed with fears that they might lose.

The sheer enormity of the undertaking mesmerised Maddie. The list of lawyers and interested parties now entering the arena ran to fifteen pages, and she wondered who all these people could be, or what they would all want? Casting her eye over the pages, she observed persons representing third parties, others who might become involved at a later date, the defendants' team, cross-defendants, claimants, cross-complainants and their representatives. The list included chemical companies, component makers, and protective clothing manufacturers. All of them were waiting on the tide of events, protecting their own interest; each was ready to do battle, to jump on or off the merry-go-round of litigation as required. Everyone was on someone's payroll, and at the forefront of these mercenary gangs was her best-known captain, Gordon J. Hugo. He was sure to be bullishly confident that Stormtree would win.

On the eve of the trial she worried more than ever about the consequence of her making a mistake. This fear was sharpened when a court official had responded to a question on proceedings she had asked, saying, 'You should know the answer to that. Counsel's familiarity with the applicable California Rules of Court, Local Rules for Superior Court of California, County of Santa Clara, and complete knowledge of the "Deskbook" on the Management of Complex Civil Litigation, is expected.'

Maddie had wanted a hole in the floor to open and swallow her. The official had charted her embarrassment, and said, 'It takes time. You'll be

OK.' Then she was enlightened as to what she needed to know; but from this point she tried to spend every available night reading.

And then, late in March, it began. There was a relative feeling of sanctuary within the court, compared to the mayhem outside. Maddie watched the battle commence. There were objections on both sides from the off – starting with every jury member; each side vied to ensure they picked the persons who were most likely to favour their argument. Watching at every opportunity, Maddie thought it was not a one-sided affair. Hugo's trial lawyer attacked ferociously, and Charles countered eloquently. Each man struck a good many blows for their clients as evidence and witnesses appeared, and the days passed. It was at times riveting; often tedious; always exhausting.

On a Tuesday night, about three weeks after the start of the trial, Maddie came home to a frantic set of messages from Isabella. Her cellphone had been switched off for most of the day while she was in the courtroom, and she hadn't bothered to turn it on again for the drive home. Now she played the messages back, and was slightly startled by the content. Nonna wanted her to know that Signora Angela, the lady who had prepared Maddie's horoscope at her birth, had called urgently to say that if Maddie had never yet opened it, tonight would be an ideal moment. The moon, she said, was very close to the Seven Sisters – the Pleiades. People right here in North America, and especially over the ocean, would have the best position for viewing them.

What a non sequitur! she thought. She had neither strength nor curiosity right now to look at astrological predictions made when she was a baby. But, mention of the Pleiades did give her pause for thought. Who could know what promise they were bound up with – what they were the timekeepers for?

By the end of April – the fifth week of the trial – Maddie started to feel that the shine was wearing off. It was hard work and there certainly weren't any of those Ally McBeal moments everyone saw on television, which she had secretly hoped to witness. Only a few days later she actually heard herself say, 'TGI Friday,' to her own front door – spoken out of total exhaustion as she turned the key in the lock. She rested her head on the back of the door in pure relief as she shut the world out behind her. She hoped for a moment to catch up with her own life over the next forty-eight hours.

It was almost nine in the evening, but at least she didn't have to be up at six thirty in the morning. She opened the balcony door to let the stale air out of her apartment and invite in the smell of the sea; then she picked up the phone to order Chinese food, and clicked the 'Start' button on her Vaio. Ten minutes after coming through her door she was in the shower; and half an hour later she took in the order and settled at her coffee table. She was ready to make contact with the other world, where her heart was.

First up on her server was Jeanette's email, embellished with a smiling face wearing sunglasses, which told her the weather was already lovely and that she had sent a personal invitation by snail mail from Borgo for the official opening of the hotel, and the unveiling of the medieval alchemist's garden. Isabella, she added, would be getting one too. Barring a catastrophe, Borgo would open as planned, and she and Claus would love them (both) to come if they were free in June. Maddie sighed as she answered that she would love to, but it depended on the court case finishing. She didn't know whether Isabella would want to make the long trip, but she would ask.

After a mouthful of noodles she gave her attention next to Barbara's mail, which asked how things were going. She reported that she had been to a rancho-style hog roast but had not been able to eat, as the dinner looked like a Damien Hirst artwork before it had been placed in formaldehyde and sold for a million dollars. She added that the Druid was still making his magic, and she ended by saying that Lord Gray had gone off the radar, but that things in the art world were struggling along without him.

Maddie replied happily about the Druid, but made no comment regarding Pierce.

She had saved Søren's two emails until last. She was pleased to read in one that the Pleiades were becoming visible in the night sky. He had been working flat out with a partner on a garden for the Chelsea Flower Show in London, but had flown down to Borgo last weekend. His 'paradise' had over-wintered well, but there were still some chores to do, especially on the old-fashioned water trough. He needed to be in London for most of May until the opening of Chelsea, but after that – if she could find some plimsolls and still wanted to go sailing – he would get up to Denmark to prepare the Folkboat for June or July. When was her summer break? It would need some work before welcoming guests.

The second email, sent a day later, contained an attachment of one of his little hand-drawn sketches, which made Maddie smile. It was in answer to an outstanding question she had put to him about the cameo Isabella had given her for *Epifania*. Remembering his skill of visual recall, she'd sent a photo to his phone and wondered if he could place the same design somewhere – perhaps at Borgo, or even in Siena that day? Before leaving her for the airport that morning in January he had looked carefully at the real thing, nodding but hardly commenting. But here was his drawing of a carved motif of two doves and a knotted garland set into the wooden cupboard in the Pellegrino room at Borgo. He thought it a close match for Maddie's great-grandmother's brooch. Maddie felt goose bumps.

Søren's note relayed Jeanette's tale: they had found the cupboard in a shabby state at the back of the old bakery when they had bought Borgo. They'd had it restored, though it was relatively modern – perhaps only a hundred years old. Jeanette had said she'd never even noticed the doves. It reminded her now of the mention in a seventeenth-century inventory of the house's contents at that time, which had included an 'old chest with doves fettered by a garland of flowers'. Søren put it to her that it was either a popular Renaissance-era symbol – perhaps tokening fidelity between a couple – or that there was a deeper connection between Maddie's people and Villa Santo Pietro.

This felt like the touch of a human hand on her head: it made her almost stop breathing. The women at Borgo were undoubtedly some-body's ancestors; and Maddie and Jeanette both felt a subtle, spiritual affiliation with them and with all those souls who had taken shelter within its walls. But, what if there really were more? This would add a layer of thrill, and perhaps of deeper identity. And yet Maddie's connection with them was quite universal, she felt, rather than singular. It hardly seemed to matter if they were 'her own people'. Those skeletons had brought home to her that life must often have been cruel and unpredictable; but that affection for others was the meaningful note in human lives.

By now Maddie was so tired that she couldn't wrestle with any more from the information Søren had sent, or the thoughts he'd ventured. She took the largely uneaten food to the kitchen to throw away, went back to close down her laptop and almost dozed off sitting back on the sofa. When she sat forward again half an hour later she had just enough strength to get herself to bed: and after a few chores of washing clothes and writing some notes from the trial, the weekend had gone.

While the trial had been playing out its drama in the courtroom, Maddie visited Neva and a few others in hospital to keep them updated. But today she collected Marilu from her home to take her into the court for her first time as a focal witness, rather than as a spectator watching other complainants. She was nervous, and even the lovely May weather couldn't bolster the hearts of those who had been watching things slowly unfold into this, the seventh week. Marilu's son had been called back to work this week and couldn't be there today, but Maddie was happy to look after her during the time she was called to the stand.

It was a beautiful morning as they seated themselves, and by way of preparation to hear Marilu's testimony Charles had been trying yet again to find a way of bringing out the general details of the working conditions without recourse to the disallowed toxicology data. He was thwarted, however, every time Stormtree's attorney objected. Such interruptions broke the arc of Charles's narrative and made Maddie anxious; but then a bomb dropped. Charles was turning to the Critical Illness Records to prompt Marilu's memory about one of her doctors, when Maddie saw frantic whispering from Gordon Hugo to the Stormtree trial lawyer – and then a very loud 'Objection'. The team, it seemed, now opposed the use of the records themselves!

Charles had just begun a suggestion to the jury that their very existence demonstrated the company had been monitoring the worsening illnesses of its clean room workers. 'You cannot prove that any single individual noticed anything unusual about the workers' health just because these records exist – which are commonplace for any company covering employees' medical insurance,' Hugo had said firmly. 'It must be proven that the employer concealed a known injury, and no such certainty can be drawn purely from the records.'

Charles was a seasoned trial lawyer with a well-deserved reputation for his style, but he was stunned; and Marilu looked terror stricken. 'How could any person paid to discharge this job responsibly not have noticed the rising number of cancer-related illnesses?' Charles complained, 'and still have deserved his or her pay check?' But Hugo and his team were adamant that no inference could be drawn just from the existence of the records, and the judge eventually agreed. He now directed the jury to be mindful that 'the issue of whether an employer has a dangerous workplace or keeps employees in the dark is not a part of our case here, and the Defence correctly states that it must be proven that the employer knowingly concealed a danger. The Illness Records must be set aside.'

Charles was speechless; Maddie was horrified; and she saw that the jury were confused and suffering from battle fatigue. They seemed to be losing track of what was supposed to count, and what was not. During a recess she tried to explain to Marilu that – from her understanding – California's laws were stringent about workers' compensation claims. The plaintiffs' lawyer had not only to prove that Stormtree's facilities caused the cancers of each plaintiff specifically, but that the company also knew this, and did not tell the plaintiffs. She admitted the judge was only doing his job, but Marilu was as angry as anyone could be. She was aware, just like the other plaintiffs, of what had been excluded from the trial. Marilu understood what Maddie had explained, and even the rationale behind the application of the law. She could not fathom, however, the disparity between what she saw as 'justice' and 'the law': they seemed not the same thing at all.

Maddie got home that night feeling as low as it was possible to feel. Without the Critical Illness data base she doubted they would ever prove that Stormtree Components Inc. knew – and had always been monitoring – exactly what their workers were exposed to. Life wasn't always fair, she thought.

But she came to her door to find a moderate size packet the janitor had propped against it, which cheered her a little. It had been posted in London by Søren. She went inside, pushed her smart shoes off and poured half a glass of wine, then slit the tape on the post bag and pulled out a bubble-wrapped copy of a book. With it was a folded white card on which Søren had executed a black ink sketch of Eleanore in her spot, sitting on top of the mound at Borgo,

'Good luck on your birthday,' it said inside. 'We are all waiting for your return.'

Maddie laughed, taken completely by surprise. My birthday is in a couple of days, she thought, and I hadn't even realised the time.

Enclosed in the card was a separate note on thin paper: he had found the accompanying book at an antiquarian seller in Cecil Court, a lane near St Martin-in-the-Fields. It was a numbered copy of a 1968 edition of Leland's *Aradia* – the book Jeanette, and Eva in Volterra, had spoken of. The short tale of the girl – '*La Pellegrina della Casa al Vento*' – was in chapter eleven. It would take Maddie minutes to read it. What struck Søren was the number of Keats' quotations Leland had peppered through the whole book.

'I can't help wondering if just a few details of Madeline's poem have found their way into this little vignette! But maybe that's part of the mystery. S x'

Madeline's poem, she thought. So Papa was right after all.

It was a week after her twenty-sixth birthday when Maddie found herself in the grounds of the Mater Misericordiae Hospital, to which she had become so unseeing that she didn't notice a new outdoor eating area with market umbrellas, which had been set up beside the beautiful Mediterranean pines. She was intent instead on something at the far reaches of her mind which had caught up with her by surprise. It concerned Gordon Hugo's remarks on the video in the restaurant. They suddenly seemed to tie in to the fact that the company's illness records, and Harden's commissioned toxicology tests, had all been disallowed.

His cocky confidence triggered something in Maddie's mind. It might have been a bit mean-spirited, but she wondered if there was an election coming up in whose campaign funds Pierce Gray was a contributor? But this was surely not possible, she thought, and just her own paranoia. It was difficult even now, after all the weeks of the trial, to understand quite why their tests and the illness files had not been admitted. But she needed to dismiss her cynicism and remember her faith in the legal process. Anyhow, she had more urgent things to deal with now.

As Maddie entered Neva's room, Wyman Walker looked straight at her. In place of anger, his expression replied to hers with sympathetic sadness. He could read her news in the disappointment and stress on her face.

'We have lost the case,' he said quietly; and he knew he was right from her reaction. 'I can see it is written in your eyes, and I am sorry for you all. You have worked very hard.'

'Yes,' Maddie nodded, her head down. 'I'm so sorry. We have failed to convince the jury. After almost three months in court they returned a "no verdict".'

Maddie and the whole team were broken, disappointed and exhausted;

but Wyman respected her for coming straight to the hospital, immediately the foreman of the jury had given the judge their answer.

Neva Walker was an ethereal beauty today, with her dark silky hair tied loosely back from skin too tightly stretched over the beautiful cheekbones and eyes that were dark pools of pain set within their appearance of light. Yet she looked in some ways as she always did, a wise and beautiful ghost offering benediction to Maddie from the pillows. Maddie had no idea what this news might do to Neva: she was acutely aware that she had been cheating time to hear the result of the trial.

Wyman stood by the side of the bed behind Aguila, with his arms around his grandson. Aguila held Neva's hand in both of his, as Maddie came to the end of the bed. All three watched her for some time. As Wyman might have put it, they felt a great sadness overtake them.

Neva still managed a smile of some strength, which made Maddie want to cry out in protest at fate, or the gods, or anyone who was listening.

'The shadow of time has fallen across me, Maddie,' she said simply. 'The spirits of my ancestors will lead me, and believe me, I am not afraid.' She took a moment to lick her lips and find a voice again. 'In a few days the men will take my ashes to Nevada, and the Walkers will see that my boy grows to be a fine man.'

She squeezed Aguila's hands and somehow – Maddie wondered quite how – the boy found the strength not to wail. His mother's voice remained clear and firm for a minute.

'It is not over,' she said. 'You will keep your promise, and my boy will have his heart fixed. They have not heard Madeline speak yet, but when they do the winds of change will blow. Time is everything, Maddie. Some things you cannot rush; but neither leave others until it is too late. Take your chance, and be happy yourself.'

Wyman looked at his daughter, and unfolded his arms from his grandson. He stepped to the end of the bed and took Maddie gently by the arm, knowing she needed his support. He escorted her towards the door, but here Maddie turned and watched Neva's face lit by the last smile she would see in it. Maddie couldn't help herself; she smiled back, though her throat hurt. Neva's extraordinary courage broke her heart.

Now, Maddie wanted to be out of the door. She didn't want to intrude on the private nature of the minutes that belonged to the father and son; and she pushed down on the door handle, but Wyman spoke as he reached the door with her, and he quietly accompanied her out.

' "Lady who understands the snow",' he said, 'we are glad you came personally to speak with us.'

For some reason Wyman began to walk with Maddie along the hospital corridor, past the smell of bedpans and disinfectant, towards the main entrance.

'For so many, it is any Friday,' he said, 'while for us it is the one my grandson will remember all his life. Mr Gray will leave town early for the weekend.'

Maddie didn't have words to answer, but she understood only too well this dislocation between private grief and the indifferent world. She nodded empathetically.

They reached the front door of the hospital, and could see outside a gentle rain had begun to fall. It had streaked the red dust on the glass front of the building, like long tears.

'You see,' Wyman indicated with his head, 'the ancestors have told the sky to weep for my daughter.'

The main door now opened automatically, bringing a gust of wind into the hospital foyer, which carried a mixture of dry leaves, fine sand and rain on its breath.

'No matter what separates us from each other, whatever different beliefs people have,' Wyman said, 'everyone feels the wind.'

Then, he was gone.

Maddie stood exposed to the elements as the door slid silently closed behind her. The wind lifted one of the umbrellas from the eating area, throwing it into the parking lot. It then came and tugged at her hair, which streamed out behind her. She leaned against the stone transom of the door, thrilling at the wind lashing her to make her sadness physical.

Then she ran from the porch towards her car.

41

Mia woke on the cool, broad ledge where she and the residents of Santo Pietro in Cellole had been sheltering under the house. She had no idea of the time: lit only by two small down-shafts, the cistern was dark, and she couldn't guess how many hours she might have slept.

She peeled her small son's arm off her chest and tucked it around her elder daughter without disturbing anyone. She checked Isabella, who was also sleeping quietly, and noticed that a dozen cottagers were still lying on makeshift pallets dotted around the cistern. She got to her feet noiselessly and looked for *la raggia*, but she wasn't with them. Her younger son, Federico, was a few feet from Barbara, but neither the angelic Luccio nor his mother seemed to be here. Mia wrapped herself in a shawl and took the steep stairs up from their hiding place to the ground level of the villa. As she emerged into the light the sun was on the horizon line, and the hour might have been somewhere between six and seven. She stepped into the courtyard and looked for signs of life, but before she could find anyone she became aware of an acrid smell hanging in the air away to the north, being borne on the light morning wind. It smelled, she thought, a lot closer than Luriano.

Walking around the perimeter of the building she noticed a seated figure that roughly equated with the shape of her aunt: but something was wrong. She got closer and found Jacquetta's normally upright body sagging where she sat on the top step of the house. She was staring blankly away over the kitchen garden and down the pilgrims' road, in

404

the direction of the strong smell. Noticing her dress was daubed in smudges of soot, Mia laid a hand on her aunt's back to make sure she was warm. Jacquetta seemed frozen to the spot; and she hardly moved, even at the touch of Mia's hand. Mia turned her head to follow her aunt's gaze, and when her own view mirrored Jacquetta's, she too slumped beside her and covered her mouth in despair.

The scene across their once immaculate paradise garden – of roses and lilacs, of marjoram and rosemary, and irises in pots – was now one of carnage. The laying hens that had not been brought to safety in baskets under the house were strewn headless among the autumn saffron and coneflowers. A pregnant sow had been stuck through with a man's sword, and left to bleed where she lay. Branches of fruiting pears and apricots had been scythed from trees, rose heads shorn from bushes, pots smashed with their contents battered on the ground. At the furthest edges of the villa grounds the chestnut huts and bales of straw were still smouldering, and to the other side of the road she could see that one end of the stable block was on fire.

Mia could say nothing. She could only sit by Jacquetta and place a second hand on her shoulder, realising that both of them were trembling.

'They slipped over the walls,' Jacquetta said in a voice without power or resonance, 'and I came out to meet them. No more than a half dozen men. They only wished to warn me.'

Mia wanted to find a question that would make sense of the wastefulness and destruction that she saw, but nothing came to her. She could only look across the spoilage and wonder, who would do that – leave the animals where they were, slaughtered yet making no food for residents or soldiers? The whole mêlée was purposeless, except for the point that it was designed to subdue them.

'They spared the house?' was all she could manage.

'I bought them off,' Jacquetta said flatly.

Her voice was husky with smoke, but it was the strange sound of detachment from everything around her that Mia found disconcerting. She had never heard Aunt Jacquetta sound so broken.

'It took no more than fifty florins, and two barrels of our best wine,' she explained. 'This time that was enough: they were already returning from more entertaining revels on the hills. I convinced them I was widowed, and that my son was on business with the council in Siena.

405

They scrupled to antagonise a man on the council, because it is the council who must pay them their real wages. But they will be back.'

Mia hugged her aunt. 'They knew nothing of the rest of us, sleeping below?'

Jacquetta shook her head.

'Aunt Jacquetta, you could have been killed by them – or raped, like my mother.'

The sound of footsteps came quickly up the lane from the stables, breaking into Mia's awareness, and she saw Agnesca. Her face was grimy with smoke, and her hands looked red and blistered, but she walked purposefully towards aunt and niece.

'Luccio was watching from above,' Jacquetta was still telling Mia, without moving her eyes from the great vista of wreckage. 'He had his father's crossbow loaded, and would have struck one of them, I am certain, if they had attacked me.'

'Luccio and Roberto are still putting out the stable fire,' Agnesca said, 'but they have recaptured the frightened horses. We must get you inside and cleaned up, Jacquetta. As awful as it is, this is minimal harm – and we are lucky.'

She gently lifted Jacquetta's frame up and walked her into the house, with Mia following.

'Go down and wake the residents of the *borgo*, and the servants, Mia,' she said. 'There is a lot of cleaning up to do.'

After four or five hours of work under a bright sun in a cool wind, the mayhem at Villa Santo Pietro looked more manageable, but Jacquetta's spirits improved very little. The needless ruination of the grounds, the waste of livestock and fodder, was not her grief. It was the impossibility of finding any satisfactory way to fight the soldiers. The residents and their servants were powerless, grossly outnumbered, with no authority in the land willing or able to hold the rebel army to book. They had no fear of God; no respect for life; and no proper code of ethics even amongst themselves. For the first time in her recall Jacquetta felt no optimism, held no belief that there was a remedy for this plague of locusts. Over any number of returning harvest seasons they would bleed the *contado* dry. What was to stop them?

The sun was close to its highpoint in the sky when Roberto opened the gate to the farmer, his second son, and Claudio, one of the servants who had arrived with the Toscano family. It was Luccio – still repairing damage in the stables – who came to find Mia and his mother and report their return while they cleaned up and ate something.

'They bear ill news about your father,' Agnesca said to her eldest son. It was not spoken as a question, and her voice seemed oddly matter-of-fact.

'It may not be so bad,' the young man answered her with a hopeful smile.

Jacquetta and Mia came to them in the hall, and Luccio moderated his voice to sound calm, for Mia's sake.

'My father and godfather succeeded in getting the whole caravan to Siena without hindrance,' he began positively. 'They had effected more than half the return journey before they were taken hostage – along with the farmer's other son – at the convent of Santa Lucia, near Rosia. I am told they are well enough and unharmed, and it is only required that I go with florins to buy their freedom.'

'Have they no money with them, then?' Mia asked in confusion.

'They had cleverly divided what they brought back between all,' Luccio answered her. 'Knowing they were likeliest to be kidnapped for ransom, they put the larger share of the money under the saddles of the farmer and Claudio. It was with a modest purse that Gennaro bought freedom for the others, convincing them it was all he had. So they are kept on a pledge to bring more from us here for their release, but it is Claudio and the farmers who have brought funds to us. If you will only allow me to take it, I will be away within the hour,' he added.

'Can we raise the sum they ask for?' Jacquetta said in the same husky voice of the morning. 'What price do they want?'

Luccio was almost laughing when he answered. 'Claudio says they were all so shabby – after the long ride in rain and slime – that they look like men who have already been beggared. The price they have fixed is one hundred and fifty florins for all three – and the ambassador for Siena, who is taken with them, requires a purse of three hundred for himself alone.'

'They ask fourteen for each of the villagers who are trapped at San Galgano,' Jacquetta nodded. 'The sum is bearable; and it is I who will take it to Rosia.'

'Then I am coming with you,' Luccio said.

Mia tried to intrude herself into the equation, to rescue Gennaro; but no one would allow it. Agnesca encouraged her instead to accept the role of negotiator at the abbey. Jacquetta directed her to a strongbox in her chamber, which contained the last earnings she had from pilgrims over two slow years. There were florins and some half-nobles, and even a few guilders from travellers from the north. She was sure they would be acceptable to the thieves for her neighbours' freedom.

On a beautiful October evening, watching the horizon once more, Mia remarked to Agnesca on the incongruity that the azure sky reflected none of the ugliness that had marked the day. The sunset had been purple rather than blood red; and the smell of the smoke had faded.

'I cannot see the Seven Sisters, however,' Mia added, 'and I always associate their disappearance with sadness. Will you be leaving us, *la raggia*, once the soldiers have quit the abbey, and our danger is passed?'

'No, dear one. I have told you honestly,' she said, squeezing her friend's cold hand. 'I am home to stay. You and Jacquetta are my family – though I will need to visit the children in Lucca sometimes!'

Mia was only too willing to accept such an assurance, but it seemed too hopeful. 'Does my brother's warning not still shout in your ears?' she asked.

Agnesca looked at Mia. Could it be that she didn't know what had happened in Volterra?

'Your brother's power and patronage are not what they were, Mia,' she said cautiously.

'Because Ottaviano died from the pestilence, just as you said he would,' Mia nodded. 'But I had heard that my brother Paolo, whom they call Bocchino, is a worse tyrant than his father. Not one visitor here has had a good word for him. He may be more brutal than Ottaviano; and I have no desire ever to lay eyes on him. I wish we shared no blood.'

'My darling Mia,' Agnesca said sadly, 'I cannot guess why Jacquetta and Gennaro have chosen not to tell you, but I would disburden you of the worry. Will you forgive your friend, if I am unwittingly telling you something that gives you pain?'

Mia looked at her, uncomprehending.

'Bocchino got himself caught between the old oligarch families in Volterra – who had held offices for generations – and the nervous Florentines, who want to keep Volterra from growing too big,' Agnesca said quietly. 'Married to a count's daughter, his only wish was to increase his power base and become a true sovereign lord; but he was squeezed between both sides. He was very unpopular, taking all the laws into his own hands when it suited him; and, like his father, he was not above seizing young women for his own pleasure. To try to hold onto his power, he asked Pisa for support, and allowed them a military garrison in the town. From that point the nobles became Bocchino's arch opponents.'

'Is he no longer in power, then?' Mia asked incredulously. For seventeen years she had avoided any return to Volterra – even to meet Gennaro's family there – so as never to see either of her brothers again. Had this been unnecessary?

'Bocchino made the mistake of offering to sell Volterra to Pisa,' Agnesca said. 'When news got out he tried to escape from the mob, but they caught him at the Etruscan gate. He was beheaded, Mia, on the steps of the Palazzo dei Priori, four years ago.'

Mia looked blank. Beheaded by the mob! She wished she could feel some compassion for this man; and she did, in a sense, regret the manner of his fall. But these people had ruined her life, her mother's life, Gennaro's family. They had condemned Agnesca, taken her property, and lived like lords at the expense of so many people. She felt very little other than relief.

'Then, you truly are safe here with me,' she said, and Agnesca nodded.

This conversation had ushered Mia to a place of strange contentment and security, and she found herself singing to her son a short time later while she bathed him. They were in the largest bedchamber, with its separate closet, which she and Gennaro had moved into at their marriage. It was luxurious compared with her old room and his: sitting at the top of the external stairs, it overlooked the courtyard and surveyed the valley. Isabella was singing with her when they both heard the farm dogs barking down the lane, and wondered if it meant Gennaro and Porphyrius were home. Sure enough the noisy dogs were soon accompanied by the sound of hoofs – slower than she would have expected – but certainly about the right number. She asked her daughter to tap on the door of Signora Toscano's chamber and ask her to greet them while she dried her son.

'You go too, Isabella,' she smiled wryly, 'for you will want to see that Luccio Toscano is unscratched.'

Isabella blushed, and then nodded. She ran away to find Signora Toscano. But after an interval, when Mia had dried and dressed the boy, she became worried: there was no sound of anyone crossing the courtyard below. By the sweet angels, she thought, it is not the soldiers returning to plunder again?

Mia hitched her son on her hip and flew down the external steps at a dangerous pace. If they were back she would tell them to leave: she had a voice, and would use it to protect her children. But as she passed the olive tree heading towards the stables, she stopped dead. A bier was being carried towards the house so slowly that there was barely a sound on the stones. Was it Gennaro? she thought. It was unthinkable that it was any of them.

She made out the silhouettes of her daughter and Agnesca; then of tall Luccio with his gold hair catching the light of the torches, and of the plumper frame of old Cesaré. She thought possibly that two men carried the bier, and that one of them was Gennaro. She turned on her heel and opened the wide front door to allow the men in with their load. And as they got near enough to her for the torchlight to offer her confirmation, she caught her breath.

'Quickly, Mia,' Agnesca said. 'Clear the refectory table in front of the fire in the kitchen, then help me get salves and tinctures.'

Stretched before her in a twisted form was the body of her aunt, the top of her dress saturated with blood. She was covered over with Gennaro's cloak and a fleece Mia didn't recognise. She fled before them, as she was asked, holding the door and crossing the slabbed stones into the kitchen. Gennaro and Porphyrius gently lifted the bier onto the refectory table.

'We were out, and away,' Gennaro said to his love, whose face was whiter than Jacquetta's. 'We were just crossing the Pia Bridge from the convent when Jacquetta looked over her shoulder – something she heard that the rest of us did not.'

Agnesca lifted away the coats and looked at the source of the blood. It was a wound wider than the length of a thumb – a tearing injury exposing flesh and bone in a grisly tangle. Protruding only about the length of a thumbnail was a dirty metal bolt, fired from a crossbow. Seeing that Mia was unable to function, Agnesca sent Isabella to the still room for thyme oil and some pincers she remembered using years before to extract a boot nail from a pilgrim's foot.

'What did she hear?' Mia finally managed to ask.

Gennaro looked at his wife and took hold of his son, who was still clinging bewildered to his mother.

'A young girl was being chased through the woods by two soldiers on foot, and one of them had just caught her,' he said. 'From the look of her clothing they had caught up with her more than once. She was younger than Isabella, and Jacquetta turned her horse, and rode at them.'

Porphyrius explained the rest of a short tale, told too soon.

'Your aunt thought to lift the girl to safety, onto her own horse, but two men of Hawkwood's company watching from the convent wall loosed a bolt, Mia,' he said. 'I think they did it in sport.'

Mia hardly heard the rest: she dimly took in that one of Hawkwood's captains – someone called Beaumont – had intervened, stopped the fun, and helped them get Jacquetta onto a bier, offering them the services of an army doctor who might remove the bolt. A rambling Jacquetta had pleaded only to come home – to let Agnesca treat her; and they had left two hours ago, taking care not to jolt her too much.

'She has been in wake and sleep, I think,' Porphyrius told his wife.

'The bolt is deep,' Agnesca said gravely. Her fingers were exploring the wound, and her expression unhappy. 'It has smashed the shoulder bone, and to withdraw it means she will lose a lot of blood.'

Leaving Mia to mop ineffectually at her aunt's face with lavender water, Agnesca made a swift concoction in the neighbouring still room from the most potent bottles. One, Mia saw from the corner of her eye, was the dangerous *aconitum*, which she knew was used only at acute times when nothing less would dull the pain.

But Agnesca quietly confided to Gennaro that her efforts were close to worthless.

'It might serve to bring one of the surgeon monks, if they would come,' she whispered. 'I am unable to dislodge the bolt because it is barbed, and to do so would cause a gush of blood I cannot turn off. The wound is too spread for me to sew. Nor can I push it through, as it is stuck hard in the thickest of the shattered bone.'

'The monks know less than you, Agnesca,' he said in despair. 'Is there nothing to do for her?'

'Limit the pain,' was all she could answer.

Mia and Alba and Agnesca sat with Jacquetta hour after hour. Mia hardly noted that Luccio and her daughter had indeed gone to the abbey for help, as Agnesca had insisted. Waived from his vows in light of events, Fra Sandro had returned with them along with one of Hawkwood's own surgeons, for the report of what occurred at the Ponte della Pia had come back with Beaumont. Sufficient embarrassment ensued, for no soldier was encouraged to fire at women of gentle birth. The soldier had been dealt with severely.

'Extraction is the first requirement,' the army doctor told Gennaro in French. 'Fever and tissue damage can be managed, but there is no route to extract this bolt, and the entry too near the neck for us to take the arm.'

Fra Sandro had brought henbane and belladonna, and these powerful herbs were added to Agnesca's thyme and monkshood. Everyone, except for Mia, seemed aware that all these ointments could do was ease Jacquetta's physical suffering.

For two days and nights Jacquetta lingered. She was not in too much pain, Agnesca thought; neither was she very aware of the world she still inhabited. On the morning three days after the injury, Jacquetta's fingers managed to stroke her sleeping niece's hair. Mia had only dozed beside her, but she woke, feeling the pressure on her head.

'Don't take me to the vault where my parents lie in Volterra,' she said softly.

Mia sat up, noticing her aunt's words were fluent. She had said almost nothing since she had been brought back.

'This has been our sanctuary, our paradise,' she said slowly, still moving her fingers over Mia's hair. 'My life has been full of joy, Mia. Nothing was a sacrifice,' she smiled. 'Put me here in the ground, my feet towards the Val di Cellole, where I can be close to you. The soldiers will go,' she said clearly, 'and though they will return, you will survive. The house has its arms around you, and even when your children leave, some will find their way back.'

Mia felt her eyes welling, but wanted to stay strong.

'I will make it our family vault, Aunt Jacquetta,' she said. 'And when it is my turn, I will sleep beside you.'

'I, too,' said Agnesca. She had come in, hearing the soft talking. 'You are my mother and my sister, and I will be buried by you both, if you will have me.'

'Agnesca,' Jacquetta looked at her clearly for a moment. She seemed to think for such a length of time before she spoke, and then said, 'I have never forgotten your words to me, long ago. Your children will have the right, and the strength, to make a difference to the destinies of human beings.'

Perhaps a quarter of an hour later, Jacquetta opened her eyes one last time and looked at Mia, who hadn't left her side.

'I think there may be unicorns after all,' she whispered.

Jacquetta said nothing more. The pain-killing drugs took her mind to another place, and a few hours later that day she slipped away. Mia was so absorbed by the loss – so distraught by its needlessness – that she was unaware the Company of St George had also moved away from the much-ruined abbey of her neighbours. And with no one from San Galgano to do the office, it was Gennaro and Porphyrius who dug her grave where the old church garden of Santo Pietro in Cellole had flourished: where its lilacs brought back by pilgrims would flower in spring next to the native irises that Jacquetta and Mia both loved.

It was three months later – in the always significant month of January, as it seemed to Mia – that her last child was born. Right at the point when Loredana was recommending the unbolting of doors and unlocking of cupboards, a blast of freezing wind blew open the shutters, and a little girl was born. She was delivered three weeks before the date she was thought to be due, and it had been a long and difficult birth, necessitating that Agnesca – a now much-practised midwife – push the child's umbilicus down and out of the way just as she was born to save her being strangled by it. In the hands of someone less skilled, the child should have been lost.

'She is certainly ours, Mia,' she laughed. 'She has been born on the wind, and with a true knot in her cord.'

Mia's first idea had been to name her after her aunt; but after long consultation with her husband and *la raggia*, she decided instead to name the little girl 'Maria Pia', in memory of her aunt's selflessness at the Pia Bridge. The name would appear every generation or two, down the long history of Mia's family.

42

LATE MAY–EARLY JUNE 2008, SAN JOSE, SAN FRANCISCO
AND TUSCANY

The fine rain mixed with red dust filled the air, lifted off the road by the heavy traffic. The wipers smeared it over the windshield and obscured Maddie's vision as she headed north along the Nimitz Freeway towards Berkeley.

Half an hour down the road she pulled off the freeway at Fremont to get gas and a bottle of water from a Chevron station. She had the boy on the pump look under the hood to check the oil and make sure there was screen-wash in the reservoir. She went into the building to pay, but her state of mind was such that she forgot the water on the counter when she left.

The weather improved as she moved further north, the drizzle giving way to clear skies as she passed the Bay Bridge just before Berkeley. Here the road name changed to become the Eastshore Freeway, but it was still the main route to the north. She thought she might stop and speak to her father, but by the time the thought had formed she found she had sped past his turn-off. There was a toll coming up, and she looked down at the passenger seat and shoved the toxicology report envelope out of the way to find change in her bag. As she approached the town of Vallejo, Maddie saw a long bank of high clouds gathering on the horizon. In another half-hour she would be climbing into the mountains, and it looked as if the weather would deteriorate again.

The rain began to fall just as she left the St Helena Highway and took the Oakville Grade for a few miles. Here she found what she was looking

414

for: a single lane macadam track leading to a set of imposing electric gates. In front of her was a long, tree-lined avenue ending in a turning circle in front of a single-storey New England-style house, with a wide porch. On either side of the avenue, picturesque rows of wonderfully tended vines extended with the first signs of fruit-set on them. The vines marched in perfect formation towards the forest that lined the mountain sides beyond.

What looked to be a winery complex stood at one end of the vineyards, and it bore a large sign:

Storm Tree Estates,
The Finest Wines in the Napa Appellation
Since 1889

While Maddie watched, the view became gradually obscured from her sight as the light rain turned heavier, and then turned into something of a deluge. She hesitated before driving on as the rain was as quickly replaced by hail, which pounded like a thousand hammers on the roof of her car and drowned out the sound of her own anxious heartbeat. A white sheet of strange weather in front of her blotted out all visibility.

Over the deafening percussion of the hail came the most terrifying sound Maddie thought she had ever heard. It rose like a scream, a noise like a high-speed express train growing in intensity and then sweeping past the car. A hand seemed to have taken hold of the little vehicle, and shaken it so violently that Maddie was sure she was going to be hit by something. It was as if the car had been parked too close to a speeding train, and was doomed to be sucked into its slipstream.

In terror, Maddie slammed on the brakes as hard as she could. She dived instinctively below the dashboard, hoping the car would not be turned over by the violence that gripped it. For almost five minutes the wind screamed and the rain and hail battered the car. Then, without reason or warning, the volume dropped to a gentle patter like spring rain. Maddie could even hear the quiet idle of the car engine again. It should not be still running now, she thought; and I should have been picked up and tossed away. With some trepidation she raised her head to survey the scene. What had ten minutes before been a scene of pastoral tranquillity was now one of devastation. On the left of the road not a vine was intact, from the winery to the far hills; to the right, there was hardly a disturbance to the pristine rows that ornamented the front lawns of the large house garden.

While Maddie sat staring, a figure stepped from the door of the house onto the porch and surveyed the remnants of what would have been the two thousand and eight Gray Lady Vintage. The man stopped and put his hands to his face in seeming incomprehension, and then he tottered forwards down the porch steps. At the bottom, however, he seemed to lose the use of his legs and sank down in the light rain. He put his head in his hands.

Safe and dry in her car, from Maddie's perspective Pierce Gray looked like a child who had lost all of his family in an apocalyptic tragedy.

She eased off the brake, and the car tyres crunched over the hail stones as she inched along the drive. It was slippery, and she was forced to move slowly up the tree-lined avenue, weaving around torn-off branches and other debris, until she came to a halt at the turning circle in front of the house.

She got out of the car and, hardly thinking why she had come, picked up the envelope from the seat beside her.

Pierce lifted his head, seeing her without recognition for a while, offering no dialogue. Eventually he found words.

'My ancestors started this vineyard in the eighteen eighties. It had to close during Prohibition, but by then my great-grandfather was in the timber business, and we had enough money.'

Maddie walked slowly towards him, understanding he had to speak. She nodded at him to go on.

'When Grandpa lived here as a boy, there was a giant redwood that used to grow out there.' He pointed towards the edge of the winery, and Maddie followed his finger. 'One day an electrical storm blew up out of nowhere, and the little boy ran for safety from the rain underneath the branches of the tree. No one had ever told him that was the worst thing to do, and it was struck by lightning and split in two. My grandfather was standing under it, and the tree was killed – but he was not. It fell alongside him without as much as a branch touching his body. That's why his son – my father – called the company Storm Tree; and when he restarted the vineyard, he felt it was providence. They could survive anything that was thrown at them.'

Maddie came up the porch steps now and sat down just behind him, out of the weather. 'I am sorry about the loss of your grapes, Pierce,' she said. 'I truly am, because I know you love this.' She nodded her head once to indicate the whole estate and its importance for him. He had been through two leggy wives and still had no son and heir; and this estate was what gave his life meaning. It was his family. She suddenly understood its relevance, and saw that possibly its flourishing status connected him to an unseen source of patriarchal approval.

'But you are very rich,' she said in a gentle voice, 'and also very protected; and your insurance will cover most of this loss. You have your health, and you have passion, and your grapes will grow again.'

'You don't understand, Madeline,' he said without looking over his shoulder at her. 'For me it's like an omen – the storm. They are not pleased with me.'

Pierce leaned over and put his head on Maddie's lap, crumpling like a small boy. She had come here full of anger at Pierce Gray, but she hadn't asked for his pain. She reached down and gently touched his hair.

'They are your grapes, but not your children,' was all she said.

She felt sadness for him at this moment, but she also knew she had to say what she had come for – what had usurped her mind of all other thought.

'I have just come from watching a friend die. She was a beautiful young woman, just a few years older than I, and she died of brain and liver cancer in the company of her small son, and her father,' she said strongly. 'You feel this loss acutely, and I understand it has taken a long effort and skilled work; but these are not living beings, Pierce. The woman I speak of worked for your company, and her death should have been avoided.'

Pierce slowly raised his head to look at her. Her face had always offered him a sense of unusual enchantment; now he didn't want to hear her, but neither could he look away from her.

Maddie sensed some of this. She spoke carefully, as she wanted to use her words well. 'Shakespeare says it is wonderful to have a giant's strength, but tyrannous to use it like a giant. Your company is that giant, and the people who work in your factories have no strength to fight such power as Stormtree commands. Their words cannot be heard above your lawyers, who shout like generals. They are destroyed, Pierce.

They have no vines to replant. Don't you see that for them, you are the wind.'

She stood up and placed the envelope on a dry step above him.

'Go in from the rain,' she said tenderly; then she touched his shoulder and passed him to walk to her car.

The Monday after Maddie had confronted Pierce Gray was the first in June, and she walked through the office door fifteen minutes late. The bus from Cow Hollow had got stuck in traffic, and Maddie's energy was too flat to run this morning. She hadn't moved from her apartment, nor spoken to anyone over the weekend. She thought of texting Søren that they had lost the case, but he had won a silver-gilt medal for his garden at Chelsea, and she didn't want to spoil his fun. She had been in something of a state of shock about Neva and the court case, and also delayed stress over how close she'd come to an accident of her own when she saw the report on the news that night of the near-cyclone that had scythed its way through just a portion of the Napa. Looking at the footage, she was aware that the wind had passed in all its fury just feet from her car, yet it had spared her. Some angel must have been watching.

Paloma stood in full bloom as the sole sentinel at the entrance to Harden Hammond Cohen; unusually, Teresa was not at her post. Maddie moved along the corridor, passing the main offices without encountering a soul. She walked down the empty passageways to place her coat in her office, and still no one was about. Mystified, she checked the other side of the hallway to find Tyler, or Charlotte next door to him. Where has everyone gone? she wondered. It was a bit like the *Marie Celeste* here today. Finally – and as a last resort – she pushed open the door to the bull ring and shook her head in puzzlement. She couldn't remember if a meeting was called, but absolutely everybody was gathered here. The whole company had crammed into all the seats, even balancing on arms and the corner of the boardroom table.

Samantha spoke as Maddie came in. Her voice was peculiar – her tone almost peremptory – which happened so rarely Maddie couldn't place the last occasion she'd heard it.

'We have been waiting for you!' she said. 'What did you say to Pierce Gray in Napa on Friday?'

'Why?' Maddie questioned. Had she done something unethical?

'Because he has had us all in here this morning before eight o'clock for an unscheduled meeting,' Samantha answered. 'I called your numbers all day yesterday, but got no reply.'

Maddie's heart sank. She had gone a step too far this time. Would they fire her?

'Have I done something very wrong?' she asked defensively. She was feeling too traumatised to go through this today.

Samantha stood up, her tone still inscrutable. 'Please read this out loud. No one here, except for Charles, has heard it yet.' She passed Maddie a single sheet of paper.

Maddie cleared her throat and began nervously.

'"Class action brought by Harden Hammond Cohen, on behalf of their clients against Stormtree Components Inc., has today been resolved."'

Then she stopped and looked around, wanting to cry. 'What?' She noticed Charles now had a big grin on his face, and everyone was beaming at her.

'Go on,' Samantha urged.

Maddie looked at the paper she held, and bit her lip. She was starting to grasp that this might be a happy ending.

'The terms of the settlement are confidential, and will not be disclosed. Neither party will be issuing any further statements on this matter. Stormtree firmly believes, based on facts and evidence, that it has no liability in this case and its workplace did not cause the plaintiffs' injuries. There will be no comment from any of the parties beyond this statement.

Signed and agreed

P. Gray   C. Hammond
CEO Stormtree Components Inc.   Attorney for the Claimant

J. M. Clemente   S. Harden
Attorney for Stormtree   Attorney for the Claimant'
Components Inc.

It took several seconds for Maddie to digest the meaning of what she had read. She looked at the signatures again and held back tears of relief. She asked Samantha, 'Why no Gordon Hugo?'

'It seems he is no longer with them,' Charles said, his tongue actually harbouring inside his cheek.

Everyone clapped.

'Charles and I have been on the phone since Saturday afternoon.' Samantha's face finally softened. 'Gray came in this morning with his new lawyers to sign the interim agreement. Whatever has caused this change of heart, we are all delighted. He mentioned very particularly that he had spoken to you, Maddie. Did you say something to change his mind?'

Maddie resolutely shook her head, unwilling to say a word.

Charles grinned, and thought he understood her silence. 'So we can say that it might have been Gray's board advising him of this course, having seen the writing on the wall.'

Tyler chimed in, 'And the writing will soon hit a lot of people's walls!'

Charles added, 'True. We made it public on Friday afternoon, intending to file a complaint in Massachusetts against Stormtree under different state laws. The toxicology information will be published on the net, making it public domain, so it can't be blocked as evidence in the future.'

Maddie's thoughts were her own. Pierce's pragmatism could never be discounted, but she thought it was his own sense of superstition that might have cast the last vote for his conscience.

She and Tyler were now asked to contact all the clients, and tell them what had happened. They would be in funds during this week.

'I can't tell you how much we have agreed,' Samantha said, 'but the undisclosed sum is big enough to be paid in several tranches.'

'Money won't give little Aguila Walker back his mother,' Maddie said with emotion.

'No,' Tyler agreed, 'but it will pay to have his heart operations, and support him to longer schooling, and that is what his mother wanted.'

After the moment of elation the truth of Tyler's words struck home, and Maddie returned to her office a little down at heart. But as she made her phone calls, everyone she spoke to was happy. They could make some plans about their lives.

Maddie took out the Janus coin from its box on her desk. She turned it slowly in her fingers, studying it, and thought for a moment of returning it to Pierce; but she decided it was a good omen – a new direction – and she replaced it in the box next to the two coins Jeanette had given her from Borgo. Maybe they had been working a little witchcraft on him, too.

'Have a week off, Maddie.' Samantha was suddenly at her door. She caught Maddie completely off guard. 'I know better than the rest; and you had a lot to do with this. Everyone will get a small bonus, so why don't you fly back and finish your holiday in Italy?' She smiled, and closed the door again.

Maddie stared at the door for a moment, and then, pulling her phone from her bag, she clicked an autodial, and a surprised voice answered.

'Madeline?'

'Thank you,' she said with emphasis. 'Thank you so much.'

'It's not me, is it?' he asked in a surprisingly uncertain voice. 'I'm never going to be the one.'

'No, Pierce,' she said, 'and you don't want to be. But today you've earned my lasting respect.'

She finished the call and sat with her chin on her hands, feeling strangely dislocated.

Later that day, while the rest of the office were in noisy spirits, Maddie phoned her father and invited him to take her out for dinner at the end of the week – 'just the two of us'. He would be delighted, he said. Next, she sent an email to Jeanette saying she would be free after all for the opening of Borgo Santo Pietro – if there was still a room for her. Her final email on this extraordinary day was to Søren. Would he be at Borgo too? His London late-night reply came back by return, but was oddly inconclusive. He would love to see her, but he was drawing up plans for his English client's roof garden in New York. He would try to make it, otherwise the Pleiades beckoned over the Baltic later in the summer. She was shocked to discover that this response felt like a really deep let-down.

'I've left it too late,' she told herself aloud.

That June evening, alone in her apartment, she poured herself a glass of Chianti for dinner and sat out on her tiny balcony to break open Nonna's other gift of a year ago. With its string, and knots, and sealing wax, it felt like a strange way to celebrate what had been an extraordinary outcome for a trial that was lost, days earlier; but could it tell her anything about her future?

The horoscope was a byzantine mix of symbols and calculations, but she understood little. There were half a dozen years plotted with what she knew must be planetary icons, where they would be at specific times in her life. She picked out two that had a resonance. 'Age 21', it said, 'moon slips past Jupiter on cusp of 9th and 10th houses. Leave home for study – Law?' Well, that was right, Maddie agreed; and it changed her life. The other was odder still: 'Age 23–24: Progressed Moon contacts Venus and natal Mars, in the Pleiades. Big love; but false start. Madeline weeps.'

OK, yes, well done, she thought, swallowing a large mouthful of the wine. But will it get better?

'Age 25:' the last entry said. 'Put on the right shoes to cross the bridge?'

Underneath this was a strange, long-hand message from the woman who had drawn the chart. It was written in Italian, and Maddie roughly translated.

Born with sun and moon conjunct the Pleiades, child of 'the doves'; 'the daughters of the harvest'; 'ladies of the sail'; and 'the rainy ones'. Pleiades are daughters of old Atlas – travel inescapable. Often associated with problems of eyesight – what don't you see? Tears of pain may change to tears of joy. You must decide if through the one, you can find the other.

It was rather occult for Maddie; but she liked the doves. They had recently become something of a totem sign for her.

It was the end of the week when she met her father for dinner. He had picked Café Tiramisu in Belden Place for their evening, one of the only corners of the city that felt like a row of local restaurants such as might be found in the backstreets of Marseilles, or even Siena. Despite the modern world of bureaucracy, by-laws and licensing, this enclave was still allowed to exist, and the outdoor café seating in the lane itself offered some of the best people-watching in San Francisco.

Enzo was enjoying this pastime when Maddie approached his table. To her delight he had two glasses of champagne waiting, and he rose to greet her with a kiss across the table. The waiter held a chair for her to sit and then placed menus before them. When they had settled Enzo raised his glass.

'To victory! It must have been a roller coaster these last few weeks. I saw the papers and thought you'd lost – but I was very pleased to read about a settlement on Tuesday. It was enigmatic, to say the least. A large cheque?'

'Yes,' Maddie laughed gently, 'very, but in the event even I don't know exactly how much. It's an undisclosed sum: and yet it's never enough to replace what has been lost. And more than that, a settlement gives no visible conclusion, of course. The people in charge are not affected personally. They just move on.'

Enzo smiled at his daughter. 'The armies of industry have pillaged the workers of one land, and leave it to recover as best it can. Then the army moves on to the next, in a poorer land. It's called "out-sourcing", I believe.'

Maddie nodded. 'Yes, Papa. But I want to talk about something more cheerful.' She smiled at her father, wondering what he really thought, now that he knew it was Pierce Gray's company after all.

'Yes, well,' Enzo looked conspiratorial. 'Did you know your sister brought home a real live Druid last weekend? I thought your mother was going to have apoplexy,' he chuckled. 'She has such preconceived ideas. I believe she thought Barbara was bringing home a devil-worshipper, but in the end he turned out to be a very interesting man. He's a Stanford graduate in physics, working in alternative energy technology. He's good for Barbara, and she's enjoying the magic at the moment.'

'Good,' Maddie said honestly.

'But these, let us wish away,' Enzo intoned, apparently light-heartedly, 'and turn sole-thoughted to one lady here. What about my Madeline?'

'I'm not sure, Papa,' she said opaquely. 'Let's wait and see.'

They ordered, the food came and they ate and conversed, talking and laughing. Part way through the pappardelle, Maddie told her father she was going back to Italy on Sunday night for a few days, and maybe stopping in London for a few more on her return leg. This raised his eyebrows a little.

'Anything to do with roses and violets?' he asked.

'But, Papa, what happens at the end of that poem?' she asked unsure.

'Is it about a girl who is too gullible, and loses her virtue to an idealised lover who only drags her out into a storm of uncertainty?'

'That's one way of reading it,' he smiled sadly, 'and critics do. But it could as easily be a celebration of the sheer vitality and hope of young love. Madeline and Porphyro are freed from the cold and the lovelessness of a place of hate, conjuring up a storm of passion, which protects them and ensures their escape. At the end of the poem Keats only offers us a beginning. You have to decide whether the potential of their love is toward ruin, or ecstatic happiness.'

Maddie nodded, immersed in thought. After another moment, pursuing an idea, she asked, 'Do you think people can control the weather, Papa?'

'What do you mean, Maddie?' he asked. 'If you mean cause a storm, or make rain, or say, "Wind blow – and move our ship" . . . Oh, to be Prospero!'

'Don't play the fool,' she laughed. 'I'm serious. It is just not possible to control the weather, is it?'

Enzo's eyes glittered mischievously. 'Do you remember my favourite algae; the ones that get together to make a cloud? They do that to keep from getting sunburned. I have my own ideas, but if I don't want to end my career as a mad scientist accused of pseudoscience . . .' He grinned. 'My peer group are so caught up in proof they seem to have forgotten that all science began with imagination. But my public answer would be, "no".'

'Put on your mad scientist hat,' Maddie teased.

'There are people who believe they can control the elements. They call on the saints, or the gods, or do rain dances,' he smiled to himself, 'and if it works, it's called a miracle. A man named Ted Owens – the so-called "PK Man" – challenged himself publicly to produce phenomenal weather; and though he wasn't much liked, he's connected with some very odd events. The record snowfall in San Francisco in the mid-seventies came when he announced it would – right in the middle of a long drought. He also had a party trick of manifesting lightning bolts.

'So, a vast body of empirical evidence tells us these events might have happened, but as they can't be produced at will, and by repeated experimentation, most scientists reject the whole idea. I am bound in fairness to say that a miracle, by definition, occurs outside the realm of natural laws. This means that repeating them for experimentation would defeat their nomination as "miracles". Maybe some of these things that occurred are unique, never-to-be-repeated events, and not really miracles; but unexplained one-offs are such a spur to the imagination.'

Maddie looked at her father. 'And your ideas?'

'I like the idea of balance, and "the one". With my algae there has to be one – although there are millions swimming around to make the group, so you will never isolate him or identify the culprit – but one organism of algae is certainly the individual that made just enough difference to tip the balance and bring on the cloud, or the wind.

'If a person, or a group of people, functioned like Mr Algae, then everything else might be in just the right state of readiness. The Native American and his rain dance *could* make it rain, or you might make the wind blow. Only belief is necessary.'

Maddie's mind slipped back to Neva and the 'snow day'.

'You know, Papa, I think . . .' She stopped. 'It's a mystery,' she smiled at him.

Acting as Maddie's travel agent, Jeanette had routed her via Gatwick rather than Rome, allowing her to hook up with Claus at the airport in London and fly with him into Pisa on the Monday early evening. Happily on this occasion the weather was loyal to the summer, and Claus drove his solid Mercedes home to Borgo without Maddie even noticing the bends. It was not dark when they reached the entrance before nine.

She was tired from a long trip, but it made her relaxed rather than exhausted. The wrought-iron gates opened by invisible command and they drove up the new avenue of pencil pines stretching from the main entrance, which was now off the Palazzetto road. She smiled approvingly: the new vista framed the place of pilgrimage to perfection.

Jeanette's hug swallowed her, and she felt the same sense of peace she had first found here a year ago. Barely beginning her second visit, she was already one of Borgo's children.

'You're too tired to look at all the changes tonight,' she said to Maddie. 'I'm taking you straight to your room.'

Maddie stopped Jeanette for a moment, and smiled at her. 'A part of me has come home, when I get here,' she said.

Jeanette nodded without showing any sense of surprise. 'I told you a long time ago that Borgo would put its arms around you.'

Eleanore greeted Maddie lazily, as though she'd only left a week ago, and Jeanette led her up the stairs by the hand with a familiar tasselled key laced through her fingers. Matteo, a handsome Italian of twenty-something, took her bag and followed behind them.

At the top of the stair Maddie lingered, waiting for Jeanette to unlock the door to the Pellegrino suite; but she shook her head.

'No, I've put you somewhere else this time,' she said.

Maddie's mouth opened. She was disappointed, having come to think of it as her own room; but she didn't want to seem ungracious. 'Oh,' she said.

But Jeanette was too in tune with her guest's mind not to hear the sadness. 'I think you've been scrubbed quite clean enough,' she laughed. 'This time you can just relax.'

They crossed the upper hall, with its antique chaises, and its French cabinets and perfume jars, its leather-bound books; and they came to a door off an alcove that Maddie had never seen. Here they stopped, and she read the name over the lintel: 'Valle Serena'.

Jeanette worked her magic with the old-fashioned key, and Maddie's face changed from disappointment to euphoria. She entered a room in gentle tones of blues and golds 'like the colours of the Tuscan sun,' her hostess said to her. It was opulent, compared to Pellegrino, and Maddie felt embarrassed to have been given, surely, the finest room in the hotel.

'It's a honeymoon suite,' she said, lost again for words at Jeanette's artistry. She had created a space of luxury and light, with lilacs spilling from vases on two tables, and a gold-leafed free-standing bath placed right in the heart of the room this time. Venus presided over the Rococo-style bed from a large canvas.

'This is the bath you can just sink into and sip champagne while you gaze at the fire; or you could just look at Søren's favourite view over the Valle Serena.'

Matteo put Maddie's bag down on a chair and quietly turned to go, when Jeanette asked him in Italian about the bottle of champagne that should have been waiting in a bucket for her arrival. He nodded and left them.

'You are impossibly wonderful,' Maddie thanked her.

'Unpack,' Jeanette beamed, 'and come down only if you want to. I'm going to go and find my husband, because he was in London this last weekend and I haven't seen him for a while.'

Maddie smiled a little shyly. 'Jeanette, is he coming . . . ?'

'I think he will,' she answered; and she handed Maddie her tasselled key and slipped out the door.

Maddie sat in the deep window-seat overlooking the beautiful Serene Valley, and she breathed in the warm twilight air. There was something about this space – this place. She was a San Franciscan through and through, but Borgo spoke to her in a language no one had ever used before.

Matteo called to Maddie at the door with 'Room Service'.

'*Sì, è aperto,*' she answered; and he came in with a small tray set with champagne in a silver cooler, and some glasses.

'Shall I open it now, *signorina*?' he asked.

'No, thank you,' she said. 'Maybe a little later.'

'Some fruit and water are coming, and is there anything else I can get you?' he asked her.

She shook her head and gave him some euros from her pocket.

'*Allora, buonasera, signorina,*' he smiled, and left without quite closing the door.

Maddie was hanging up some of her best clothes and considering whether to run the enormous bath when the knock came at the door with the fruit.

'*Sì, grazie,*' she said over her shoulder, vaguely aware of someone slipping behind her with a second tray and placing it on a far table.

'. . . jellies, soother than the creamy curd,
And lucent syrops tinc't with cinnamon;
Manna and dates, in Argosy transferr'd
From Fez; and spiced dainties, every one,
From silken Samarcand to cedar'd Lebanon.'

She stopped still, with her head in the cupboard, and then slowly took one step backwards.

'You,' she said, without quite looking at him, not trusting her expression in the wake of rising emotions, 'crossed the globe to see me for one night; and you left the next morning; and you didn't even kiss me.'

Her tone was light and ambiguous: it might have been teasing, or it might have been a little cross. It sounded rather vulnerable, and unsure.

'That wasn't our night,' he smiled at her honestly. 'It belonged to another man. But I've worked hard to make this one our own.'

He walked across the space between them and put his arms around her, as though they were in the comfortable habit of doing such a thing every night. He put his fingers through her hair and drew her face towards his, and then, he did kiss her: and it was slow, and very easy, and loving. It felt as natural to Maddie as laughter, but it spoke in gentle passion. She knew she was too invested in Søren to pull back, and her body was already lost to him. But she heard a tiny voice of caution, and needed to get something off her mind.

'If I get naked with you in that bed,' she said, 'I won't want it to stop; and I don't know how to manage things.'

He slipped his arms low around her waist and pulled her tightly against his body.

'Because you're there, and I'm here?' he asked.

She nodded. 'I can't wait for you off planes. I can fly to you, but I can't be counting down days to airport pick-ups. I just can't do it.'

He shook his head and brushed a thumb sensuously over her lips. 'You want to know the middle already; and even the ending. But we don't know that part,' he smiled softly. 'We only have the beginning: and the sense of possibility.'

After a moment, her eyes shone an answer for him, and he lifted her onto the exquisite linen of the turned-down bed. Then he moved quietly to the door, opened it, and slipped the privacy tassel over the knob.

If there were owls, or doves, or dogs, or spirits anywhere in the outside night, they were unheard and unseen by the couple in the Valle Serena suite. The first kiss had preceded the second by a calendar year: and a single night was not long enough to begin to address the lost time in between. With the windows open wide for the warm air, only the scents from the garden below casually intruded on their privacy.

It was some time after sunrise when Maddie woke, only dimly aware of the time zone where she was. She stretched, moved Søren's arm and slid gently from the bed to tease open a heavy curtain from the large window that overlooked the valley. A breath of summer wind followed her back to bed and she leaned up on one arm, watching Søren dozing. A long strand of her hair moved in the breeze, and tickled his cheek, successfully waking him.

'You're hungry,' he smiled, barely opening one eye.

She nodded, but her expression – unseen by him – spoke of an appetite quite indifferent to croissants and scrambled egg.

'And when you want something, the wind always speaks for you,' he grinned, turning to face her fully.

She positioned herself over him and looked into the hazel eyes, which were full of intensity and imagination – what Jeanette liked to call his 'poetic, dreamy eyes'.

'You really think I can do that?' she asked amused.

'What, call up the wind?' he smiled lazily. 'No question. You're an Etruscan, and it's in your DNA.'

Without a word spoken that might break the spell of their intimacy with one another, fruit, pancakes and coffee were brought to a table laid especially for them near the fountains in the rose garden. It was a sublime June day.

Jeanette had wanted to give them plenty of time and space on their own; but she was also restless to show them something. When Matteo at last reported they had finished their coffee and asked for a second pot, she decided she might be allowed to interrupt them.

'Good morning,' she said in her voice of familiar sunshine, and gave them each a kiss.

Søren stood up and kissed her warmly. 'Join us,' he said; and she nodded and sat down. Both Maddie and Søren were aware that a very large grin had chased away her usual smile; and he finally asked her: 'OK, what is it?'

She looked very pleased with herself as she passed him a copy of an Italian morning newspaper, which had been discreetly tucked under her arm. Maddie moved her head sideways to see what was so important.

There, in the middle of the front page, was a headline announcing that a 'unicorno' had been found in Prato, near Florence. It was accompanied by an enchanting photo of a wide-eyed baby roe deer, and in the absolute centre of its head was a beautiful single whorled horn. 'It is proof that the mythical unicorn, celebrated in legend, was probably not a fantastic creature but a real animal, with an anomaly similar to this deer,' was a rough translation of the text. The extraordinary 'unicorn' deer made them all smile in disbelief.

'The sense of possibility,' Søren told Maddie.

'You see,' Jeanette said, 'there are the most wonderful things, just out there.'

'And by believing in them,' Maddie took Søren's hand, 'maybe we make them true.'

AUTHOR'S NOTE

Years ago I was given a copy of C. G. Leland's *Aradia: The Gospel of the Witches*, and I have been intrigued ever since by its blend of myth and folklore, as well as the tantalising glimpse of a possible lost aural history it offers us. Motivated to record folkloric traditions in both his native America and in Europe – specifically Tuscany – Leland's document, published in the late nineteenth century, has long fascinated serious scholars and those interested in pagan lore.

Leland's source for his book, which is essentially a collection of rituals in a so-called 'gospel' of medieval Italian witchcraft, was a young woman called Maddalena, from the Emilia Romagna region. He employed her to help him research the underground survival of spells and charms, curses, invocations and healing rituals that had remained – alongside Christianity – with the people of her native Romagna. What excited Leland was the possibility that these popular practices might trace their descent from antiquity, particularly from the Etruscans who were (and are) the parents of Tuscany. They presented him then – as they do for us today – with an inviting riddle: much exquisite Etruscan culture is preserved in tombs, masonry and artefacts, yet we are still largely unable to read their language and know exactly what they believed.

The rituals outlined in *Aradia*, dedicated to the goddess Diana, offer a conundrum for academics, who must grapple with the question of how reliable Leland's source, Maddalena, might have been in presenting him with a 'genuine' tradition, and also ask about his own scholarly methods when he was so keen to find in the material a tangible link with the Etruscans. Raven Grimassi, who has the advantage of a verbal family tradition of his own, writes that he has been taught by his maternal ancestors that 'Aradia' was a real person from the fourteenth century, and that she preserved a rare and fascinating heritage of Italian witchcraft, which she eventually passed on to others.

Without my entering the debate about the historical 'truth' or otherwise of Leland's research, the chapter most of interest to me in his book is the teasing vignette of the 'Beautiful Pilgrim of the House of the Wind', which appears almost as a throwaway. This character, outlined in my Prologue, of course inspires 'Agnesca'; but I have always been curious about the elements of the tale that remind us strongly of Keats' pair of lovers in 'The Eve of St Agnes'. They, too, escape from the family-imposed veto on their love into a night under the protective cloak of a storm, and run away together to an unknown history – much as the unnamed *bella pellegrina* does in Aradia. Leland quotes many lines of Keats' poetry in his book, and it was this curiosity that prompted my own departure point for *The House of the Wind*.

ACKNOWLEDGEMENTS

As I started work on this book I suddenly became aware that I had climbed up to a place where I had long wanted to be: and then, I made the mistake of looking down. The following special people helped me to overcome my vertigo: –

Thank you to Fran Slater, for sharing your very personal responses to a loss closely related to Maddie's, and helping me to an understanding of my character; and to your own daughter Maddie, who welcomed me in spite of a prolonged weekend intrusion. You are brave, beautiful women. I am very grateful to Janet Opie, Fiona Donaldson and Philip Whelan, for reading the manuscript in instalments. Your comments and intelligent insights helped me hugely – as always. Jeanette and Claus Thottrup generously opened their home and their lives for me. I came looking only for a location to set the Tuscan end of the story, and found instead the heart of the tale in the true paradise they have created out of ruins. Your perpetual striving for excellence is a lesson. John Harmshaw was kind enough to read, and correct, the legal proceedings in the Oxford chapter.

To the indefatigable Eva, at the Tourist Office in Volterra, and to her colleagues, Claudia and Lorenzo – *molte grazie*. Surely no tourist office in Italy could be more helpful than you have been, answering email after email about medieval facts and history in your haunting city. Thanks, too, to Lola, and to the well-stocked mind of Alessandro Furiesi, for giving me excellent grounding on the pattern of life in the medieval city, and for whisking me into building after building. Thanks to Sergio, Matteo, Max, Ivan, Appollonio, Simona, Sabrina, Gori, Peter, Milo and

Justina at Borgo Santo Pietro. You are superb at your jobs. In Sydney my sister, Wendy Charell, spent hours at the start talking over several points in my planned story, and was very encouraging of the whole. Thanks also for recently sending me Judyth McLeod's delightful horticultural book, *In a Unicorn's Garden*, which spiritually has so much shared ground with *The House of the Wind*.

Finally, I am deeply indebted to the professionals in my life. To Flora Rees, for bearing up against my grumblings and for a light hand and excellent insights as my editor: thank you dear Flora. All remaining mistakes are certainly my own, and in spite of your urgings! And I am in awe of the wonderful, thorough job of copy editing from Yvonne Holland. To my Spanish editor at Santillana, Gonzalo Albert, in Madrid: thank you for help with your beautiful language, and for your constant stream of kindnesses. Ditto to Julietta, Pablo and Maria. Maria-Giulia at Piemme, in Milan, was kind enough to drive down to visit Borgo Santo Pietro and fall under the spell of the place and the story: thank you for your enthusiasm. A huge hug and thank you to architect Chris Boehm for the unicorn drawing which graces the end of the story: a worthy substitute left hand for Søren! For sunshine, language, accounts and research, bouquets to Daniela Petracco, Giulia Mignani, Vicky Mark and Lisa Brännström at Andrew Nurnberg and Associates. And though no longer at Nurnbergs – but very sadly missed by all – my special love and thanks to Barbara Taylor. Robin Straus, Sarah Branham and Judith Curr in NYC: thank you from my heart. To my agents, Andrew Nurnberg and Sarah Nundy, what can I say? You are extraordinary, in my most need being by my side. I will borrow your words if I may, Andrew, and say truthfully, 'I do not deserve it.' Lastly, I offer up most inadequate thanks to the person who spent months researching more than a dozen cases of the kind at the heart of this book, and who held my hand tightly jumping across the chasm. To my husband, Gavrik Losey: thank you for sharing the 'sense of possibility'.